Praise for Mary Ann Marlowe's debut novel, *Some Kind of Magic*

"Marlowe makes a name for herself in this hilarious and sexy debut. . . . It's filled with frisky sexy scenes set to the backdrop of rock music, and Marlowe makes the chemistry scientific and literal in this fun read."

—*Booklist* STARRED REVIEW

"This love potion romance, which pairs up the lead singer for a rock band with a biochemist who's also an amateur singer/songwriter, is light and fluffy."

—*Publishers Weekly*

"This fun, romantic and sexy novel explores the instant connection that manifests between two people and what happens next. The chemistry between Adam and Eden is instant and electric, and watching them bring out the best in each other gives the story warmth along with the heat. . . . This love story will make readers smile!"

—RT Book Reviews

"Frisky, Flirty Fun!" —Stephanie Evanovich, *New York Times* bestselling author of *The Total Package*

"Sexy, engaging and original. I completely fell in love with Eden and Adam. An amazing first novel."

—Sydney Landon, *New York Times* bestselling author of *Wishing for Us*

Books by Mary Ann Marlowe

Some Kind of Magic

A Crazy Kind of Love

Published by Kensington Publishing Corporation

A crazy KIND OF LOVE

MARY ANN MARLOWE

KENSINGTON BOOKS
www.kensingtonbooks.com

KENSINGTON BOOKS are published by

Kensington Publishing Corp.
119 West 40th Street
New York, NY 10018

All Kensington titles, imprints, and distributed lines are available at special quantity discounts for bulk purchases for sales promotion, premiums, fund-raising, educational, or institutional use.

Special book excerpts or customized printings can also be created to fit specific needs. For details, write or phone the office of the Kensington Sales Manager: Kensington Publishing Corp., 119 West 40th Street, New York, NY 10018. Attn. Sales Department. Phone: 1-800-221-2647.

Kensington and the K logo Reg. U.S. Pat. & TM Off.

eISBN-13: 978-1-4967-0809-0
eISBN-10: 1-4967-0809-1
First Kensington Electronic Edition: December 2017

ISBN-13: 978-1-4967-0808-3
ISBN-10: 1-4967-0808-3
First Kensington Trade Paperback Printing: December 2017

10 9 8 7 6 5 4 3 2 1

Printed in the United States of America

To Kelli
I'm forever your Gayle

Chapter 1

Stalker. When you put it that way, what I did for a living sounded despicable.

Paparazza had a nicer ring to it. Slightly.

My editor, Andy, said I was too fresh to work the street. The way he told it, I still had the stink of human about me. *Josephine, you have to figure out if you want to work in this profession or have a soul.*

That Andy was a joy to work with. But I'd seen him in action, walking backward down the sidewalk, shooting pictures and asking questions, right up in the faces of people who behaved as though he was completely invisible. He still hadn't let me live down the one time I apologized to a mark before taking her picture. In my defense, it was my first week on the job, and she'd just come out of the hospital with fresh bruises.

That was months ago, and I'd hardened up.

I'd been called "loser" and told to "get a real job." One time, an innocent bystander intentionally blocked my shot of an incognito Jeff Daniels slipping through the airport unnoticed. In addition to ruining my chance to call it a day, said Good Samaritan accused me of being a vile parasite before sitting back down to ogle Jennifer Aniston in another entertainment magazine's photo spread.

Most people assumed it was an exciting line of work. But

while I clocked more celebrity sightings in a week than most people would their whole lives, most days, I simply leaned against a brick wall for hours, shoulder cramping, hoping the stars would align. Literally.

On other days, like today, a tweet would take me on a journey to Brooklyn where I'd narrowly missed getting a shot of Emily Mortimer rehearsing her lines in Prospect Park. Cursing the waste of the morning, I had no choice but to head back to the subway with nothing to turn in to my editor. But as I rounded a corner, I spotted Maggie Gyllenhaal coming out of the Park Slope Food Coop with her two daughters. I raised my eyes to the heavens in gratitude and then steeled myself for the kill.

I wore two cameras strapped across my chest bandito-style. When Maggie stopped to adjust her bags, I grabbed my work camera off my right hip and caught her in my crosshairs. I disengaged my conscience and prepared to pester this person whose only crime was to have achieved a level of celebrity that made people willing to pay money to read about her and invade her privacy. It was my job to cater to that need.

Centering her in the frame, I got off one shot just as some oblivious jerk crossed right in front of me, completely obscuring my line of sight.

I threw my hand in the air. "Seriously?" Aggravated, I angled myself around the interloper for a better view of Maggie, but as I peered through the eyepiece, my viewfinder filled with a plasma-colored blob that autofocus slowly resolved to reveal Mr. Oblivious now staring directly into my lens. I let my camera drop against my sternum with a growl of frustration, but my new friend didn't register my impatience.

Rather, he moved in closer with a disarmingly friendly smile. "Who are you shooting?"

"It's Maggie Gyllenhaal." Still irritated, I spoke too loud, and a nearby woman gasped and repeated the news. My heart sank as the whispers grew, and I watched my last chance at a celebrity sighting disappear into a vortex of autograph-seeking passersby. A long exhale left my body along with my hopes of returning with anything Andy might want.

I glared at my nemesis, but even as I formulated a murderous plot, I became aware of how deliciously pretty he was. With his blond hair, blue eyes, broad shoulders, and tanned skin, he should have been holding a surfboard on a poster for a California travel agency. He really was too perfect to be roaming the streets without a chaperone.

But none of that mattered. He'd thrown a wrench into my morning, and I arched my eyebrow a fraction higher in reproof.

And yet, he continued to stare at me with a look of curiosity, as if somehow *I* were more interesting than the famous person half a block away. A famous person I still couldn't see for the crowd surrounding her. He pointed at my camera. "Are you paparazzi?"

His fascination made sudden sense—he'd probably never seen the paparazzi up close and impersonal. I sucked on my teeth and considered the situation. "Look. I'm sure you don't care, but you've cost me a candid shot of that actress, and that's my bread and butter. The least you could do is give me a boost so I can maybe bring something back to my editor."

His eyes narrowed for a beat, and he glanced down the block, then back at me, as he pieced together my dilemma. I wasn't short, but I'd need to stand on a bench to see over that crowd. A slight smile played on his lips. "You want to climb on my shoulders?" He waggled his eyebrows salaciously.

The idea seemed preposterous, but desperate times and all. I'd gone to greater lengths for less in the past. And somehow I felt like this guy might be a good sport. He'd maintained a devil-may-care grin throughout this entire exchange. And I really needed that shot. I closed my eyes and swallowed my pride. "Would you mind?"

He dropped to one knee with the speed of an eager suitor, and I winced as his bare knee hit the concrete. He merely bowed his head and said, "At your service."

I couldn't help but giggle at the absurdity. But then he lifted his eyes, and my laughter caught in my throat. Until that moment, he'd just been an annoying interference, but his smoldering gaze brought me thundering to reality. I took a half step away and drank in the beauty of my kneeling knight. Golden hair glinted in the late morning sun. Bright blue eyes shined with mirth and intelligence. Well-muscled biceps peeked out of a T-shirt that stretched across his broad chest. Thigh muscles flexed, and his smooth, taut skin cried out to be touched.

I swallowed.

He held a hand out toward me. "Come on, then. I don't bite. Well, not in full daylight."

I circled around him, hearing everything my mom would say in this situation. But this total stranger didn't appear to be suffering from typhoid, and I hadn't seen a gutted panel van in the vicinity, so I felt reasonably confident this wasn't the way I was going to die. I laid my hand on his left shoulder and immediately yanked it away from the shock of how toned and solid he felt.

He twisted back and looked up at me. "You don't need to be scared. I carry equipment all the time. I've only dropped a few." His lips, lips I noticed for the first time, grew into a full-fledged smile, white teeth flashing like an ad for Crest, and I wondered if I could muster the nerve to climb on this beautiful man.

One of Andy's many lectures came to mind: *Get the shot at any cost.* And just like that, fear of losing my job overcame my self-respect. Honestly, I'd been chipping away at that virtue ever since I traded art school for tabloid photography.

With a last farewell to my dignity, I swung my right leg over that mouthwatering shoulder. As soon as I felt his hand on my shin, I hopped up and sat square across the back of his neck. My human crane held my legs tight and stood.

And wobbled.

My free hand instinctively latched onto his hair, and he yelped. "Sorry," I hollered down. A hint of coconut wafted up, and I fought off an overpowering visceral reaction—the desire to touch him, smell him, even taste him. I wanted to lean forward and plant my face into the top of his head.

But I'd spent months focusing on preserving my job and wasn't about to crumble just because I straddled a Fifty-Most-Beautiful-People level of beautiful person. With those sexy lips. And his hands on my legs.

Focus, Jo.

The crowd below had begun to thin, and I was tempted to abort plan A, but I couldn't take the chance that Maggie would walk away once she'd signed the last autograph.

I lifted my camera and zoomed in. There in the center stood my target. And she was facing the wrong way.

Crap.

I yelled down, "I can't even tell it's her from here. Do you mind walking closer?"

He began to move down the sidewalk, and my self-control faltered thanks to his neck, now rubbing against my inner thighs—and more. His shoulders tensed and relaxed beneath my legs, heat intensifying in the most intimate way. My fingers gripped his neck, and goose bumps appeared. He lifted his arm and caught my hand in his. It was a miracle I didn't fall from a spontaneous swoon.

Despite our conspicuous approach, we'd nearly reached our destination before Maggie turned her head up and locked eyes with me. I quickly lifted my camera, but the appearance of a desperate pap precariously perched on a lumbering accomplice must have spooked her, because in the time it took me to point and aim, she'd lifted her bags, grabbed her youngest daughter by the hand, and fled down the block in the opposite direction.

I palmed my forehead. Unless I'd inadvertently captured something during that mortifying display, I had nothing at all.

My accidental hero lowered me back to the street, and I found myself out of breath even though he'd been the one exerting himself. He ran a hand through his hair, and I followed it with greedy eyes, already regretting my descent to ordinary earth after my perch atop a golden god.

He eyed me with equal interest. "Perhaps we should be formally introduced? I'm Micah." He stretched out his hand. "And you are?"

"J-Jo." I took a deep breath and let it out.

"Jo Jo?" In ordinary circumstances, his constant teasing might have put me off, but Micah had an air of easygoing charm about him. And he had just agreed to be used as a parade float for no other reason than generosity.

"Jo," I repeated, a bit more confidently. "Josie."

"Well, Jo-Josie." His hand gripped mine, and his half smile hovered somewhere between charming and devilish. "Where are you from?"

I took another shuddering breath and tried to get my heart to stop galloping in my chest. I prayed my lack of composure had nothing to do with a sudden drop in my blood sugar, please, God, and rather everything to do with the proximity of the most attractive man I'd possibly ever laid eyes on. And I'd seen a lot of attractive people in my line of work. "Georgia," I said, then clarified, "Atlanta."

He gently pushed my shoulder. "Get back, Jo Jo."

I snickered at the dated song reference as though that joke hadn't fallen from the lips of every class clown I'd ever known. I put on my twangiest Southern. "You shooin' me on home?"

His blue eyes crinkled at the corner, and his playful smile stretched all the way to flirtatious scamp. Dimples emerged in his tanned, smooth cheeks, beneath a hint of blond stubble. His skin looked as soft as a baby's. "Absolutely not." He reached over and pulled one of my ash brown curls out straight, and I shivered. "It's just, you don't look . . ." He bit his lip and seemed to think twice about finishing that sentence. "You barely have an accent. I wouldn't have guessed you were Southern."

" 'Fraid so. Dekalb County, born and raised." I took a step closer. "And you?"

"Actually, you've wandered into my kingdom." He twirled his hands out as though to present his domain. "Might I ask, what is your quest here?"

I gave him points for nerd humor and chuckled. "I seek the holy grail. Have you seen it here about?"

"Alas, no." He winked. "I was just on my way to find it when I was accosted by a fair maiden in distress." His bratty-little-brother smirk felt like a challenge.

"Is that so?" I flashed him a smile. "And do you make it a habit of photobombing innocent maidens?"

He exhaled with surprised laughter. "You might say that."

I narrowed my eyes at him and, before he could react, lifted my camera and clicked the shutter. "Aha! I've captured a consolation prize." I shook my camera at him, defiant. "Now we'll see what you go for on the open market."

He made a gesture as though to swipe my camera away, dramatically failing and clutching at his chest. "Touché. But I can tell you it's not much."

Thoughts of payment hit my stomach like a runaway freight train and sucked all the fun out of this enchanting encounter. The probability of running into yet another celebrity in this part of Brooklyn was slim. I needed to head back to the office immediately and do more research to scout my next lead. Maybe I could still bring something to Andy before the end of the day. I couldn't afford to let him down again. I knew he'd begun counting down the days until he could fire me—I could feel it. And I needed this job.

I frowned. "I have to be getting back."

Micah chewed on his pretty lower lip for a beat, then said, "Hey, you wouldn't happen to have a business card? You know, in case I'm ever in the market for my own personal paparazza."

That made me laugh again, and my momentary gloom lifted. I reached into my camera bag and produced a plain white card with just my name and contact info. "And you?"

Micah patted his pocket and came up with a wallet. He slid a card out and held it toward me. I started to scan it when he laid a finger on my shoulder, and my eyes closed for a beat as I leaned my head against his hand. What had come over me?

"It was good to meet you, Jo-Josie from Georgia, Atlanta. I hope I see you again." He looked into my eyes once more, more serious than before. "And don't let this business change you."

He gave my arm a quick squeeze, then turned and headed away from me, and I stood planted in that spot enjoying the view as he walked away. I sighed, hoping maybe he'd asked for my card so he could call me. I dropped my eyes back to his and read, *"Micah Sinclair. Theater of the Absurd."*

My jaw dropped.

I'd been talking to Micah Sinclair for a good thirty minutes. *Micah freaking Sinclair.* My head fell back, and I stared at the clouds passing. He'd been in my clutches, and I hadn't asked him a single hard-hitting question. And the picture I'd shot—I didn't want to think about it.

My boss would eat me alive. If I didn't kill myself first. I could have delivered a click-bait-worthy photo if I'd had the first clue I'd been hanging out with a sought-after commodity.

In my defense, I didn't have an encyclopedic mind like Andy. And I didn't have the experience to recall every single minor celebrity who graced the tabloids. In fact, I had to wrack my brains to think of the last thing I'd even heard about Micah. Something about a girlfriend, I thought. It didn't matter. None of my excuses would hold water in the court of Andy.

I considered chasing after Micah. I could take a picture of his backside. It was a worthy subject in my estimation. But I was already going to catch hell for the one crazy-ass shot I'd taken—especially without a printable quote. I could have deleted the picture and pretended this never happened. But Andy would make my life even more insufferable if I returned altogether empty-handed.

An ember of hope began to bloom as I remembered I had Micah's contact info. What if I called and sweet-talked him into a quote? I lifted his card again and read the words *"Please contact my agent at—"* And all hope died.

Fixated on Micah's last statement, I trudged back toward the subway. *"Don't let this business change you."* All along, he'd known I was missing a golden opportunity, and he must have been laughing at me the whole time. I squared my shoulders and decided to chalk it up to a learning experience. Yet another one.

Ordinarily, such a humiliation would have left me near tears. But as I walked, I began to laugh. At the very least, I'd have a hilarious adventure story to tell Zion. And in spite of everything, it had been the most fun I'd had since I couldn't remember when. Micah had turned out to be the bright spot in an otherwise cursed day.

As I neared the entrance to the subway, a young girl wearing face paint and holding a bright red balloon caught my eye. I reached left and switched to my personal camera, pressing the shutter to capture a burst of images. Bright sunlight created a halo in her wild curly locks. Her parents hunched over a map, blind to the masterpiece of their child. The girl glanced up and saw me. I knelt on the sidewalk and winked at her. She tilted her head and looked directly into the camera. A guileless smile broke out. She was missing her front tooth.

Click click click. Beautiful.

Chapter 2

I giggled as I rode the elevator to the newsroom floor, mentally reliving my madcap morning. In the few months I'd been tracking down celebrities, I'd never interacted with any of them like that. Like people. I wondered why Micah had approached me when he had nothing to gain from it. Not gonna lie. It made me feel a little bit special to be singled out by him. I lectured myself not to go and develop a crush on someone so completely out of my reach, but it was too late. I was smitten.

A stomach growl warned me I needed to grab something to eat soon, but I wanted to catch Zion before Andy came back from lunch.

Thankfully, the office was practically deserted. I skulked toward my desk, trying not to attract the attention of the office busybodies. Derek was too busy shoveling forkfuls of tikka masala out of a Styrofoam box to pay me any mind. A blob of brown sauce clung to his hipster beard, and I suppressed a gag. A few tables over, Leonard quietly blew steam from his coffee as he read a competitor's paper, squirreling away more gossip into his encyclopedic memory.

We didn't have cubes like the other offices. Our open-concept department looked like some kind of art studio or architectural firm. Black wooden tables lined one wall that had tall bright windows. Instead of watercolor paper or blueprints, these work-

stations held state-of-the-art flat-screen monitors—usually two
or three per dock. Simply drop a laptop onto the port and stalk
away. And instead of rolling around in comfy office chairs, we
had to perch on high stools. Andy thought it encouraged us to
work in the office as little as possible. We were meant to be out
on the street.

As I settled in front of my computer and connected my camera to the server via WiFi, I caught Zion's eye and silently invited him to come hither with a stealthy sideways jerk of my
head. He dropped off his stool and sidled up beside me.

While I searched the share drive for the picture of Micah I'd
just uploaded, Zion laid his chin on my shoulder. As soon as the
image opened, he sucked in a sharp gasp. "You ran into Micah
Sinclair?" Zion had been at this job for years but still got excited about celebrities, especially the beautiful ones. He leaned
forward, as if he could touch Micah right through the screen.
"Yum. Did you ask him about his breakup?"

That was the story I couldn't quite remember.

Zion's wiry hair nearly poked me in the eye, and I shoved his
head out of my face. "Uh. No."

On my second monitor, I typed Micah's name in the search
bar. The first headline that popped up read: "Micah Sinclair
Single Again?"

Competing aches twisted in my gut. The word *single* might as
well have stood in thirty-foot-tall neon letters in my mind. The
thought of an allegedly available Micah Sinclair flirting with the
very available me made my nerves effervesce.

But the word *again* knocked me back to reality, reminding me
that he only showed up in the news in conjunction with a brand-
new, or a recently former, girlfriend. He might be available, but
he probably flirted in his sleep.

Still, I couldn't contain my grin as I studied Micah's adorably
bratty expression in my photo. Even though I'd surprised him,
he looked like he'd somehow gotten one over on me instead of
the other way around. Like he'd tricked me into taking his picture. And, damn, was he ever photogenic.

Zion said what I was thinking. "He sure is pretty."

I zoomed in, and Micah's features filled the screen. He'd been so close when I'd snapped the picture, I hadn't gotten much below the neck. What a shame—he had a great build. Still, those eyes. Blue like sapphires. Sparkling like the sea.

"I'd kill for that skin. So smooth." Zion's dark skin was dotted with black spots. To me, they were just a part of him, but I knew he felt self-conscious. "It's not fair. He looks Photoshopped."

I patted his cheek. "You're beautiful, Zion."

He dismissed me with a quick roll of his eyes. "Can you filter out the glare?"

"I'm not sure if it's worth bothering. Without a comment, Andy's not likely to use it."

Zion nodded at the photo and graciously said, "If he'd been looking at me like that, I might have been a little tongue-tied, too."

I rested my elbows on the table and dropped my chin on my hands, appreciative of the spiritual pat on the back but tired of always needing one. "I wasn't tongue-tied, Zion." I looked around for eavesdroppers and whispered, "I didn't have a clue who he was."

"What?" He spoke too loud, and nosy Leonard glanced up at us. "How'd you get a picture of Micah Sinclair if you didn't even know who he was?"

That comment released the kraken. Leonard left his desk, holding his coffee mug in both hands. "Ten bucks *he* approached *you.*"

I double-blinked in shock. "He did. How did you know?"

He set his mug on my desk. "Micah Sinclair is attracted to paparazzi like a moth to a bug zapper."

I recalled how Micah had gotten right up in my camera, how weird I'd found it that he didn't even notice the celeb down the street, how curious he'd been about me. And everything clicked into place. So much for feeling special. Still, something didn't add up. "If he wanted the publicity, why didn't he tell me who he was? I would have at least interviewed him."

He shrugged. "Dunno. Maybe he figured you should already know."

Ouch.

"I just didn't recognize him at first. I should have, but he started talking to me like a regular person, like *I* was the interesting one." My tone sounded defensive even to me.

Leonard's shoulders relaxed as though he remembered I wasn't any competition, that I was the hapless fresh meat who still needed to be patronized like a newbie. "Ya know, I've noticed he's friendlier to photographers than reporters. Maybe he's a narcissist. Or maybe he likes the publicity without embracing the invasion into his privacy. Can't say I blame him considering what he's usually asked." He shook his head and mimicked, *"Micah, did you break up with your girlfriend?"* He tsked. "Poor kid. He *is* a musician after all."

Leonard had worked here longer than Andy even. He had war stories about everyone, and his words hung in the air like an invitation to ask him to share more.

"Have you ever interviewed him?"

He twisted his lips, like I'd asked him if he'd ever ridden the subway. "Of course. Several times."

"And?"

He paused to rifle through his mental filing cabinet a moment, then proceeded with an air of authority. "The first time I'd even heard of Micah Sinclair was when that *Rock Paper* article came out."

Zion said, "Oh, right," at the same time I said, "Huh?"

Douchelord Derek, forever eavesdropping on everyone, called over. "That was over a year ago. They might not have run that story down in Podunk."

I shot eye daggers at him. "We get the Internet in Georgia, Derek."

Zion started Googling. "I remember that. 'The Pretty Boys of Rock.'" I assumed he was repeating the title, though knowing him, he might have been waxing nostalgic over eye candy past.

Leonard grabbed the reins of conversation back. "The *Rock*

Paper had put out a spread of the hottest chicks in rock. It was fifty pages of sex kittens in leather and heavy makeup. They got a ton of blowback from it for focusing on women's looks instead of their music. Sexist, you know? So a couple of issues later, they put out an equally offensive article, featuring as many attractive male rockers as they could dig up."

"Offensive, *sure*." Zion had found the article and was slowly clicking through the ad-riddled slide show, ogling photos of huge rock stars like Jon Bon Jovi and Adam Copeland. I reclaimed the mouse from him and powered through a series of people I didn't recognize until I found Micah, showing more teeth than the rest of the brooding rockers, and dressed like he'd dug up his wardrobe at a rummage sale: tight garish red pants, green Converse high tops, and a ripped T-shirt for a band I'd never heard of. But with that face, Micah easily filled the "pretty" quota for "The Pretty Boys of Rock."

I read the blurb out loud, *"Micah Sinclair, thirty-one years old. He's a Libra, and ladies you should know that means he's a lover."* I snickered and couldn't read the rest without laughing. *"But what you may not know is that this bad boy of rock was raised strictly religious. Touring the country in an End Times cult as a child, young Micah Sinclair sang uplifting church songs years before he brought everyone down with a song called 'Gravity.'* Oh, good Lord."

"Exactly," said Leonard. He strolled over. "May I?"

I gave him control of my mouse, and he Googled something else. Before he clicked the link, he said, "So reporters latched onto that bit about the church and immediately began publishing articles like this." He clicked through to an article topped by an enormous image of Micah snuggling with a gorgeous blonde on what must have been a private beach. The photographer had been so lucky as to catch Micah with his pants down, literally. His entire body would have been exposed if not for the pixelated fig leaves obscuring the very thing that made the picture interesting.

Zion shook his head and said, "Mm-mm-mm. That boy is delicious. Look at those shoulders."

I was looking. I'd been sitting on those shoulders less than two hours earlier. My stomach flipped at the thought. Out of nowhere I felt a stab of irrational jealousy toward the girl on the beach. I probably should have felt sympathy for her. He'd probably dumped her soon after the picture was taken.

Leonard gave us a chance to drink in our fill before picking back up. "The hint of hypocrisy fueled these kinds of stories for a while."

The things I learned working in this department never ceased to amaze me. "Fascinating."

"Oh, I know. At the time, I thought it was going to be like watching a total train wreck. I even went and did a bunch of research on this cult he was in. His parents anyway."

"Yeah?" I leaned in, intrigued. Gossip sold for a very good reason.

"They were called Maranatha, which I learned means something like 'the return of the Lord' or whatever—you know like the what-do-you-call-it?"

"The Second Coming," said Zion. Leonard and I turned and stared at him, eyes wide. He put a hand on his hip. "What? I was raised Southern Baptist."

I said what we were both thinking, "You said 'second coming' with a straight face. Not even a 'That's what she said.'"

Leonard cracked up. I enjoyed working with these people when they weren't all jockeying for the best stories. That is, when Andy wasn't around to drive everyone to compete.

Leonard still held everyone's attention when he continued. "I happened to run into Micah soon after, and I asked him about it. You know their family had toured the country on this bus they called the Salvation bus. They crisscrossed the U.S. like the Partridge Family, except instead of pedaling pop music, they were selling the apocalypse."

Nobody said a word for a moment, until we couldn't handle the suspense, and a chorus of "What happened?" sprang up. Leonard smiled, always the attention whore. "Ah well, that's what was funny. He told me about how great it was to travel town to town and meet people, playing his guitar. The way he talked about it, you'd think I'd asked him about his latest musical tour."

Zion said, "You mean his parents went around the country preaching the gospel and what he got from it was how to become a traveling rock star? That's kind of hilarious."

Leonard pointed at Zion in agreement. "I think that's why the story never really went anywhere. Micah didn't let the religion aspect catch and hold. He deflected it without really denying it or apologizing, so the story never got very big. But it did make him one of those people who are interesting for being interesting."

The door swung open, and everyone flew to their stations. Andy rushed in on some kind of mission. He'd probably caught a celebrity dropping her baby. The newsroom bustled with renewed activity. Fingers clacked on keyboards, and every eye turned away from our fearful leader as he wended his way toward his office. When he approached my desk, I ducked my head, but it was too late.

Andy's eyes landed on me. "Jo! How'd you make out with Emily Mortimer? Get anything we can use?"

Zion straightened up, my personal savior. "She got a pretty picture of Micah Sinclair we could use for an out-and-about shot." Since he'd talked me into taking the job here, he always tried to help me navigate the trials and tribulations of working for the devil.

Andy's ruddy face moved through the calculations quickly. "No text?" Zion's silence answered his question, and he went on, "How'd she run into Micah Sinclair and get no text? Did she ask him about his breakup?"

"I'm right here, Andy." I didn't want to confess I hadn't recognized Micah. "He didn't stop. I barely got this picture."

Andy glanced at my monitor and clucked. "That's not the face of someone in a hurry. What did he do? Stop and flirt?"

He took a few more steps toward his office, and I sputtered out, "It was the best I could get."

Wrong answer. Andy spun around, drawn to me like Sauron's eye to the one ring. "I bet you I could go on Twitter and in five minutes find a better amateur fan photo of him from to-day." His mouth hardened into a frown, which was how Andy showed perverse pleasure. "Slide over."

He opened my Twitter tab and searched for Micah's name. Sure enough, within seconds, he had a dozen tweets showing Micah out on the street today. The one at the very top said, "Micah's new girlfriend?" Andy clicked a link to a shaky video, and there I was, very clearly perched on Micah's shoulders, wearing a crazed look of determination on my face.

I knew I was about to get the lecture of a lifetime, but all I could think about was sending that video on to my mom who would get an enormous kick out of it. I made a mental note to watch it two or three hundred times myself—if I survived the next few minutes.

Andy's head swiveled around. "You said he didn't stop. What's your explanation for this?"

I wrapped my arms around myself, starting to shiver. And did my head feel light? I needed to get something to eat and soon, but I'd have to make it through Andy's harangue first. I closed my eyes a second, but Andy had less than zero empathy for my health.

"I'm waiting."

When I looked up, Andy hadn't lost his sneer.

"I'm sorry, Andy. I didn't know who he was. He came up to me. He actually blocked my shot of Maggie Gyllenhaal, so I talked him into giving me a boost."

"Nice." His mouth curved slightly up, and he nodded, considering. "Fast thinking. Shows initiative." He turned and took in the others who were all completely absorbed in the unfolding drama. "This is what I like to see. Get the shot any way you can." He rounded back on me. "So where's the picture of Maggie?"

His praise had lifted my hope, but the last question blew it to smithereens. "I never got it. She saw me and fled."

He pressed his lips together, and I saw the words *incompetent rookie* in his eyes. He exhaled. "There may be a silver lining here, though."

A muscle in my cheek twitched from the stress of dealing with Andy's mood swings. "What?"

He grumbled, "If you want to get something I can use, stake out the townhouse of Hervé Diaz in Brooklyn Friday night."

"Friday night?" Ugh. I looked from Andy to Zion, trying to make sense of the assignment. "Who's Hervé Diaz?"

Zion said, "She wouldn't know." He turned to me. "Hervé's the drummer for Adam Copeland's band, Walking Disaster."

Andy rolled his eyes. "You *have* heard of them, right?"

"Of course." I'd heard their music to death, and Adam Copeland's image graced the covers of legitimate big-time magazines.

"Hervé always throws huge parties before their band goes on tour, and his shindigs have become a magnet for all kinds of interesting people. Your new friend Micah will probably show up there, too. See if you can catch his eye. He's been known to bring the wolves right into the pen."

"Micah Sinclair is friends with Adam Copeland?"

Andy exhaled his exasperation. "You could say that. Adam Copeland's engaged to Micah's sister. Eden Sinclair?"

Of course. I should have made the connection myself. "You want me to use Micah to gain access to his sister?"

I regretted it as soon as Andy's eyes took on that gleam of zealous self-righteousness he got whenever I talked about the marks like they were people. He loved to hear himself wax prolific on the subject of our holy mission. "Look, Jo. It's business, and they're the commodity. If you wanna get paid, you're gonna have to change your mind-set. You can't befriend them. They won't befriend you if there's nothing in it for them. And without publicity, they cease to exist. Really, by doing your job well, you're doing them a favor."

"Right. Thanks for the assignment. I won't let you down."

Andy pointed his finger at me. "No, you won't. Jo, a lot of people would kill for your position. Don't blow it." He glared at me, reminding me again of the unblinking eye of the dark lord. "The marks don't care about you, so don't you start worrying about them. Okay?"

When Andy used the word *mark,* he intended to turn the celebrities into an impersonal product. I repeated his words in my head, trying to learn to approach this job with the same ruthless instinct. But when I looked at the picture of Micah laughing while carrying me like an old friend, he seemed so guileless and sweet.

Then again, he'd only approached me because of the camera.

I straightened my back and nodded to Andy. "Okay."

Chapter 3

Friday night, I sat alone on the bottom step of a quiet Brooklyn brownstone and settled in for a long wait. I'd arrived early, before any other photographers had staked out a spot, long before the first guests had begun to arrive. A muscle-bound bouncer type peeked out the front door and eyed me a couple of times, filing me away in his *you-shall-not-pass* mental database of creepy stalkers. Nights like this, I felt like a loser two times over, uninvited and unwanted.

I thought Andy was delusional for suggesting Micah might invite me in, but what could it hurt to give the plan a chance? I'd even dressed a little nicer just in case. Not so nice as to feel stupid when Micah inevitably snubbed me—just a flattering scoop-neck T-shirt and a pair of dark jeans. I still wore comfy tennis shoes, but I'd taken a little more time on my hair and makeup.

If Andy was wrong, at least I'd be in a great position to get clean shots of any other big-name celebrities as they entered. And if he was right . . . My heart beat a little faster, in fear and anticipation.

After twenty minutes of inactivity, I rummaged in my backpack and unearthed my emergency reserve of SpongeBob fruity snacks. I chewed on a gummy Squidward and opened Facebook on my phone to check the comments on the video I'd shared on my wall, the one of me riding Micah like a mechanical bull. I'd already watched it so many times I had all the subtle changes in Micah's facial expressions memorized, from his wide goofball smile to the round "oh" of surprise when I toppled forward and grabbed his hair.

My mom cracked me up with her naughty comment: *Ooh, does he have a father?*

Mom's obnoxious neighbor Marisa Bennet, mother of perfection-incarnate Kelsey Bennet, wasted no time posting a link to an article titled "Lothario Rocker Micah Sinclair Confirms Split with Girlfriend." Marisa added, *Are you aware of this guy's reputation, Annie?*

My mom never appreciated unsolicited parenting advice and replied, *Thanks for the article, Marisa. I'm sure Josie can make her own decisions.*

I clicked through and frowned as I read the article. *"Ever reluctant to settle down, Micah Sinclair has dropped his latest in a string of groupie-turned-lover girlfriends in record time."*

The reporter had somehow gotten a quote from Micah. *"We simply agreed to go our separate ways."*

The editorial judgment was predictably harsh. *"Going separate ways seems to be a recurring habit for Micah, forever on the prowl. When his tours come to an end, so do his short-lived relationships."*

The rest of the article veered off into related gossip with clickbait links to companion articles. *"Fear of commitment must run in the family. Micah's sister, Eden Sinclair, and her fiancé of two years, Adam Copeland, have yet to set a wedding date. Will they ever get married?"*

I couldn't understand why people obsessed over the marital status of engaged celebrities, as if anyone else had a chance with Adam Copeland as long as he didn't say "I do."

Likewise, I couldn't understand why the gossip surrounding Micah bothered me at all. It wasn't as if *I* stood a chance with him, even if he couldn't keep his dick in his pants. Not that I wanted to be "the latest in a string of girlfriends." I was still holding out for my happily-ever-after, despite how that hadn't worked out for my mom.

Knowing the way tabloids took a concept and stuck to it, I couldn't help wonder if there might be more to Micah's story, and I wasn't going to find the truth in the judge-jury-and-executioner gossip pages. I caught myself wanting to give him the benefit of the doubt even though I barely knew him. Maybe I was already under Micah's spell.

But I'd seen how the sausage was made. Some of the gossip sites posted total lies, and everyone knew it. At least Andy made us track down actual stories. He liked our newspaper to be a reliable source of trash. Granted, he considered speculative journalism to be an offshoot of the truth. *"Are they dating?"* is a close enough hand grenade.

As streetlights began to pool soft circles on the sidewalk, other paps appeared and set up their equipment. I stood and put away my phone, checking my camera to make sure I'd be all ready to do my job.

Before long, the first car pulled up. Immediately, two walls of cameras created a kind of arched entrance for whoever would emerge. A young girl with long sleek blond hair climbed out and blinked. A few cameras clicked, but the whispers grew like an oncoming wave. "Who is she? Does anyone know who that is?"

Still the cameras flashed—just in case. I hated night shots. It was bad enough I had to get in people's faces in broad daylight, but at night, I had to blind them, too.

The girl swept up the steps and in through the front door. Nobody had figured out the identity of the first fish out of the sea. She was probably nobody. Most everyone would be a nobody.

With the excitement over, the camera wall broke into its individual pieces. The others uploaded photos and texted like crazy to see if anyone would recognize the girl with the long, blond hair. I did the same.

Andy texted, *That's Victoria Sedgwick. She's a hanger-on. Don't worry about her.* Andy had worked so many events over the years, he was a font of expertise on even the lowest ranks of the wannabes.

The levels of celebrity were nothing compared to the levels of nobody-ness. Hangers-on, fans, friends, managers, reporters . . . As a gossip page photographer, I didn't even rate as an A-list nobody. And that was fine by me. I'd much rather be on this side of the camera.

To kill time, I looked through the pictures I'd shot to make sure the lighting was good. Victoria Sedgwick flashed by like those cartoon images animated by flipping the pages of a book. She was still one moment, and then the forward button sent her into spectacular motion. It was hard not to envy the elite. Victoria had the kind of stunning beauty money could buy. Her shoes alone probably cost more than I was willing to spend on the new laptop I sorely needed. And yet she didn't merit the storage she took up on my camera. These photos would get archived and forgotten.

After working in this field awhile, I'd become somewhat inured to how fast the interest in someone dropped off the further they got from the center of the celebrity Tootsie Pop. In most contexts, a girl like Victoria would command the room, but here, she didn't elicit another thought—not unless she came in on the arm of someone famous. The paps around me were hoping to catch a glimpse of one of the big names. If someone like Adam Copeland or even Micah Sinclair appeared, the frenzy would begin. But someone as close as Adam's mom could show up, and nobody would care.

Then again, Micah's sister . . .

"Eden Sinclair!" The guy to my left practically shouted a whisper, and I looked up, thinking he'd read my mind. But in fact, Micah's sister was walking quickly down the sidewalk, head down. And she was alone.

I aimed my camera and started bursting the shot. But as soon as the cameras *click-clicked,* she put her hand up, palm out, blocking a clear view of her face. The guy to my left shouted, "Eden, where's Adam? Is he on his way?"

Another voice raised above the din. "Is Adam already inside? Why are you alone? Is everything good with Adam?"

The questions overlapped. "Eden, have you and Adam set a date yet? When are you going to finally tie the knot? Where's Adam? Have you set a date? *Have you set a date?*" It was a chaotic song with a repeating refrain.

I framed her in my shot and zoomed in on her, watching her once removed through the lens. I'd never seen her before in person. She had a song that played on the radio a little, but she was more well-known for her connection to her boyfriend. She was surprisingly small, maybe five-three if that. Her dark hair contrasted with her porcelain skin. Her clothes were also all black, and there was a tear in her jeans at the knee. She wasn't beautiful in the same way as Victoria Sedgwick, but I'd noticed no matter how traditionally attractive people were, if they had charisma, they were always compelling. Eden was captivating.

She closed in on me and threw a glance my way. Her dark eyes flashed anger at me as though I was the one bombarding her with questions she clearly wouldn't answer. She tossed her mess of black hair back and took the steps two at a time up to the front door, and I heaved a sigh. If looks could kill, I'd be lying in a chalk outline on a Brooklyn sidewalk.

"Boy, she's really nothing like her brother," I muttered.

The guy to my left laughed. "Can't really blame her." He pointed at my credentials. "You work for Andy Dickson, don't you?"

I nodded.

"You're public enemy number one around here. Persona non grata."

I swallowed hard. "I'm just doing my job."

"Preaching to the choir."

He looked somewhat familiar to me, but I hadn't formally met every single pap in Manhattan. "What's your name?"

He rested his camera against his beer belly and reached in his back pocket for an overstuffed, cracked leather wallet. With one hand cradling the camera and the other manipulating the wallet, he managed to slip out a bent business card with nothing on it but his name and phone number. Why couldn't he just say "*Wally*"?

I thanked him for the card and handed him my own. "I'm Jo. It's nice to meet you. Have you been doing this long?"

Rather than answer, he hoisted his camera up. Another car slowed in front of the townhouse. This time a driver stepped out and came around to the side. Out stepped a man I didn't recognize, but the paps closed in, questions flying, cameras clicking. I dutifully crammed in and flashed directly in his face before he ducked his head and bounded up the stairs. I uploaded the picture for Andy to decipher.

More people rolled in, either on foot or via personal motorcade. The feeding frenzy intensified as the level of fame increased. Some celebrities disappeared as quickly as possible. Others walked the runway, stopping to give the photographers ample time to capture them, only answering questions about whichever project they wanted to publicize.

By the time Micah Sinclair emerged from a black sedan, tall and confident, voices had reached fever pitch.

"Micah, over here!"

As his car drove away, Micah stood a moment to take in the scene. Rather than escape the fishbowl or pose for publicity shots, he shook hands with one of the reporters and chatted for a few seconds before he came my way. He tilted his head back, and his face lit up.

"Wally!" He crossed over, hand outstretched. "Haven't seen you around in a while. I hope everything's good at home."

Wally actually put his camera down to shake Micah's hand. I glanced around. Nobody was taking pictures. Was there something inherently un-newsworthy about a guy talking to the media? I lifted my camera and started shooting. The whirr of my camera caught Micah's attention, and he turned away from Wally with a wide-eyed look of recognition.

He put his hand up against the flash and peered around his fingers. "Jo-Josie from Georgia! I didn't expect to see you again so soon."

Since he was facing me, I kept snapping pictures. Knowing that Andy would want me to at least get a comment if I could, I blurted out, "Hey, Micah. Are you here alone tonight?"

I knew I should have asked him something more specific, but he was smiling that cocky-bratty grin, and it was messing with my killer instinct. If I had a killer instinct.

"I am. Or at least I came here alone." The cameras around us began to flash, but Micah kept his cool, eyes on me, as if we were still standing on the sidewalk in Park Slope, all alone. His lip curled up on one side, like he was gearing up for a challenge. "How'd you like to be my date?"

Now I dropped my camera, and it slammed into my gut. *Oof.* Damn if Andy hadn't called it. I still couldn't process the invitation. "Sorry, what?"

He gestured with his head toward the steps. "Come on. You'll get better pictures inside."

I threw a glance at Wally who looked as envious as Charlie Bucket when the last golden ticket was found. He nodded me forward. Now that fantasy had turned into reality, I realized I wasn't remotely prepared to rub elbows with the same people I needed to exploit. "Sure. But are you sure it's okay? Nobody will mind?"

"Eden will, but I owe you one. And besides I have an in with the guy throwing the party." He offered me his elbow. "Come on. Don't be shy. You might get that Pulitzer prize shot."

I gathered my gear together. Micah stopped and looked down at me while I threw my camera bag and backpack over my shoulder and straightened up. At my full height, he only had a couple of inches on me. I put my hand around his proffered bicep, completely aware of the feel of his skin on my fingertips. He turned his blue eyes on me, and I forgot how to breathe.

The smile dropped from his face for a second, and he asked, "Everything okay?"

I sucked in a lungful of air and laughed off my nerves. "Entering enemy territory for the first time."

His confident, charming smile returned, and he led me up the steps into the brownstone—my own personal Trojan horse.

Micah nodded at the burly man inside the door as we passed. "This is Jo. She's with me."

The bouncer shot me a look of grudging respect. "Good luck."

As Micah pulled me along, I looked back, unsure what the bouncer meant by that, but he'd already turned his attention away, so I faced forward, glancing around wildly for any A-list celebrities.

And it hit me for real. I was on the inside.

Chapter 4

We glided through the partygoers lining the hall, straight into a darker room that appeared to be an entertainment center. A large flat-screen TV occupied the far wall, and a long counter ran down the side of the room in front of a fully stocked bar.

Micah placed his hand on my back and directed me to one of the bar stools. "What'll you have?" He lifted a finger, and an auburn-haired woman appeared out of nowhere, attentive to my needs.

"Club soda please? Could I get a twist of lemon?"

As she occupied herself, Micah slid onto a stool next to me. "Don't drink on the job, Jo Jo?"

There were two answers to that question. I went with the second and confessed. "Don't drink." That answer would leave him wondering if I was straitlaced or overly religious, but whenever I told people I was type 1 diabetic, I ran into even weirder assumptions and judgments. Or people who would want to police my every choice and give me advice based on their experience with Great-Aunt Sally who nearly lost her leg to complications.

Something caught his eye, and he tapped my arm. "I'll be right back. Don't go anywhere."

I surveyed the room, feeling way underdressed in my T-shirt, jeans, and Converse combo. Not that anyone was in tux and tails, but I got the distinct impression that if I asked, "What are you wearing tonight?" nobody would answer, "Something I found at the Mall of Georgia two years ago."

At the end of the bar, Victoria Sedgwick sat, nursing a drink. She looked like that Degas painting, the one where the woman's got her glass of absinthe and a vacant expression. I pulled my camera out of the bag and lifted it slowly. The shutter made the quick whirring sounds that always gave me away, but Victoria was too far away to hear them, in every sense.

I scooted down the bar next to her. "I hope you don't mind, but I've shot some pictures of you. You remind me of this old painting."

"Who are you?"

"I'm a reporter. Is everything all right?"

She took a sip of her drink and grimaced. "I'm supposed to meet Mark Townsend." Her eyes met mine, and I could tell she was assessing me for signs of envy. I didn't know who Mark Townsend was, but obviously she thought he was a big deal.

"Is he not here?"

"He's not here. And now nobody cares that I'm here."

"I care that you're here," I offered.

Her head tilted toward me, her eyebrow arching directly at me. "And who are you?"

My hand ran across my press badge of its own accord. Victoria eyed it. "No, sweetie. You are not your credentials. Do you think you'd be invited in here without that? You're here because someone wants something from you. My guess is free publicity. But you could walk out that door, and nobody would notice any longer than it would take to fish another rat out of that snake pit of paparazzi out front."

Ignoring the mixed metaphor, I couldn't argue with her point. I moved back to the stool where Micah had left me right as he showed up at my side. He laid his hand on my shoulder, familiar, and apologized for abandoning me. I happened to look up and caught Victoria's face change from cool disdain to cold envy and realized I might have trumped her. I'd need to know who Mark Townsend was to say for sure. And I didn't really care.

Micah saw my camera sitting on the bar, the viewfinder still lit up with a photo of Victoria. He winced playfully. "Sorry about this, but . . ." Then he turned to the room and raised his voice. "Excuse me. Everyone, this is Jo—" He hesitated and glanced at me.

"Wilder."

I watched the inevitable reaction—lips pressed into a line, one eye squinted—as he searched for a hilarious joke, then fought the urge to crack it. He turned to face the room, his eyes lingering on mine until the last possible second. "Jo Wilder. She's a reporter and a photographer. And she's a guest. Please be on your best behavior, or whichever behavior you want to see in the morning paper." He winked at me.

"So you don't mind me taking pictures?" An echo of Victoria's bitter spiel ran through my head. Of course he didn't mind. I was free publicity, just like Andy had said. I didn't know what I'd been thinking.

"Nah, but you're gonna have a harder sell with my sister. Come on with me. All the fun people are downstairs."

There'd been a dramatic uptick in the number of guests. The halls were harder to navigate, and we walked turned a little sideways. People stopped Micah every couple of feet. Hands slapped shoulders. Exclamations of greeting were exchanged. Introductions were made. This guy was a local congressman. That lady did the evening news.

I recognized some people. I'd already met or photographed some of them. They didn't recognize me. Their eyes landed on my credentials before they looked in my face. The camera was more interesting still. I didn't take any pictures. Andy wouldn't like that, but Micah was pulling me forward, and I was curious to see what the basement held in store.

As we started down the stairs, Micah asked, "Do you like music?"

I snorted. "Who doesn't like music?"

"You'd be surprised." He offered his elbow again. I hadn't needed help climbing down stairs since I was two, but I eagerly wrapped my hand around his arm. His bicep flexed, and he winked, letting me know he'd done it intentionally. In such close quarters, I could smell his skin. Feigning a slight stumble, I tightened my grip on him, and then as though readjusting, I slid my hand down his arm to better feel his muscle.

Involuntarily, my eyes rolled at my own ridiculous reaction to this guy. I'd met honest-to-God celebrities before. I'd met senators. I grew up surrounded by notable notables on account of my dad. I couldn't remember ever being starstruck. And Micah Sinclair was barely a star.

If anything, he acted as though I were someone worthy of attention. He made me feel like I was someone. But somehow I got the impression he had that effect on everyone. I repeated Andy's admonition, reminding myself that these people didn't really care about me. Without publicity, they'd cease to exist—and I was the publicity. Tonight I was nothing more than Micah's personal paparazza.

The basement turned out to be a recording studio, but so crowded with people, it might as well have been a frat house. Snatches of music drifted over the chatter, coming from one corner. I stood on my toes to try to see who was playing.

He gestured to his shoulders, "You want me to lift you up?"

That elicited a rather unladylike snort. "Do you think anyone would notice?"

We began to move toward the sound. I no longer had any reason to be latched onto Micah's arm, but when I let go, he caught my hand in his and led me across the room.

As we weaved through groups of people, he asked me. "So who's your favorite musician?"

"Of all time? Or current?"

"If I say 'of all time,' what are the chances you'll say my name?"

Without hesitation, I said, "Micah Sinclair." I could flirt, too.

He squeezed my hand. "I won't ask you to name one of my songs. You can do that next time, and I'll pretend you already knew."

I looked away from him, so I wouldn't have to admit he was right. I swore I'd remedy that.

When we reached the other side of the room, we came upon Adam Copeland strumming a guitar and singing. I figured he might be there, but I hadn't seen him come in, and it took me by surprise to find him hanging out like any normal guy. Micah was a bit of a fascination in the tabloids, but Adam was the real deal. I stood in the presence of a huge rock star.

But as weird as it was to see someone that famous in this intimate setting, it didn't make me feel anywhere near as nervous as I'd been moments ago making small talk with Micah.

Adam didn't notice us as he sang quietly without an audience or a microphone. Only his guitar carried into the room past a few feet, but as close as we were, I could hear his voice, too. Another voice wove in, and I located Eden, standing in the shadows, leaning against the wall. Her eyes were closed, and she was harmonizing with Adam, but it was as if she sang to herself. I wasn't used to musicians, and I gaped, completely awed listening to them create something so private right there in the chaotic cacophony.

As the song ended, her eyes opened slowly like she was reluctant to come out of a sweet dream. Adam put the guitar down and jumped up. He took two steps and pressed her up against the glass separating them from a soundproof booth as if the song served as some kind of aphrodisiac. I worried these two were about to share an even more intimate moment surrounded by partygoers.

Micah reached over and picked up the guitar. When he hit a chord, Adam drew away from Eden and looked over. His face lit up. "Micah! When did you get here?"

Maybe Andy was right. If I were cut out for this, I'd have thought to get pictures of Adam and Eden lip-locked in that hot embrace. By the time it occurred to me, it was too late.

The expression Eden shot at Micah was equal parts frustration and forbearance—until she saw me. Then storm clouds gathered. "Micah, what's she doing here? Isn't it enough you're dating your groupies? Do you have to feed the strays as well?"

My camera bag weighed my shoulder down, as if I carried a baby elephant in there. I hadn't taken a private picture of her when I could have. She had no reason to be angry with me. And yet, I felt like I should leave.

Micah swung an arm around my shoulders, protective. "Hey. You need to remember that reporters are people, too."

She scoffed. "You need to remember that they are not your friends, Micah. She's probably looking for an angle right now that she can sell to her editor."

She wasn't wrong. In fact, I worried I'd never be allowed to take my camera out now that she'd seen me.

Micah retracted his arm and lifted his hands, palms up. "I've got nothing to hide."

Eden wasn't having it. "Like they care. You of all people should know she'll twist reality if she can't find any actual dirt."

"But Eden, she might have some good in her yet." He elbowed her, and any doubts I had these two were siblings dissipated. "If you could save just one, wouldn't you want to try?"

She burst out laughing, and her face transformed into a radiant beauty. No wonder she'd hooked Adam Copeland. "I'd love to see one of them redeemed. It would be one less soulless bloodsucker in circulation. But I don't think she came here to be converted. Your mission is doomed to failure, my friend."

I felt like I should say something in my defense. After all, I hadn't asked to come inside. But before I could open my mouth, Micah followed through with his request. "Let her shoot pictures tonight, okay? It'll be fine. I've already cleared it with Hervé—as long as you give your blessing."

The laughter she'd shared with Micah melted off her face. She sucked on her lip for a minute, then appraised me. "You've got three options." She held out her index finger. "First, you can pack up and leave."

She was so tiny, I could have laughed, but right then, I thought she might bite my face off, so I nodded to let her know I was listening.

Her middle finger joined the first, making a sideways peace sign. "Second, you can leave your camera with me and enjoy the party."

I shook my head. I couldn't relinquish my camera. For one thing, it wasn't mine.

"Third, you can move around and shoot any pictures you want. But there's a catch. And if you don't agree to my terms, I'll personally escort you out. Okay?"

I swallowed hard. "Sure." It came out a croak. I glanced over at Adam, standing with his fist covering his mouth like he was trying to hide his laughter. I wondered if he was laughing at me or Eden.

She started over with her index finger. "First, you will let me see everything on your camera before you leave here. Anything I don't like, you'll let me delete."

Damn, she liked lists. I wondered if I should tell her I could upload pictures to our server via a hot spot on my phone periodically anytime I wanted, so waiting until the end of the night to check my pictures was going to be pointless. But I agreed and actually meant it. I could tell Andy I didn't have good service if he'd even hung around this late on a Friday night.

"Second, you will not alter any of the pictures in any way that would change the context in any meaningful way. I understand you need to clean them up, but you will post nothing intentionally misleading."

I could make that promise for myself, but Andy liked to frame a photo with a context meant to lure readers. He specialized in rampant speculation.

But Eden wasn't a fool and said, "Those are my conditions. I recognize that you can agree to them and then do whatever it is you do. But if you break your word, it will be the last time you come to any party I'm at."

I nodded. "No problem. And thank you."

With Eden's permission to shoot the party, I wanted to start moving around, but Micah stuck to my side like a chaperone. Every time I'd lift my camera to get a candid shot of a group of people, Micah would tap one of them and say, "Hey, guys. Say cheese!" Then he'd throw an arm over someone's shoulder and smile perfectly. Confirming my fears that his true interest lay in my camera, Micah insinuated himself into every single shot. But if he hoped to show up in the morning paper, he was wasting his energy. Unless any of the others revealed themselves to be Banksy or Daft Punk unmasked, I didn't expect Andy would use any of these posed pictures.

Yet, I followed Micah from group to group, my lip firmly caught between my teeth as I fought the urge to ask him to let me work alone. After all, if it weren't for him, I wouldn't have been there.

Besides, despite my frustration with the results of my labor, I didn't mind Micah's company one bit. Even if he hadn't so brazenly photobombed every picture, my camera would have sought him out on its own. He was the prettiest thing in the room.

After a short time, I ran out of people in the basement to capture. I certainly didn't need twenty identical posed pictures, so I leaned against the wall to flip through what I'd gotten and see if I could identify anyone worth seeking out later. Most everyone appeared to be musicians which—with the exception of Broadway musicals—wasn't my scene at all.

Micah apparently didn't intend to lose sight of his pet paparazza and peered over my shoulder. "So how'd you get into this business?"

The back of his hand brushed against my arm, standing every hair on end, and I inched away for fear of succumbing to a crazy, dead-end infatuation. "My dad's a photographer. He taught me everything he knew—when he was around." I flipped through the last few pictures. "Unlike him, I can't make a living off my photos yet. That's where you come in." I looked up to find him hunched over my camera.

His eyes met mine, and my perfidious heart fluttered. "What kinds of photos do you like to take? I'm guessing since you came to New York, you're not interested in capturing nature in its wildest state."

Nobody at work had ever bothered to ask me, and they'd be horrified at my silly answer anyway. "To be honest, I like to capture people at their most vulnerable." When Micah frowned, I realized that made me sound like the worst kind of paparazzo. "No, I don't mean—"

"*Micah!*" A short, rotund man whose face was mostly mustache slapped Micah's shoulder. "Aren't you going to introduce me to your friend?"

"Of course! Hervé, this is Josie Wilder. She's the photographer I told you about. Jo, meet Hervé, our host and the best drummer in the world."

We shook hands. "You're Hervé? Your place is incredible."

Hervé tipped an invisible hat. "Micah's not making you work, is he?"

Micah nudged me with his shoulder. "I'm not making her do anything. She's one with her camera."

Hervé winked. "Micah will co-opt all your time if you don't watch him. But you're in luck. I need to borrow him away for a bit. If you don't mind."

"Of course not." I had a compulsive urge to bear hug him. Micah was impossibly sweet, and he tempted me to ditch my camera and enjoy his company, but I couldn't afford to squander this opportunity. I needed just one fortuitous shot to appease my boss.

Before Hervé pulled Micah away, he asked, "Can I at least bring you something to drink?"

"Um, sure. Some water would be fine."

With Micah gone, I moved around like a deer hunter, seeking out camouflage and trying to blend into the woodwork and eavesdrop on conversations, hoping to hear anything I might be able to carry home to Andy and lay on his doorstep like a dead mouse. But nobody was confessing infidelity or plans for divorce. It might have been too early or else my presence had them on high alert, but every snippet of conversation I overheard was innocuous and useless to me.

"No, I didn't go to the VMAs this year."

"How are you enjoying South Hampton?"

"My wife and I went on that cruise line two years ago."

I inched around to where we'd first encountered Adam playing guitar and settled in to shoot pictures from that angle.

A movement in the soundproof booth caught my eye. Adam leaned against the wall, gazing intensely into Eden's eyes. When my shutter snapped, they couldn't hear it.

He brushed a strand of hair off her face. *Click click.* His hand stopped at the back of her head and clutched her hair in his fist. *Click click.* Her hand came up and grabbed his. Her engagement ring caught the light. *Click click.* They stared at each other like they were seeing each other for the first time. A pang of jealousy hit me. I'd never felt anything close to that kind of connection to another person. They were so obviously in love. *Click click.*

Then Adam stepped back and laid his hand on Eden's stomach, caressing. He said something, directed at her midsection. *Click click.*

He leaned down and pressed his ear against her belly, as if listening for a second heartbeat.

I dropped my camera, and the strap pulled taut against my neck.

Oh, my Lord.

Chapter 5

When I registered what I'd seen, I lurched and encountered something hard. And wet.

"Dammit! What the hell?" The man I'd backed into lifted his arm in the air, out of my way, but beer dripped off his elbow. I'd gotten it on my shirt, too, but I ignored it and looked into the recording booth. Adam had just kissed Eden's belly. I grabbed my camera up and paused. Eden looked out, and our eyes met. I hesitated for a half a heartbeat. And the moment was gone. I laid my camera down at my side, turned, and walked away.

My mind reeled with the valuable information I thought I'd discovered. I had no evidence, and I'd missed the money shot, but what I'd witnessed along with the pics I did take would give Andy a story he could spin for major traffic. The question was: would I tell him?

As I crossed the room, lost in my own internal conflict, Hervé caught me and handed me a plastic cup filled with sparkling water. "So you're a photographer? I've always loved those huge pictures of the great western expanses. Ansel Adams stuff, ya know? And pictures of Manhattan that make it look as majestic as a national park. What kinds of pictures do you take?"

These people were so damn nice. I wished I could tell him I took pictures of the Brooklyn Bridge at night. "I work for Andy Dickson over at—"

Recognition registered in his eyes, but his face remained friendly. "Ah, right. So Eden gave you permission to shoot?"

"She was hesitant, but she said I could."

He whistled. "Wow. Never thought I'd see the day. But she always humors Micah."

"Does she? She doesn't seem like the type to humor anybody."

"Eden's a sweet girl once you get to know her, but she's been burned by the media, so she tends to treat you guys with a shoot first, ask questions later kind of attitude." He chuckled. "Kind of like you, if you think about it."

I smiled at his little joke, still processing his appraisal of Eden. Maybe there was more to her than met the eye. From everything I'd seen, Eden was a stone-cold bitch. Except when she was alone with Adam. But who would know better than Hervé? That led to another burning question. "What about Micah? Has the media gotten him all wrong, too?"

He grunted a little grizzled grumble. "Tread carefully with Micah, sweetheart."

I lifted a hand, protesting his inference. "No, I'm just curious if there's more to him than what's been reported."

He half shrugged. "Eh. With Micah, what you see is what you get." He stepped an inch closer, confidentially lowering his voice. "Although the reporters like to paint him as a serial womanizer, you know? It's not fair to him."

"But he does go through women at an alarming rate."

"He does. But numbers aren't the only story. If journalists reported more than the who and the what, you'd know that he treats the women he dates very well. He's respectful and kind. Someday, a girl will come along and appreciate him."

I laughed. He made it sound like Micah was the victim of a string of women using him.

Hervé abruptly broke into my thought. "I don't know if you're going to get anything tabloid-y tonight. This crowd doesn't appear to be interested in making your job easier."

He had no idea I was sitting on a story that would get Andy off my case for a very long time. And it would only cost me Eden's trust—followed quickly by Micah's. Not that I had much chance of securing Eden's, but for whatever reason, at that moment, I valued Micah's opinion more than Andy's. And if I didn't squash that instinct, I'd never make it in this industry.

I shared a secret with Hervé that I'd never told anyone. "To be honest, I much prefer taking candid pictures of ordinary people. I understand why people want to see celebrities doing fabulous things, but I'd almost rather capture people here in everyday life. It would be more interesting for me to see Hugh Grant making a sandwich than climbing out of a limo."

He laughed in a way that was part grizzly bear, part indulgent uncle. "That sounds great. This mug might not be worth photographing, but if I decide to make a sandwich later, I'll let you know."

As he peeled away from me to go mingle with his other guests, I peered through my lens and tried to find a subject worth capturing. In a group near the basement stairs, I found Micah. He was looking directly at me. Andy had claimed he was a media whore, but I didn't think he'd be so conscious of where the only camera in the room was at all times. I snapped a picture anyway. The camera loved him as much as he loved the camera. I didn't want to stand in the way of that great romance.

He walked over and put his arm around my shoulder. "I want to introduce you to some friends if you don't mind taking a break."

I was there at his behest, so of course I didn't mind. "Lead on."

Without withdrawing his arm, he walked along with me, ducking his head a little to speak into my ear. "Are you getting any good shots?" His breath tickled and sent goose bumps down my neck.

"Well, nobody has danced on a table yet, but I'm doing my best with what I've got to work with."

"The night's still young, Jo Jo. Surely someone will suitably shame themselves for posterity."

Near the foot of the stairs, two weathered old men, wearing what could only be described as vintage rocker attire—jean jacket on one, leather vest on the other—stood, arms crossed, heads bent in conversation. Micah approached and pulled me around by his side.

"Josie Wilder, I'd like you to meet Lars Cambridge and Stuart Michaels. Lars is a reporter at the *Rock Paper*—"

"Yes, I know who Lars Cambridge is," I cut in, hand out in greeting. Lars was a legend in his own right. Editor of the hottest music magazine, he'd cut his teeth as a concert photographer. They say it's not what you know, but who you know. Maybe this was a chance to know someone whose career I'd love to emulate.

Once Lars shook my hand, I turned to Stuart and added, "And Stuart Michaels with the Haverford Gallery in SoHo." Two giants of the art world in this small room.

Stuart nodded and shook my hand. "Did Micah say your name was Josie Wilder?"

"Yes." I nodded.

He glanced at Lars briefly as if to confer, but then back to me. "Your name is familiar. Have you ever submitted your work?"

"No, though one day maybe, once I've developed a portfolio." I held my breath a beat to moderate the gushing speed of my vacuum-like sucking up.

He rubbed his chin, eyes narrow. "Did you take a class with me at the Arts Annex?"

"Nope." I pressed my lips together. Stuart dealt in photography and would figure it out sooner or later, so I fed him the bread crumbs. "Maybe you know my dad. Chandra Namputiri?" Only a true photography aficionado would be able to connect the dots from my dad's name to mine.

Apparently Stuart was an avid fan. His eyes lit up. "Ah, yes. That's it." He turned to Lars. "I'm sure you've seen his work in *World GeoPolitical.*"

"Of course. Stunning photographs."

Of course. My dad's photos hung in the National Gallery of Art.

The pieces clicked into place, and the features on Stuart's face lifted like he'd been injected with helium. "And you must be *Anika Namputiri.*" He said it as if my name was the title of a book. I hadn't gone by Anika since I started kindergarten. I'd never gone by Namputiri. Mine was the most obscure fame imaginable—a trivia question for photography geeks.

Lars nodded as if he knew, but his eyes glazed with lack of recognition.

Among my dad's more popular works were a couple of portraits of a daughter he must have once viewed with the same curiosity that drove him deep into the Serengeti or around the corner to Little Five Points, his mind translating the world into compositions of color and shapes. They hung in private collections or galleries, usually with my Indian name, a name I tried to forget.

My favorite photo of his caught me, perpetually tan, running through our backyard sprinkler, rainbows of water spraying, my eyes closed as a smile of pure delight spread across my face. That one hung in a hallway at my mom's house, though. At some point, I'd become another piece of the furniture, inconsequential backdrop to more interesting people in the world.

Stuart held his plastic cup toward me. "I see you've followed in his footsteps. How is he?"

"I wouldn't know. He lives in India with his wife." Stuart's eyes slid away from me briefly. But it wasn't my shame that my dad allowed his parents to pressure him into returning home, that he'd chosen a new family over me. It was his life. Still, it wasn't Stuart's fault the situation was awkward, so I tried to pull the conversation out of the nosedive. "I'm sure he'll get the itch to travel again sooner or later."

In every picture I'd ever seen of my dad, he held a camera. He'd left me with that same love of photography—and abandonment issues when he never returned.

Lars indicated the camera hanging from my shoulder. "Are you here on assignment, or are you permanently attached to your camera like your dad?"

"Assignment."

"Oh? Who do you work for?"

"Andy Dickson at the *Daily Feed*."

His mouth twisted into a subtle sneer. He caught it and corrected it, but I saw it. "Well. It was nice to meet you."

Their heads bent down, and Stuart began talking low to Lars. "Did you say Marta's at Johns Hopkins?"

The conversation changed to things that obviously didn't concern me. And just like that, my dream of making connections in high places burst into flames. I stood awkwardly, casting about for a convincing escape route.

I took a step away and ran smack into Micah's chest. "I thought you'd left."

"Nope. Thought I'd give you a chance to talk to your own kind."

"I don't have a kind." I meant it as a joke, but the truth of my statement right on the heels of such a stinging rejection and invasive thoughts of Dad made my lips twitch into a frown. I swallowed down the traitorous emotion.

As if Micah caught my emotional upheaval, he laid his hand across the small of my back and led me to the far corner, near the soundproof booth. "Is everything okay?"

I forced a smile. "Yes. Thank you for introducing me to Lars and Stuart. I've admired both of them for years."

He relaxed and sat on an amplifier, indicating a stool beside him. "I'll tell you a secret. I've always wanted to be featured in the *Rock Paper*. I mean, as a musician, not as—" He blushed adorably.

"You haven't been?" I recalled the Pretty Boys spread and winced. "Hasn't your band ever been featured?"

"You'd think so. I've known Lars for a while, and I can't get him to do a friend a favor." He laughed, and I got the feeling he was intentionally abasing himself to cheer me up. I was grateful to him for that kindness. "Maybe I should pay him more."

I didn't have to force a smile at that. "It's his loss. I could offer to do a full-length article on you for my paper, but you might not like it quite so much."

"I might if it meant you had to spend some time getting to know me." He struck a teasing tone, but the sincerity in his eyes knocked me for a loop.

I double-blinked, searching for an appropriately flirty, casual reply, but someone approached us and usurped his attention, saving me from navigating the land mines of ambiguity.

When it became clear he'd been sucked into that conversation, despite the apologetic glances he shot me, I excused myself and slunk into the shadows, invisible and unimportant.

Time passed, and people came and went. The volume increased as the alcohol flowed, and I became transparent to the naked eye. It always amazed me how quickly people forgot to notice someone recording their lives. And so I moved around the party, fading into the periphery, forgotten—but the camera remembered everything.

Near two a.m., Eden caught up to me and pulled me upstairs into the kitchen. I hadn't been out of the basement except to use the bathroom in hours. I saw Adrianna LaRue, a ridiculously famous pop star, in the kitchen, huddled with Adam. She flashed brilliant white teeth my way, and I stopped to snap pictures, but Eden grabbed my arm and tugged as the shutter clicked. Those pictures would end up blurred and useless.

Eden led me to a small office and shut the door. "Let me see what you've got."

I flipped the settings on the camera to the viewer and handed it over. "There are a lot of pictures on here." It was going to take me hours to figure out which ones Andy might like to see. He'd go through them all in any case, but I'd want to make sure he saw the best ones.

"These are really great." She rolled through the pictures I'd taken of Victoria. "You have an interesting perspective on the world, don't you?"

I blushed. "I just like to watch people. I mean, to see how they tick."

She nodded. "Yeah. I guess."

As I expected, she slowed down when she got to the pictures of her with Adam. She forwarded through the shots of them talking, kissing, gazing into each other's eyes and then stopped. "Delete these."

She scrolled through five pictures of Adam touching and talking to her belly. "And I know I can't ask it, but I'm asking. Could you please not mention any of this. To anyone?"

I wasn't sure how to respond. It had to be awful to trust her secret to someone paid to spill the beans. But she'd luckily crossed paths with the world's most reluctant pap. "Yeah. I didn't see anything."

She appraised me for a minute, searching the truth through the windows to my soul. I hardly blinked for fear of failing the analysis. Her features relaxed. "Micah might have been right about you. Maybe you're not so bad."

She flipped through the rest of the pictures, with a *hmm* and an *ahhh*. Finally, she handed me the camera. "Do you think you could do some work on the side? Unlike Micah, I'd pay you. I'd love to get some shots of one of my shows. I loathe the pictures up on my website now. They make me look like a 1960s folk singer."

"Sure. Sounds like fun."

"Excellent. Do you have a card?"

I fished one out of my wallet, then hesitated. What if she'd somehow forgotten who I worked for? I still didn't know the story there, but I didn't want to accidentally blow this tentative trust with her. She pursed her lips, so I went ahead and extended the card to her. "Look, I don't know what went down with Andy, but I just work for him."

She studied the card. "Try not to learn anything from him if you can. He's concentrated evil as far as I'm concerned."

"I'll do my best. As it is, he thinks I'm not long for this job."

She snorted. "You do good work. I'm sure you'll make a name for yourself eventually. Keep at it." She paused. "The photography that is. Not the stalkerazzi."

As she stood to leave, I reached out and touched her arm. "Not that I know anything, but congratulations. You both look very happy."

Her expression moved through a complex series of acrobatics—fear, suspicion, appraisal, acceptance, relief, and finally honest guileless joy. "Thank you. But really—not even Micah knows yet. It's way too early. But thank you."

She slipped out of the room, and I felt like I'd made a tentative friend. Hervé was right. She'd been a lot sweeter to me once she dropped her guard. She seemed like someone I'd really love to get to know in a different world, one where I didn't live on another plane of existence. One where celebrity didn't create a caste system. I took out my phone to turn on the hot spot and began the process of submitting my photos.

The door clicked open, and Micah stepped through. "Hey there. I was going to head out. Can I give you a ride? Do you live around here?"

"I live in Williamsburg."

"That's not exactly on my way home, but not too far out of the way. I could give you a lift if you like."

"And where do you live?"

"Brooklyn."

I tilted my head. "Right. Where exactly?"

He shrugged, defeated. "Park Slope."

"Not too far out of the way, huh? I live in the exact opposite direction."

He dropped to his knee before me. "Would you do me the great honor of letting me give you a ride home?"

I could not for the life of me figure this guy out. If there was an angle he was working to get something more out of me, I couldn't find it. "You know I've already uploaded all the pictures from tonight."

He knit his brow. "So . . . you're off the clock?"

"I won't be taking any more pictures tonight."

If I thought he'd change his mind once I was no longer of any service, I was wrong. He held out his hand. "Okay. You wanna go?"

As he opened the door to the townhouse and we emerged into the night air, a dozen cameras pointed at us, shutters *click-clicking*. I picked Wally out of the crowd and waved at him. He didn't smile or wave back. He moved his finger up to the zoom and continued snapping.

Chapter 6

A dozen cameras clicked and flashed in a syncopated rhythm. Voices overlapped with undecipherable questions from both sides, calling out to Micah. Micah put an arm around my shoulder and ushered me to a waiting town car. The driver touched his cap and opened the door for me. Unnerved and somewhat thrilled by my moment in the spotlight, I turned to gawk at the crowding paps. A bright light blinded me temporarily, and I saw spots as I slid across the leather seat of the sedan.

Micah climbed in, and I had a brief moment to wonder if any of my friends or loved ones would yell at me later for taking the risk of riding home with a relative stranger. Both Zion and my mom popped up on my shoulder, alongside the devil, shouting, "Go! Go! Go!" I secured my seat belt.

Once the driver had taken his place behind the wheel, he turned around to ask for my address, and then we were off, leaving the crazy cacophony behind us.

The inequality of our status slammed home all at once, and the sudden dark silence exacerbated my awkwardness. I had no idea what protocol I should follow when crammed into such a small space with my natural prey. Should I make small talk? Or maybe Micah wanted me to interview him. I stared into the night, overwhelmed with shyness and uncertainty.

Fear of Andy's disapproval knotted my gut, and I made up my mind to come right out and ask Micah for a statement on his recent girlfriend. I turned to face him and found him leaning against the door, watching me with interest.

Before I could start my interrogation, he launched the first strike. "I overheard some of your conversation with Stuart. I thought you were from Georgia."

I sat up straighter. "I sure am. Born and raised."

His features changed with the alternating light and shade striping his face as we passed through Brooklyn. "But that's not the whole story."

"No. My dad's Indian. There's a fairly vibrant Indian community outside of Atlanta."

He narrowed his eyes. I could see he wanted to pry. I took a deep breath. People could never quite understand how two people from totally different life trajectories could end up romantically entangled. So I gave him the basic outline. "My dad came over to get an MFA in photography." I smiled, thinking of this bit of shared history. "Same school and department I went into. But I never went for the Master's."

"I never went to college." He said it conversationally with no trace of bitterness. "My sister did. She used to be a biochemist if you can believe that." It was sweet to see him speaking with pride about Eden. "So is that where your parents met?"

"Actually, yes. Mom started an MFA in interior design, but she never finished it."

"Because of you?"

I put my finger on my nose. "Yup. But she does okay without the degree. She has her own business. We always got by."

He shifted but never took his eyes off me. Thankfully, he dropped that line of questioning and opted for something safer. "Did you ever get a chance to go to India?"

"Once. I must have been nine or ten. Dad was from the southwest, a region called Kerala. He took me over to meet my grandparents."

"That sounds like a great trip for a kid."

"Oh. My dad took me everywhere with him. France, Kenya, Tierra del Fuego. But until that summer, he'd never taken me to his home."

I thought back to that summer. Dad had been uncharacteristically quiet and irritable the whole trip over. I'd traveled with him enough to know he was a life-is-about-the-journey-not-the-destination kind of guy. He normally loved every aspect of our trips from planning to packing to boarding the plane to messing with the in-flight music stations. So I knew something was off.

Micah leaned forward, as if listening intently. "That's crazy. I've always traveled, but my entire family lives within a fifty-mile radius. I can't imagine meeting my grandparents like that. Must have been kind of scary."

I tilted my head and poked at emotions packed into memories that were two decades old. "I was a little nervous but mostly excited to finally meet my cousins and grandparents. My dad had taught me enough basic Malayalam so I could grasp some snatches of meaning from context. And most everyone spoke some English."

"But you were the foreigner."

"Exactly. Everyone there treated me as a curiosity. I asked them about their foods and other customs, and they were all eager to repair my ignorance. But really, just seeing where Dad came from—the people he looked like, the places he'd known before—gave me a sense of connection to that other half of me."

I didn't know how he was doing it. I'd never talked so much about my dad to anyone but Zion. But Micah seemed genuinely interested.

"I've never been to India. What was it like?"

"Beautiful. Dad showed me around his city and took pictures of me in front of this amazing temple. And he showed me these gorgeous beaches on the Arabian Sea. We drove up into the Ponmudi hills. There's a reason Kerala is known as God's Paradise. I fell in love with the whole region."

I left out how much I wanted to stay and grow up with a true dual heritage. And I left out the fact that the whole time we were there my grandfather, a man so stern I never could call him the more familiar *Acha-cha,* didn't look me in the eye once. I could hire a therapist to talk about all that. It was nice to remember there had been some good times, too.

"You make it sound irresistible. Now I'd like to see it for myself."

"It is. I can't believe you dragged all that out of me. Are you sure you're not a reporter?"

He laughed. "I'm naturally curious."

"My coworkers all told me you were easy to talk to."

His eyebrows shot up. "Did they? What else do they say?"

I hedged. The answer to that question could get ugly. "Leonard says you're cagey."

"Oh, cagey. I kind of like that. I always figured that, behind closed doors, they'd say I'm easy prey."

"Yeah, kind of. But in a good way."

"There's a good way to be easy?"

I adjusted my seat belt. He waited, so I expounded as sweetly as I could. "Andy says you're savvy because you're so open that anything you say loses value to any specific outlet. And yet, they obviously still all seek you out."

He considered a beat. "So tell me this. Why'd you decide to become a pap?"

"Oh. Well . . ." I wasn't expecting a sort of Spanish Inquisition.

"I mean, I don't mean to judge, but you haven't been here that long, so I was wondering if you came up here specifically for that job."

I cleared my throat. "I did try to find other jobs, but the market for straight journalism is tough right now." I looked down and picked some invisible lint off the end of my shirt. "But a friend of mine from college works there and got me an interview."

"Ah, nepotism," he teased, not condescendingly. "You just wanted to work in New York City, eh?"

I nodded. "I need the job. It pays the bills. It beats flipping burgers." The statement hung in the air, and I thought Micah couldn't have forgotten what it was like to be broke and barely making it. "Can I ask you a question?"

He smirked. "I thought you were off the clock."

"I am. But I'm curious. What went down between Eden and Andy? It must have happened before I got here, and nobody's ever mentioned it to me."

"Yeah, well, I'm sure that for Andy, it's hardly memorable. But for Eden . . . Let's just say that she and Adam are still together despite the articles he ran about her."

"Oh. That bad, huh?"

"Eden thinks so. She fails to remember that Andy couldn't have reported dirt if she didn't have anything to hide. And it all worked out, right?"

"You approach things entirely differently, don't you? I mean, I'm here with you now, so you clearly aren't afraid of the media."

He shrugged. "Eden holds a grudge, but I figure it's the times we live in. Tabloids aren't going away, so why not just be up front and open?"

I could never resist playing devil's advocate, and he'd taken my position, so I rebutted with Eden's point of view. "That only works until you have something you want to keep private. Maybe you've never had a secret? What would you do if you did?"

"That's the thing. I live under the assumption that there are no secrets. It will all come out. I might as well be the one talking about it first, right?"

That gave me a perfect opening for the so-easy-anyone-could-have-gotten-it story I'd failed to get earlier in the week. "So whatever did happen with your last girlfriend?"

His smile disappeared for half a second, and I realized I'd taken him totally off guard. But he recovered fast. "I guess I can't ask you to turn your work off, huh?"

Busted. Any reporter worth her salt would have pressed the point and gotten something to print in the morning paper. I, however, took in his disappointed slump and his guileless blue eyes, knowing I could take advantage of his openness, and I caved instantly. "What? No, sorry. I was asking off the record. I'm sorry. Consider it a residual echo. I'll shut up, now."

He sighed. "First of all, she wasn't my girlfriend."

"No? But you were linked with her for the past month." I'd done my research. In every article, she'd been listed as *"Micah Sinclair's girlfriend, Isabelle Montreuil."*

"Because tabloids are so accurate." He rolled his eyes with a laugh. Not for the first time, I wondered what it must be like to be on that side of the camera, always misinterpreted with no way to put a shattered reputation back together or fight the stories manufactured for someone else's profit.

"So what then? Didn't you break it off with her?"

"Don't you read the gossip pages?" He chuckled at that, and I exhaled, relieved I hadn't offended him.

I had read them. Of course I had. It was like salt in the wound to see other papers easily getting the information I could have had if Micah hadn't flummoxed me. "You said you'd had fun together, but it was never serious." No wonder he had a reputation as a mimbo.

"To be honest, it would be more accurate to say *she* had her fun and was ready to move on. That's what usually happens. I meet a girl, she hangs around for a while, and then she meets someone else, usually someone more famous, and climbs up." This time his laugh rang a little false. The corner of his mouth twitched, and I thought I saw past the perpetually charming facade for a moment. "It's almost like a business transaction."

"That sounds so sad." I faced him, looking into his eyes for any signs he was lying. "Why do you always say it's your fault? You know you've got a bit of a reputation."

"I never said it was my fault. I said it was a mutual breakup, but for some reason, that always seems to read as an admission of guilt." He lifted his shoulders in a slight whatcha-gonna-do shrug. "But it can't hurt my image much, right? I've already been cast as the partying bad boy."

"Well, you do only seem to date party girls."

"No. I've dated nice girls."

"Really? I have a hard time believing I wouldn't have read about them in the gossip pages."

"Nice girls don't like the paparazzi." He winked.

"Like that would stop the paps." I should know.

"I know." He looked out the window. "That's why those re-lationships don't last."

"So what? You just gave up?"

His shoulders sagged, and he faced me with the most seri-ous look I'd seen on him. "I haven't given up. Maybe I've taken the path of least resistance." He leaned toward me. "Maybe I haven't found the right girl."

Was he smoldering? I groaned. "Does that line work on any-one?"

His face lit up in a playful smile. "You'll have to let me know."

"You sure are a smooth operator."

"Nah. Just direct."

I laughed. "Hardly. Interviewing you is like trying to catch a greased pig." He snorted at that, and I considered him, sitting there with his cocky grin. "So why are you telling me all this?"

"I don't know. I probably shouldn't. I can see the exposé to-morrow. However, you did say my three favorite words: *off the record*."

"I honestly don't know what to make of you."

He scooted closer and brushed against me. He'd never strapped on his seat belt. "Copy that. I've been trying to figure you out all night."

"Me?"

Ignoring my mostly rhetorical question, he reached up and pinched a strand of my hair, sliding his fingers down before let-ting the lock drop onto my shoulder where it sprang back into shape. "You really do have beautiful hair."

I shook off the mini-thrill his touch sent through me. I didn't want his flattery to take me in. "You didn't answer my question. Why are you being so nice to me?"

"Journalist, through and through." He took my hand, so gently it was as though he were afraid it would detonate any minute. "And yet, I can tell your curiosity isn't cynical, not yet."

I felt the rough calluses on the tips of his fingers, and as he squeezed a little tighter, his pulse and mine became an inter-changeable rhythm against my own fingertips. I concentrated on holding still, afraid to encourage him to move any closer, afraid he'd pull away.

The cab was dark, and I spoke softly. "Tell me why you picked me out of all the other photographers there."

"It's not that easy, Jo." He sat quiet, and I waited for him to collect his thoughts. "Eden gives me a hard time for running mostly on instinct. But even she grudgingly admitted I may have been right about you. You're like the sheep in wolf's clothing."

I didn't laugh. "You don't think I can do my job?"

"I didn't say that. Eden praised your photography skills. And you've got me here alone, sharing my secrets."

"Because it's off the record. And you don't think I have it in me to take advantage of that information."

He ran his thumb along the back of my hand, and I couldn't contain the ensuing shiver. His lips curved in the slightest knowing smile. "I think you have it in you to be an amazing journalist. But no, I don't think you'd pass the tabloid journalist aptitude test."

I snatched my hand away, indignant. "So you plucked me out of the paparazzi pool to take pictures of your party because I'm so bad at it?"

"I never asked you to take pictures. I offered so you'd agree to come in."

I replayed his invitation, his promise that I'd get better pictures inside, his reaction to finding my camera on after he'd left me alone for a few minutes, his sudden announcement to the party guests. "Oh. I assumed."

He'd slowly moved closer as we talked, and now his face was mere inches from mine. It would take so little to lean forward and taste his lips. A butterfly twisted in my gut at the thought of kissing Micah. If we took a sharp turn or hit a pothole . . .

But this was Micah Sinclair. *Micah Sinclair.* He'd probably seen the longing in my eyes on the faces of a million other girls. I scooted another inch away. "Do you always pick up girls from the paparazzi pool? Or only the incompetent ones?"

He licked his lips, and my first traitorous thought was how

much I wished I could do the same. I swallowed. I didn't want to become a notch on his belt.

"I'm sorry." He had the audacity to smile that charming half smile—more mocking than sincere. I nursed my wounded pride. "I didn't mean to insult you. Honestly, I do sometimes invite photographers into our parties, but when I've invited Wally Stephens inside, I never had any thoughts of doing this."

He closed the gap and brushed his lips against mine. He smelled slightly of cigarettes and tasted of liquor, two vices I denied myself. I drew back and sucked the air into my lungs. He gazed into my eyes, so close, my rapidly blinking eyelashes butterfly kissed his. A million and one questions exploded in my head, all of them screaming, "*What does he want?*"

I shut off the protesting voices and looked into his intensely curious eyes. He was waiting for me to say something. Or do something. I leaned forward and pressed my forehead against his, closing my eyes, leaving the ball in his court. When my shoulders relaxed, he pressed his lips against mine again, harder, but still soft, and I couldn't resist running my tongue across his lower lip. He pulled away and inhaled sharply. He looked back and forth between my eyes and must have seen how much I wanted him to do it again.

He ran his fingers through my hair, holding tight at the nape of my neck and drawing me toward him. When he kissed me again, everything I thought I knew about Micah Sinclair flew out the window. My hands lay flat across his chest at first, but I dared to reach up and touch the side of his neck and the tight muscle running along his back to his shoulder. He groaned, and my heart wouldn't stop pounding.

The car came to a stop.

I glanced up. "Oh," I croaked. We were outside my apartment building.

Micah's breath came shallow and fast. He was looking at me more intently than any person had ever looked at me before. I shook my head to clear the confusion. Would he expect me to stay in the car or get out? Would he expect me to invite him up? Should I invite him up? What did he want from me?

Before things could get awkward, I gathered my camera and my things and opened the car door without waiting to find out what the driver intended to do.

Micah climbed out after me. "Jo."

I could see a light on in my apartment, meaning Zion was awake.

Micah grabbed my shoulder and turned me toward him. "I'm sorry. Did I make a mistake? I shouldn't have—"

"No. God, no." The shaking started in my legs. I needed to bring up my blood sugar, but I thought I could make it upstairs—if I left immediately. I said, "I have to go. I'm sorry."

I lurched away. My hands trembled as I punched in the key code outside the front door. Micah was still saying my name, but I was desperate to make it inside at least. The lock released with a sharp buzz, and I was in, thank God.

Chapter 7

The door clanked shut behind me as I collapsed on the bottom step with my head in my hands. I didn't think I could climb the stairs, so I fumbled for my phone and texted Zion.

Downstairs. Help.

I laid my head down on the filthy step and hoped Zion would come quickly. A door slam echoed down the stairwell. Steps boomed closer. Zion was taking them two at a time, jumping over the last few to get to the landing. Then he was there. He picked me up and carried me up to the apartment where he laid me on the sofa. He grabbed a bottle of grape juice from the fridge, opened it, and handed it to me.

"Have you eaten anything tonight?" he scolded me.

"Yes." I sipped on the juice, ignoring his skeptical expression. "I *did* eat something, but it was earlier. Then I sort of lost track of time."

"That's not like you." He shook his head. "You're lucky I was here. What were you going to do if I was out? Pass out in the stairwell?"

"I saw the light on. I knew you were here." I swallowed the juice and closed my eyes, waiting for the dizziness to subside. "But thanks for coming to my rescue."

He bowed deep. "Prince fucking Charming. That's me. So how did you manage to get home like this? Did you take a cab?

Should I go pay a cab?" He handed me a cold, wet cloth, and I laid it across my neck.

"No. It came on all of a sudden. And I got a ride home from Micah Sinclair." I grinned at him and waited for him to give me the envious glare I'd hoped for.

"You bitch," he said. But his envy quickly turned to curiosity. "Tell me everything."

"It was an interesting night."

"I wouldn't mind five minutes alone with that hot man."

"I don't think you're his type."

Zion huffed. "I might be. His type is generally anything that moves." He stepped into the kitchen.

I called over the back of the sofa. "That's just a rumor."

"Hey, rumors are often based in truth. You might be too new to the gossip pages to realize how often he shows up with a new girl, right on the heels of ditching the last one."

"But I think maybe the tabloids are creating that image of him."

He returned holding my glucose meter out to me. "Why would you think that?"

I rubbed my thumb with an alcohol wipe and pricked it. The blood beaded, and I laid the test strip against it. "On the way over, Micah told me—off the record—that he'd rather take the rap for the breakups, but it's usually him who gets dumped when girls tire of playing with him and move up the ladder."

The meter still read below seventy, and Zion went to the kitchen and came back with a banana. "So Micah just happened to confide that to a girl who works in the gossip business? You don't think he's maybe trying to clean up his image through you?"

My stomach sank. "But it was off the record."

"Yeah, but he has to know that information will color anything you write about him in the future."

"I hadn't thought of that."

He peeled the banana and handed it to me. "Eat this."

I concentrated on chewing and swallowing, more worried about getting my numbers up than about Micah for the moment. As soon as the banana was gone though, another thought occurred to me. "But then why did he—"

"Why did he what?" He dropped into the chair beside me, chin on his hands. He was a worse gossip than my mom. No wonder they got along so well. No wonder he was so much better at this job than me.

My face flushed with embarrassment at how easily I'd let Micah take me in. That kiss bamboozled me, and he'd known it would. "Nothing."

"What happened?"

I flailed my arms. "I let him kiss me, okay? Oh, Lord. I'm such an idiot."

He sat back, his budding afro snapping into place a microsecond later. "Way to bury the lede, Josie." His eyes closed and then opened wide. "You aren't serious."

"Yeah."

"You kissed Micah Sinclair."

"Yeah."

"Micah fucking Sinclair."

"Yes."

"Good God. How was it?" Now he leaned forward, looking at me like I might levitate at any moment.

"It was amazing. Up until I nearly passed out and abandoned him on the sidewalk."

"What?" He jumped up and peered out the window, as if he could see the sidewalk from that angle. "Did you say anything to him?"

I looked at him through veiled lids. "I was kind of too busy trying not to drop into a coma at his feet."

"You didn't tell him anything?"

I crossed my arms. "Drop it. It's probably for the best anyway. Can you imagine if I'd asked him to help me up here?"

His eyes rolled up to some invisible thought bubble over his head. "I'd like to imagine that."

"Zion!" I laughed. "You're the worst."

He shrugged. "But yeah. It's probably better that you don't

get involved with him. He'd end up breaking your heart. And he wouldn't even mean to."

"Yeah." I stretched, and that caused Zion to yawn. "I should get some sleep. Why are you home, anyway? I figured you'd be at Robert's."

He fell into the sofa beside me and grimaced. "He's ghosting me. I thought about going out anyway, but my heart wasn't in it."

I scooted over and lay my head on his chest, snuggling against him, drowsy. "I'm sorry. I wished I'd known you were here eating your heart out."

He wrapped his arms around my shoulders and squeezed. "No worries. Plenty more fish in the sea. At least one of us got some action." He dialed his Southern accent to eleven and said, "After all, tomorrow IS another day."

I woke up to the sounds of sizzling in the kitchen. I gravitated to the living room, dropped on the sofa, and checked my glucose. Over the months I'd lived with Zion, he'd become part-time roommate and full-time best friend. We'd been close in college, but since we worked and lived together, our relationship had morphed into one of family. And I suspected he'd made some kind of deal with my mom to keep an eye on me. Once in a while, he hovered—especially when he thought I was overdoing things. I didn't mind so much. I knew he cared about me as much as I cared about him.

He fluttered around, fixing breakfast, so I got up to straighten, but he told me to sit and relax until after I ate. Since I'd moved in, I hadn't had a serious hypoglycemic episode, but he'd been there in college when I'd landed in the hospital after a particularly stressful finals week. He obviously still wore a cloud of worry about the night before.

It was a good thing it was Saturday morning. If we'd been at work, his behavior would have irritated Andy. Andy only grudgingly put up with extra accommodations, like allowing me to keep juice and insulin in his minifridge. Andy told me his college roommate had been able to control his diabetes through diet and exercise as if my precautionary syringes were further proof of a character weakness. No use explaining to him that my body did not actually produce insulin.

I felt fine, but I'd never convince Zion of that. So I sat down to read a book, but my mind wandered as I daydreamed about the night before. Or more accurately, fretted about what Micah must be thinking after I'd left him standing on the sidewalk without an explanation. Did he think I was still angry at him for insulting me? (I was.) Or offended by him for kissing me? (I wasn't.) Or repulsed by him physically. (Definitely wasn't.) I had no way to reach him to apologize and tell him I'd loved every second of that kiss. (I had.)

Did he feel like an idiot? I did.

In addition to worrying I was putting him off, I couldn't shake the idea he was putting me on. Was he serious about why he invited me into the party? Surely, he just charmed his way through everything. Did girls ever say no to Micah Sinclair? How many questions had he silenced with those lips?

Zion was right though. If I let myself fall for Micah Sinclair, he'd break my heart without even knowing it. Better to acknowledge he was having a bit of fun and let it go.

When my phone rang, Zion was handing me a plate of something yellow and orange—either cheese eggs or undercooked eggs—and I didn't bother to check the incoming contact before hitting Answer.

"Josephine, what the hell?" I pulled the phone away from my face and stared at the screen. I kicked the leg of the coffee table.

"Morning, Andy. What's up?' For him to call on a Saturday morning did not bode well.

"I waited last night for your pictures. I finally gave up and went to bed only to discover you uploaded everything in the middle of the night."

"I know but—"

"And then all the pictures are completely useless." I held the phone out so Zion could hear the tinny insults barreling out my speaker. "People standing around mugging for the camera. Who wants to see that?"

"I know, but everyone was hyper aware of the camera, Andy."

"So that's when you turn it off and mingle. Did you get any story at all?"

I thought about Eden and her secret. "No, Andy."

"The really funny part is, the biggest scoop of the night was captured outside the townhouse by another paper."

"Why? What happened?"

"Well, I could have sworn I saw a picture of you leaving the party and getting into a car with Micah Sinclair. I must be looking at some *other* Josephine Wilder on Page Six of the *New York Post*."

I mouthed *"Oh, shit!"* at Zion. I pointed frantically at the laptop, rolling my hand in a circular fishing motion. He opened it up and slid it to me.

"What do you mean?" I was stalling. I knew I was dead, but I had to see. I pulled up the website and clicked the links to get to the gossip page. And there I was, right beside Micah Sinclair. I should have expected that. A dozen flashing cameras had surrounded us as I'd climbed into that town car with Micah. The caption did me in: *Micah Sinclair leaves party with paparazzi photog Anika Jo Wilder, daughter of famed photographer Chandra Namputiri.*

"Oh." I felt the blood drain from my face. It was worse than I could have imagined. I hated that they'd printed my name like that and felt the cruel irony of getting pissed at a tabloid journalist for digging into my life. "I can explain."

"Did you at least get any kind of statement from Micah?"

"Andy, he went off the record."

"And so what? Am I paying you to party with these people?"

"He was just giving me a ride home. It wasn't like that."

"Listen, Scout. You've given me nothing I can work with all week. Do I have to remind you what your job is?"

"No."

"Then understand that you can't befriend these people. You have to make a choice between work and play. If I see you hanging out with celebrities, I'm going to expect something I can actually print. Do you understand?"

"Yes, Andy." It wasn't like I'd be hobnobbing at another party any time soon.

"You take great photos, Jo, but we're not in the business of flattering people. And I need you to step up your game." His tone relaxed, and I knew the storm had blown over. "You know, I do hear the complaints from human resources, so I am well aware you guys think I'm too hard on my staff." I held my breath. I didn't know how to respond to that. "But it's only because I want you to be your best, right?"

I gave a noncommittal grunt.

He paused as though waiting for a vindication that would never come. After a beat, he went on. "Okay, then. I'm going to comb through these pictures. Maybe I'll find something I can use. Maybe someone brought a date instead of a wife to the party." He hung up.

My eggs were cold, now. I pushed them away and said to Zion, "How have you managed to work for him for so long?"

The notification ringtone dinged on my phone, reminding me I needed to get on my computer and catch up with emails and social media. Since my mom had discovered Facebook, it was the only way she communicated. If she did call, she'd say, *"Did you see what I posted on Facebook?"* I'd have to log in and read it even though she had me on the phone. And then she'd ask to talk to Zion because he'd actually tell her what was going on with me.

Today's ding resulted from a mention when my mom posted a link to the article about me. *My daughter Josie Wilder out on the town with a celebrity!*

She was the worst name dropper. She still bragged about knowing that guy who hosted all those reality competitions because they went to the same high school. Didn't matter that she was eight years older than him and would have already graduated by the time he even started. And this despite her connections to an artist whose name meant something in some circles. They say familiarity breeds contempt. Apparently, so does emotional desertion.

I typed, *Mom, I was just working,* and then surfed the rest of my usual points of contact. Why everyone couldn't agree to reach me the same way, I couldn't understand. Mom Facebooked, Zion texted, and my dad still emailed.

Speaking of Dad, an unread message from him sat in my queue.

"Oh, no."

Zion snuck up behind me and leaned over the sofa. "What?"

"My dad."

"Has he contacted you once since you've been here?"

"Once." I swallowed hard before I answered completely. "On May twenty-third. Two days after my birthday."

"Do you think he saw the article?"

He'd left the subject line blank, so I couldn't predict. I braced myself for whatever he'd have to say.

> Anika,
> I have received a forwarded article today with my name below a gossip rag photo of you. I am disappointed to find this. Please remember that my name is forever yoked to yours, and your actions reflect on your family. I expect better from you, Anushka.
> Papa

By "my family," he meant himself. His wife didn't acknowledge I existed, and my mom was clearly delighted by my antics. That's what I had to deal with. One parent I never disappointed and one parent I always let down. I put my laptop on the coffee table and curled up on the sofa, hugging a pillow.

"Bad?" Zion could ask invasive-as-hell questions, but he wouldn't read over my shoulder.

"No." I covered up the warble with a nervous laugh. I sat up and took a drink of water. I would not cry. He wasn't worth it. He didn't have the power to upset me.

Zion didn't seem to notice. "So what did he want? Did he see the article?"

"Yeah. He's just irritated." I laughed again, even though I'd said nothing funny. "He used my pet name, so he's going with shame instead of threats." That was kind of hilarious.

"What can he do, Josie? Tirovanillapooram is eight thousand miles away. And you're an adult."

I corrected his pitiful attempt to say the name of the city where my dad lived. "Thiruvananthapuram."

"Right. What I said. But seriously, what can he do from there?"

"He can still make me feel like I'll never measure up."

Once upon a time, my dad sat me on his knee while he dismantled his camera or picked through slides to find photos to submit to magazines. He would talk to me with an accent he never lost and tell me about exciting treks into Nepal or a chance to meet a traveling dignitary. I always associated those memories with the smells of the *beedi* he smoked and the Robusta coffee he imported from Kerala.

Back then his name held no special recognition. But he had to work, and among his future prizewinning shots of exotic peoples, less artistic photos of run-of-the-mill celebrities mixed in. And I still recalled his pride and joy when his image appeared in the local newspaper in black-and-white, catching him speaking to the actor Mohinder Khan. But he conveniently forgot that he'd had to start out somewhere. In his mind, he'd always been *the* Chandra Namputiri, world-class photographer—no longer "world's greatest dad."

I could live without his hypocritical condescension. I deleted the email.

In the inbox, another email caught my attention. "Oh, Eden wrote me."

Zion had settled on a chair with his feet propped on the coffee table. "Seriously? Look at you moving up the social ladder. What's she want?"

I read the email. "She wants me to come photograph her performance at some club in Lower Manhattan. And she said my three favorite words."

"Micah loves you?"

I threw my pillow at him. "She said: *I'll pay you.*"

Chapter 8

Since Eden had said I could bring a friend, Zion insisted on escorting me to her show. I couldn't tell if he was hoping I'd get to hang out with Micah again or if he was actually concerned for my health. But either motive was invalid. He had no reason to expect Micah to show up for his sister's show. And I could take care of myself. I wasn't likely to forget to eat again after last night. My pocketbook held sandwich bags filled with emergency snacks.

The entrance to the club hid under scaffolding, but even without the obstruction, the door was nondescript, dark. A neon sign lit the window behind a curtain of advertisements and posters. Zion pushed the door open, and I followed him through, unsure whether I should hold my breath. The room was so murky, I assumed there would be smoke, but the delicious aroma of coffee and food hit me. Underneath that, I could detect a slight underlying stink of cigarettes and body odor—the smell of dark places.

Several feet in, we approached a podium where an Asian woman leaned on her elbows watching us. "Tickets?" she asked.

"No, uh, we—"

"This is a private show. Tickets required in advance."

Zion spoke for me. "We're on the guest list?"

She scanned the page. "One minute. You stay here." She left

us and dropped farther into the club. We probably could have simply walked in, but it seemed bad form. And I would have rather been admitted properly. After all, we were invited.

The woman returned, trailing a man wearing a Pussycat Dolls T-shirt and sporting well-groomed facial hair. He put his hand out to me. "Hi, I'm Tobin. You must be Jo?"

I nodded. "And this is my friend, Zion. Eden said I could bring a guest."

Zion put his hand out in the way he did like he was at a debutante ball and he'd been asked to dance. Or like he was the Pope, and he expected someone to kiss his ring. It always made me blush, but I'd long since stopped trying to cajole him into normalcy. He told me it was like a white cane for a blind man. It was one way to test out the world.

Tobin took Zion's proffered hand, and to my surprise, he leaned forward and planted a kiss right on the tops of Zion's fingers. Zion flashed me a satisfied side-eye. *You see?* Tobin looked up into Zion's eyes for the first time, and the two appraised one another. I felt distinctly invisible. And with the darkness of the club, I practically was. Tobin led us toward the stage.

An alcove held several tables with merchandise for sale— T-shirts, CDs. I saw Eden's album and stopped for a minute to pick it up and flip it over. A woman behind the table asked if she could help me, but I didn't want to buy anything.

I caught up with Zion, who'd found a seat close to the stage. The club provided tables or stools along the bar, but the stage area held nothing but rows of chairs. I threw my camera over the back of one. "Do you think I should look for Eden?"

He shrugged. "I wish you'd let me bring my camera. I bet there will be some interesting people here tonight."

I shot him a warning glance. "You wouldn't be here if it weren't for me. And I wouldn't be here if I wasn't asked to do this privately."

He craned his neck around. "Hey, isn't that Adrianna LaRue?"

Sure enough, on the other side of the room, the pop singer preened on a chair no different than the one I sat in. But somehow she made it look like a throne. Her enormous hair eclipsed the entire row to her right. She was the definition of larger than life. Something struck her funny, and when she giggled, she covered her face with both hands and leaned back. And then I saw him sitting beside her. Micah Sinclair twenty feet away from me, breathing the same air.

Zion saw Micah at the same time as me and pulled at my sleeve. "Come on. You have to introduce me."

I swatted his hand away. "You've interviewed him before, Zion. You've talked to him countless times I'm sure."

"Yeah, but I've always been a nameless face, a reporter. I've never just sat and talked to any of these people. And Adrianna. Oh, shit. You should be shooting pictures." He sat back into his chair and pushed my camera bag at me.

Despite my earlier protestations to the contrary, I gratefully wrapped my hand around the strap and unlatched the clasp. "I totally shouldn't be doing this."

Once I had my camera poised, I cut a glance over to where Micah sat, but his chair was now empty. Before I had a chance to spin my head around, surreptitiously of course, to relocate him, I felt a hand kneading the muscle between my neck and shoulder like the start of a massage. I dropped my head back and looked straight up at the bottom of Micah's chin. His face was upside down. His smile was a frown.

"I saw you over here. Why don't you come sit with me and Ade?" He gestured toward the other side, and Zion was already up and moving.

"Micah, this is my friend Zion. Zion, Micah."

Micah put his hand out to Zion, and Zion forgot to offer his dainty handshake. He clasped Micah's hand and said, "It's great to meet you."

Adrianna stood as we came over. I couldn't make my brain process that she was a real person, hanging out in this dingy club, wearing a massive boa with a blond afro teased out about a foot in every direction. She was like a living Barbie doll, a freaky living Barbie doll. Zion was about to bow down before her.

Micah intervened to make introductions. "Ade, this is my friend Jo-Jo from Georgia. Or should I call you Anika?"

I knew he teased, but he couldn't know the depths of my anger toward that name. "Please don't. That's what my dad calls me. I go by my middle name."

"You have many names, Jo Jo." He turned to Adrianna. "And this is her friend Zion. . . . Where are you from, Zion?"

Adrianna lifted her hand up in the exact same way Zion had earlier. He took her fingers in his hand and lifted them to his lips for a benediction, but his eyes were absorbing every detail of her hair, and I knew he was trying to figure out how he could re-create that. I'd tell him later it was probably a wig. He couldn't make his real hair do what her fake hair could do. But right then, it was all possibilities. Right then, he was working out how many times he'd have to bleach it to go from midnight black to virgin white, and his eyes were saucers.

Adrianna cooed, "Aren't you adorable?"

I answered Micah's question for him. "Zion lives in Williamsburg. You dropped me off at our apartment last night."

"Right." He tsked. "But I only saw the sidewalk. You left in a bit of a hurry."

"Yeah, sorry about that. I wasn't feeling well."

Micah sat down and indicated a chair to his right. I moved around Adrianna and sat beside him, on the end. That left Zion alone with Adrianna. From the looks of things, I didn't think he'd mind. I couldn't tell if it was the celebrity or her mesmerizing beauty, but Zion was a goner. I hoped I wasn't gawking at Micah so openly. I was thankful for Zion's complete loss of composure since it took the focus off my own.

"Zion from Williamsburg." Micah said that as though he were considering the title of a novel. "Nope. I can't work with that at all. Surely he's not *from* Williamsburg. Nobody's *from* Williamsburg."

"No. He's from down South. Like me." I'd already Googled the basic facts about Micah and knew his family lived somewhere in New Jersey, but for the sake of conversation, I asked, "And where are you from?"

He scrunched up his nose. "Sometimes I wish I could say I'd been born and raised in West Philadelphia."

"Huh?"

"Like *The Fresh Prince of Bel-Air*?"

I stared at him blank. No clue.

He frowned at my silence. "It's a TV show."

"Oh, right. I didn't watch that."

His eyes opened wide. "How old are you?"

I snorted at the impertinence of the question. "I'm scandalized."

The dimple in his cheek made an appearance when he laughed. "I mean, you must be a lot younger than me if you don't remember *The Fresh Prince of Bel-Air*."

I sat up to my full height as if that would make me look older. "I'm the same age as you."

"Thirty-two?"

"I turned thirty-three in May."

"Hmm." He scratched his chin. "You're older than me."

"Only by a couple of months. You'll be thirty-three in a few weeks." My face flushed with the realization I'd basically admitted to stalking his online bio.

"You've done your homework." The corner of his mouth turned up. "So how'd you miss out on a classic nineties sitcom?"

A memory stirred. I used to sneak out to my neighbor Kelsey Bennet's house to gorge on ice cream and forbidden TV, before my diagnosis. "I do kind of remember that show, but I wasn't allowed to watch sitcoms. Brain rotting."

"What a sad childhood. We'll have to make up for it sometime. You should come over, and we'll marathon all the junk sitcoms and eat all the junk food."

I appraised him to figure out if he was being serious. It would be embarrassing to say yes if he was only fooling. "Sounds fun."

He clasped his hands in supplication, like he was praying. "Think about it. Crappy food and television. You totally want in, right?"

"Yeah?" I fiddled nervously with my camera lens.

"If it would entice you more, you could do a whole photo

spread of me eating pizza and watching sitcoms in my boxers at home."

And there it was. I cringed at how easily I'd let him convince me he was hitting on me. I'm not sure why he wanted to float pictures of himself being a regular guy. Maybe he'd talked to Hervé and found out what I'd said about that. But I drew the line at shooting pictures of guys in their underwear anyway.

I settled in my chair, trying to pretend I couldn't feel the gravitational pull of the hot celestial being to my left. He leaned over and started to say something else, but a movement caught my attention. Two women had taken seats behind us, and one of them tapped Micah's shoulder before they fell back, heads together, giggling. When Micah looked at them, they burst into full hysteria.

The one with short-cropped gray hair said, "I'm sorry. My girlfriend thought that was you." She was still recovering. "She wanted me to ask you for an autograph."

Micah had already turned around with a hand outstretched. "Hi. What are your names?"

"I'm Martha," said the gray-haired woman. She had incredible skin. It made me wonder if she was prematurely gray or if she had great genes. I had no idea how old she was. "And this is my friend Lynn." Lynn had long brown hair, tied back at either side of her face. They both wore loose yoga wraps over tighter T-shirts and jeans. Lynn had accessorized with dangly earrings.

"Do you have something for me to sign?" Micah waited, and both women knocked each other as though he were on display at a museum and couldn't see them.

Martha looked at Lynn. "Do we have something he can sign?" Her face contorted like she was stifling another onslaught of hilarity. "Here. Can you sign my arm?" She held out a ballpoint pen.

Micah took it with a dubious scowl. "I can, but you have to promise you won't go and get a tattoo of it or something. Just take a picture. Trust me."

That sent Martha into a convulsive fit, and she held her stomach. She obviously couldn't believe she'd been so bold tonight.

Her friend held her arm out and shoved up the sleeve. Lynn was the brains of the operation apparently.

Micah wrote, "What a crazy night that was. Micah Sinclair." Or I assumed it said Micah Sinclair. Only the *M* and the *S* were legible.

Lynn showed it to Martha, and Martha shoved her sleeve up, too. "Me, too?"

"Sure." He wrote, "We'll always have TriBeCa," and the same scrawl of a signature. Anyone could have scribbled that on their arms.

Lynn fished out her phone. "We have to get a picture with you. Our friends are never going to believe us." She handed the phone to me. "Do you mind?"

Suddenly a part of this situation, I took the camera and leaned back so I could get all three of them in. Martha and Lynn held their arms up so the signatures were visible. I said, "One, two, three." The camera clicked, and the two ladies flopped into their seats, content. The invisible boundary went back up.

Micah faced forward again. His face registered no difference in attitude, but I felt his shoulders sag and the energy seep from him.

"That seems exhausting," I whispered.

"Better than flipping burgers."

"Good point. How'd you end up a musician anyway?"

"When I was in high school, I started a band with some of my friends and let my sister sing with us sometimes." He cut his eyes at me. "I never told her our audience doubled if we announced that she'd be singing. I didn't do great in high school, but I worked summer jobs and saved up money so I could move to Brooklyn and join up with some guys who were looking for a front man. The rest, as they say, is history."

"What else do you do? I mean when you're not onstage, at a party, or supporting your sister?"

His eyes narrowed briefly. Did he think I was trying to get him to talk about all those women he dated in his spare time? Would it be horrible of me if I was? But he relaxed back into that cocky half grin. "Music takes up about eighty percent of my life. I'm either touring or rehearsing or writing or going to see other musicians. I spend the rest of my time blowing off steam—or sleeping."

"How do you blow off steam?" I was incorrigible. But I wasn't asking as a journalist. I really wanted to know.

A wry little devilish light gleamed in his eye, and I knew I'd pushed too hard. "Treks through the Amazon mostly. You know, saving the rain forest."

I pushed his shoulder, but he didn't budge. His shoulder muscle was hard as a rock. "Tease."

He pretended to be pushed over, a second later. "Yeah? Then why was I the one left standing on the sidewalk last night?"

Before I could formulate words again, the sound quality of the air changed noticeably. People stopped milling around their chairs and all settled in. If there'd been a cue, I'd missed it, but moments later, the lights dimmed. Eden had advised me that there'd be an opening act that I could use to set levels on and get in some test shots. She also told me to get up and move around, but all the chairs were full, and people were leaning against the walls on either side. I'd be in someone's way anywhere I went. But I was being paid to be in someone's way.

Tobin, the guy we'd met up front earlier, hopped up on stage to a smattering of applause and a couple of catcalls. He pulled the mic up and scanned the audience. "So good to see so many familiar faces out here tonight."

More applause.

"The fact that you were all so willing to give up five times the normal ticket price for this event just goes to show how much you all take advantage of me."

The audience laughed.

"Starting tomorrow, the cover charge will be adjusted accordingly." Tobin smiled. "Seriously, though, I'm appreciative that all of you were willing to come out tonight. The proceeds will go to a great cause:"

Tobin paused for a minute, and the smile faded from his face. He cleared his throat. "Some of you here remember my mom, Elena." His hand rubbed across his cheek, almost of its own accord, brushing off a tear maybe. "Mom fought a long hard battle. She was my fiercest supporter. She stood for things and made a difference despite her own frailty. She had so much strength, but—" He took a deep breath and heaved it out as though he couldn't contain it.

Someone in the audience hollered. "We love you, Tobin!" And others applauded and shouted encouragements.

Tobin raised his hand to indicate a banner hanging behind him for an organization that specialized in muscular dystrophy research. "Together we'll find a cure." His voice was pitched and the tears fell unchecked. "Let's give a huge round of applause to Eden Sinclair and Kelli Hind for volunteering their own time for this special evening."

The applause from the crowd was powerful and clearly in support of Tobin more than in support of the fund-raiser. I got the feeling these people would've come there if he'd asked them to support clown school. Even though I didn't know Tobin, his speech affected me. My heart constricted at his loss. I fought the urge to go back to the door and pay my way in. But I didn't have a hundred bucks on me. Or in my bank account.

When Micah leaned over and asked if I'd ever seen Kelli Hind, I shook my head, afraid to speak for the lump in my throat.

At last Kelli took the stage, gave her own short speech, and started to play. I lifted my camera and shot off a picture. Hearing the shutter open and close, I cringed. I glanced at Micah, but he continued to nod his head to the music. I hoped that I was just being hypersensitive to the noise and shot another. Then I checked the pics and readjusted for lighting. After I was confident I had the right settings, I relaxed and enjoyed the music. It wasn't the style I usually listened to, but the woman sang and played well. It beat leaning against a wall out on the street hoping for a celeb to wander by. Or flipping burgers.

I turned my head slightly so I could take in Micah without him noticing. He was completely rapt by the singer. Even his fingers tapped along. His blond hair shook lightly in time with the beat. He was so pretty I couldn't even stand it. The cord running down the side of his neck tightened and relaxed along with subtle changes in his mouth. He moved his lips slightly like he wanted to sing along. Like he was singing along to himself.

My skin sparked with the awareness that he sat half a foot from me. I didn't know if I'd ever be that close, that comfortable, that familiar with him again. I wanted to bump him, pull his hair, pinch his arm. Anything to be able to put a hand on him.

Like a wish come true, he brought his arm around the back of my chair and leaned over without turning his eyes away from the stage. "What do you think?"

I didn't know how he managed to make me hear him without disrupting anyone else around us. I couldn't trust myself to speak at such a perfect volume, so I made a show of twisting toward him, as if I hadn't been staring at him, and whispered close to his ear, "She's good." I wanted to push my shoulders against his forearm, but I also hoped he'd forget to move away from me. If Andy knew I was sitting this close to Micah and hadn't asked him a single investigative question, he'd crucify me. But what Andy didn't know wouldn't hurt him.

Micah said, "Yeah. Wait till you see Eden."

But right then, I only wanted to see him. And I wondered how I was going to do the one thing I'd been asked to come here to do while Micah Sinclair had his arm across my shoulders in a dark club. I sat back a little farther, experimentally, and his fingers grasped my arm, tightening with a little squeeze.

Kelli sang about the shadow of a feeling, and I wondered if she'd written that song about me.

Chapter 9

After six songs, Kelli thanked the audience and exited the stage. The lights came up slightly, and people stood, stretched, headed to bathrooms or the bar. Micah turned in his chair, his arm pulling a hair'sbreadth away from my back. "I used to play this club a lot. Did Eden explain the best places to shoot from in here?"

And just like that, we switched to publicity-hound Micah. I straightened up. "No. Tell me."

"Start here. Eden doesn't move around so much that you'll miss some exciting stage dive."

"Okay."

"After you have what you need, then you should go to the bar." He twisted his shoulders around and pointed. "There. See those tables? They're on a riser. You can get some great shots from that angle."

"Got it."

"Then over there." He pointed to the other side of the stage. "There's a set of steps leading to the stage. Go stand over there. You can even get up on the stage some as long as you don't draw too much attention. You should try to get there before her last song."

"Why? What's the last song?"

"Just trust me."

"Sure." I was a professional. I could take direction. "Where's the fourth place?"

He turned again toward a location he'd already pointed out. "There."

"Again?"

"No, not there." He touched my temple and pushed my head ever so slightly so I was looking directly back—at the door to the club.

"Outside?"

"Yeah. When you're done here. Meet me outside."

I looked up into the Caribbean of Micah's blue eyes. "Meet you outside," I repeated it like it might mean something different to him than to everyone else.

The charming half smile called his dimple out to play. "Yeah. You should come hang out after the show. Unless it's too late for you."

"Oh." I was at an actual loss for words. "Yeah. Maybe."

The night before flashed in my memory. He'd implied that his kiss hadn't been a spontaneous decision, and I wondered if his plans might lead us back there. My eyes fell on his lips, curling wickedly, and I thought, yes, he might also wish we'd finished what we'd started. Before my near loss of consciousness.

Whether or not it would be wise to toy with Micah, I found him impossible to resist, and I didn't break eye contact with him until the lights dimmed, and the show went on.

I'd come prepared tonight so I wouldn't be caught with low blood sugar again. I reached down into my pocketbook and rummaged around to find a plastic bag holding a handful of cut carrots. I slipped one out and crunched into it, wincing at the explosion of sound in my own head.

Micah glanced over. "You might want to save the rabbit food till later, Bugs."

I didn't know why I'd packed nothing but nuts and carrots and things that go crunch in the night. I put the bag away. I'd be okay for a little while, and it was time to get to work.

Eden stepped up on the stage to a burst of applause. She took some time getting the mic situated and dragged a stool forward to lean against. Watching her, I was struck again by how different she looked from her brother. Micah was tall and fair but not pale, whereas Eden was small and nearly alabaster. And while Micah had obviously taken care to style his blond hair, Eden's wavy black hair had been pinned in a barrette as an apparent afterthought.

They both seemed to have paid almost no attention to clothes, opting for comfort over style. Eden had on a pair of faded blue jeans, worn-out leather ankle boots, and a T-shirt advertising a band that had broken up last year. I wondered if she remembered I'd be shooting pictures. I hoped she'd pay me either way.

Finally, she leaned into the mic. "Hey, everyone. Thanks for coming out in support of this great cause. I hope none of you were hoping to see Adam tonight 'cause he's halfway to Tokyo. We're going to have a good time without him."

I didn't even realize Adam Copeland singing in a small club like that would have been an option. Part of me was devastated to lose out on an opportunity to get some close shots of him there in the club, performing. But the ethical side of me was relieved not to have to wrestle with that dilemma. I wasn't there to take tabloid photographs for my own profit. I was being paid a set wage to take professional shots to give to Eden. I didn't think she could sue me for turning them in to Andy or selling them to an agency, but she'd probably murder me. And I'd never work for her again. Because I'd be dead.

While she began to strum, I trained my lens on her and took several close-ups, several full frame shots and then tried to get her in the context of the stage. I was too close for this, so I got up and moved to the area Micah had indicated. Sure enough, it was a perfect location for taking pictures. And as Micah had promised, Eden didn't vary her performance so much that I needed to take many. Instead, I sat and listened to her perform, quickly forgetting I was there for a job as I drifted into the music. She had a lot more talent than the girl who'd played before. More talent than I'd realized. Maybe I'd pick up her CD after all.

I'd never paid much attention to Eden's music. Zion had filled me in on her background on our way over. She'd reputedly used nepotism to break into the music business. Twice actually—through her brother, Micah, and her boyfriend, Adam. She'd met Adam a few years ago through Micah when their bands toured together. A year later, she had a song that played occasionally on the radio. It would probably get more airplay if people respected her as a musician who'd paid her dues. Or if people came out to hear her play live. I liked what she performed tonight better than that song on the radio last year.

Eden strummed a chord one note at a time and said, "Thank you," to the applause. When she announced she'd be playing one last song, I followed Micah's advice and moved over to the side of the stage. As she bantered, I climbed partway up the steps so I could get a close shot of Eden from the side with the faces of her audience beyond. I peered through the lens and zoomed in on Zion with his phone in one hand. I lifted my head from my camera to check the rest of the audience. A dozen smartphones were positioned in the air, snapping a picture or capturing video. I reassessed the value of selling any pictures taken during a show.

The lighting from that angle fell differently and shrouded the audience beyond in a pale gray mystery. In that shadow, Zion caught my eye again, and I noticed him turning his phone at an angle away from Eden. I realized at once that he was taking secret selfies with Adrianna and rolled my eyes at his audacity. I casually let my gaze drift to the spot where Micah'd been sitting. I'd been trying so hard not to obviously stare at him that I hadn't noticed he was gone.

Had he left already? Would he leave after asking me to go out after the show? Had he taken my response as a no? My stomach clenched. His offer might have just been polite. But why would he walk out on Eden's performance?

With that thought, I felt pressure on my right side. I turned and found Micah standing behind me on the stairs with his hand on my waist. A chill ran down the length of my body, and I leaned into him. He breathed in my hair as he rested his chin on my head. His arm slid around to the front of me and tightened. Without thinking, I twined my fingers in his, and his other hand wrapped around and pulled me in closer. A thrill forced my shoulders into a shrug and my head fell to the side, eyes closed. I felt his cheek brush mine. Or it might have been his lips.

I wanted nothing more than to melt into him, but at that precise moment, Eden said, "If you'd all welcome my brother Micah up—" and she turned to look at the side of the stage, where I stood encircled in his arms.

Micah chuckled and whispered into my ear, "Stay here." Then he bounded onto the stage.

My heart raced, and small drops of perspiration began to form across my forehead. I caught Zion out in the audience flashing me a huge grin. He shot a thumbs-up at me, but I wanted the floor to swallow me. I couldn't believe I'd thought Micah had been standing there for me, but he'd evidently put his hand on me to nudge me out of his way so he could perform. He could turn into a flirt on a dime. I made a mental note to watch out for him and not to imagine him as a romantic prospect. It would be insanity to start thinking of him like that.

Though it would be fun to think of him like that.

He put his guitar strap over his shoulder and stood to Eden's side, strumming his guitar, singing into the mic, harmonizing with his sister. Their voices fit together beautifully. Micah's fingers flew across the strings, and Eden played something that looked incredibly intricate. Together their guitars sounded like something out of some seventeenth-century baroque period. Utterly gorgeous.

I remembered my camera and focused in on the two of them. I could get them both in profile if I leaned a little bit forward. I put my knee on the stage and shot. Then I stopped and gazed through my camera lens. This was the most openly I'd been able to sit and stare at Micah.

The women in the front row weren't as shy about it, and those that weren't training their phone cameras on him were either gawking at him or whispering with their friends and sighing, hands clenched over their hearts. I wouldn't want to have to compete with all the women in this room. If I wanted a chance with Micah Sinclair, I'd obviously have to get in line.

Finally, they finished their song and took a bow. As they came down the stairs, Micah touched my elbow. I turned with him and headed down, but Eden grabbed my arm. "Come with me real quick. I've only got a few minutes."

The loud applause grew muffled as I ducked down a hallway and into a small side room. I assumed this was where the musicians went to hide before the show. A nice leather sofa overwhelmed one wall, and plates of half-eaten food balanced on a coffee table.

Eden dropped onto the sofa, and I joined her. "Thanks for coming out tonight. I'm sorry I didn't find you before the show. Were you able to get any pictures?"

I pulled out my camera and flipped through the images quickly. "I like these the most." I showed her the ones from the side of the stage.

"Great." She scratched something onto a notepad and tore off the paper. "Here's the email address of my webmaster. Can you send us both whichever pictures turn out the best?" She reached into a backpack and got out her wallet. "What did we agree to?"

I folded up the note, feeling incredibly uncomfortable suddenly. "Could I ask you a favor instead?"

She shrugged. "What sort of favor?"

"Instead of paying me, would you mind if I keep any pictures you don't use for my own portfolio if I promise not to sell them to the tabloids?"

"What portfolio?"

"I don't always intend to make money spying on celebrities. The pictures you liked last night, the interesting pictures . . . I can't keep those unless my boss releases them to me because I was on the job. Tonight is my own time, my own camera."

She thought for a minute. "Will you put these up in some kind of photo display at some time? Like a gallery?"

I nodded. "I might. I haven't thought that far ahead."

"I did like those pictures you took. And I'd love to see what you'd come up with. I'll make a deal with you if you promise not to use anything without getting written consent first. Would you agree to that?"

"Absolutely."

The applause in the front of the house had picked up into a near rhythmic stomping. Eden paused a moment longer. "I'll still pay you for whichever pictures I end up keeping. Okay?"

"Deal."

She jumped up. "Thanks again for coming tonight. I hope to see you again. You've got my email, so let me know how it goes with the photos."

And she flew out the door. By the time I left the room, she was already performing an encore song. I squeezed around to my chair and scooted over next to Zion. Adrianna and Micah had left. I knocked Zion with my shoulder, and he leaned into me. All around us, people were singing along with Eden's song, but I'd never heard it before. I wanted to leave now, but it would've been rude, so I sat and waited for Eden to sing another song and say good night.

The lights came up, and Zion immediately asked, "Have you eaten anything?"

I found my carrots again and took a bite out of one. "Okay?"

"So? What now?"

"Micah said something about meeting him out front. Do you want to see if he's there? I don't have any idea where they were planning to go."

"You sure you're up for it?"

It was a valid question. I knew he meant because of the night before. But I processed it a little differently. Was I up for tagging along with Micah Sinclair who seemed up for anything? Had he only asked me along to get some favorable press photos? Would any of that be so bad?

"It beats going home and turning in. Let's go check it out." I grabbed my pocketbook and pushed through the people crowding around the alcove with the merchandise table. I expected to see Eden back there, signing her CDs, but the line abruptly ended at the girl I'd seen there earlier. I guessed people were waiting until Eden came out to greet them. I wondered if Micah had gone backstage, too.

Zion's thoughts must have followed my own. He muttered, "I hope we don't have to wait for him out front for an hour."

Then I saw Micah's hair through the blank spaces in the window that the posters didn't cover. His back faced the window. My face brightened of its own accord. I didn't expect to feel so . . . what? relieved? . . . to see him out front. I grabbed Zion's hand. "Are we going to do this?"

"Why not?"

He swung the door wide open, and I saw Micah talking to someone I'd seen before. Someone holding a camera in one hand, resting it on his shoulder for a moment. I placed him all at once. Wally, the guy I'd seen the night before. Possibly the same guy who'd published pictures of me with Micah.

Micah was engaged in conversation with Wally, but when I stepped out on the sidewalk, his eyes turned my way, and a smile broke out across his face. Just like that, my heart slammed in my chest. He lifted his hand up toward me, reaching out to pull me into him if I'd let him.

Everything started running in parallel time. My pulse raced like I'd pressed Fast Forward, like I'd inhaled a pound of sugar. But Wally moved on another time line, in slow motion. First, his eyes lifted and met mine. His eyebrows followed the upward trajectory as recognition registered. Then, his head swung toward Micah. Then back to me. When his gaze dropped down to Micah's rising arm, his mouth formed a tight O.

And then he reached for his camera.

Time clicked into place. I grabbed Zion's arm and pressed him to keep moving down the sidewalk. I skirted behind Micah, throwing one glance at the confused paparazzo. His wrist went limp, and the camera didn't pursue us. Zion's mind must have caught up with his body because he resisted me slightly.

I tugged him. "Keep walking."

At the first opportunity, I turned the corner and abruptly stopped.

Zion pivoted so his whole body turned in a wide circle back toward me. "What are you doing, Josie?"

"I can't go back there."

"What? Why not?"

"I just can't. Andy will kill me if I get caught in the news again with Micah with nothing to report."

"You're on your own time, Josie."

"Zion, you don't understand. He told me I have to choose between work and play. What if he fires me?"

Zion's eye roll was a study in dramatics. "He's not going to fire you. But if you wanna be a big baby, we can wait till that guy leaves and then go back." He peeked around the corner.

"What if he doesn't? Or what if Micah comes over here looking for us? How lame would it be to tell him I'm hiding from the paparazzi?"

Zion just laughed. "I'm guessing you didn't foresee this problem at the beginning of the week."

I leaned against the wall. "I've never known Andy to be so weirdly overinvested in any other celebrities. I don't get why he even cares about Micah that much."

"Probably because his sister and Adam like to fuck with him."

"How do you mean?"

"Like how Adam and Adrianna somehow had the entire tabloid industry chasing after an engagement that turned out to be completely fictional."

"I think I remember that." I'd been aware of the tabloids from glancing at them in the Publix while waiting to check out. But at that time, I'd been using my useless degree in fine arts to cover the local interest stories for an Atlanta newspaper. If a soldier returned from Afghanistan, I'd be at the airport snapping pictures of his tender embrace with his wife. I'd jumped at the chance to come work with Zion in New York City without questioning what I'd be doing.

I readjusted my camera strap. "I didn't know they hadn't been engaged. I figured they broke up."

"You need to go and read the articles about Adam and Eden

back then. Back when Andy made Eden look like the worst gold-digging home wrecker, before Adrianna put out a press release denying the engagement. Ever since then, Eden and Andy have had a kind of low-level vendetta. Although, for the past several months, she's been off his radar."

I thought about Eden's pregnancy. Had she shown me something on purpose so I'd feed it to Andy? Was I a pawn in her game? "Lord, I'm naïve, huh?"

"Naw. You're normal. This world makes people crazy."

I laughed and relaxed. And that's when Micah rounded the corner and stopped cold. He looked from me to Zion. "Oh." It was the first time he'd ever met me without a smile on his face. "I assumed you'd left."

"No, I—" I what? *I can't ever be seen with you? You who have never seen a camera you didn't pose for?* My feet shuffled.

He lifted his hand and rubbed the back of his head. "Yeah, okay. Well, I'm heading off." He put a hand out to Zion. "It was good to meet you."

Zion shook and said, "Yeah, you, too," but he stared at me. The whites of his eyes practically glowed from bulging out of their sockets. If I could read his mind, it would've said, "*Ask him to tag along.*" But I couldn't do that.

Micah's hand stretched out to me again, but unlike the last time when he'd so casually raised it in expectation, this time it was a formal gesture. I took his hand in mine and gripped tight. I gazed into his blue eyes, wondering if I could pull him toward me and steal that second kiss. My mouth twisted into a frown, wishing I could find the words to say. I got out, "I'm sorry for—" right as Micah spoke.

"It was good to see you again, Jo Jo." He gave my arm one good businesslike shake before he walked away from me, down the sidewalk and out of reach.

"I expect that's the last I'll ever see of him." My voice cracked, and Zion put his arm around me.

"Not so fast, my friend. While you were talking to Eden, I got us these." He slipped a pair of tickets out of his back pocket.

I snatched them from him and read the print. "Theater of the

Absurd at the Dobbler Theater? You got tickets to see Micah's band?"

He waggled his eyebrows. "Yup. He said he'd intended to give them to you earlier." He nudged me. "He said he hoped he'd run into you again."

Hope and disappointment vied for supremacy. "That was sweet of him, but what do you think it means?"

"I think it means you're going to have to tell Andy to back off."

I stared at the tickets, processing the competing emotions. For the second night in a row, Micah must have thought I'd blown him off fairly blatantly. He'd apparently recovered from the rejection of the night before. He couldn't have failed to read my reaction to him when he kissed me. Would he forgive a second cold shoulder? Or was I reading too much into what he'd said to Zion? There could be more than one explanation for wanting to invite me to his concert. More than one reason he'd want to run into me again.

And I hadn't even processed what I thought about Micah Sinclair. It would probably be better to let him slip away before I felt anything for him.

"I'm not going to need to tell Andy anything, Zion. There's nothing to tell."

Chapter 10

Sometime during the weekend, Andy had sorted and archived the pictures from Friday night's party without posting any of them online on the newspaper website. In case they might become useful in the future, he left me the daunting task of tagging them. I scrolled through the images, wishing I could steal them back. Some of them would have made great additions to my portfolio, and Andy wouldn't use them anyway. The pics of Victoria Sedgwick were beautifully tragic but worthless to anyone trying to make a buck off her name. I jotted down the image numbers in case I caught him in a good mood. Maybe he'd let me have them.

Kristin and Jennifer argued loudly over who had aged better: Brad Pitt or Johnny Depp. Leonard threw out anecdotes about stalking each of them, saying Brad was nicer to him, slightly. The chatter became a kind of background noise I heard but wasn't listening to.

When Derek sidled up beside me, I jumped at the sound of his voice close to my ear. "So, you're Indian?"

I glanced at him but then went back to scrolling through photos. "My dad is. I'm actually American."

He leaned an elbow on my workstation and openly scrutinized me. " 'Cause you don't really look Indian. I mean, I always figured you just tanned easily."

Did he think he was complimenting me? I turned an arched eyebrow at him to let him see that I didn't really care for the direction this conversation was taking. It opened up way more worm cans than Derek could ever imagine because I did look Indian—just not enough.

I inherited my spiral locks and sepia-toned skin from my dad, but the ash brown hair from my American-as-apple-pie mom separated me from an entire subcontinent. My hybrid coloring was only the most obvious indication that I never quite fit in.

It was the great curse of my existence that I was never enough. Not Indian enough. Not American enough. Not artistic enough. Not tabloid enough. Not healthy enough. Never enough.

This became apparent the summer my dad took me to India. One afternoon, after we'd been there for almost a week, my dad and grandfather argued. My dad, who rarely raised his voice to me, spoke so loud, I heard him from outside the house where I leaned against a banyan tree eating the coconut *sukhiyan* Achama had cooked for me.

The words *"aval malayāḷi alla"* carried out the open front door, followed by my livid father, who gave me one look and told me to go pack my bags.

I repeated the phrase: *"aval malayāḷi alla"*—she is not Malayali. I didn't know if my grandfather was talking about me or my mom. In any case, we left the house in a taxi, my dad talking to my mom about how his father could not decide his life. But when we got home, he and Mom argued, and he began to travel more often. And then he stopped coming home.

The kicker was that I'd always expected my Indian family to accept me since my mom's mom had apparently taken one look at me and decided I was too Indian.

How could I be too much and not enough at the same time?

This memory flashed through my mind more as a fleeting feeling than a thought and disappeared in the blink of my bone-dry eyes. I turned away from Derek and swallowed down the stupid frog in my throat.

Derek attempted a course correction. "I mean, it's cool if you're part Indian. Kind of hot, really. I just didn't know." I ignored him, but he persisted. "Hey, if you're free tomorrow night, I was wondering if you might like to go out and do something."

"On a Tuesday?" I turned and leveled him with a what-kind-of-idiot-do-you-take-me-for look. He'd never asked me out before. Either he had an Indian fetish or he was after something. The trouble with working in the gossip industry was that everyone always had an angle. I trusted no one. Except Zion. I trusted Zion with my life.

He ignored my skepticism. "Yeah, there's this club opening, and I'm on the guest list."

"Sorry. I've already got plans."

"Oh, yeah? Whatcha doing?" He was way too interested and not nearly disappointed enough.

"Washing my hair." I threw him a withering glance. I wasn't about to tell him I had tickets to Micah's show. He could pry into my business the old-fashioned way, by rummaging through my backpack when I wasn't looking.

The door opened and bounced hard against the wall. Andy walked through it before it could swing back and hit him. He slowed as he passed behind my desk. "Wilder. In my office. Now." His pace picked up. He didn't even check to see if I followed behind him.

I climbed from my stool and caught Zion watching me. I mouthed "*What?*" at him, but he shrugged, hands outstretched, palms up. I sucked in some air. Andy was no fun on his best days. He seemed to be riding a storm cloud today.

When I entered his office, he had his phone cradled between his shoulder and his ear. Clumped strands of unwashed hair striped his forehead. His right index finger scrolled across images on his tablet, making them careen off, chasing after each other. In his left hand, he held a pen over a temporarily forgotten copy of the competitor's paper. I suspected it may be the paper featuring a photo of me.

He fluttered the pen at a futon chair and readjusted the phone on his shoulder. I shoved over a stack of week-old papers and took a seat, awkwardly eavesdropping on his phone call.

"I have to say I was pretty annoyed Friday night."

I settled onto the seat and glanced up to discover the phone lay abandoned on the desk, and Andy now stared directly at me, waiting for a response. "Oh, uh. Friday night."

His eyes bored into me. "I didn't think I'd need to give you a deadline, but I also never expected you'd send in your work past midnight."

My fists clenched, damp from the anxiety. "I can explain."

Andy tsked. "Zion already filled me in."

"Zion?"

"Right. He explained why you were so late."

"He—" Zion wouldn't have sold me out. I squirmed in my seat but resolved to wait for Andy's explanation rather than undermine both of us with the wrong panicked guess.

"You need to be better prepared, Scout. You know there are things you can carry to recharge on the go."

"Yeah." I relaxed, relieved that maybe he'd become more understanding of my medical issues. "But that's not exactly why—"

"You can borrow this for now, but you should invest in some." He reached into a drawer and pulled out a rectangular white plastic box, the size of a cell phone. He tossed it to me, and I recognized it as soon as my hand wrapped around it. I had about six of them in my camera bag. "Next time, you won't be stuck with a camera full of photos you can't send in."

I clutched the portable battery pack. "Thanks, Andy. That would have been a big help last weekend."

He'd already forgotten me and started scrolling through the pics on the tablet. As I stood, he lifted his head again. "Those pics of you and Micah that Wally Stephens captured trumped your pics anyway." He had to get that last dig in.

I laid my hand on the door handle and twisted it. "Right."

A beat before the latch disengaged, he added, "Did you get pics of Eden on Saturday night?"

I released the door handle, blinking fast. How did he know about that? "I—"

"Don't worry. I'm not going to ask you for your pics. That

was on your time. Wally Stephens said he saw you there, though. Called to ask if there was something going on between you and Micah."

"Between me and Micah?" I shock-laughed. "That's preposterous."

"Yeah. I laughed it off, too." He froze, hand mid-scroll. His forehead wrinkled as his caterpillar-like eyebrows levitated. "You'd let me know if you had an in with Micah, right?"

"What?"

"Because if you do, I'd like to see you work that angle."

"You want me to exploit Micah Sinclair?"

He set the pen down and placed his fists on the table to support his weight as he loomed forward, focusing now on nothing but me. "Josephine, do you know what you do for a living?"

"Of course."

"Does Micah Sinclair know what you do?"

I swallowed. I didn't like where this was going. "Yes."

"Then who do you think is exploiting whom?"

I wanted to argue with him, but I had nothing to prove that Micah hadn't been using me for free publicity. So why shouldn't I use him back? We could have a symbiotic relationship. "You're right. I forgot who I was dealing with."

He waved his hand. "Rookies. You need to get a thicker skin."

He was right. I nodded. "Sure. But I don't know if I've got as much access as you seem to think."

"With Adam out of the country, maybe you could buddy up to Eden. Information is currency, Jo. Befriend her. Try to find out if they've set a date for their wedding. Prove to me you're more than just one more skilled photographer. Go after the story."

I pictured her with Adam, happy about a pregnancy only one other person knew about—a tabloid journalist of all people. What would Andy do with that information? But I didn't want to sell her out. I knew there was a line between public and private information, even if Andy no longer saw it.

But I said, "I think you've overestimated my connection with her. She only hired me for pictures. Since I sent them off, she'll have no more need of me."

"I think she will." He maintained eye contact with me until I dropped my gaze. Then he returned to checking all the pictures his photographers had sent in, panning for gold.

I slipped out of his office, feeling the need for a Silkwood shower. Maybe I could apply for a position in another division. I caught Zion's eye, and he tilted his head, "Everything okay?"

"Everything's fine. Thanks for covering for last Friday."

He nodded once. "Payback for Saturday night."

I still couldn't believe how fangirlish he'd been all weekend. After we'd returned home from the club, he'd watched videos of Adrianna and changed his ringtone to one of her songs. And now his screen saver was a picture of Adrianna.

I started to tease him for acting like a besotted teenager, but I knew that as soon as I pulled my stool up to my laptop, I was going to go through my Friday night pics for any shots of Micah.

And indeed, I climbed on my stool and played Where's Waldo with the party pics.

In the first pic I found him in, he was talking to a group of people, smiling, wide-eyed, engaged. But after one or two shots, he inevitably locked in on the camera. It may have been my imagination, but he never seemed to look directly into the lens. His eyes were always a smidgen off to the left like he was looking past the camera. Like he was looking at me. I shook off a shiver and grabbed a sweatshirt from a hook on the wall.

Zion interrupted my stargazing with a "Whoop!"

I figured he'd gotten some pictures that turned out well, but when I swiveled around, he was staring fixated at his phone, his face contorted in uncontained glee. "Omigod!"

"What?" I slipped off my stool and tried to look over his shoulder.

He hid his phone against his chest, but I could tell by his shining eyes and pudding face that he would tell me. "Omigod. So this morning, I tweeted at Adrianna." He turned his phone to face me so I could see his notifications. "Look! She just favorited my tweet."

As I looked at his notifications, another popped up. "And she just followed you."

"WHAT?" He fumbled the phone but caught it before it dropped to the floor. "OH MY GOD!"

"I hate to be a naysayer, but are you sure it's her and not a bot? Or some auto-follow thing? Or her manager?"

His expression darkened, and I regretted my words, but I didn't want his fawning to lead to disappointment. "It's her. Look. It's official."

"Yeah. Okay." I patted his back. "That's awesome, Zion. How cool for you."

I caught Derek watching us with a smirk on his face. He thought he was too seasoned to get excited over any celebrities. I pursed my lips at him, too grown up to stick out my tongue.

As soon as I was at my desk, I sneaked my phone out of my bag and searched for Micah on Twitter. When I found him, I followed him and wrote, *It was good to see you last weekend. Thanks for the tickets to your show!* I stared at the message for a minute and then hit Send. I didn't expect to have the same luck as Zion, but it was worth a shot.

It had been a long time since I'd used Twitter in such a personal way. I pushed my phone into my pocketbook and scooted up to my desk. My laptop was docked. Three enormous monitors stretched across the workstation. On the left, a folder displayed thumbnails of the images from Friday night. A Twitter app dominated the center console, flashing constantly with new updates. The right monitor currently showed a map of Brooklyn.

I scrolled through various feeds on Twitter watching for any indication of a celebrity sighting. I'd hit the streets in the afternoon, but for now, I needed to tag any pictures Andy had missed. Halfway through the pictures, I'd started yawning so loud, Zion went and fetched me a cup of coffee. The groups of people repeated again and again in slightly different configurations. I'd been introduced to most everyone, but if nobody in the office could recognize them, they weren't generally of any interest. But in a crowd like this, it had to be assumed that anyone could be someone or might one day become someone. Better to tag what I could.

Aaron Silver. I typed the name in, trying to recall when I'd taken his picture. How did I manage to get a shot of Aaron Silver without noticing that? Aaron had played the lead in an off Broadway production of *Hair* earlier in the summer, but I remembered reading in our own Arts and Leisure section that he'd recently taken a smaller part in a larger production. I could have asked him about that if I'd seen him there rather than here, through the lens.

The next picture clued me into why I'd missed seeing Aaron. Micah had stepped in front of the camera and walked toward me. That must have been right before he took me to meet those snobby old farts.

Zion snuck up behind me. "I'm heading out. Someone spotted Peter Dinklage walking his dogs."

"Okay. I'll see you at home later. I'm gonna go poach Andy's turf later today."

"Don't work too hard." He mussed my hair and left.

When I turned back to tag the next picture, I noticed Eden standing in the background, Adam's arm wrapped around her, caressing her belly. She'd missed that one. The gesture could mean anything, but Andy missed nothing. I glanced over my shoulder, finger hovering over the delete key. But if a picture disappeared, Andy might ask why. So instead, I clicked on the tags and made sure Eden and Adam weren't listed.

Chapter 11

Andy's favorite stomping ground was a restaurant that catered to the stupid rich. The menus had no prices, and the chefs prepared tiny portions of elegantly plated and delectable food, though from what I could gather, money couldn't buy unicorn meat or other rare cuts unavailable at any ordinary steak house. The patrons here paid for prestige. The restaurant faded into the urban landscape and looked like any of the hundreds of hip and trendy spots all over town. An innocent couple visiting the city might inadvertently walk in and ask for a table. Lucky for them, they'd be turned away, not because they didn't have reservations. One didn't need reservations at a restaurant like this. The right people could stroll right up, unannounced, and be seated. Meanwhile, I'd never been through the front door. I pictured the A-listers inside shaking hands with each other, making jokes only famous people would get. *"Did you flash the paparazzi out front?"*

At times like these, I wished I could drink to numb the sense of rejection. I had no true desire to be accepted by this disparate group of people who shared little in common with each other except for their exceptional spheres of influence. I'd observed them long enough to know they were all just people. Some had been born with money and power. Others had earned it. Some were gracious despite their blessings. Others behaved as though the universe owed them even more. But all of them needed the same basic things. All of them had to eat. And it didn't matter that it was six o'clock on a Monday. Time bent to their whims.

I staked out a position close to the corner near the parking garage. And waited. I slipped an earbud in one ear and loaded up a playlist to block out the street noise. My phone buzzed, so I knelt down on the concrete to slip it from my backpack and make sure Zion wasn't trying to reach me. But it was only a Twitter notification. I clicked it.

Micah had replied to my earlier tweet. *Glad you had a good time. See you at our next show?*

I checked his feed and found it littered with recent replies he'd made to others like he'd just logged on and started going through all of his tweets, and it made my heart sink to discover he'd answered me at the end of a chain of obligatory fan management.

He wrote, *Thanks! Love you, too!* to a number of fans who'd expressed their love for him.

And *I hope you have a happy birthday!* to people begging him to tweet that, or who casually mentioned it was their birthday. Either way, he had it covered.

When I saw the tweet where he wrote, *Yeah, that Micah Sinclair's the worst,* I had to click through to find out what inspired him to respond that way. The original tweet hadn't even been addressed to his Twitter handle. Someone had claimed, *Micah Sinclair sold his soul to the devil. How else can anyone explain his popularity?*

It tickled me that he wasn't only reading tweets directed at him, but searching out comments about him. It made me laugh that he interacted with his haters as much as his fans.

The phone buzzed again while I was spying on his tweets. He'd sent a direct message following up. *Stop at the will call before the show. I'll leave some backstage passes.*

I sat down hard on the sidewalk and read the message over again. With my back pressed against the wall and my feet crossed under my knees, I hit reply and typed, *Thank you. I look forward to it.* But when I hit Send, I got an error message rudely informing me that the recipient didn't follow me. I retyped the message on the public feed instead. It occurred to me to let him know he wasn't following me, but I couldn't think of a way it wouldn't sound desperate. I considered unfollowing him and following him again. How pathetic could I be?

Before I could decide my next step, hip-hop legend L.L. Stylez appeared around the corner, and I was on my feet in seconds, snapping pictures. He acted put out by my attention, but he preened for my shots nonetheless. I called out, "L.L., could I get a comment about the announcement you're retiring?"

One of his handlers followed behind, speaking for L.L. "His comment was his press release. Please take a step back."

I swung wide around them and beat them to the front of the restaurant so I could get some shots of him strutting toward me. He wore sunglasses and a track suit, but he vogued like he walked the runway. I blurted out, "You're looking fine, L.L.," and he stopped dead.

He pulled his sunglasses up an inch and scanned my entire body, starting with my feet. "You're looking fine, little lady. Who you with?"

I handed him my card, and he eyed it. Cursory.

"You want a statement?"

I flipped the switch on my camera from still photo to video and began recording. I could do this without looking down. If L.L. made a statement, I wanted it on camera. I wouldn't get the video, but I'd at least have a documented record. And I needed him to say it without uttering the three deadliest words: *Off the record.*

"I'd love to get your thoughts, L.L." Could I pull off cool and flirty?

"I'll give you a statement." His handler had grown skittish and had started to urge L.L. toward the restaurant, but he swatted the hand away. "Yeah, I'm retiring. Not from music. I'm going to be helping young musicians grow, sheltering them from the agents and the snakes that prey on the creative. This industry is a cesspool of no talent wannabes looking for the next buck. Where's the integrity?"

He glanced down toward my camera, and I knew he was aware everything he said had been recorded. I still didn't dare lift the camera to shoot video. He clearly had more to say, and I didn't want to blow the moment. He leaned in close now. Inches from my face, and I could smell the traces of liquor. He didn't appear drunk, but at some point that day, he'd had a drink. He looked in my eyes and waited until I stopped and locked eyes with him. He laid a finger on my chin, this legend of hip hop and blues. The stubble on his chin had begun to turn silver. I suddenly felt humbled by his intense attention—until he whispered, "This industry ain't no place for a pretty little thing like you."

And just like that, he whipped away from me, dragging his entourage in his wake. For half a second, I felt dejected for standing out on the street chasing after photos and scandal rather than finding ways to make photographs of trees interesting. But as the last of his entourage disappeared through the doors, it struck me that he wasn't any better than me for all his lofty criticism. He retained a cadre of personnel whose only job was to cater to him. He was fixing to spend the money he'd earned in the industry on an eighty-dollar sirloin.

At the thought of food, my stomach growled, and I remembered I needed to eat before I got sick. I walked a few blocks to a street vendor and ordered a bottle of juice and a whole lot of spiced lamb. I sat down on a nearby bench to eat it and scroll through my pictures. This was my chance to get some respect from Andy finally.

When I got home, Zion lay on the sofa watching a game show, half asleep. I shoved him over so I could start writing.

"Listen to this." I hit Play on the recording, and L.L.'s voice sprang to life.

Zion hit the mute on the remote. "Who is that?"

"L.L. Stylez. I got him to talk about his retirement."

Zion's mouth became an O. "Ho-ly shit. Start it over."

I played it all the way back. "I have pictures, too. You think Andy's gonna shit or what?"

"If he doesn't try to steal it. That's gonna print on the front page of our whole website." He stuck out his foot and hooked the coffee table leg so he could drag it over without getting up. Once it was close enough, he grabbed my laptop. "You better get this in tonight. If L.L.'s talking to you, he might be talking in general."

"Good point."

I folded my feet under me on the sofa and shoved a pillow behind the small of my back. When I opened the laptop and fired up an empty document, the cursor flashed at me, taunting. I'd never been much of a writer.

"Transcribe the interview," suggested Zion. "Nobody cares what you say around his quotes. His words will take up eighty percent of the article."

"Right."

I typed a temporary headline: "Legendary hip hop artist L.L. Stylez opens up about recent retirement." Andy would clean it up anyway. I chose a picture from the group that showed L.L. in all his glory, sweeping down the sidewalk. Zion was right. The only thing I needed to write was a little contextualization. "Last week, L.L. Stylez announced his retirement from the music industry with little explanation. Speculation has run hot over the past week, but L.L. has offered no further insight into his decision. Until Monday night."

The rest wrote itself. I uploaded the article with all the pictures to the work server. Then I opened my email client to let Andy know to look for it.

"Hey, I got an email from Eden."

Zion had disappeared into the bathroom. Instead of yelling louder, I opened the email.

> Jo,
> Thank you so much for the pictures. They turned out even better than I expected. If you go to my website, you can see what my webmaster did with them. I still look like a folk singer from the sixties, but that's on me, not you. I liked the pics you took with me and Micah best, but I

couldn't use those for the site. Feel free to keep
those for yourself. I've emailed one of them to
this digital picture frame my mom keeps on her
mantel. Micah likes to send over pictures of
himself making faces, so she was happy to have
something nice of us for a change.

I feel bad that you wouldn't take my money for
your time. At least let me know what I owe you
for the twenty pictures we ended up using.

Eden

I had no idea how much a picture was worth in non-word
currency. And even if she could probably pay my rent without
missing the cash, I couldn't bring myself to name a price. And
not because of any my-pictures-are-priceless nonsense. I literally
didn't have the first clue what they might be worth.

I wrote back:

Eden,

Since you're letting me keep so many pictures,
I can't in good conscience ask you to pay for the
few you kept. Consider them my gift in return
for the chance to do some honest work for a
change. :)

Thanks for the offer though and for giving me
such a great opportunity.

Jo

Zion came out of the bathroom with a towel wrapped around
his waist. He had no modesty at all, but he at least covered his
dangerous bits for my benefit. His chest and arms were rock
hard. I used to think about trying to trick him into hooking up
with me, but he'd never once batted an eye at any woman.

At least until Saturday night. But then he was more starstruck
than anything else.

"Did you say something?" He plopped down beside me. His
hair dripped on me, smelling of oranges and ginger.

"You're using my shampoo, again."

"You're using my sofa."

"Touché."

"Did you get your article done?"

"Yup. And I got a nice email from Eden."

"Oh, yeah?" He jumped up to grab some boxers in his room and then shamelessly sat on the sofa half-naked to watch TV.

I threw my comforter over him. "Have mercy on a poor girl."

We companionably fast-forwarded through his favorite DVRed entertainment shows, him hoping to find out which celebrities might be coming to New York, me hoping to figure out how to do my job. About fifteen minutes into *Access Hollywood,* my phone buzzed, and I discovered a response from Eden.

> Could I at least take you out to lunch on
> Wednesday? If you pick a place near where you
> work, I could come meet you. You'd be doing
> me another favor actually. Until Adam gets back
> home, I don't know what to do with myself.
> If I don't get some real company, I might start
> remodeling the kitchen or something insane.

There was no possible way Eden Sinclair had nothing to do with her time. I knew she'd only couched it that way to make me more inclined to accept her invitation without feeling weird about it. But I did feel weird about it.

I hit Reply.

> That sounds fun. Do you know where the
> NY Daily Feed is located? There's a Bon Appetit
> sandwich place right around the corner from
> where I work. Do you know the one?

That restaurant would be on the cheap side, but still pretty good. As soon as I hit Send, I hit my forehead. Eden wouldn't want to meet in a cheap sandwich shop. She probably had her own chef, preparing micro cuisine for her. Whatever micro cuisine might be.

I lifted my head from my phone screen. "I'm going to have lunch with Eden later this week."

Zion pushed me. "No way!"

I pushed him back. "Way!"

The corner of his mouth turned up. "You're gonna be best buddies. See if you can find out when she's getting married."

"You're as bad as Andy. I'm not going to exploit this friendship."

He shrugged. "Then find out when she's going to see Adrianna again, and get her to invite me along."

"What is it with you? It's like you've got a crush."

His eyes grew wide. "I know! I'm starting to wonder if I'm bi after all."

"I think you're just infatuated. She's pretty impressive." I leaned over and kissed his cheek. "But you'd have beautiful babies."

I scanned Eden's email once more. "That's odd. She uses the same excuse as Andy did for us to meet."

"Whatdya mean?"

"Andy said that I should befriend Eden while Adam's away. And then get dirt on her."

"You're not planning to, are you?"

"No, I wasn't. But now Eden's saying that she's bored while Adam's away. It's weird. You don't think she's trying to befriend me for some reverse espionage?"

"To get dirt on Andy? Who would even care?"

"No, I mean, maybe there's more to her apparent friendship than meets the eye. She's got a vendetta against Andy. How could she use a friendship with one of his employees?"

Zion shrugged. "To feed him bullshit stories?"

I chewed on my thumbnail. "You don't think she'd use me that way, do you?"

"I dunno. Does she think you'd use her that way?"

That was a great question. How could either of us trust the nature of this tentative friendship?

Chapter 12

*Look at this interview my daughter published. **Josie Wilder!***

I woke up to the notification ding that followed my mom's weird reposting of the article on Facebook. Zion had correctly predicted it would show on the front page of our website even if it was only a teaser with a link to the entertainment section. He'd incorrectly predicted that Andy would take credit. But when I saw the headline, I wished he had.

"Creatively Bankrupt L.L. Stylez Lashes Out at Music Industry."

The picture centered below the headline showed L.L. at his worst. The burst feature on the camera will capture every change in expression. Some flatter the subject, while others . . . not so much. The one printed in the paper caught L.L. with an expression that could be described as entitled. His frown, combined with a curl of the nose like he'd smelled something rotten, gave the impression he merely condescended to share the sidewalk with the handler who, unfortunately, appeared harried to L.L.'s left.

Had I misjudged the entire situation, or had Andy found a way to pull a story out of thin air?

I scrolled through my photos, wishing I'd taken video. When L.L. had talked to me, his face had looked beatific. But distracted on the street, under the fire of a paparazzo, he came off frustrated. Still, there were pictures Andy could have used to put L.L. in a better light, and he'd chosen not to. And my name stared out at me in black-and-white.

Here was my moment in the sun—a front page headline. Not just for an opportune picture, but with news. Something relevant for a day. And I felt a cold finger down my spine. This article was ugly and unfair. But I knew Andy's version would generate more clicks and bring in more ad revenue.

As Zion and I rode the train in to work together, I asked him, "What should I do about this?"

He leveled a shut-up-with-your-first-world-problems stink eye at me. "You got on the front page! That's awesome."

But I felt like I needed to tell Andy I wasn't comfortable with his changes. On the other hand, he already saw me as weak. So I went into the office and suffered through the "Huzzah!" from my coworkers as I walked through the door. I pantomimed a modestly proud response, waving and ducking my head until I got to my desk.

Andy's mood was uncharacteristically upbeat. He didn't criticize me at all and even complimented me on the solid interview. I bit my tongue and swallowed down my discomfort with his sketchy tactics. But for the first time in days, he didn't ask me anything about Eden or Micah. I hadn't told him Zion and I would be seeing Micah at his show later that night. I didn't question the silence or poke the sleeping bear.

After about an hour, my Twitter stalking paid off, and I got a tip that Chris Hemsworth was walking around Greenwich Village, heading toward Washington Square Park.

In order to avoid raising suspicion, I slunk out of the office and then high-tailed it uptown to the park, where a crowd had gathered. I grabbed my camera and ran over.

A mega-famous celebrity is like a spontaneous energy source. Magnetic. The initial mob that formed around Chris generated more interest from passersby, and so by the time I reached the edge of the park, I couldn't even see through the mob. The buzz itself attracted more people, and ladies holding shopping bags whispered, "Who do you think it is?" And they waited for a turn to meet a celebrity, whoever it was. It didn't matter to them.

A girl broke free of the expanding ball of humans with a piece of paper clutched in her hand. "It's Chris Hemsworth! Oh, my God!"

At her words, the frenzy redoubled.

I looked around for something to climb on. I couldn't snap a picture of him from where I stood, and if I jammed in there, I wouldn't get a good angle. A line of benches ran along the path, but even standing on these, heads obscured my shot. I put my hand on a nearby tree and dared to stand on the back of the bench, praying it was securely bolted down. The view was clear enough to identify Chris, and I managed to capture the insanity of the scene.

If I could give him a word of advice, I'd have suggested he find himself a decent disguise—something other than Thor.

Once I had collected my prize, and Chris had dragged his swarm of human beings farther away, I threw my backpack onto a bench near some chess tables. I turned on the hot spot and uploaded my pictures. Andy couldn't possibly complain I didn't get a comment today. As if I could have combated the fray.

It wasn't much, but that little score bought me at least an hour to myself. The sun felt nice, and I leaned back on the bench and closed my eyes, listening to the sounds in the park. Before long, my curiosity won out, and I had to see the things I was hearing.

At the chess tables, an elderly man with his cane leaning against the table looked on as a college-aged kid studied the board in deep concentration. I couldn't tell who held the lead, nor did I care. I grabbed my personal camera and rested my foot on the bench to better prop my elbow up on my knee as I focused in. I snapped pictures until the players glanced up at me, eyes deglazing momentarily as their brains tried to force them to take in the world outside their own heads. The pull of the table proved too great, and they forgot about me and continued to play.

A young girl crossed in front of me, chasing after a Pomeranian she held on a leash. Her hair was pulled up in tight pigtails.

The tiny dog dragged her along in its excitement, sniffing at everything it came across. Behind her, a disinterested woman stared into her phone, saying without conviction, "Slow down, Sadie."

My own phone buzzed. I laid my camera aside and checked my notifications. I had a new direct message, and it was from Micah. I scrunched down onto the bench and huddled over my phone to cut the glare so I could read it.

Heard you're having lunch with my sister. I hope you won't call her washed-up in your newspaper. :P

I wanted to respond and tell him I hadn't written that headline about L.L. Stylez, but he still hadn't followed me back. The significance of his quip registered a moment later—he'd read my article. Maybe he had a habit of checking the tabloids for any stories about himself. He clearly hovered over Twitter. I had a dim hope he'd only read it because I wrote it. Crazy.

Frustrated, I tweeted at him on his feed. *Hey, do you like talking to yourself? Follow me back.*

Then I thought that felt too pushy and nearly deleted it. But I couldn't think of any better way to clue him in, so I left it.

While I waited for a response that never came, I scanned Twitter for hints of any other celebrities out and about. When I'd applied for this job, I had an inkling I'd have to chase down stories but wasn't at all prepared for the cutthroat nature of the business. And at first, Andy had praised my photography skills while training me in his art of war. Little by little, the praise evaporated, replaced by an irritation that worried me. I couldn't afford to lose this job.

Leery about returning to the office with nothing more than my word that I'd spotted a Hemsworth in the wild, I decided to head uptown to the theater district. Stalking exit doors at the matinees was an act of desperation, but sometimes a big name celebrity would step out to greet the fans. I hated to poison the well with my presence, but I worked in a parasitic industry. And I had a selfish motivation—I adored Broadway.

On my way, I happened upon a mesmerized flock of young Buddhists huddled near the TKTS booth, gazing up at Times

Square in every direction. When I raised my personal camera, I heard my father's voice in my ear. "*Illa,* Anushka. Don't take the obvious shot." I peered through the viewfinder, framing the composition that would make him say, "*Nalla.* Good."

This shot would be my little secret—a side benefit of my day job.

The theater stalking paid off when stage queen Miriam Blackwell, still painted in her costume makeup, emerged from the fire exit into the side alley and greeted fans. I shot pictures from several feet away, and she stopped for a moment and posed for me.

Encouraged by her indulgence, I flipped my camera to video and approached her. "Ms. Blackwell. I'm a reporter for the *Daily Feed* and a huge fan. *Candy* was the first musical I ever saw, and I caught this show again last month. You were amazing as always." She thanked me, and I went on. "Is it true that you're stepping down from the show at the end of the season?"

She nodded, considering, and said in that famously smoky voice, "I originated this role, you know. I played Candy when this show began in 1992 and again in 2001. It's been an honor to come back to reprise the role, but to be honest, my dear, I'm getting too old for the rigors of theater. It will be good for someone younger to take over again. I've grown spoiled and lazy." She laughed unselfconsciously. She'd never been one to mince words, and I thanked my stars I'd come up here today. "Don't get me wrong. I'm not going anywhere. I plan to keep making movies until I shrivel up and die. But I shall part ways with the theater." She winked. "For now."

I'd been a fan of Miriam Blackwell since the first time my dad brought me to New York and took me to three different musicals. He'd let me pick one show, while he and my mom chose the other two. I was nine and didn't have any interest in seeing a musical at all. I chose *Candy* thinking it might actually be about chocolate. My parents were equally shocked by the bawdy review, but I never forgot the spectacle and eagerly went to the next two shows of our visit.

I assumed Andy would be excited about an interview with someone of Miriam's stature and hurried to a corner café to upload the photos and video. I didn't want to take any chances that I'd somehow lose them. I plugged my headphones into the camera to play the audio and transcribed it into my phone email app, wishing I'd lugged my laptop uptown.

When I returned to the office, I expected to be greeted with fanfare equal to the morning, but instead, Andy stormed out of his office. "What the hell is this? Nobody cares about some crone of a theater actress. If this is the kind of garbage you call content, maybe you should walk downstairs to the Arts and Leisure department and apply for a job there."

"I thought this was entertainment news, Andy. Theater is entertainment." My voice wavered. Sometimes out of nowhere and at the most inopportune moments, I sounded like I was on the brink of an emotional breakdown, even though I was completely in control. Zion said it was because I bottled everything up, but I figured it was nothing more than fatigue. Whichever, I certainly didn't want Andy to think he got under my skin. He'd either single me out to torment or find a way to fire me.

His lip curled in a sneer, and I wondered if he could already taste blood. "Let me explain it to you in a way you might understand, Scout. Our news *is* the entertainment."

And just like that, I'd gone back to being the goat. Thankfully, Andy got called out of the office, and Zion came back in, so I spent the next hour hovering at his desk, complaining about how I couldn't ever win in this suckfest of a job.

"And if I could find another job—" My phone dinged, and I absently glanced at it, intending to finish that sentence, but when I saw the notification that Micah had followed me on Twitter, I lost my train of thought.

Directly on the heels of that, he sent another message: *Can I get your phone number? It's easier for me to text.*

I sent it to him, and a minute later my phone buzzed with a text from him. *What are you doing right now?*

Working. I abandoned Zion and walked back to my desk with a smile on my face. I moved my mouse to wake up my monitors and tried to make myself focus on copyediting the document I'd emailed in earlier. Andy might not want to print an article about

Miriam Blackwell, but someone somewhere might be interested in it.

Another buzz distracted me. *Are you going to print this?*

Maybe.

In that case, you should know I'm reading War and Peace *and performing surgery on an orphaned puppy.*

I bit my thumbnail and giggled. *Pictures please?*

When my phone buzzed, I held my breath hoping for a photo, but it was even better. *Screw texting. When can I call you?*

Zion and Leonard lifted their heads when I squealed. I had at least another hour left to work. But I wrote, *Now?*

I set my phone aside to flip through my afternoon shots, but my stomach felt like it might burst with rainbow-colored exploding butterflies. I barely dared hope that he was calling because he might be interested in me and not my camera. The last time I saw him, he'd been all business. But then hadn't he flirted a little bit just now?

Minutes later, my phone rang, and I snatched it, but made myself wait for at least a second ring. "Hello?"

"Jo? It's Micah." His voice directly in my ear made me swallow hard.

"Hey, Micah. What are you doing?"

"Sitting in my backyard, talking to a pretty girl."

I bounced on my stool. "Yeah?"

"Are you going to be able to come to the show tonight?"

"Planning to."

"Cool."

He paused, and I couldn't think of anything to fill in the silence.

He broke in. "Hey, I can put a press pass in with the backstage pass if you want to take pictures. I think they'll confiscate your camera otherwise."

Like a punch in the gut, his intentions hit me hard. "You want me to take pictures?"

"That would be cool. But only if you want to."

"Yeah, that would be great." I wondered if he'd found out I hadn't made Eden pay for her pictures. Now he'd expect me to show up wherever he wanted me to and give him free publicity. I started to tell him exactly what I thought of that, but he found his voice.

"So will you have time after the show to come out with us? It won't be anything special, but we like to go out after and get some food and relax. It will mostly be the band guys, but you'd totally be welcome."

"Will you need pictures of that, too?" At my irritated tone, Zion glanced up at me with a curious expression.

"What? I hadn't thought . . . I mean, it will only be . . ."

Why was I blowing this? I changed my tone of voice. "Yes. I'll be happy to come out. Can Zion come, too?" Zion waggled his eyebrows and continued to mess on his laptop.

"Zion? Oh, right." He exhaled. "Zion's just your roommate, right? I mean, he's not—"

I chuckled. "Have you met Zion?" It suddenly hit me what he was asking. I pushed my hair behind my ear. "He's just my roommate. And my best friend. But he's not—"

"I'm sorry. That was pretty nosy."

"*You're* apologizing to *me* for being nosy?"

He laughed. "Yeah. I guess that's a twist. But can I ask you something personal?"

"Sure."

He cleared his throat and waited a beat. "Are you seeing anyone?" His voice cracked halfway through the question.

"Not at the moment." I pressed my lips together to hold in the *Yippee* that threatened to escape. I ventured a volley. "And I happen to know that you're not, either."

"What else do you know about me?" He'd lowered his voice, making me feel like we should be alone.

I got up and walked to the window as if it would give me privacy. I looked down at the street below and talked low. "That you read everything anyone writes to you on Twitter. And respond."

"Easier than answering fan mail."

"I suppose it would be." I glanced back. Zion peered at me over the top of his computer.

Micah said, "Now you have to tell me something I don't know about you."

"Okay." I leaned against the windowsill for a minute to think what I should share.

"Come on, Jo Jo. I can't just look it up in the papers."

I wracked my brain for something that felt safe enough. "I'm kind of obsessed with the theater."

"Oh yeah? Like musicals or plays?"

"Musicals mostly. I own all the soundtracks and love the performances. Is that corny?"

"Uh-uh," he said. "You've never seen my band perform, right?" It sort of bugged me that he switched the topic back to him without even listening to what I'd said.

"Nope."

"Do me a favor. Don't look anything up before you come tomorrow night. Promise?"

"Sure." I didn't know where to go with the conversation. It was too awkward to return to the topic of theater, but then he'd just effectively shut down any questions about his band.

He hesitated a second, too, then said, "God, I'm no good on the phone. I'm all discombobulated."

I had to give him that. Still, I jabbed. "Hey, you're the one who insisted on it."

His laugh came across like a sigh. "I do like the sound of your voice."

Down on the street, Andy marched head down toward the front of our building. I remembered I had a dozen things to finish if I wanted to leave early. "Hey, I've got to scoot. I'll see you tonight?"

He quickly threw in. "Don't forget to stop at the will call."

"Oh, yeah. The backstage passes."

"Right. And there will be a press pass."

My budding hopes wilted. "Yup. I'll be sure to bring my camera."

Chapter 13

Knowing I'd be seeing Micah (and he'd be seeing me), I got home from work as soon as possible to kick off my street clothes, shower, shave, and change into something more alluring, hoping I might get him to see past the camera lens. I picked out a flirty skirt that would show off my long legs and settled on a loose-fitting blouse with a low neckline to flash a little cleavage. I tried on a pair of sling-back heels that would put me at eye level with Micah, but considering how long we'd be on our feet, I went with my Roman sandals. When I started fixing my makeup, Zion barged in on me and asked if he could borrow my mascara.

Neither Zion nor I wanted to sit through an opening act we'd never heard of, so we didn't get to the venue until much later than the doors opened. Outside the theater, nobody waited in line or hovered near the doors. Loud but muted music pulsed through the walls. I could almost feel it more than hear it. The ticket windows were eerily quiet. The man behind the speak hole had no trouble finding our names and slid us an envelope with *Wilder* written on it in black sharpie.

I peeked in to verify it held a pair of backstage passes and press credentials. "How cool is this?"

We handed our tickets to another portly man on a stool right inside the doors. He scanned them and handed them back. Another checker had me open my bag to make sure I wasn't carrying a camera. Of course I had one, but I flashed him my press pass.

He pointed out a plastic baggie filled with small cookies. "Can't carry food into the venue." He indicated a trash can. "There's food available in the concessions." He sounded bored like he was repeating a script from rote. He didn't even make eye contact.

"This is emergency food. I'm type 1 diabetic." I said as sweetly as I could muster.

He lifted his eyes, and I could see him processing me as a human for the first time. He tilted his head toward the lobby like it made no difference to him. "Go on in."

"Thanks," I called from several feet away as Zion shoved me inside.

The lobby bustled with people milling about, buying tiny clear plastic cups of beer or wine. We found the main doors, showed our tickets again, and entered another world.

What struck me at first was the fluidity of the crowd. We had assigned seats, but nobody sat. Some people stood in the aisle, not entering or exiting, just dancing. We located our seats near the front and slid across to occupy them. I fell into mine, and nearly fell back out. The seat was broken and stopped about two inches below level. I jumped up. Zion did the same and complained that his seat was crooked.

I started to put my pocketbook on the floor, but my feet stuck to some syrupy glue. I wrapped it over my neck the opposite direction as my camera strap. I immediately hunted for something to eat. This experience promised to be far more draining than an evening with Eden Sinclair.

The theater was dark, but spotlights crisscrossed on the stage. The music coming from the speakers had a distant quality. Maybe the sound system sucked, or maybe the band did. A mass of black bangs obscured the lead singer's eyes, and he sang with his mouth crushed against the microphone so that his lyrics came out muffled. Every so often, he'd bounce and spring in sharp angular motions. The rest of the band concentrated on their so-called craft. I couldn't make out a melody at all.

When those sounds came to a stuttering halt and the audience applauded, the lead announced that they had one song left. He must have spoken the title or else people knew what to expect, but they started the next song to a roar. After a few bars, I realized the song sounded vaguely familiar.

"Who is this?" I yelled at Zion.

He reached into his back pocket and produced our tickets. "Halcyon?"

I'd definitely heard the song somewhere. It sounded awful live, and I wondered if all their music sounded better in a studio. I had low expectations for Micah's band.

As the lead singer waved and ran off stage, a red curtain dropped, and the lights came up. I had a chance to take in the theater. After the last performance, I wouldn't have been surprised to find a burned-out shell of a hole in the wall. But in fact, the place was old school classy, with a focus on old. The seats were all red velvet but less posh and more scary. A pair of once shiny gold balconies peered down on us, now dull and decaying. I wouldn't have trusted my life to the stability of those structures. The crowd in the venue would have looked more at home on a field at a festival. And they smelled like it, too.

After another fifteen minutes or so, the lights double flashed, and the people to either side of us pushed out of the row and into the aisle. At first, I thought they were taking advantage of intermission or maybe leaving before the show even started, but they moved forward, jamming in with others who now pressed against the stage. Security ineffectually directed people to move back. The crowd amassing in the aisles had to be a safety hazard.

"Don't shout 'fire.' " I whispered to Zion.

"No shit. What's going on?"

I shrugged. My experience with rock concerts was practically nonexistent. My mom would never have let me blow out my eardrums and brain cells on rock music. Once, in an act of rebellion, I went with some friends to see a Nine Inch Nails concert, but I didn't know their music and regretted the decision. We left after three songs. I had a suspicion tonight might be a repeat.

The lights dropped. A moment later, loud music broke out through the speakers at the same time the red curtain opened. Micah stood at the mic, wearing a ridiculous pair of bright blue pants and a ratty T-shirt. Somehow they'd fixed whatever technical issues had plagued the first band. The sound system functioned perfectly. Micah's vocals came through clear.

I sucked in my breath at the sight of him. It was one thing to sit beside him while he was just some other guy, but seeing him onstage, lit from above, in complete control of his audience made me want him in a weird, visceral way. I wondered if that was the feeling other people got when they went to church. It was nearly spiritual, and Micah was the cult leader.

And the mystery of the crowd behavior resolved itself as Micah grabbed his mic out of the stand and walked to the edge of the stage, touching all the outstretched hands and then pulling one person up on stage with him. This guy immediately fell backward off the stage into the waiting arms of the fans, who carried him on a wave all the way to the back of the group. When it happened a second time, I noticed Micah wasn't pulling people on stage. He would give a tug, and whatever guy climbed up on his own. But every time someone had surfed to the middle of the crowd, Micah would choose the next volunteer victim.

"You should go up there," Zion yelled.

"Hell, no. You go."

It was a moot point. When the song ended, many people in the crowd returned to their seats. Clearly this was an insider first-song-only stunt. But when the second song started, an inflated ball appeared out of nowhere. I craned my neck up to the balcony and watched as another dropped into the audience.

Micah's band was living up to its name: Theater of the Absurd. I remembered my press pass and slung my camera around to start shooting. The show went on, half rock concert, half performance piece, with more crowd interaction. Zion followed me as I moved around the venue, trying to get the best angles.

I almost considered testing out the structural integrity of the balconies but decided I didn't need to risk my life if I wasn't getting paid.

When Micah announced the last song of the night, people moved up to the stage, and Zion and I returned to our once-upon-a-time seats. I expected more of the same crowd surfing, but they all jumped up and down in time with the music—until Micah started into his last verse. At that point, he fell backward into his sea of fans, completely trusting them to catch him and deliver him unharmed to the back of the theater. And he continued to sing. When he finally landed on his feet again, he said, "Good night!" and walked out the door.

The band stopped playing without winding down or fading out. They just stopped and walked off stage. Then the theater erupted in a chorus of "Encore."

Zion leaned over. "Is that the same guy who sang with Eden last week?"

"That is a guy who does whatever he wants."

"Probably a guy who gets whatever he wants, too."

It took me a minute to process what we'd just seen. Now I understood why Micah had asked me if I'd ever seen him perform after I told him I loved theater. His band had taken a page from some of the musicals I'd seen where the stage actors moved through the crowd or where they came in and exited from the back of the theater rather than the stage. What I'd interpreted as a non sequitur so he could talk about himself made sense now. He knew I'd appreciate his show. And I did.

The band came out and wrapped up with a few more songs. He'd saved his radio hit for the encore. Everyone in the crowd sang along. Me included. It felt like a communal event. I wanted to hug the strangers around me.

And then the show ended, and the lights came up. People left the theater, laughing and singing. Normally, leaving a theater had an anticlimactic, returning-to-normal isolation to it. But I overheard people talking to each other, already reliving their favorite parts of the night. I'd noticed the crowd consisted mostly of guys, but there were a handful of girls, giggling together over how hot Micah was and trying to figure out if they'd be able to catch the next show.

I smiled, smug in my knowledge that I had backstage passes and feeling so special until one girl said, "Do you have the backstage passes?"

Zion nudged me to keep walking since I'd come to a complete halt to eavesdrop, but the girls were moving with the crowd.

"Yup. I'm gonna go for Noah."

"Not Micah?"

"As if."

Their voices drifted away, and the crowd swallowed them up. A surge of adrenaline had left a strange metallic taste in my mouth. The girls had triggered some kind of competitive drive in me. I had an overwhelming urge to rush backstage and stake a claim on Micah to show those girls up. And I didn't even know what they looked like. They were a pair of voices.

"Remind me not to get involved with a rock musician," I said to Zion.

"As if," he giggled.

The laughter helped diffuse the pent-up nervous energy. "Maybe we should just leave."

"And miss this weird experience? No way." As we merged into the lobby, he tucked a hand under my elbow and navigated the crush of exiting people.

"Where are we going?"

"Following those girls."

Then I saw them. They both had two-toned blond hair and wore interchangeable clothes. They might as well have worn T-shirts that said "Sleep with me." I glanced down at my skin-baring outfit and wondered if I looked any less obvious.

We followed them through a plain red door and down a narrow hallway to another door covered in peeling black paint. Through this door, we were confronted by a member of the theater staff who studied our backstage passes and handed them back to us.

"Vince, take these two to the visitor room."

We eventually entered a kind of surreal cocktail party where groups of people clumped together around band members like they were planetary objects. I scanned the room for Micah, but since he didn't seem to be there, Zion and I hung back to figure out the dynamic.

A pair of friends would slowly circle up to a band member, who stayed fixed in one place, chatting, signing things, taking photos with fans, and then chatting some more. The pair of friends would awkwardly attempt to engage in conversation, but only a few people managed to get the band member into an interesting discussion. Most of the talk seemed kind of lame. The pair of friends would then move around to another band member.

Others, like me and Zion, stood off to the side like wall-flowers, waiting for the action to come our way. But it clearly wouldn't.

"I wonder if we're allowed to feed the animals," Zion whispered.

I chortled. "And on your right, you'll see homo musica in his natural habitat."

Zion laughed out loud. "Please keep your hands to yourself at all times."

"I hope not at all times," a voice said in my ear from behind me. I turned and discovered Micah had snuck up on me. He'd changed into a different T-shirt, but his hair glistened either from sweat or the world's worst shower. His scent hit me a second later—musk, smoke, Tide, and something indefinable. Something that made me breathe in deep and tremble.

Before I could formulate a response, all the people in the room siphoned off whichever band member they'd been trying to approach and encircled Micah.

He completely ignored the press of people and kept his eyes on me, a true professional. He clearly knew how to handle a mob.

"No camera?" he asked, looking down at my pocketbook.

"Right here." I sighed, swinging it out from behind my back.

"Oh, right. I loved the pictures you took of Eden's show."

He touched my elbow. "Can you hang out here a little while? I'd love to look at them, but I've got some people to meet first."

That was an understatement. I swallowed the disappointment at his obvious interest in my photos and agreed. Maybe I should have bared more cleavage. But I couldn't say no to spending another ten minutes shoulder to shoulder with him. And while I waited, I shot a few more pictures of him talking with his fans. It made me happy when he signed autographs for a couple of girls, chatted with them, and then turned to the next waiting pair of fans without any hint of flirtation or interest in meeting later.

One of the girls we'd followed backstage approached me. "Are you with Micah?"

That was a tricky question. "With Micah?"

She lifted her hand to her hip. "Are you his girlfriend?"

"No. Just a friend."

She took a step back and ran her eyes from my head to my feet and then half smiled, like she'd won some imaginary contest only she was aware of. "Then if you don't mind, I'm going to try my luck with him."

As if he was an overstuffed toy at a carnival. "*Step right up! Win yourself a Micah Sinclair.*"

I usually tucked my Georgian upbringing away, hiding it from New Yorkers who mistook it for rank ignorance. But the only thing I could think to say to this girl was, "Well, bless your heart."

She relaxed as if I'd just given her my approval, but Zion had a wicked grin on his face.

Encouraged by our apparent bumpkin-ness, she went on. "I've hooked up with even bigger musicians."

Zion said, "How nice for you!"

I thought I might burst out laughing. I feared she'd go into graphic detail, so I pointed out, "The line's gotten shorter. Here's your chance!"

She fluffed her hair and readjusted her bustline. Then she threw me the shittiest expression of superiority I'd seen since high school.

My dad had taught me to reserve displays of arrogance until after I'd achieved a victory, but this girl had obviously never gotten that lesson. In fact, I got the impression she was putting on a show for my benefit. I'd given her no reason to think I'd be jealous, and I wasn't. Maybe she lived in a world with a different currency than mine.

Zion asked, "You got any popcorn?" and nudged me forward so we could hear the entire exchange.

As she moved closer, I checked my own smug arrogance. I'd forgotten that Micah's last three girlfriends had been groupies. Maybe this was how it had started. The realization made me feel queasy. I laid my fingers on my wrist to check my pulse and make sure the queasiness wasn't a sign of imminent danger. My pulse hammered. I slipped a cookie out of my pocketbook and handed another to Zion. Nibbling cookies while intent on the unfolding drama, we looked like we were watching a TV show.

At last, the girl had her moment. "Hi, Micah. My name's Kendall. I'm a big fan of your music. Great show tonight."

"Thank you, Kendall. It's great to meet you."

I had to hand it to Micah. He didn't show any signs of exhaustion or boredom. Every smile seemed real. He engaged 100 percent with whomever he talked to. And each of them had to feel special. I knew how it made me feel when he focused that charm on me.

Kendall went on. "I'm only in town for the night and wondered if you'd like some company. Maybe you could give me a personal tour of the city?"

I nearly groaned out loud. I wondered if that had ever worked for her. She could have just as easily said, "I'm available for free sex, no strings attached." Though I supposed it would have been more awkward to turn that down.

As it was, Micah put a hand on her shoulder. I'd noticed he did that frequently. A little tap on the arm or a handshake that lingered. He seemed to make a concerted effort to touch every single person he spoke to. And most of them weren't even aware he was doing it. I tried to recall if he'd done the same with me, suppressing a chill as I pictured all those little moments when he'd touched my hair or tapped my shoulder. Or wrapped his arms around my waist.

I suddenly wished this meet and greet would end and I could find a way to get Micah alone. Maybe I could ask him for a personal tour of the city.

"That's very generous of you, Kendall. Unfortunately, I've already got plans for the night." He lifted his eyes in my direction and winked. Right at that moment, I empathized with Kendall, fervently wanting to tell him I was free for an evening of no strings sex. One night with him was all I was asking.

She flipped her hair. I supposed that was her signature move. "I don't mind waiting."

"Oh, no. I wouldn't want you spending your only night in the city waiting around. But thank you. Would you like an autograph or a picture?"

And just like that, he'd reduced her from potential hookup to fawning admirer. She politely declined and turned toward another band member, perhaps hoping to have better luck. She never again glanced my way. I tried to muster up some sympathy, but the well had run dry.

Eventually, the band members began to leave the room. Micah successfully extricated himself from the last fan and made his way over to me and Zion. "Ready?"

"For?" I asked.

"Come on. I told someone I had plans with friends tonight. Don't make me a liar." He held out his hand. I stared at it unsure what he expected. I took a chance and placed my hand in his. He closed his fingers over mine and began moving toward the door. He led us down the hall to an exit. It hit me as I trotted along that he'd never stopped to see my photos—like he'd completely forgotten about them.

As the door opened to bursts of light, I had this horrible fear that Wally would be standing on the other side. I took advantage of the transition from inside the nearly deserted backstage and the eruption of sound and light outside to twist my hand free from Micah's. The last thing I needed was to be featured in a news story pitting me as Micah's next conquest.

As generous as Micah had been with his time in the visitor room, he barely acknowledged the fans waiting outside the venue. A handshake here and a flash of a smile there. But he didn't stop moving until we reached an idling car. He opened the door and waited for Zion and me to climb in. He slid in next to me and shut the door on the clamoring horde.

There was no possible way I wouldn't end up in tomorrow's paper.

Chapter 14

The car took us only a few blocks and pulled up in front of a trendy bar. I groaned. There was little I hated more than going out with people who would order round after round of drinks and proceed to get tanked while I remained on a different plane of sobriety. I resolved to hang out for the first round but abandon Zion if I had to when the party switched gears.

The doors opened onto a crush of people, fighting to get into the bar. Micah caught the eye of the hostess, and she motioned with her fingers. "Follow me."

We pushed through packed bodies as the black-clad blonde wended her way toward the back. Moving through the crowd, I heard Micah's name pop up in conversations nearby, but like a wave trailing always behind us. Micah moved too quickly for anyone to stop him. If he'd hesitated half a second, he would have been down there all night fending off requests for photos. Or knowing him, he'd be stuck down there granting everyone's requests. It didn't seem to make a difference to him either way.

At the bottom of a set of stairs, the hostess paused and pointed up the dark wooden steps. "Go on up. Martin will take care of you."

Micah laid his hand across my back and waited until I'd taken the first steps before he climbed away from the curiosity seekers with Zion following. We sandwiched Micah like a pair of shadows nobody would ever take note of.

The upstairs room had its own door, further separation from prying eyes. It was a testament to New Yorkers that nobody had climbed the stairs after us, hoping to crash the party. And evidence nobody downstairs worked for Andy Dickson.

Micah's bandmates had already made it to the bar and were engaged in an intense conversation. I scanned the room for Kendall, but she hadn't made the cut. There were a couple of girls, but none of them looked as eager to please as Kendall had. For all I knew, these were their sisters or wives. Or groupies of long standing.

Micah planted himself at the end of a table, and I took a seat facing him. Zion sat beside me.

A waiter approached. "Can I bring you a drink, miss?"

The others were nursing beers or mixed drinks. I always felt like such a freak. "Could I get a club soda with lime?"

He nodded. "Sir?" he said to Zion.

"Uh." Zion scratched his head. "Could I get a mojito?" When I rolled my eyes, he said, "What? It's still technically summer."

The waiter nodded and turned to Micah. "The usual, sir?"

Micah looked at me for a beat. "No, thanks, Martin. I'll have a club soda with lime. And could you bring us an assortment of appetizers? Boneless wings? Chips and dip?"

"Certainly, sir. Right away."

When the waiter left, I asked, "What's the usual?"

Micah wrinkled his nose. "Would you believe seltzer water with lemon?"

"Not likely."

"It's not important."

"You don't have to forgo your appletini or whatever on my account."

He smirked. "You think I drink appletinis? For your information, I drink nothing but boilermakers with a side of Jägermeister."

I snickered. "Is that so?"

"Seriously. I usually grab a beer or two after a show. That's all. It's Eden you want to watch out for. She and Adam have their fridge so full of beer, there's no room left for actual food. Which is fine since they seem to live off pancakes."

I laughed at that image. "They're so lucky. I haven't had pancakes with *real* maple syrup in fifteen years." He lifted an eyebrow, and I realized I'd opened up a subject I didn't want to pursue. And since I didn't want to spoil his night, I waved my hand at the mugs of beer on the other table. "Again, don't let me stop you."

He raised his voice loud enough for the room to hear him say, "I only drink because this company here is intolerable without a pint or two."

Instantly, the insults hurled back his way.

"Micah gets his talent from a bottle, you know."

"Micah gets tanked off a pint of Ultra Lite."

They all behaved like family, and I realized I had no idea who anyone was. "Micah, could you introduce your friends maybe?"

His eyes widened. "Oh, God. Sorry. Right."

He stood and banged on the table until the room quieted, and everyone looked up to him. I wondered if I was getting a glimpse into how band practice went down. "Everyone, this is Josie Wilder, the photographer from the *Daily Feed* I told you all about." This was met with a mix of shouted greetings and catcalls. I might have to reassess my earlier judgment. Maybe some drunk people were fun to hang out with.

"And I'd like you all to meet her friend, Zion, who I believe also works at the *Daily Feed*. So we have double the spies in our midst. Bear that in mind, folks." His Cheshire grin disarmed the insult.

He pointed at the red-haired cutie facing me at the adjacent table. "This here is Shane. You'd best stay outside a four-foot perimeter from him because he has a long reach. By that I mean, he's our drummer." Shane nodded his head as though he were acknowledging a lady at a ball.

"That fat bastard is Rick, my bass player. He's off-limits. Not because he's married with two kids, but because as I just mentioned, he's a bass player." Micah pretended to shudder as though that were self-explanatory.

"Noah, our lead guitarist, is the only one of us with a lick of talent. The only reason he hasn't abandoned us for another band is because he's so damn ugly." Noah was in fact quite pretty, but he laughed in a way that only someone with no issues of self-confidence could.

"And let's see if I can get anyone else's names right." He then proceeded to mis-introduce the girls in the room, leading me to hope he hadn't slept with either of them.

The door opened, and servers brought trays of food in. The conversations changed course like a flock of birds in flight, converging, diverging, chaotic, yet responsive. The room never fell silent. Shane lit into Zion with loud but hilarious complaints about tabloid coverage, and I turned my gaze back to Micah.

As gregarious as Micah had been with the introductions, he didn't engage with the debates and reminiscences of his bandmates. He sat quietly across from me with his chin on his hand and an elbow on the table, eyes on me.

"What?" I asked. Self-consciously, I touched my face expecting to find something stuck to it.

"Nothing. I was just wondering why it took such an elaborate ruse to get you to come out with me."

"This was a ruse?"

Splotches of red appeared on his cheeks. "I'm exaggerating a bit. But you have to admit, you make it tough on a guy."

My own cheeks felt warm. "How do you mean?"

"You're kind of hard to read."

I shot him a pot-calling-the-kettle-black look. "And you're not?"

He opened his mouth to say something more but then thought twice and turned his eyes away with a small smile playing across his lips.

Zion shoved a plate toward me, and I took my eyes off Micah. Zion had carefully chosen a variety of appetizers that would make a decent late night snack for me: a couple of boneless wings, celery, three corn chips and spinach dip, and more celery.

"Uh, thanks Zion."

He nudged me. "Eat."

Micah watched the exchange and asked, "Does he usually do that?" He started piling food on his own plate.

I took advantage of the situation and shoved a round ball of fried chicken in my mouth so I wouldn't have to answer. Zion filled in the silence. "Girl's high maintenance." He knocked my shoulder with a laugh and twisted around to return fire with Shane.

Maybe I should have just explained it all to Micah right then. Why Zion was watching me like a hawk after last week. Why I refused to order a simple pint of beer. But it sucked. It sucked to be the one who couldn't do everything everyone else wanted to do all the time. It sucked all through high school to have kids think I wouldn't drink because I was uncool. It sucked to drink anyway and then spend the night in the hospital. And it doubly sucked to get left out of everything when people learned why. I knew by now that a drink wouldn't kill me, but I fought hard enough to eat right. I didn't need to factor in the added complication.

And I didn't need to complicate Micah's view of me when he barely knew me.

But Micah didn't let it go, and as we ate, he peppered me with questions about how Zion and I met. "So how long have you two known each other?"

"Almost ten years, now. There weren't many students pursuing a BFA in photography, so we saw each other all the time and eventually started hanging out. We had almost nothing else in common, but when you're away from home, the strangest people become family. Emergencies happen, and you fall back on each other. Bonds are forged."

"Emergencies?" He glanced at my plate. "I get the feeling he took care of you."

I blotted the corner of my lips with a napkin and took a drink before answering. "We watch out for each other. When school ended, he moved up here, while I found a job in Atlanta. It's funny that neither of us appreciated how strong our friendship was until we were miles apart. We always knew we were friends, you know, but it always still seemed like we were from different worlds and we'd return to our respective corners when we were no longer forced together. But as it turned out, we have more in common than we realized. He's been trying to get me up here for years."

"Why'd you finally decide to come?"

I crunched on a celery for a bit. "It's not that I think tabloid journalists are beneath other photographers. But there's a difference between feeling good about what I do and feeling good about how other people perceive what I do. And I knew my dad wouldn't approve."

"And so?"

Did I want to lay out my whole history—how I'd watched my parents make choices in the face of their own parents' disapproval? Micah's expectant expression encouraged me to give him a piece of the truth, but this wasn't the place for unburdening the past, so I gave him the short version. "And so, one day, I decided I could wait until my dad died to start making decisions for myself, or I could live down his disappointment."

He leaned back, considering that. "And what about your mom?"

"Mom? She supports whatever I want to do. She worries a whole lot, but she knows and loves Zion, so she believes I'm in good hands."

He caught the attention of the waiter and had him refill our drinks. Before I could grab the reins of the conversation and make him answer some questions, he asked, "So Anika Jo, what's your ambition? Do you have any long-term goals?"

I squinted at him. "I will answer your question if you tell me your full name. It's only fair."

He laid his elbows on the table. "Oh, you're a negotiator."

I licked my lips and crossed my arms. "Waiting."

"I'm Micah Jordan Sinclair. Pleased to meet you." He reached one hand out.

We shook, but then he didn't let go. We rested our arms on the table, now joined together between the baskets of food and drinks. Half my brain zeroed in on the feel of his skin against mine while the other half lurched around for words to say to keep up the pretense of acting normal.

I processed his name for a second. "Jordan? So I'll just be calling you Jor Jor from Jersey from here on out."

"Oof. Anika and Jor Jor? Sounds like the world's worst *Star Wars* porn."

"It does!" I had to laugh. "Jordan's nice, but Micah suits you better."

"That's just because it's what you know me by."

His finger stroked along my wrist, and it triggered a reaction down every corridor of my nerves. I could only manage a single-word response. "Maybe."

"Now you owe me an answer. What are your plans?"

I'd hoped he'd forget. Nobody my age should be without a long-term plan. Instead, I cheated and told him something different. "I used to want to follow in my dad's footsteps, but when he's working, he spends way too much time away from people, way out in isolated locales. As much as I hate the invasive nature of my job, I love that I get to be out on the streets, meeting all kinds of people." I squeezed his hand. "Like you."

"I love meeting people, too. It's half the fun of what I do." His face suddenly lit up like a lightbulb should have popped out of the top of his head. "Have you ever considered becoming a concert photographer?"

The sudden change in conversation gave me a sense of vertigo. "What? No. What I did for Eden was the first time."

"You should come out on the road with us and shoot our shows."

My hand pulled away from him of its own accord. "You want me to be a groupie?" Even as I said it, I realized how passive-aggressive it sounded.

He sat up stiff. "I'm sorry. I get an idea and say things without thinking."

I unclenched my fists. "I shouldn't have said that. That was—"

He relaxed some, but he'd lost his friendly tone. "It just occurred to me that it wouldn't be that different from what you've been doing, but maybe your dad would approve more. There are some very successful concert photographers. I looked up your dad's photos after I saw his name in the paper last week."

"Yeah?"

"Yeah. And then I saw what you did with Eden. You're talented. I bet you could sell your photos to the *Rock Paper*."

"Oh, so you want me to help you get your picture in the *Rock Paper*?" It would have been better if I could tell him what was really troubling me rather than tear him apart by lobbing these sarcastic barbs at him.

"Ouch. Is that what you think?"

I took a shuddering breath to get my disappointment and irritation under control. I should have remembered he was just a big old flirt.

But even so, even if he was trying to find a way to use me to further his own career, I didn't want to start a fight with him, especially not here among his friends. He hadn't needed to bring me along. And he'd been nothing but gracious. "I'm sorry. Can we start over?"

He reached his hand back across the table toward me, but not like a greeting. His hand was palm up, vulnerable. I reached mine out to him in return, and he clasped my fingers in his. "I don't want to start over. I want to go on."

A wave of dizziness swept over me at his words. My eyelids fluttered and closed, and my head rolled around to the side. When I opened my eyes, Zion reached over and felt my forehead. "We should be going." He pushed his chair back and offered me his hand.

I wanted to communicate with Zion in giant semaphore flags to let him know I was fine. But I couldn't easily explain the situation either to Zion or to Micah. "*Oh, hey Zion. It's fine. I'm just swooning over something Micah said, though I'm sure insulin shock must appear the same to you.*"

Micah jumped up when I stood. "One second. Let me at least call my car."

As Micah texted, Zion handed me my pocketbook. I glared at him although he meant well. "I'm fine, Zion. Really."

Micah led us down the stairs, through the crowd and out into the night. "My driver should be here in a second." He reached into his coat pocket and pulled out a pack of cigarettes.

As soon as he lit one, I moved several feet away from him out of long habit. He blew out a cloud of smoke, then threw the cigarette on the ground and twisted it out with his shoe. "Oh, right. Don't drink, don't smoke."

I glared at him. "I'm not a Goody Two-shoes, if that's what you think." My voice faltered, and I felt like an idiot. Tears welled up in my eyes, but I didn't want Micah to think I was going to start crying on his account. So I walked toward the street and turned my back on him, choking in huge breaths of air to calm down. Just because I didn't want to stand in a cloud of smoke, did that make me too lame for the rock star party?

Micah laid a hand on my shoulder. "No, I didn't mean—"

"Are you Micah Sinclair?" A couple of girls in short skirts, low necklines, and high heels flanked Micah.

Micah's head jerked toward the interruption. "What? Yeah."

The redhead said to her blond friend, "Told ya so." She flung her hair and inched closer. "God, you're even cuter in person."

The car entered the street, and I took a step toward the curb. Micah's hand fell from my shoulder.

"Mind if we take a selfie with you?"

I couldn't even look. I willed the car to hurry up so I could dive in and get away, but the road was clogged with taxis. I contemplated hailing one, but I couldn't find one that wasn't occupied.

"I'm sorry. This isn't a great time." Micah stepped closer to me, away from the girls.

"Oh, please. It's just a quick picture." The blond one pushed her way beside Micah with her back to me and her arm around Micah's waist, without bothering to ask him if she could touch him. Like he was a cardboard cutout instead of a person.

"Do you mind? I'm in the middle of a conversation." Micah eluded her grasp right as the car pulled up.

Zion opened the door for me, and I bent to climb in, but Micah caught my arm and said, "Hey, is everything okay?"

I turned my face away so he wouldn't see the tears already falling. Zion ushered me into the backseat and threw over his shoulder, "Everything's not okay, Micah. She's diabetic."

Of their own volition, my eyes cut sideways to check on

Micah's reaction. His mouth hung slack for an instant, and his eyebrows drew together as he ran through everything he'd ever known about me. I didn't want to stand there watching him reprocess our every interaction through the filter of disease, so I looked away and climbed into the car.

Zion followed and closed the door. "Hey, if he's not cool about that, he's not good enough for you anyway."

I dropped my head into my hands, and Zion rubbed my shoulder.

When the car didn't start moving right away, I looked up to see why just as the door on my side opened up. Micah stuck his head in. "Is there room for an asshole?"

I wiped my eyes on my shirtsleeve. "You're not an asshole, Micah. You didn't know."

"I do now. Can I ride with you? Can we start over?"

I scooted over to let him in. He closed the door and told the driver where to go. He laid his hands in his lap and stared at them. "I'm sorry, Jo."

"Why?"

"Why am I sorry?" He adjusted himself so he could look me in the eye. "I don't know why, but everything I say or do seems all wrong. I'm all feet in mouth with you. And then all that—" He waved back in the direction of the bar that was receding quickly behind us. "So I'm sorry."

"You couldn't help that."

He put his arm around me and held me close. "I know I'm impossible to be around."

That made me laugh out loud. It was the complete opposite of the truth, and suddenly all I wanted to do was relax into him, but my guard had gone up. And it remained fortified. "Why are you being so nice?"

"Oh. I thought that part was pretty obvious. I really like you."

"But you barely know me."

He leaned forward far enough to see past me to Zion. "Can you give me a reference?"

Zion was laughing. "Yup."

"Is Josie Wilder from Georgia?"

"She is."

"Is she a tabloid photographer?"

"Indeed."

"Is she pretty terrible at her job?"

Zion guffawed. "She's a great photographer. She's a terrible tabloid photographer."

"And why is that?"

"Because she focuses too much on the humanity and not enough on the sensational."

I sat up. "I'm not terrible at my job. I just haven't been at it long enough."

"I have one last question."

Zion said, "Shoot."

"Does she like me back?"

Zion, bless his heart, actually looked like he was torn. I gritted my teeth and waited for him to show my full hand. But instead he said, "Isn't half the fun finding that out for yourself?"

When the driver parked in front of our building, Zion opened the door and then turned and said to Micah, "She shouldn't stay out too late. She has to be up early in the morning. But I'm going to bed." He jumped out and slammed the door behind him, leaving me alone with Micah. And his driver.

He still had his arm around my shoulder, and I couldn't decide if I should push back and talk to him, or shut my brain off long enough to give into whatever was happening.

"How are you feeling?" he asked. He rubbed my shoulder, and I looked up into his face.

"I feel fine. Zion overreacts sometimes where I'm concerned. I'm like his only family."

"He obviously cares a lot about you."

I leaned back to see him better. "Micah?"

"Yes?"

His eyes met mine, and I wished I could read his mind. I wished I could make him tell me point by point why he thought he liked me. I wanted him to make guarantees he couldn't make. I wanted him to promise not to hurt me.

Instead, I gave him back the one point he'd already earned. "I like you."

He smiled the big smile, the one that brought out the dimple in his cheek. He ran a finger across my forehead to move loose strands out of my face. Then he kissed me. The first kiss was sweet. Our lips tested each other, tasted each other. Then he put his hands around the back of my neck. I pulled away and listened for the dangerous sounds of my heart pounding in my ears. He opened his eyes. "Everything okay?"

I reached for him and wove my fingers in his hair. I pressed my lips on his. The second kiss felt like an invitation to open myself up to him. When his tongue brushed against mine, a delicious queasiness spread through my belly.

"Can you come back to my place?" he asked.

The clock on the dash showed two a.m. My quick math told me that I'd be up all night if I went home with him. As it was, I'd be lucky to be up by eight. "I have to be at work by nine tomorrow. I should be going to bed."

"Okay." He pulled me in for a tight hug. "I'm sorry again." He shook his head and leaned back. "You must think I'm a jerk."

My mind was racing.

Zion had brought his boyfriends home occasionally. Not often, but it wasn't unprecedented. . . .

Micah took my hand. "But thank you for coming out tonight."

And I could be a little late in the morning if I made it up at the end of the day.

His thumb stroked mine. "When can I see you again?"

And that kiss. My legs were still shaking from that kiss. And . . . "Can you come up?"

He inhaled sharply. "Jo. You don't have to."

I laid my hand on his cheek. "Would you please come up?"

"Are you sure?"

In response, I pulled him in to me and kissed him until his lips parted, and his hands roamed into uncharted territory. I broke away. "Yes. I'm sure."

Chapter 15

All the lights had been turned off except for the one in the range hood, and the apartment was dark and quiet. Zion had obviously gone to bed or had pretended to in the event I might bring Micah up. That was adorably sweet of him, but it left me awash in nerves. It left no doubt about why I'd brought Micah up.

To cover my awkwardness, I opened the fridge. "Do you want a drink?" I unscrewed the top of a bottle of water and drank half of it in one pull.

Then he was behind me, his hands on my shoulders, fingers running down my neck. A chill shot down my spine, and I set the bottle down and closed the door. He spun me toward him and pushed me against the fridge. He kissed me so deep, my legs almost gave out. I took his hand and led him to my bedroom.

He'd carried a kind of canvas messenger bag with him like an old army medical supply bag. I wondered if he kept a pair of spare clothes with him at all times. I wondered how many times he'd hooked up with a girl exactly like this after a show.

Had I been seduced?

If so, I was still under the spell, and I lured him with my own dark temptation toward my lair. I hadn't been in New York long enough to have brought anyone into my bedroom. It seemed utterly preposterous that this guy I'd met on the street last week,

whose pictures I'd seen in my own newspaper, was in my tiny
bedroom, about to lay himself in my fortuitously large bed.
About to lay me . . .

I sat on the edge of the bed, watching him. Without hesitat-
ing, he kissed me, pushed me over, and climbed in next to me.

And my brain caught up with my body, protesting with all
the reasons I couldn't go through with this. Maybe it was my
Georgia upbringing, but the logical side of my brain threw up
alarms that said, "*You'll never see him again if you let him sleep
with you tonight.*"

Another part of my brain countered that I'd be the worst kind
of tease if I told him no now. He'd sent his driver away. I'd told
him I was sure. I'd all but advertised my availability to him tonight.

But how many women had thought the same exact thing?

His thumb pressed against my cheek, and his hand slid
around to the back of my head, and then down my neck and
across my chest. He only lingered on my breasts for a moment
before reaching for the hem of my shirt—the hem that hid my
insulin pump attached to a white tube. I grabbed his hand before he could discover it. Even though he knew, mentally, that
I was different, it was a whole other thing for him to see me. It
wouldn't be the first time someone turned away, repulsed by the
"hospital patient."

He stopped kissing me and looked down into my eyes. He
drew his hands back. "It's okay if you just want to go to sleep."

"What?" Had I turned him off entirely already?

"Look. This is a really weird situation. I get that. And I really
don't want to screw it up with you. If you don't want to do this,
I'd be happy just to sleep next to you. I'm obviously attracted
to you, but I'm not going to do anything that might make you
doubt that I like you." He traced my cheek. "You're probably
thinking that I picked you up like any one of the girls who show
up looking for a night with a musician."

That was an understatement. I leveled my gaze at him. "It
had crossed my mind."

"If I wanted sex, I could get it. And I know how bad this

sounds, but sex has never been something I had to work hard for. You know my track record. I can't pretend things aren't what they are. But what I can't find is someone I just want to spend time with, someone I want to get to know. That's priceless to me."

"But why me?"

He scooted over and sat cross-legged next to me, stroking my hand. "I could ask you the same thing. Why me, Jo?"

I'd been so fixated on trying to understand how he could possibly have any idea who I was in only a week that I hadn't stopped to wonder how I'd developed such a strong positive feeling toward him beyond physical attraction in the same amount of time. This despite fairly damning information I'd assessed objectively. This despite the swarm of queasy doubts that plagued me when I imagined how many casual relationships he'd flown through. Why him indeed? "I don't know. Gut instinct."

"Exactly." He gazed at me with his bedroom eyes and his soft lips turned in a perfect smolder.

I'd never felt so conflicted. I wanted him to kiss me again, but I hesitated. "You know what I want to do?"

"What?" He interlaced our fingers together.

"I want to lie here and listen to you talk. But I am nearly desperate to lay my hands on your skin. I want to get to know you better—but slowly. Can we work something out?"

"Yeah." He slid in next to me, and we each laid our heads on a pillow. Then he turned to face me, letting me run my hand along his arm and wrap my fingers in his. I found the hem of his shirt and touched the soft hair along his tight abs. I followed the trail up to his chest. If he was dying, he didn't say.

"Can I ask you something first?" His voice at that volume made me willing to answer anything.

"Yeah." I'd reached his collarbone and tiptoed across it until it ran out, then I spread my hand out and caressed his shoulder.

A small groan escaped him. "Mmm. That feels so nice."

"That's not a question." His neck felt warm and tense. If I didn't think it would lead to anything more, I would have laid my lips on his skin there. Micah needed kissing.

"I kind of had the feeling at first that you wanted to be with me to get better pictures. When you left me on the sidewalk that night, you said it was because you weren't feeling well."

"I hadn't eaten, Micah. I was afraid I was fixing to pass out right in front of you. I would have rather died."

He nuzzled the top of my head and kissed my forehead. "I believe you. But then you snubbed me outside the club the next night, and I figured I didn't stand a chance with you."

"Micah, I can explain. Wally was out there and—"

He laid a hand on my arm and said quietly, "Let me say it all. I feel weirdly safe right now, and I want to say it all. Okay?"

"Yes. I'm listening."

"So when you tweeted me about the show, I had a fleeting hope you might be interested. But when I messaged you and you never wrote me back, I figured you only wanted to keep things friendly or professional. Obviously, that was my stupidity."

"Yeah, I wanted to write you back, but you weren't following me. That was so frustrating."

His breath tickled my cheek, and I turned my face up toward him. He met my eyes. "I was afraid you wouldn't come to my show if you couldn't take pictures. I thought I'd need to entice you with press credentials."

I pulled his hand to my lips and kissed his palm. "You still haven't asked me a question."

His nervous laughter sounded false, equal parts relief and sadness. "I just want to ask when you stopped thinking of me as someone who could help you with your career and started to see me as someone you might like to spend time with." I pressed my lips against the ends of his fingers, one at a time. "You have started to think of me that way, right?"

I stopped kissing him and lifted myself up on an elbow. "Are you asking if I'm using you, right now, to advance my career?"

"I'm sorry. It's Eden in my head. I want to trust everyone at face value, and until tonight, I wouldn't have asked the question. But now it has the potential to really hurt. So I have to ask it. But I swear, I never will again. If you tell me I can trust this, I will. Completely."

I poked at my inner sense of righteousness for the *How dare he?* but I couldn't find it. It had absconded with my *What will the neighbors think?*

"Micah, those are fair questions. To be honest, I had the same concerns about you. I thought at first you only wanted me around for the publicity."

"Really?"

"Yeah, of course." I laughed my no-duh laugh. "Try to see things from where I'm sitting. You've got a solid reputation for soliciting publicity. I thought you brought me in only so I could photograph you at that party."

"Whoa. I didn't ask you to photograph my party. You started taking pictures the minute I stepped away."

"Yeah, you already explained that. But every time you invited me with you, you offered me an opportunity to document it. The press credentials you enticed me with convinced me you only wanted me at your concert for my camera."

He ran his fingers through my hair and tugged on a strand. "The first time I saw you on the street, I wanted you to lose that camera so I could look at you."

"And the first time I saw you, I completely failed to do my job. Do you know why?"

"Because you're terrible at it?"

I jabbed him with my finger. "No. Because you took me off guard. You confused the hell out of me, too. And later, when you kissed me, that was the moment you stopped being anything more to me than someone I'd like to get to know better."

"Then that was smart of me."

I poked him again, gentler. "Yes. That was very smart of you."

He pulled a pillow up behind him and relaxed into it. His muscles lost their tension, and he yawned. "You're tired. I'll shut up."

"No. Keep going. I want to fall asleep listening to you. Tell me a secret."

"A secret?"

"Not a big secret. Something I can't find on Wikipedia."

"Hmm." He wrapped his arm around me and kissed the top of my head. "Okay. When I was five, I had a stuffed gorilla named Clark."

"Clark," I mumbled, yawning.

"I dragged him around so much that one of his arms became longer than the other. My parents tried to wean me off Clark the deformed gorilla when he started to ooze stuffing out the gaping hole in his side. But I wouldn't forsake my monkey. So I hid him under my pillow. Later when my parents took us on a trip across the country, Clark stowed away in my suitcase. . . ."

As I snuggled against him, his quiet voice in the dark lulled me. What felt like a moment later, my alarm went off, and it was morning.

Micah's arm lay across my waist, his hand tight across my belly. Snuggled against him, I hated to move, but Zion was already up and about, cooking breakfast. He wouldn't wait around for me forever, and I didn't want to have to ride in to work alone. So I carefully slipped out from under Micah and hunted around for some clothes to carry out.

When I clicked the door shut behind me, Zion stopped what he was doing, spatula held aloft as though he were in the middle of casting a spell. "Are you still wearing your clothes from last night?"

The door opened behind me, and Micah stepped out, wearing his bright blue skinny jeans and looking like he'd spent the night in a tent. His disheveled hair made him seem more real than he had since I'd met him, and I bit my lip at how endearing such a little thing could be. He yawned and said, "Good morning. Is it time to go to work?"

For a moment, I stood paralyzed in suspended animation. Should I kiss him or play it cool? But he rubbed his eyes, stretched and yawned, scratched his side, and then staggered over to the kitchen.

Zion asked, "You want eggs?"

"I don't want to trouble you. Could I just get some coffee?"

While they talked, I slipped into the bathroom and checked

my appearance in the mirror. My makeup had turned against me in the night, and my hair defied gravity. I brushed my teeth and did what I could to tone down the horror of morning me.

Coffee was brewing when I came back to the kitchen, and I fetched the mugs.

While Micah excused himself to use the bathroom, Zion reached into a drawer, pulled out my glucose meter, and dropped it on the table. "Sit. You're pushing yourself too hard," he warned.

"It's been a weird week. I'm fine."

"Look. Your mom said, 'Don't you leave her, Samwise Gamgee.'" He clutched at his chest dramatically. "And I don't mean to."

I put on my best Irish accent. "Do you mean to share the load?"

He grew serious. "If I could carry it for you, I would, Josie. I hate that you have to work so hard just to hit normal. And you gave me a scare last week. And then again last night . . ."

"I was fine, Zion. You totally misread my reaction." I dropped my voice a little. "If you'd heard what Micah had said to me . . ."

He sighed. "I heard enough in the car. You sure he doesn't have a gay brother somewhere? Beautiful *and* thoughtful."

"Mmm, yeah, he is."

The toaster dinged, and Zion plated our breakfast. I tested my blood sugar while he set everything down on the table.

Micah returned, looking like he'd also tried and failed to salvage his hair.

I'd already taken a bite of my toast when he sat beside me. "By the way, I'm having lunch with your sister today. Should I tell her you said hey?"

He sipped his coffee for a second before responding. "Can you maybe not mention this to her until I have a chance to? I mean, I don't think she'll get bent out of shape, but I'd rather be the one to talk her down."

"Won't she be mad that I lied by omission?"

"Don't worry. I'll explain everything."

Before I could probe further, Zion sat down and cajoled Micah, hoping to convince him into coming to the office with us. "Imagine the look on Andy's face if you walked right in with us. He'd piss himself."

Micah wisely excused himself, saying, "That's like asking a murder suspect to just stop into the precinct for a couple of questions."

"But think of the hijinks!" Zion changed course. "Could I take pictures of you eating breakfast with Josie?"

I choked and coughed. "NO! God, no!"

Micah leaned back, smiling. "Let me crawl into her bed first."

Zion laughed. "Maybe if you draped her blanket over your bare body?"

My eyes bugged out. "Now you're trying to take advantage of the boy for your own sick entertainment." I acted put out, but the image of Micah half-naked in my bed left me regretting my decision to put him off the night before. On the other hand, I loved that he hadn't made any attempt to convince me to change my mind. And that was worth a little morning-after regret. Better than regretting the reverse.

Micah's poor beleaguered driver arrived and carried him out of my life. But I was armed with his phone number, his email address, and a promise that he'd contact me later in the day.

When Zion and I got to the office, Andy had assembled everyone together for some kind of stand-up meeting. The second we came through the door, he said, "Are we all clear?"

Everyone nodded and went to their workstations. I glanced at Zion. "What was that about?"

Andy said, "With me, Jo."

Somehow I'd devolved to rank newbie in a little less than a week. I entered his office, unprepared for whatever he had on his mind. "Sir?"

"I've asked Derek to cover anything regarding Micah or Eden Sinclair from now on. I think you have a conflict of interest."

"What? Why?"

He pushed his iPad toward me, and I saw the back of my head as I ascended the stairs in the bar, a couple of steps above Micah.

"Did you expect me to take pictures? I wasn't even on the clock!"

He rolled his eyes. "Jo, you're paparazzi. You're always on the clock."

I fumbled in my bag for my camera. "I did shoot some pictures from last night's show."

"Are you kidding? Micah's a pretty face, and we can always use provocative pictures of him. But his band is low interest news."

"I've got some with his fans in a private meeting after the show."

He thought about it. "The problem with you, Jo, is that you think like an amateur. Fans in a private meeting? Every single person in that room will have already tweeted a half dozen pictures."

"You wanted me to get closer. I have."

"That's what's so frustrating. You're *right* where I want you."

"So what's the problem?"

"You, Jo. You've gone native."

I chortled. "Native? Seriously?"

He thumbed toward the office where reporters with blood-shot eyes scanned their computer monitors for any sign of a lead. "You find yourself in a position all of them only dream of and you're not taking advantage. You're hanging out with Micah, but I can't count on you to bring me anything you might learn about him. Or his sister." He pinched his fingers together. "I'm this close to sending you out to cover the airports."

"No. Andy. Not the airports." I'd lose my mind.

"I think you might need to take a step back, regain your focus. You've been wandering around, haphazardly stumbling across half stories."

"I got you the L.L. Stylez story."

He gave me a what-planet-are-you-from wide-eyed stare. "You got me the raw materials. I had to mold it into something provocative." His shoulders relaxed with a sigh that seemed somehow calculated. "I'm giving you opportunities to grow. I just need you to give me something I can work with."

"I'm trying, Andy. I honestly don't know what more I can do."

He pushed his tablet toward me. "Did you see this?"

It was a picture from the set I'd taken at Hervé's party five days before. I raised my eyes to meet Andy's. "I looked through all the pictures."

"Right, but did you see this?" He laid his finger and thumb on the photo and spread them to zoom in further. As soon as he did, I knew which picture it was. The group in the original photo was of no interest, but Andy had brought the scene in the background forward, cropping out the people who'd been in frame. The resulting picture showed Adam standing behind Eden with his arm wrapped around her. His hand lay on her stomach. My stomach dropped.

"I'm not sure what you're seeing." If he ran a story about Eden's pregnancy now, she'd never speak to me again.

Andy tapped his finger right on top of Eden's belly. "The ring. Adam's wearing a wedding band. Look."

I exhaled and looked closer. Sure enough, there was a band on the fourth finger of his left hand. "I see."

"How did you miss that?"

"I wasn't looking for it."

He stared at the photo, chewing on his upper lip. Finally, he put down the tablet, and said, "This would be a huge story, if we could prove they secretly married." He tapped his finger absently on his desk. "I've been through all the pictures, trying to get a good view of her ring finger. I can tell she's got a ring on, but is she wearing two? Is she wearing an engagement ring and a wedding band? I can't quite tell."

I wanted to tell him it was none of his damn business, but sweat beaded his lip. He looked like a junkie in need of a fix. If I didn't intervene, he might start digging through their trash and find out even more than he'd bargained for. I needed to throw a stick out for him to chase after.

"I'm going to see her today. I'll look at her rings. Okay?"

He lifted his hand to his forehead and rubbed his temple as he worked through his options. His lizard-like tongue ran over his lower lip, and he came to a decision. "Okay, sure. I'll give you another shot. If you can bring me that story, I'll let you keep your freedom, maybe even let you keep reporting on the Sinclairs. But if you can't do it, you might as well head straight to JFK after lunch."

Caught between two terrible options was no way to live. But what other choice did I have if I wanted to keep my job?

"I'll get the story," I promised.

Chapter 16

I found an empty table outside the restaurant. The day had turned overcast and cool, but still nice enough to enjoy the open air. Eden walked up a few minutes later. She moved through the New York crowd as though she were cloaked in invisibility. Considering what I did for a living, it always amazed me how unfazed New Yorkers could be when lower level celebrities passed in their midst. They'd perk up at someone really famous—like Chris Hemsworth. I'd wager that Adrianna LaRue would turn some heads.

Eden waggled her fingers in a gesture so girlfriend friendly that it made me forget to get a closer look. She reached me and laid a hand on my arm. "So good to see you, again."

As soon as she sat down, a lady wearing a visor and a fanny pack stopped at our table. "Excuse me. Aren't you Eden Sinclair?"

Eden smiled graciously. "Yes."

"I thought so. I don't want to interrupt your lunch, but I just wanted to tell you I loved your CD. I downloaded it and gave a copy to my daughter. Would you mind if I got an autograph?"

"No, of course not." She waited patiently for the woman to conjure up some kind of pen and paper, but as the woman continued to stare helplessly at Eden, I reached into my pocketbook and rescued her from the awkwardness, handing her a pen.

"Thank you!" She relayed the pen to Eden, who still had nothing to write on. "Oh, right!" She fumbled in her fanny pack for something and came up with a checkbook.

Eden asked for her name and scrawled a message on the registry while the woman nattered on about how nice it would be for Eden to come play Indianapolis.

Eden kept writing. "Yes, I played there in June. So sorry you missed that." She added her Twitter handle and website URL to the registry. "I hope you'll sign up for my newsletter so you won't miss me next time."

As soon as the woman left, I asked Eden. "Should we go inside?"

"Maybe that would be a good idea."

We grabbed our things and found a table at the far corner of the restaurant. I hoped that nobody else would want to stop and have their moment with her. Or take pictures and post them in a tabloid.

While we waited to order, she made some small talk about how great it was that we could meet. I reached out and touched her left hand, turning it for a better view. "I'd noticed before how gorgeous your ring is."

"Ah. Yeah. I love it. Adam surprised me at one of our shows with it." There wasn't a wedding band.

"I thought I saw a ring on Adam's finger."

She balled her fists. "Do I need to tell you this lunch is off the record?"

My cheeks burned. "Of course not. I'm sorry. Natural curiosity. A great characteristic in a journalist. A terrible characteristic in a friend." I had an urge to come out and tell her that Andy had charged me with the task of investigating, but then she might wonder why I'd even told Andy about our lunch. I already felt like this friendship was precarious.

"Well, it's actually no secret. My mom's Swedish." She said it as if that answered some mystery. That explained where Micah got his coloring, but not why Adam was wearing a wedding band.

"And?"

"And in Sweden, men wear an engagement ring. It's actually just the wedding band, worn a little early. As soon as he heard about this tradition last month, he insisted on getting one." She shook her head and smiled fondly. "He's really good at sucking up to my mom."

I laughed. "That's a great characteristic in a future husband."

"I should just be wearing a band now and wait to get the diamond when we're married. Adam didn't know that either when he got me this." She flashed her hand. "And I wasn't about to wait to wear it. I have no need to impress my mom."

The waitress arrived with her pen poised on a notepad. "What'll you have?"

Eden ordered a cheeseburger, fries, and a soda. That sounded tempting. I ordered the same, but replaced the fries with a side salad and the soda with water.

As soon as the waitress left, Eden said, "So you're going to want to know if we've set a date."

The abrupt shift in topic took me off guard. "What?"

"Since we're talking bluntly about your interest in my life, aren't you going to ask when I plan to get married?"

"It does seem to be driving everyone crazy. You were engaged two years ago, right?"

"Yup. But we have a hard time coordinating. It's been a crazy busy two years. It's hard to plan far enough in advance to know for sure we'll both be in the same town at the same time. Adam tours all the time."

"Do you ever worry about him out on the road?" I wished I could take that back. So nosy. I wasn't even trying to pry. "I mean. I would, but I think I might lean more jealous than you. You both seem completely smitten."

"I used to worry. But Adam's a keeper. I think it would kill him to cheat on me even more than it would hurt me. And then I'd kill him. He's never been into on-the-road romance with groupies."

"Unlike your br—" I clipped the last word when I realized how awful the question was. Did I really want to dig into Micah's private life?

Our food came, and we fussed with settling in to eat. I could tell she had something on her mind, but she didn't speak again until she'd taken a few bites and then a swallow from her drink.

"You think my brother's a slut, don't you?"

I nearly choked on a crouton. I'd always hated that word ever since the neighborhood gossips leveled it at my mom. "Look, I'm in no position to judge him. But he sure has had a lot of relationships with his fans."

"Not his fans."

"But—"

"His fans go out and buy his CDs. They may or may not go online to talk to other fans. They live in places like Iowa and go to community college while working a part-time job so they can eventually get a job as a manager of a Best Buy. They come out to his shows when he's in Des Moines and scream their heads off in the audience with their girlfriends. And then they go home to their Iowa apartment and listen to his music while they study for an exam. At most, they come out after a show and try to get his autograph."

"But—"

She waved a fork-impaled fry to punctuate her next point. "The people Micah dates are groupies."

I held up a hand to interrupt. "But aren't groupies just bigger fans?"

"Sometimes. There are definitely devotees of the band who live on the road, following the tour from town to town. But for a large number of them they may not even care about the music. They may not care which musician or even which band they're in with. They somehow make friends with security and find ways to get passes backstage. They like the musician's life, and they make it really easy for a boy who has no attachments to have something like a relationship out on the road—or even if he does have other attachments. They sometimes call themselves 'road wives.' "

My food sat uneaten. I gaped at Eden while she talked, more and more unnerved. She said all this so matter-of-factly, I wondered how she sat there casually scarfing down her lunch while her fiancé currently thrived in an environment of casual invitation. "And they don't want anything more? No commitment? Just sex?"

I thought of Kendall and her "one-night personal tour of the city." I pushed the lettuce around my plate.

"For Micah, when the tour ends, and he goes back to his normal life, these girls don't usually follow him. They'll use their connection with him to work their way into the whole groupie culture. It's not unusual for them to go out looking for another musician to latch onto."

"He was telling the truth, then?"

"About?"

"About the girls breaking it off with him?"

"Well, it's not as if he really cares. Once upon a time, he used to date girls who didn't seem to even know that he was a musician. I guess it's getting harder to find one. To be fair, he's never cheated on his groupies. I'm not sure they ever returned the favor. He's not a man-whore. But he's definitely not a monk."

I felt a blush creeping up my cheek. Eden blotted her lip with a napkin and leaned in. "But you should probably keep a low opinion of him. I love my brother, but I can't vouch for him. I don't know if he's ready for anything more than the easy commitment-free relationships he's burned through in the past two years."

I took a sip of water, but my throat had clenched up, making it hurt to swallow. "He's definitely a big old flirt."

"That he is." She sat back in her chair and watched me for a second. "Look. Micah's got a big heart, and he's had legitimate girlfriends—though mostly back before this whole rock star thing took off. It's a hard life for regular people." Her eyes bored into mine. "I don't have to tell you how invasive the media can be, especially when it involves new relationships. And new relationships are the most vulnerable. The paparazzi drive away anyone who values a shred of privacy."

"But you put up with it?"

She snorted. "Do I?"

We declined to order dessert when the server came, but Eden

ordered two coffees. I folded my napkin absently. "My boss would be so pissed if he knew I spent an hour talking to you about Micah."

She steepled her fingers. "You want to fuck with him?"

"What? With Micah?"

"With Andy."

"How?"

She leaned on her elbows. "We could feed him something bogus but innocuous."

My heart sank. "Like what?" Her eagerness confirmed my suspicion that she wanted to use me to get to Andy. And maybe she already had. Maybe the pregnancy was a complete fabrication. Would she go that far?

She cast her eyes up toward the ceiling, thinking. "I don't suppose you could make him believe I'm Elvis in disguise?"

I snorted. Her ridiculous suggestion dispelled the nagging doubts about her ulterior motives with me. "Ooooh. Or we could say you're in contact with our alien overlords?"

Her face lit up with laughter. "Yeah."

A waitress cleared our cups away and spoiled the moment. "Anything I tell Andy about you will get published in my name. He's probably not above stealing credit, but you'd most likely be messing with my career."

"Crap. I'd really love to get him good."

Knowing what drove the tabloids as well as I did gave me some insight on what might actually entice Andy, and I couldn't help share with Eden. "There is one thing we could do. Is there a jewelry store nearby?"

Andy ambushed me the second I came into the office. "Well?"

"She said it was off the record." Not that Andy would care. He wouldn't print it, but he could mine information for gold for future research. And nothing would get him more interested than starting off by telling him he couldn't print whatever I knew.

"What did she say was off the record? Did they get married or not?"

"She says, 'Not.' "

He pouted like a little kid. "Did you at least get any pictures of her ring?"

"That I did." My conscience stirred slightly. I'd told Eden this could cost me my job if Andy found out I was lying to him, and she said that would put us into a state of détente. We both knew a secret about each other.

Andy reached for my camera without waiting for me to offer it. He rolled through the pictures Eden had posed for outside. We'd gone into a boutique that sold cheap jewelry and bought a ten-dollar silver band that she'd worn with her engagement ring, flashing her hands about while I took pictures. Andy zoomed in on every picture and finally got one that came out clearer than the rest.

"Is her engagement ring a double band?" He kept flipping through pictures. Then he started looking through older pictures trying to compare. It was impressive but scary to watch him work. "Here. There's only one band." He zoomed in on a picture from weeks earlier.

He narrowed his eyes and went over the pictures. "Something doesn't seem right about this. Eden doesn't ever pose for pictures."

I held my breath.

He stood for a minute in thought. "And she told you she's not married? Then why would they go around wearing wedding bands in the open?" He straightened his tie and ran a hand through his hair. As he walked to his office, he muttered, "I wouldn't put it past Eden to pull another stunt."

So much for operation *Fuck with Andy*. At least he hadn't suspected my involvement in the prank. No harm, no foul.

When he came out of his office, I made the mistake of asking him if I'd fulfilled my end of the bargain. He scowled. "Do I have a story I can print?"

He hadn't answered my question. After I hadn't moved, he finally said, "Are you waiting for an invitation?"

But I had to play the cards I had. "Andy, didn't I bring you the picture of Eden's ring?"

"Yeeeeah." He tapped his finger on the table. "About that. I'm pretty sure she's using you to get to me. You'd know that if you made it your mission to take candid shots instead of the ones they pose for. But she's up to something, and I want to know what it is. I've asked Derek to keep an eye on her."

He sent Derek to stalk her. My throat constricted, and I had to fight stupid unintended emotions. If I choked up now, Andy might suspect I was hiding something. And he'd be right. "What's he going to do?"

"The fact that you have to ask that speaks volumes." He leaned against my desk. "Go to the airport, and bring me something good. If you can show me you've finally discovered your edge, we'll revisit the whole situation. If not, well then we'll have a different discussion next week."

I grabbed my backpack to head out of the office, but before I'd made it to the door, Andy added, "And Jo, if I see you in the paper with Micah again, I hope it will be because you've found me a story I can run." He tilted his head toward me with an ominous expression. "You need to understand that nobody who works for me would fail to take advantage of that situation."

I bolted with a growing pain in my stomach. As much as I hated Andy, I couldn't lose this job, or I'd lose my health insurance. And then I might as well just move back to Georgia and live with my mom. But there were other departments at this paper, so on my way downstairs, I stopped in the Arts and Leisure department and asked the rail-thin Audrey Hepburn look-alike if I could see the managing editor.

She waved her hand toward a desk in the far corner, and I squeezed through the small office.

"Excuse me," I said to the gray-haired man reading his monitor intently. "Are you Sang Moon-Soo?" The question was rhetorical. How many grizzled Koreans worked in this department?

"Yes?" He looked up, but I waited until his eyes lost their glaze and focused on me.

"Hello. My name is Jo Wilder and—"

"Have a seat." He indicated a chair at an unoccupied desk. I rolled it over. "What can I do for you?"

"Mr.—" I stopped, unsure how to address him. I was 99 percent sure other journalists referred to him as Moon-Soo as was the Korean way of putting the first name last. Tentatively, I finished, "Sang." He nodded, and I continued with more confidence. "I was hoping you might have some openings on your staff. I'd love to transition to Arts and Leisure if possible as a theater reporter."

He rubbed his nose. "Theater reporter, eh? I don't have enough staff down here to be able to hire on anyone for such a specific role."

"Oh. Well, I could do other things, too, but I had an interview with Miriam Blackwell last week."

He perked up. "Has it printed?"

"No. I'm currently working up in the entertainment department, and they aren't interested in stories about theater actors."

"Yeah. Well, shoot it to me. I can evaluate it and let you know." He started to turn back to his monitor but glanced up over his glasses. "But I can tell you I can't pay you whatever you're making now. This department fights for space, and we're usually the first to suffer cuts when the newspaper is losing revenue."

"But would I keep my health insurance?"

"That you would keep."

I thanked him and headed out toward the airport to collect entertainment news. *Entertainment news.* It was both an oxymoron and a lie. Nobody in my department cared about the creative entertainment provided by the people on the other end of the camera. It was all about their personal lives.

As the subway came above ground, my notifications buzzed, and I read the text from Micah. *What are you doing today?*

Working. You?

Also working.

I tried to picture Micah in a coat and tie, punching a clock. *You got a nine-to-five job?*

You could say that. We have a show in Asbury Park tonight. Packing up now. Wish you could come.

It's okay. I'm on my way out of the city. Have a good show.

Have a good night. I'll talk to you tomorrow. okay?
Yes.

It was a simple exchange, but I hugged my phone to my chest. I might have been kicked out of the office for carrying on with Micah, but it was worth it. Or so I thought.

Then I remembered that he'd be surrounded after his show with groupies throwing themselves at him brazenly for all they were worth.

And I remembered Eden's admonition that Micah couldn't do a committed relationship.

I deep-breathed and told myself not to get ahead of myself. He liked me. I liked him. Nothing had really happened between us yet. And besides, if he did turn up with some other man-stealing whore, I'd be among the first to know.

or maybe even recognized him, and crowded around for auto-graphs.

Andy wouldn't care about the interview, but it was better than nothing. I'd started to feel serious hunger pangs, so I went in search of a restaurant with plenty of seating. Bonus if they served healthy food. I passed a bakery, dying to go in and shove an entire chocolate croissant in my face. That was a bad sign. When my sugars dropped, I'd start craving any kind of sugary junk. It's not that the pump couldn't handle the sweets, but I'd found that giving in to temptation only made me want to fall into a vat of liquid chocolate. Like scratching a mosquito bite— it only made the itch that much stronger. I was always hungry, but I could usually manage to ignore my sweet tooth as long as I kept on top of my diet.

At last, I found a kiosk selling fruits and salads. I got some nuts and strawberries and splurged on some yogurt. Not a bad snack.

I had to settle for a seat in a high traffic area, but after stand-ing out on the street waiting for hours, it was nice to have a place to rest. I couldn't remember why I'd been so dead set against coming back to the airport. Seats, food, free WiFi, and no Andy. It was like a mini-vacation.

I opened my laptop and took advantage of the airport's hot spot. First, I checked my email and found that Eden had written me earlier.

Subject: Micah.

I hesitated for a minute before clicking on the link.

> Jo,
> You're very sneaky, sitting there at lunch not letting it slip that you and Micah have something going on. And I just sat there telling you to steer clear of him. Now I've got egg on my face. :)
> I hope I'm not way off base here, though I'm sure I am. This is hard for me to write, but I feel like I have to say all this, once.

Chapter 17

Exiled.

I hadn't worked the airports since I first started on the paper. It's a despicable job. The exhausted celebrity encumbered by carry-on luggage and sometimes children, too, must push through a sea of cameras and shouted questions. The beleaguered traveler exits the terminal too haggard to pose for a picture or compose a well-constructed response. Most just walk on by as though the paparazzi were invisible.

I wondered if Micah walked on by or if he stopped and chatted. He probably offered to take the reporters all out for a beer.

Celebrities who didn't have their own plane had to use the same entrances and exits as everyone else. They stood out with all their elaborate camouflage. Anyone wearing a hat *and* sunglasses inside was suspect. Sometimes travel routes were predictable from telegraphed information dropped on Twitter or elsewhere. Whenever anyone flew into JFK or LaGuardia, there'd be a good chance they'd be ambushed. Keeping other paparazzi in my sights often clued me in to some action.

Wednesday had been a total bust, but by Thursday afternoon, I'd gotten lucky and shot some pictures of a young stage actor who hadn't yet made it so big that he was above free publicity. He stopped and chatted with me about his current projects before some passersby saw him talking to a reporter,

I like you and I think you like Micah. Of
course, everyone likes Micah.

Here's the thing. Micah likes everyone, too. He
trusts people, and he puts it all out there. People
think he's like this because he's never been hurt
or because he's lived a charmed existence. And
that's partly true. He's never been badly hurt. He
chooses to live his life open and vulnerable and
happy. I love that about him, but it also worries
me. I worry that one day, he's going to more than
like someone and he's going to get hurt in a way
he can't brush off and get back up.

I've never bothered to say this to any of
Micah's girlfriends because none of them had any
substance. But the way he talks about you . . . He
would kill me if he knew I was writing you this.
If I scare you off, I'm never going to hear the end
of it.

What I'm getting at is that Micah doesn't have
the first clue how to actually date anyone, like
really court a girl. He's going to do it all wrong.
He's going to be too intense or too fast or just
weird about it. You don't have to let him rush
you, and if he freaks you out, you need to tell
him. He doesn't scare easy. Once he knows what
he wants, he'll work hard for it. But you might
have to work, too. He's worth it, Jo.

Call me if you ever want to talk about
anything.

Eden

Although we had only just begun *something,* her warning
the day before had loomed in my mind like a portent. I was still
freaking out a little about Micah's lifestyle choices until I read
her email. I could handle a bumbling boyfriend if that's where
things were headed. As long as I wasn't one of *those girls* he
slept with for a month before parting ways with no hard feel-

ings. If Eden thought he could treat me differently than he'd treated the women he'd burned through so fast, maybe I could relax and go with it. I hoped so because I really did like him.

I started uploading the pictures I'd taken and wrote down the questions and answers I'd recorded. If Andy declined to run it, I'd ask to send it down to Sang Moon-Soo.

It occurred to me that if I waited to upload the story closer to five, Andy wouldn't know whether I'd stayed at the airport or gone home. I gathered my things and started to head toward the exit when my phone buzzed with a text message ringtone. I dropped everything and sat down. I'd hoped it would be Micah and squealed a bit when it was.

What do you usually do on Thursday after work?

I texted back: *I go home, eat a snack, have some hot tea, change into my gym clothes, and walk two blocks to a step aerobics class.*

A minute passed. Then another. I had no idea if he was flakey or responsive with communication and didn't want to be stuck in the airport all day waiting for an answer, but another text came before I'd even moved to gather my things.

Should you be exercising? I mean is it safe?

I took a deep breath and let it out. He knew nothing. *Safe. Necessary. Everyone should exercise.*

Okay. Can I come with you?

You want to come to my aerobics class? The visual of that made me giggle. I lifted my eyes expecting to make eye contact with someone to share the hilarity of it, but the strangers trudged by, lost in their own worlds.

Can I? Everyone should exercise. He had me with my own words.

My fingers flew. *On one condition. You have to let me take pictures. For the paper.* Andy would have to give me back my freedom if I gave him Micah's head on a step aerobics platter.

I thought we weren't going to exploit each other for personal gain. :)

I sat for a minute trying to come up with a witty, flirty response, but the phone buzzed again. *Fine. It's a deal. What time should I be at your place?*

Six.

The girls in my aerobics class owed me. Big-time.

I hurried home so I could test my blood sugar without Micah there. I knew he'd have to see it at some point. And frequently. But I didn't want to plant that image into his brain quite yet.

I hit the Suspend button on my pump and fetched a glass from the cabinet and poured some orange juice. In my fridge, I discovered a boiled egg Zion had left me and swallowed it in two bites. Then I had the presence of mind to brush my teeth and check my hair and makeup. Would it be overkill to wear lip gloss to exercise class?

The buzzer rang as I was heating some water for tea. I pressed the intercom. "Micah?"

"Yup."

"What's the magic word?"

"Uh. *Alohamora?*"

I buzzed him in. I stood in my open door until he climbed the stairs. He panted. "Is aerobics any harder than those stairs?" He had on a goofy pair of running shorts that looked like something from a middle school gym class. One leg said "*Broo.*" The other leg said "*klyn.*"

"Where'd you get those shorts?"

"You like them? I found them in this great store up the street from my apartment."

I covered my mouth with my fist, hiding my smile. "Do you want some tea? I was fixing to make some."

He grimaced. "Water?"

"In the fridge." The water came to a boil, so I threw in my tea bag and then excused myself to change into my gym clothes.

The tea had steeped when I came out. I stood at the counter to discard the tea bag. Micah slipped up behind me and laid his hands on my waist. His lips grazed the back of my neck. I froze in place, wanting him to keep touching me. My chest rose and fell, and my heart rate sped up. His fingers dragged across my back and under the hem of my shirt. His hands on my skin sent tingles to the tips of my toes. But I wanted those lips on mine. I wanted to press myself into him.

As I turned around, he loosened his hands and pushed the teacup away. Then he lifted me onto the counter. We were face-to-face. He stopped and looked at me, and I looked at him. I was asking myself how I could have ended up with someone like him—a literal poster boy of rock star boyfriends.

He traced a finger along the side of my neck. "Has anyone ever told you how beautiful you are?"

I resisted the urge to laugh. It would have totally spoiled the mood. "Does Zion count?"

His head tilted. "No."

"Micah?"

"Jo?"

"Do you think you might kiss me now?"

"What about step aerobics?"

I hooked my foot around his back and pulled him closer. "I can tell you're not in good enough shape for that. You need to work up to it."

"How about I lift weights first?" He placed his hands under my thighs and hoisted me up.

I wrapped my legs around him and laid my hand against his chest. "You'll need to add some cardiovascular."

His arms flexed and showed off his tight muscles. "Can we start now?"

Breathless, I whispered, "Yes."

He carried me to my room and set me down on my bed, pushing the door closed with his foot. He sat beside me and took my hand. "Jo, am I rushing this?"

I brought his hand up to my face. "Would you just kiss me?"

He brushed my hair over my shoulder and bent down to kiss my neck. "Here?"

I shivered. "Mmm, yes."

He ran his lips up to my ear and caught my earlobe in his teeth. He trailed kisses across my cheek. "Like this?"

My body was electric. "No. Like this." I tangled my fingers

in his hair and dragged my tongue across his lips, teasing and pulling away when he'd try to catch me in a kiss. Finally, I gave in, and we melted into each other. He grabbed me by my upper arms. But I moved my hands along him, finding out where I could cause a shiver or a rise of goose bumps. He loosened his grip, and I dragged my fingernails down his back.

His eyes closed and he groaned. "Oh, my God."

When he reached down and lifted my shirt up and off, his hand brushed against the insulin pump attached to my shorts. "What's this?"

I detached the tube and laid the device onto the nightstand. "That's my insulin pump." If I hoped he might just ignore it, I wasn't so lucky.

"What's it for?" He returned to the exploration, touching the adhesive disk covering the needle insertion point.

"Basically, it keeps me alive."

He stopped and glanced over at the pump. "Shouldn't you be wearing it?"

"Relax. It's okay." I took his hand and put it back on the adhesive disk. "Are you weirded out?"

He tapped the plastic connector. "Does it hurt?"

"Not really. Only sometimes when I put it in."

His eye drifted to the device on the nightstand. "Are you part robot?"

"I guess so."

"Cool." He ran his fingers around the edge of the white fabric circle. "Sexy robot."

Every time he touched me, my skin responded with tingles, and I wanted to see his body and touch him, too. I slipped my hands under his shirt and peeled it off, then helped him with the insanity of my sports bra.

His fingers moved across every inch of exposed skin, bringing me to such a state of arousal, I needed him more and more until I couldn't wait any longer. But when I reached for his waistline, he put a hand on mine. "Are you sure?"

My answer came in the form of a guttural moan.

He jumped up and left me lying on the bed, wondering if he'd taken "Argh yeeees," as an ambiguous invitation. But he came back and tossed a square packet onto my nightstand next to my pump. Good thing one of us was thinking.

As soon as he lay down, I ran my finger down his side and along the waistband of his shorts.

He stopped my hand with his and twined our fingers. "Slow down. I want to make the moment last."

I laughed. "*You* want to slow down?"

He laughed, too. "Yeah. I don't want to just have sex. I want to get to know you. I want to take our time."

"Micah? Do you think we could take our time *next* time?"

"You sure?"

"Micah, I need you right now. Please. I am dying."

"Well, I don't want you to die." For all that, he took forever sliding my shorts off and then touching me until my back arched, and I begged him to stop toying with me.

I clutched at his ridiculous shorts and dragged them off. And then I made sure he'd want to seal the deal sooner than later by touching him in delicate places to heighten his arousal.

He groaned as I stroked him slowly. "You sure you don't want to go to your step aerobics class instead?"

"Yeah. Let's go to aerobics." I pretended to sit up, calling his bluff.

But he caught my arm. "Come back here."

And we lay on our sides, driving each other more and more insane with need. It was like a game of chicken. Who would blink first? I didn't honestly know what the toll of this much excitement was going to be on my blood glucose and hated that I had to stop and wonder. So I threw my leg over him and rocked him onto his back. He stretched his arm over to the nightstand and tore the condom open with his teeth. I straddled him and let him guide himself into me.

I'd had sex before—frenetic dorm room sex in college mostly. Never had I been made to wait so long. Never had I been so near the edge at the moment of impact. So almost as soon as I felt him deep inside me, a sharp explosion of pleasure shook me, and I collapsed onto him. Then horrified, I realized he was still hard as a rock, still in me. I lifted my head and looked into his eyes. They glittered as he smirked.

"Never had that kind of response before," he said, literally all cocky. "Do you want to stop?"

I wasn't ready to stop touching him, to stop feeling him in me. "No."

He flipped me over onto my back and thrust in me again. As I watched him, I touched his tight abs, his nipples, his shoulders. He was beauty in motion. His eyes closed, and his face moved through various expressions until he said, "Oh, God."

Then he slumped over to my side. He kissed me hard, sucking on my lips, skimming his tongue against mine. He fell back panting. "I can't get enough of you."

He wrapped his arm around me, and my head rested on his shoulder. My heart rate hadn't slowed, and I was starting to feel almost euphoric. High. Like a sugar rush.

I reached for my pump and reattached it. "Stay here. I have to do something." I threw on a bathrobe and left my bedroom.

I pulled out my testing strips and pricked my finger, hoping everything was normal. The last thing I needed was to find out sex with Micah would kill me. The numbers were high for me, but not dangerously so.

Micah joined me in the kitchen, clad only in his gym shorts. "Is that something you have to do a lot?"

"Only like six times a day. Or whenever I want to be sure. I can't always trust my body to tell me. And you saw what happened when I let things go last Friday."

"So are you good? Did I hurt you?"

"I'm fine. I felt too good. And that could be bad. But everything's fine. Everything's good."

His shoulders dropped, and I realized he'd actually been worried. This seemed like as good a time as any to ground him in reality. I opened a drawer and took out a small notebook. I sat at the table and opened it up to today's date and wrote down the time, the readings, and the words *Amazing sex.*

I raised an eyebrow at him. "My weird diary. I keep this so I can get a handle on how changes to my routine affect me. *You* are a change to my routine. And I need to make sure I can predict and adjust my diet—and possibly this." I lifted the hem of my shirt to reveal my pump. "It might take a little time to work out the kinks."

He knotted his brow. "So maybe next time, I'll listen to you a little better."

I stretched like a satisfied cat. "I like the sound of next time."

He stretched, too, showing off his beautiful torso. "So what do you want to do now?"

I got up and opened the fridge. "Throw something on. I'm gonna fix supper."

"You cook?"

I peered over the open fridge door at him. "You don't?"

He put up his hands. "I eat."

Zion had been shopping recently and stocked the fridge with red, yellow, and green peppers; onions, and strips of beef. I grabbed a pair of peppers and laid them on the counter, then went back for the rest.

I glanced up and caught Micah's expression. He looked panicked like a diabetic about to be served a plate full of candy. "What's the matter? Are you allergic to peppers?"

He cleared his throat. "No. It's just . . . You're not a vegetarian, are you?"

"Seriously? Would that be a problem?" I closed the fridge and laid my hand on my hip, daring him to tell me I needed to eat meat.

"No. I mean." His eyes darted around as if the words he was searching for were hiding in the cupboards. He took in a sharp breath and exhaled as quickly. "I can live without alcohol. And I guess I'll learn to live without the cigarettes." His whole face was a comedy of tragedy. "But meat?" He rubbed his eyes with his palms. "Meat!"

I opened the fridge, pulled out the package of steak, and dropped it on the table. "We're having fajitas."

"Oh, thank God."

"Micah." I sat down at the table. "Why do you think you have to give up alcohol? And cigarettes. Well, you should give up cigarettes. But you don't need to change for me."

He sat beside me. "But isn't it hard to be around people when they have things you can't have?"

"Totally. But I've been living with this disease most of my life. I've learned to deal with it. Would you expect me to start drinking and smoking just because you do?"

"That would be dumb."

"Yeah." I knocked his chin with my fist. "Don't be dumb."

"But I will quit smoking. My mom's gonna love you for that."

The door rattled with the clattering of keys, and then Zion came in. "I thought you were going to—" He stopped dead. His eyes grew three sizes when he saw Micah sitting half-naked at our kitchen table.

The thought hit me a second later. *Micah Sinclair was sitting half-naked at our kitchen table.*

It hadn't seemed so extraordinary until I thought I'd need to hand Zion a tissue to wipe the drool from his chin. Micah had nothing on but those stupid shorts. He didn't have an ounce of fat on him. For a guy past thirty, he had the body of a twenty-five-year-old gym rat.

"Micah, can I ask you something?"

"Uh-huh."

"How do you look so good when you drink, smoke, eat like shit, and apparently never go to the gym?"

He beamed. "You think I look good?"

I snapped a dish towel at him. "What's your secret?"

"Amplifiers."

Zion got a knife and sat at the table to help cut up the peppers. "Amplifiers?"

Micah pointed at the peppers. "Should I be helping with that? It doesn't look too hard."

I shook my head. "You just keep us entertained. Tell us about your magic amplifier regimen."

"Okay, but give me a second. I feel weirdly out of place suddenly." He stood and headed into my bedroom.

Zion blew through his lips. "I hope that doesn't mean what I think it does."

But sure enough, Micah returned, pulling a shirt over his head. He started talking before he'd even gotten to the table. "So do you guys know how heavy amplifiers are? They are crazy heavy."

"Do you bench them?" Zion asked.

"Close enough. I push those suckers down hallways and up ramps at least once a week. It's a workout."

"Don't you have roadies?" I hadn't seen him push a single amplifier when we'd left his show.

"Well, yeah. But I help. And they don't come and unload everything into our practice studio. We aren't made of amplifiers and roadies."

Zion stopped chopping. "Don't the venues have their own sound systems?"

"Not always. During the summer we play some gigs outside in places where they have nothing but a stage. And carrying all the equipment . . . The drums take us about forty trips. Most of the drum pieces are small but all that walking. It burns a lot of calories."

The skillet had heated up, and I started browning the onions. When I threw on the meat, Micah started making sex sounds from the delicious smells filling the kitchen.

Zion set plates on the table and put the tortilla wraps in foil to heat in the toaster oven. "Micah, could you open a bottle of wine?"

The poor thing wanted to do what Zion asked, but he shot a glance at me. "Wine?"

"Zion drinks. You can drink, too."

Zion reached into the cupboard for two wineglasses. "Josie, you could have a little, right?" He hesitated, then pulled down a third glass.

"I guess I'm having wine tonight." I started plating the veggies and meat.

I hadn't thought about what a messy meal this would be, but

it was one of Zion's favorites, and he didn't mind getting it all over his hands and face. Micah didn't stand on ceremony either. So I dug in, too. We were all too busy "mmming" to care. I sipped the wine economically. I knew Zion only wanted to help me fit in, but I didn't even like wine.

Micah said, "Sho whajyu wanna ju?"

"What?"

He swallowed his food. "What do you want to do? What do you normally do?"

Zion said, "I usually read up on the latest medical discoveries. Josie practices jujitsu."

In truth, usually I tied up any loose ends from work or— "Oh, shit. I never submitted my story." I jumped up and froze, trying to remember where I'd left my gear. "Stay there. I have to do something."

While I hunted for my camera, Zion grilled Micah about Adrianna. Micah said, "Sorry. She's more friends with Adam and Eden than me."

I sat on the sofa and eavesdropped on them while uploading the day's pictures. I just sent everything without going through it all. Then I turned on my laptop. Thankfully, I'd already written the story, so I hit Send. "Done."

Micah pushed his chair back and turned it around to face me. "I have a question for you."

"Shoot."

"What do you like to be called?"

"What?"

"When I met you, you introduced yourself to me as Jo and as Josie. And I know you don't want to be called Anika. Zion calls you Josie. I like Josie. It's pretty. It fits you."

"Then I like Josie."

"Josie. I might need to write a song."

Goose bumps shot down my arms. Then I thought about his concert and asked, "A hard rock song called 'Josie'?"

Micah scowled. "You don't know any of my music, do you? I have several solo acoustic CDs, you know."

I blanched. "I—"

He jumped up. "Now I know what we're doing tonight. Get your things."

"Where are we going?"

"My place."

He pushed his chair in as though that were the end of the debate, but Zion held up his hand. "Wait a second. Will you be coming back here tonight?"

Micah shrugged as if he hadn't thought about it. "She can stay the night." He looked at me. "You can stay the night, right?"

"Uh, yeah. I just need to pack some things." I got up and fetched a small travel case so I could carry all the crap only I had to worry about.

I opened the fridge and took a deep breath before I began the rundown. "First, I'm packing a couple of syringes. These are for emergency only, in case my blood glucose spikes. I'm pretty good about watching my sugars—"

Zion butted in. "Too good probably. You shouldn't need those."

"Just in case." I held up a small black phone book, saying, "Emergency phone numbers."

Zion added, "The hospital, the pharmacy, me, her mother, her doctor, everyone you might need to reach is in here."

I tucked the phone book in with the syringes. "We can program your phone with the numbers, too. But I keep them on paper for traveling."

Micah's eyebrows drew together. "Do you normally need all this?"

Zion laid a hand on his shoulder. "She hasn't ever needed any of this since she's lived here. But you have to be prepared. She lives in between the margins." He kept talking while I packed a couple of juice boxes and glucose tablets. "Her worst habit is letting her blood sugar drop too low. She doesn't eat enough or at the right time. She can usually tell you if she's feeling faint, and a juice box will do the trick."

"Now for the worst." I let him see my strips and blood stick. "I'll have to show you how all this works. Zion made a cheat sheet for the readings in here." I flipped through the phone book until a small paper fell out. "Here."

Zion said, "If she's unresponsive or falls outside these ranges, get her to the hospital immediately."

I took a glance at Micah, hoping my love life hadn't just gone up in flames. It was worse than the time Molly Johansen walked right up to Danny Burke and told him I had a crush on him. Micah rubbed his temples clearly overwhelmed by it all. I walked behind him and wrapped my arm around him. "Don't worry. It's all a precaution. I just have to be a little careful."

He nodded, eyes glazed over. And I had an idea. "You want to come help me pick out my pajamas for tonight?"

His face relaxed, and he looked at me again like I was human. "Yeah."

By the time we had everything ready to go, with my clothes, cameras, laptop, and medical crap, I looked like I was going to stay a week. I gave Zion a hug before I left, and he whispered in my ear, "Damn, girl. Don't blow that."

I whispered back, "That's what she said."

Chapter 18

The driver arrived moments after Micah texted for him to pick us up. I couldn't believe how quickly he had responded. "Does that poor guy just sit in his car constantly waiting for you to call him?"

Micah looked at me confused. "It's a service. They work in shifts. Haven't you noticed it's not always the same guy?"

I hadn't, and I felt like an unobservant heel, so after we climbed into the car, I changed the subject. "What are we going to do at your apartment that we couldn't do at mine?"

He slid over and put his arm around me, his hand brushing lightly against the exposed skin on the back of my neck. "You don't have a guitar."

I marveled at the power in a single touch. We'd been together only a couple of hours earlier, and already, I longed to be alone with him again, in his bed, slowly undressing him. I shivered at the thought, and he wrapped his arms around me more tightly.

The driver let us out in Park Slope on a tree-lined street with a coffee shop on the corner. We climbed a few steps and entered near the ground floor. It took seeing the stairs inside his front door to realize all three floors of the building were his.

Normally, my next question would be "How can you afford this place?" But then I remembered that there were people at an Iowa community college who knew his name.

Micah moved around picking things up and closing doors. I still hovered in the vestibule. Both of us had transitioned into awkwardness. Somehow Micah put me at ease so much that I went long stretches forgetting about who he was. I knew he'd dated groupies, but it didn't matter. I knew he was a celebrity, but he didn't act like it. *But* at odd times, I felt like the looking glass cracked, and reality would creep in. Right at that moment, I wondered how I'd ended up standing in Micah Sinclair's Park Slope apartment ready to stay the night.

And then he came back to take my hand and pull me into his living room with its cherrywood floors and high ceiling. All I could think about was biding my time until we could call it bedtime so I could take those stupid shorts off him again.

He led me through the living room on a tour of his apartment, stopping in the kitchen to put my snacks and syringes into the fridge. His fridge was frighteningly empty and dwarfed my small stash of emergency energy. His kitchen opened onto a patio and yard. I didn't know the true meaning of jealousy until that moment.

"You have a yard." I opened the door and took a step out into the night air. The brick patio spanned a few feet before ending in a patch of dirt and crabgrass. The plastic table seemed cheap and out of place compared to the interior decorations. A single lounge chair told me that Micah didn't host many backyard barbecues. The cigarette butts on the ground revealed Micah's tendency to sit out here. Alone.

"Is this where you were when you called the other day?"

"Yeah. It's peaceful out here in the evening."

I jumped when a cat rubbed up against my leg. I knelt down. "Well, hey there." The cat flopped onto its back, purring, so I rubbed its tummy. "Where did you come from?"

"That's Oscar." Micah squatted beside me and scratched Oscar behind the ears. "You're not allergic to cats, are you?"

"No. I love cats. Is he yours?"

"Sort of. Felix is around here somewhere. He's mostly blind, so he gets a bit shy sometimes."

Micah picked Oscar up and carried him inside. He set him

down on the floor and grabbed a bag of cat food from a cabinet. I supposed in an emergency, I could always eat the cat food. Or I could eat the cat.

"Where did you get them?"

"I got Felix while doing a benefit concert for the SPCA last year. With his condition, he couldn't find a home. But he's a great cat. And Oscar buddy just showed up here and wouldn't leave. I let him go out in case he's got a home nearby, but every time I come home, he's there."

"But who takes care of them when you're not here?"

"Anna." He put the cat food under the sink. "She's my house-keeper. She'll come by when I'm not here and check in on the cats."

We went upstairs to drop the bag with my clothes in a bed-room. And then I followed him down the narrow steps to his basement. There, he had divided the room into two purposes. On one side, he'd lined his walls with musical equipment. The other side looked like a personal gym. A treadmill faced a flat-screen TV, and a huge weight machine ate up a chunk of real estate.

I raised an eyebrow. "Amplifiers?"

He sat down on a small amplifier, laughing. "It's plausible. I have nightmares about these things."

A notebook lay open next to the treadmill, and I thumbed through it. He had a routine, regular in regimen, irregular in execution. "You sure skip a lot of days."

"I travel a lot."

He did. I flipped back. Page after page showed blanks. "When do you travel next?"

"Tomorrow."

My eyes shot up at him. "What?"

He shrugged. "Just going up to Connecticut. You wanna come?"

"You're asking me to go to Connecticut tomorrow?" I put my hand on my hip. "You know I have a job, right?"

"No worries. I'll be home Saturday. You'll barely miss me."

He pulled up a guitar and started picking at it. I found a stool

and leaned against it to watch. His fingers moved smoothly between chords, totally professional. He kept his eyes on me. He
wasn't really playing, just doodling.

I struck a teasing tone. "Are you gonna write me that song
now?"

He changed chords and began playing a song that sounded
almost familiar. Then he sang. "Josie came up from Georgia.
She was looking for a soul to steal."

I squealed. "No no no!"

He stopped playing. "I'd love to say I wrote you a song in my
head over the last hour. Eden could do it, but if I'm going to
write you a proper song, I'll need a little more time. I could play
you something else. I won't put you on the spot for a request."
His smile took the barb out of the jab.

"I want to hear something. I really loved hearing you sing
with Eden last week."

He started into a quiet song. I tried to imagine what it would
be like to sit in a club like the one Eden had performed at while
he sat onstage playing songs like this. It was so different from
the music his band had performed. Would he stage dive at the
end?

While he played, a scraggly black-and-white cat peered out
from behind the amplifier. Its eyes were milky, and I recalled
Micah mentioning that Felix was blind. He'd failed to mention
the cat's ear was half missing. The little guy was so beat up, it
appeared to have survived a tragic combine accident. Whatever
possessed Micah to take that pathetic thing into his house was
beyond me, but it emerged from hiding and began to rub its
head against Micah's ankles while he played, apparently a fan
of the music. Or a fan of Micah.

The whole scene was utterly incongruous. At the concert on
Tuesday, Micah had been larger than life on a huge stage, com-
manding adulation from a thousand screaming fans. Here in his
small spare basement with a cat making love to his feet, he'd
disappeared into himself. But his stillness couldn't disguise the
power he held in his fingertips. He overwhelmed the acoustic
guitar. He overwhelmed me.

When he stopped playing, my voice trembled a little as I said, "Wow."

"Yeah?" He grinned and set the guitar down.

"Yeah. You can write a song about me." I bit my lip. "If you want."

He slipped onto the floor with his back against the wall. When I started to sit down in front of him, he reached out his hand and pulled me next to him. I leaned against his shoulder.

He said, "I've never written a song about a real girl."

"You write about blow-up dolls?"

He snorted. "I write about fictional girls. There are a ton of great, sad stories in old country songs. Tragic love songs. That's my go-to inspiration."

"I feel like I should be writing all this down."

His chest rose and fell as he chuckled. "You want to interview me?"

"Is there anything left you haven't already said?"

"Ouch." He sat silent for a minute, then said, "There are lots of things I've never said. Things I haven't told the media. Things I've never told my mom. Things I'll *never* tell my mom." He grew quiet. "Things I've never said to a girl before."

I shifted so I could meet his eyes. "What have you never said to a girl?"

"You do ask the tough questions."

"You're not going to tell me?"

His cheek rose as he half smiled. "I have a feeling I might." He stood and offered me his hand. "But not tonight. Come on."

I followed him up the narrow stairs and then up to the next floor and into his bedroom. The foreplay had taken a steep nosedive since earlier that evening. He stood in the doorway and asked, "Do you need anything?"

I answered him with a look of confusion. Was I supposed to ask him for the condoms this time?

But he clarified. "Towels? Extra pillows? Toothpaste? More food?"

Realization dawned. "Are you sending me to bed?" Dread curdled my stomach. Had I done something to turn him off?

Had I killed his interest in me by giving it all away too fast? Or was he more repulsed by my health issues than he'd let on?

He took a step forward and rubbed my arm. "I know you need to be up early, and I kept you up way too late last night. If I stay in here with you, I'll never let you get any sleep. I was able to resist you one night, but I can't get my mind off earlier today. With you—" He heaved in a shuddering breath that echoed my own palpitating desire. "I'd never be able to keep my hands off you. Besides, I don't think I can fall asleep this early."

"But I don't have to go to sleep right away." I took his hand. "I want you to stay."

He hesitated. "Zion asked me to make sure you get your rest. He said you're wearing yourself out." He looked into my eyes, as serious as a brain surgeon. "I want you to know I can take care of you, too."

This was maddening. "I don't need taking care of." My budding arousal had been cut short from irritation, and I did need to eat something before bed. "Fine. Would you mind getting me a juice box?" My stomach rumbled. "And the peanut butter crackers." I was decimating the reserves I'd brought, but that was better than crashing in the middle of the night. I'd deal with the ramifications in the morning.

After Micah went downstairs and brought me my late night snack, I climbed in his oh-my-God amazingly comfortable bed, phone in hand, and texted Zion.

Thanks a whole lot, Z. You've scared Micah into thinking I'm made of glass.

He wasted no time replying, *Good.*

He's sleeping on the sofa.

LOL. You're kidding.

I wished I was kidding. Micah's king-size bed could have accommodated both of us with room to spare. I never could have predicted I'd end up sleeping in Micah's bed. But I never would have believed I'd end up there all alone. I recalled Eden's admonition about how weird Micah would be. She couldn't have foreseen this.

Honestly, I needed the sleep. I'd been on the go all day with very little sleep from the night before. And then uncut extended bonus sex earlier in the evening. Then cooking. And I drank wine. I slid under the covers and laid my head down, suddenly annoyed by a noticeable lump pressing into my head. I reached under the pillow and encountered a bulky mass. I realized what it was before I'd pulled it out: Clark the deformed gorilla. Micah still kept it after all this time. It was truly the ugliest thing I'd ever seen. But I hugged it tight to my body and drifted off, snug and secure.

Chapter 19

When I eventually opened my eyes again, it took me a few moments to get my bearings. My head hurt, and the soft light breaking through the curtains didn't help. I found my finger stick and measured my blood glucose. I needed to eat.

I snuck downstairs and passed Micah draped on the sofa without a shirt on, bathed in the morning light. I wanted to memorize that image, but if I lost consciousness on his floor, I was pretty sure I wouldn't remember anything.

His kitchen was a barren nightmare. In the fridge, a lone juice box remained beside a couple of slices of leftover pizza. I considered the pizza but went for a glass of milk instead. I rummaged through his pantry until I found a box of Cheerios, a jar of peanut butter, and crackers. I shook my head in disappointment. I went in search of a knife. Another day of peanut butter crackers—at least it would tide me over until we could go out for real food.

Finally, my head cleared, and I felt human again. I meant to sneak upstairs and get another hour of sleep, but Micah's sleeping form looked like something that should be hanging in the Louvre. I carefully slid my camera out of my bag and sat crisscross on the floor, trying to find the perfect angle.

The shutter whirred open and closed. Micah stirred. I scooted back to get the length of him, with the crimson throw sliding off him and exposing his toes. His arms and chest needed to be chiseled out of marble. Would nobody preserve this work of art but me?

I shot off another picture, and his eyes opened. I couldn't stop shooting because every movement of his face was more beautiful than the last.

"Hey." He yawned. "Were you taking pictures?"

"I couldn't resist. You're so gorgeous when you sleep."

He frowned. "Only when I sleep?" He held out his hand to me and drew me close. "Have you been eating peanut butter?" He ran a finger across my chin and popped it into my mouth. I licked off the peanut butter, and he groaned.

Encouraged, I ran my tongue down his finger to his palm. Then I took that hand in mine and continued to graze my lips along his forearm, then his bicep, and finally I licked the nape of his neck. He wrested his hand free from me and wrapped his arm around my back. As he pulled me to him, he sat up, letting the crimson throw finish its descent to the floor. He had nothing on underneath. And boy was he happy to see me.

He hid his mouth behind his fist. "You have that effect on me."

"Where's my camera?"

"That kinky, huh?"

"Just feeling selfish keeping all this to myself." I laid my hands on his abs, and a shiver vibrated along his muscles. "You should be dipped in gold."

"How about chocolate?"

"Not chocolate. Then I couldn't do this." I bent forward and sucked on his nipple. My hand ventured down, and this time, I made his back arch.

"Oh, God." His voice cracked. "Josie, stop. You're driving me insane."

"Stop?" I drew my hand away.

He caught my wrist and kissed my arm, all the way to my shoulder. Then he started working on the buttons of my pajama top. "I need to see you."

I helped him undress me. Then he touched me with gentle

fingertips. Slowly. And every square inch he touched made me yearn for him. And so I touched him in kind. I laid my finger on his lips and let him kiss me. I caressed his forehead and his cheeks. I wrapped my hand around his neck and pulled him to me so I could taste his lips.

But he had other ideas and ducked his head and kissed my neck instead. "You are so delicious. I could spend an eternity learning your body."

He teased me with ticklish circles along my inner thighs. I would have been happier if he grabbed me by the hair and dragged me to his cave to take me from behind at that exact moment. But I wouldn't beg. Not today. I wanted to leave that honor to him.

I reached down and gently massaged his balls and earned another "Oh, my God."

He upped the ante, dragging one finger straight up right where I wanted it. At that, I grasped him and ran my thumb along his shaft. We looked into each other's eyes. I could see he was about to break, but he had to see the same on my face.

At the exact same moment, we both said it. "Please."

Then "yes."

His bag lay on a nearby chair. He reached for it and dug around for a packet. Then he took my hand and led me to the chair. He kissed me between my legs. His tongue found my most sensitive spot, and I moaned. He lifted his head, but kept working that pleasure point with his thumb as he entered.

With him on his knees and me in his chair, we fit together perfectly. I draped my arms over his shoulders and bit his neck. The noises coming from him only heightened my ache. I dragged my nails across his back and sucked on his earlobes. And he came with a shudder, panting.

"You drive me wild, Josie. I swear I can last more than five minutes."

I still felt turned on and sultry, so I may have looked like a drunk person. He licked his lips.

"Can I?" And without waiting for an answer, his finger slid inside as his tongue and lips circled and sucked and darted, excruciating and delicious. The pleasure concentrated to a pinpoint, and then spiraled out in geometric shapes in every direction, both sharp and diffuse. And then I bucked and lurched away, suddenly overwhelmed by the physical contact.

I sat up and slouched into him. He tugged me down into his lap and hugged me tight. I wrapped my arms around him. "It's never been like this for me. I've never been like this. You turned me into a sex toy, Micah."

"You're not a sex toy. You are a goddess. Do you think it's ever been like this for me?"

I'd seen his girlfriends. I'd seen his infinite stash of condoms. I wouldn't want to see what this apartment would look like under a black light. "I wouldn't know."

"It hasn't. When I'm with you, I want to tease out every second. I don't want the end to ever get here."

"Like a never-ending book."

"Or a song that keeps getting better."

"Yeah."

"Are you sure you can't come to Connecticut? Do some gambling? See a little rock show? Couldn't you call it an interview?"

"I wish. My boss isn't interested in rock shows. That's for another section of the paper."

"Well, why don't you work for that section?"

"Too much competition."

"I could put in a word." He waggled his eyebrows as if the animals at the zoo could choose their own spectators.

"You are free to try. But I have to go serve out the rest of my punishment today."

His winced. "Punishment?"

I grabbed his comforter and draped it over us. I'd started to feel a distinct chill. "It's nothing. Andy wants to teach me a lesson, so he's sent me off to cover the airports."

"Why's he teaching you a lesson?"

"He says I'm too soft. I'm supposed to grow a spine or something."

Micah ran his hand across my back. "You have a nice spine. Solid."

The shiver turned into goose bumps, and I'd started to sweat. "Micah?" I tried to stand up, but I staggered. I found the sofa and lay down.

He was up in a second. "Oh, shit. What do I do?"

"Juice."

He left the room and returned, jabbing the plastic straw at the juice box, swearing the whole time. Purple liquid dripped from the puncture, and the straw had bent so badly there was a hole in it. I sucked it down and relaxed into a pillow. "Meter," I said.

"Where?" His face was white panic, but I focused and pointed up.

He bounded up the stairs and came back with the meter. I fed the strip in, then pricked my finger and pressed the blood against the strip. It was low. "Can you bring me that pizza in your fridge?"

He ran and got it. I said, "I'm sorry for this," and ate like a starving wildebeest. Then I curled up, wrapping my arms around myself. It hadn't even registered I'd done all this butt-ass naked until he placed the comforter over me. But then again, so had he.

"Are you going to be okay? Should I call the doctor?"

"I'll be fine. It looks scary, but you did everything perfectly. Could you just buy more food?" I offered a weak laugh to help lighten the mood, but it made me feel nauseated, so I closed my eyes and tried to wait out the dizziness and light-headedness and cold, clammy sweats.

Micah sat beside me for ten minutes, holding my hand with a look of serious concern on his face. "I'm going to kill you, aren't I?"

"Yeah, but not how you think."

"Huh?"

"Sorry. My sense of humor is off."

"Should I stay here with you? What do you need?"

"I'm going to be fine in a few minutes. And then we go on with our day as planned. This is what my life is like. Usually not so dramatic. I'm going to have to figure out what I need to adjust. Maybe I'll get to eat more now." I tried to laugh again, and it didn't make me want to puke, so I sat up and threw my feet on the floor. I took one more reading to make sure and then asked, "Can I use your shower?"

He must have run to the deli while I got ready. When I finished showering, he proudly displayed the various things he'd bought, from an apple to a breakfast sandwich with egg and cheese and bacon.

"I should be going. I've got to catch two trains to get to the airport's air train."

"No, you don't. I'll call my driver. So sit down and eat something."

I liked bossy Micah. "Show me what you got."

From everything he brought, I managed to fish out an egg with some cheese still clinging to it, the apple, and a couple of slices of whole grain toast. "How'd you know to get whole grain?"

"Easy. I just asked myself what the worst possible toast would be. Whole wheat."

I snorted. "Why'd you want to get me the worst toast?"

"I figured it would be the healthiest."

He stood behind me and combed his fingers through my long hair. "Your hair is the first thing I noticed about you. Silky."

"What if I cut it all off?"

He wrapped his arms around my waist and kissed the top of my head. "It wasn't the only thing I noticed about you."

"No? What else?"

"Positively shameless fishing, Wilder."

I spun around and cocked my head at him. "Waiting."

He twisted his mouth, and for a second, I thought he was going to tease me. But he touched my cheek and said, "Your skin glows like a golden statue." He ran his finger down to my mouth. "That first day I saw you, I had to drag my eyes away from your lips so I wouldn't creep you out with lusty attention. When you smiled, all I could think about was how one day, I'd like to kiss you."

My cheeks heated with flattered embarrassment. "You're just saying that so I'll kiss you now."

"Maybe." He smiled his bratty smile. And I let him kiss me anyway. He leaned an inch away. "Did you notice me at all that day?"

Despite his professions of first crush, I hesitated to let him peer into that strange part of my brain where I was still nobody and he was still somebody. Even standing here with his arms around me, I worried he'd be repulsed by what I still saw as early unrequited desire. "I may have thought you were cute."

"Cute," he said, like a parent whose child has just told a whopping fib.

His phone vibrated, saving me from a thorough investigation. His driver had arrived, and Micah walked me out so he could give me a kiss and send me on my way with many promises to call and text and see each other when he got back from Connecticut.

Twenty-four hours had never seemed so daunting.

Time in an airport is like perpetual déjà vu. Different people repeating the exact same tasks for the billionth time. One day here had felt like a reprieve. Three days felt like a prison. I texted Zion, *Find out anything you can about people traveling through JFK today. I can't take this.*

But it gave me plenty of time to think about my relationship with Micah. He was right. He was going to kill me. Not from the sex—which incidentally is how I'd choose to go—but from total ignorance. He meant well. I gave him about a week before he hit the wall and couldn't deal anymore. And then he'd walk away. I hit that wall constantly. But I couldn't walk away. Maybe I should make it easy on him and just let him go.

On the other hand, he was a flibbertigibbet and went through women faster than I went through glucose meters. He'd probably get bored with me soon anyway.

Bored. I was so bored. I walked through the pre-security area of the terminal, looking for my people. Around eleven, I spotted a cluster of photographers and approached. I asked one, "What's the scoop?"

"McCauley Leffert is coming home from rehab today."

The poor kid. Walking into the same fishbowl that had brought him to the breaking point. I considered leaving the feeding frenzy to these other guys. They had huge video cameras and would walk side by side next to the kid, prompting him for any words. McCauley would be smart to say nothing and get out of there. On the other hand, how much worse could I make things for him, and Andy would love to get a shot of the returning washup. People loved stories of celebrities falling from great heights and then climbing up from the depths of their own personal hell. Especially when they were only seventeen. So I stood there and watched the crowd exiting the terminal for any signs of him.

When he came out, I had to shoot around the horde, and in the end, Andy would have to mostly take my word on the pictures being of McCauley. Most of them were of baseball caps and microphones.

That meant I needed to stay and try to catch at least one more celeb. Zion texted to alert me about an actress who hadn't acted in several years but had recently been in the news for some controversial statements she'd made during an appearance on a reality show featuring "where are they now" celebrities. He sent me a link to the article so I'd have the background.

The other paps had cleared out, so I had a clear shot of her, wearing exaggerated sunglasses and an outrageously wide-brimmed sun hat.

"Miss Walker?" I called, snapping pictures. "Are you here to talk about last night's show?"

She veered around me, and I followed her. "Were you misquoted? Do you want to tell your side of the story? Is that why you're in New York?"

She stopped, and I hit record on my camera instantly. "You people. You take moments of people's lives and twist them and—" she ground her teeth "—reconstitute them into garbage. A whole person's life is not one statement made in confusion."

Her voice choked. "People make mistakes. Sometimes there's a context around a mistake that would make anyone do the same thing at the same moment. But you people—" she poked her long fingernail at me "—you sit around waiting to pounce. You wait to ruin a person's entire life, and for what? Money? Your own twisted curiosity? Why do you do it?"

I realized she was talking to me, not asking a rhetorical question. "It's my job."

"You should be ashamed. Get a job waiting tables if this is all you're good for. You'd at least make someone happy."

And with that she turned and left. I had the entire video recorded, but now felt sick about transcribing it. Andy would love it. Maybe he'd love it so much he'd give me back my freedom to work the streets again.

I'd had enough, so I packed it in and took the subway home. I tested my blood, got some food, and then crashed on the sofa to close my eyes and get some rest.

Zion woke me in the early evening. "You feeling okay? Did you catch the has-been?"

"I'm okay. Worn out. Would you mind uploading my pictures and video? I forgot to do it." And truthfully, I didn't want to listen to that woman's accusations one more time. I yawned and rolled over on my side, pulling the blanket up over my shoulders.

Zion flipped on the TV and clicked on my camera. "Everything?"

I still hadn't deleted the pictures of the theater kid from the day before, but I didn't want to make Zion hunt through and figure out which ones he needed to send. Andy could delete the duplicates. "Yeah. Thanks."

We watched the evening news, and then Zion said he was going to make Jamaican jerk chicken. "But then I've got plans tonight. Are you sure you're okay? Micah sent me crazy worried texts earlier today."

"Yeah, I freaked him out pretty bad."

"I told you you're pushing things too hard. Stay in tonight and rest. Promise?"

It was an easy promise. I had nowhere else to be, and besides,

Micah called before his show and again right after. And we talked for hours. He'd recovered from whatever awkwardness he had on phones. I wanted to know everything about him, and his curiosity about me seemed equally limitless.

When I said, "Can I ask you a question?" he answered, "Ask me anything." And so I started the process of getting to know Micah Sinclair.

"What was your favorite thing about high school?"

He didn't hesitate. "The parties. Yours?"

"Cheater. If you can say 'parties,' then I get to say 'summer vacation.'"

"Fine. But do I have to lie and say I liked learning about Shakespeare? Because seriously, my fondest memories of high school involve sneaking into my house late at night and not getting caught."

I pulled my feet under my legs. "Okay, let me ask it a different way. What was your favorite book as a kid?" I kept my voice low like we were sharing secrets.

"Don't laugh. I wasn't allowed to read a lot, but I read *A Wrinkle in Time* until it fell apart. And Narnia. I was allowed to read Narnia. But not Harry Potter."

I'd never heard of a kid being forbidden to read. "But that came out while we were in high school."

"And? If I lived under my parents' roof, I followed their rules. I have seen the movies."

"Oh, but you have to read Harry Potter. Promise me you'll download it and start reading it tomorrow."

He laughed. "Deal. But then you have to promise to marathon some yet undecided sitcom of my choosing."

"Okay. It's funny. I wasn't allowed to watch a lot of TV growing up—mostly PBS or BBC America." A vision of my dad leading me by the hand into the public library swam in front of my eyes so powerful I had to shake my head to clear it. "But if I could manage to read a book, I was encouraged to try it. Why weren't you allowed to read?"

"Satan."

"Satan? What?"

"My parents worried that books might corrupt me. They worried to a lesser extent about music. Obviously, they got their priorities backward."

"So you're telling me you're a devil worshipper?"

Soft laughter. "Don't tell me you're not."

I recalled all the stuff Leonard had said about Micah's parents' mission trip, and wondered if I should mention it. I snuggled into my blanket and took a sip from my water bottle, thinking of a better question. "So are you religious?"

"I don't know. Maybe?"

"How can you maybe be religious?"

"I mean, I don't really think about it. Sometimes I think it seems ridiculous to believe in God when we're just this tiny speck in a huge universe. Then I think how could there not be a God. It's easier not to think about it."

"So you like to drift through eternity?"

"Yeah. I'm a drifter. What about you?"

"My parents disagreed about religion. Dad's vaguely Hindu, and Mom's vaguely Southern Baptist. By the time Dad left, and my mom started going back to church, I'd missed a window. I can kind of see why people believe, but I could never feel it."

"I can feel it. My mom would say feeling is proof that my soul is searching. But I also sometimes feel like inanimate objects have emotions, you know? Have you ever felt sad to throw away an old pair of shoes that have been nothing but loyal?"

I snorted. "You're crazy."

"I mean, feelings can be misleading."

"Yeah, they can." I sat up and took a deep breath. "Micah?"

"Uh-huh?" He was quiet, too. He'd told me they'd all gotten rooms at the casino for the night—gaudy, expensive rooms. A room perfect for a one-night stand with a groupie.

"Can I ask you something serious? About us?"

"Yeah."

"Are you just drifting?"

"With you? No. I'm anchored. Positively moored."

I smiled to myself. I'd never known anyone to lay it out so openly. It encouraged me to ask a trickier question. "So, would you consider this exclusive?"

"You want to know if I'm flirting with other girls?"

"No. You're gonna flirt. That's just you. But I want to know what to expect."

"What do you want to expect?"

"Micah, you are talking in circles. You can't answer a question with a question."

"I can't? Why not?" He started laughing.

"You are a brat."

"I'll tell you what to expect then. Expect me to be home tomorrow around noon. What are we doing?"

I laid my head down and rolled on my side, switching my phone to the other ear. "Going to a flea market."

"A flea market?"

"With Zion."

"Sounds fun."

I lowered my voice, quiet. "Micah. You haven't answered my question."

"No? I thought I did." If I closed my eyes, I could imagine his low whisper coming from beside me.

"I must have missed your answer. Could you say it again?"

"Josie. Unless you tell me to take a hike, or, in some dystopian universe, I tell you we're through, you're the only girl for me."

Chapter 20

Zion must have carried me to my bed during the night. I slept late into the morning and woke more rested than I'd been in days. I got up and made some tea, checked my glucose, and then started scrambling eggs.

There was a message on my phone from Andy: *Good work, Scout. Maybe I misjudged you. Come on into the office on Monday. We'll talk.*

Zion opened his door, wearing his ratty bathrobe. His hair stuck out in every direction, an homage to Adrianna perhaps, though far shorter.

"What time did you get in last night? You look like a horror show."

A woman emerged from his room, wearing Zion's silky kimono. Without her blond wig, it took me a second to recognize her.

Zion waved back at her. "Josie, you remember Adrianna?"

"What the—" I clamped my mouth shut. "Of course. Hey, Adrianna." I shot Zion a you-better-start-talking look, but he yawned and went into the bathroom.

Adrianna hugged the kimono tighter around her rail-thin body. "We met last week at Eden's show, right?" Her natural hair was cropped short and reddish brown. She had noticeable acne scars that she must have hidden under all the makeup she usually wore. Her appearance reminded me of nothing so much as a shaved poodle. Still beautiful, but strangely different without all her usual trappings.

I threw another egg into the skillet. A little warning would have been nice. Zion had some explaining to do. I had my chance when they swapped places in the bathroom, and I arched an eyebrow at Zion, waiting for him to fill me in.

He pulled out a chair and sat at the table. "So I've been chatting with her, and we decided to meet last night."

"I gathered."

He stood and reached into the fridge for juice. "Want some?"

"Why'd you bring her here?"

"She can't exactly bring someone to her place. I mean, someone's likely to notice and report it. Even people who go in her apartment alone are probably scrutinized."

"And they wouldn't notice her coming over here?"

He popped a strawberry into his mouth. "She camouflages well."

After seeing her this morning without her wig, I could almost believe that. "But her face is constantly on magazines. She's instantly recognizable."

"Ever notice how few out-and-about pictures ever turn up of her?"

I hadn't, but now that he mentioned it, I'd never seen her myself. I guess I'd always assumed she was a recluse.

She emerged from the bathroom, wearing a navy FDNY T-shirt and a pair of white nylon sweats with two bars of stripes running down the sides. She put on a baseball cap backward, and joined us at the table. To say she was perfectly androgynous would be understating things. Dressed as she was, with her height, she could even pass as a boy.

"Oh," I said. "OH!" All at once, I understood why Zion had been so attracted to her. To him? She looked up at me, but when Zion opened his eyes wide, I recovered and managed to blurt out, "I just remembered Micah's coming over soon."

I couldn't stop staring bug-eyed at Adrianna though. Was she still a "she" when she was dressed as a "he?" I'd need to get Zion alone and make him answer every single question, but for now, he covered for me and explained. "Jo's seeing Micah Sinclair."

Adrianna smiled, coy. "Seriously? You are so lucky."

I shot her a dirty look. Zion was sitting right there. I was sitting right there.

She held up a hand. "No, I don't mean it like that. Although he is a fine piece of ass. Am I right?"

"Mmm. You are so right." Zion horrified me sometimes.

"Oh, Lord, give me strength." I finished my last bite of egg and pushed my chair back to start clearing.

"Seriously," said Adrianna. "Micah's a really beautiful person, inside and out."

Zion burst out laughing. "That's what she said."

"Zion, are we still going to the flea market?" I shot a glance at Adrianna. Zion's plans might have changed.

"Yeah. You wanna go?" he asked Adrianna.

"Sure."

I frowned at them both. "We have to wait for Micah." I got up to get a shower. Zion could clean up the table.

When I came out of the bathroom, towel wrapped around my chest, hair dripping wet, Micah sat on the sofa, talking to Zion and Adrianna. He jumped up. "Need some help?"

"I think I can manage. But you want to keep me company while I dress?"

He followed me into my bedroom. I dug through my drawers for a nice T-shirt and flattering shorts, but he opened my closet. "This is pretty."

"A dress?"

"Is that wrong? Am I not supposed to have an opinion?"

"No. You get an opinion. I'll have to rethink my shoes. We're going to be walking quite a way."

"Never mind. Maybe you could wear this tomorrow?"

"Why, what are we doing tomorrow? Going to church?"

"If you want. But I was thinking of going to see my parents. Eden will be there."

"You want to introduce me to your parents?"

He shrugged and dropped onto my bed. "It's no big deal. We don't have to."

"No, it sounds fun. Are we going to West Philadelphia or Bel Air?"

"I thought you didn't watch TV growing up."

"I never said I always followed the rules."

Once I figured out what to wear, I had an awkward moment, wondering if I should turn around and dress with my back to Micah. He sat on my bed, eyeing the knot in my towel, waiting for the big reveal. So I dropped it. But before I could step into my underwear, he reached over and drew me toward him. In a reversal of the morning before, I stood naked before a fully dressed Micah as he ran his fingers across my skin.

"Watch it. Zion and Adrianna are waiting for us."

"And we're going to be out in public for how long?"

I hadn't even thought about what that would mean to him. "Oh. I mean. If that's a problem. Do you want to stay here? Or do you need a hat?"

He stifled a laugh and handed me my bra. "A hat won't keep me from wanting to take this back off you."

Getting dressed was an exercise in frustration because he handed me every piece of clothing and then followed my hands with his as I put them on. When I stepped into my underwear, he ran his finger along the inside of my leg all the way up. I climbed onto his lap, facing him, knees on either side of him and kissed him. "You are making this very hard."

"Nothing on what you're doing to me."

He pressed into me, and I groaned. Our lips barely touched. I felt his breath against my face and knew he'd passed the tipping point, too. "Your bag is in the other room."

"Wallet." His hip lifted slightly, knocking me off kilter as he pulled his wallet from his back pocket. I didn't want to know why he had a veritable Easter egg hunt of condoms in his possession. At that moment, I didn't care.

I unzipped his jeans, and helped him shimmy until he was free of the confinement. He didn't bother kicking them off before he slipped on the condom, pushed my underwear to the side, and lifted me up. And then he was in me. I sat on him, not moving, feeling him deep inside me. He pushed my wet hair back and kissed my neck and shoulder. "Can we stay like this?"

It was an impossible request. The slightest movement produced an ecstasy. I pushed him over and rocked, panting and then groaning loud enough that there was no doubt Zion would know what we were up to. I didn't care.

Micah pushed me off him to the side and ripped off his jeans and then my underwear. Then he was over me and in me, kissing me, sighing, moaning, saying my name, saying "Oh, my God."

Saying "I love you."

My eyes flew open. "What?"

He stopped, and his eyes opened. "Did I just say that out loud?"

"Uh-huh." I pushed my hips up, urging him to keep moving.

"I wasn't supposed to say that. I know that. I'm sorry. You don't have to say that." He still wasn't moving.

"Micah. Could we talk about this later?" I put my legs over his back and forced his shoulders down to me. His eyes closed again, and he fell into rhythm.

He hadn't lied that he could go longer than five minutes. He took his time, and only after I shuddered with a groan, did he hit a faster pace until he dropped to one side, dripping sweat and breathing heavy.

"Is Zion going to be pissed?"

"Um, no." I'd already picked up sounds from Zion's adjacent room. "They found something to do while they waited."

I got up and started to dress. "Come on. I'm going to need to eat something and check my glucose levels before we leave."

He lay on the bed. "Do you want to talk first?"

"We'll talk later."

I closed the bedroom door and went to the bathroom where I'd left my pump when I showered. I reattached it and started making turkey wraps for everyone. Micah joined me, dressed again. Zion and Adrianna emerged, thankfully also dressed. I handed out sandwiches and said, "Let's eat and walk."

It was a hike to the flea market. Adrianna and Zion walked

about two blocks ahead of us. Adrianna's anonymity would be compromised if anyone recognized Micah next to her. We stopped along the way and bought drinks. I carried my water bottle in one hand and held Micah's hand with the other. Occasionally, we'd pass someone who did a double take at Micah. Nobody stopped us on our way to the flea market, but once we arrived, we slowed down to look at all the wares. And then someone tapped Micah's shoulder and asked, "Are you Micah Sinclair?"

He turned and said, "Yup. What's your name?"

"Mark."

"Hey, Mark. Nice to meet you." He held out his hand, and they shook.

Mark said, "Would you mind if I got a picture with you? My roommate's never going to believe this. He's a huge fan."

"That's awesome." Micah didn't point out that Mark had basically just said he wasn't a huge fan.

Mark handed me the camera. I guessed this was going to be my new job. Selfie photographer to the stars. I said, "Say cheese," and clicked.

Micah put a hand on Mark's shoulder and said, "Tell your roommate thanks for the support."

"He's going to die. Thanks, man."

Other people had watched the exchange, which prompted more people to gather the courage to approach him and talk to him. Every time, he'd ask the person for their name and lay a hand on their shoulder or across their back. He'd find something nice to say to each and every person, no matter what.

"You should run for office," I said. "You're a natural politician."

He draped an arm over me, and we passed through the flea market, looking at everything. The nice thing was, there were no paparazzi at the flea market. Well, there were two, but neither Zion nor I were interested in shooting pictures of Micah.

At one stall, he stopped and tried on a knockoff Gryffindor scarf. "Would this be my house?"

"You read it!"

"Some. What do you think? Where would I be sorted?"

"Yes. Gryffindor. Definitely."

"And you?"

I thought about telling him I'd been sorted into Ravenclaw via Pottermore, but shrugged. "I'd have to be in Gryffindor, too. Someone would have to keep you in line."

"Hey. Take a picture of me here wearing this. Nobody ever prints any pictures of me having any fun."

"What?"

He froze. "I mean. If you want to." He tugged on the scarf and let it fall back on the table. "Never mind. I wasn't thinking. It was a dumb idea."

I scanned the crowd around us—under the adjacent tents or passing between. So many people held their phones in their hands. Any one of them could have just snapped a picture of Micah and uploaded it to Twitter. I sighed. "Put the scarf back on. Might as well kill two birds with one stone. My boss will love it." Andy would probably never print this fluff, but it didn't hurt to humor Micah and shoot the picture.

"Nah. Let's keep moving."

We wended our way through to a stall filled with hilariously smutty dresses. Micah held one up. "I changed my mind. I want to see you in this."

I fanned out the skirt, what there was of it. "Seriously?"

"Maybe tonight?"

I laughed. "Sure. Anything you want."

He bought the skimpy thing. I doubted it would even fit, but I'd rather deal with that later. I had so many other things to sort out. Not the least of which was the problem of his profession of love.

My first impulse—to ignore it—had only caused it to grow in my mind. And I knew it would grow between us if I didn't address it. But how could I without ruining things one way or another? Why'd he have to go and say that? And if he went around saying that so easily, what words had he never said to another girl? "*Would you like to eat squirrel?*"

The flea market went on forever. I led Micah in the direction of the waterfront and spied an unoccupied bench. "You mind sitting for a bit?"

We'd barely situated ourselves when a kid who'd been playing Hackey Sack walked over. "Hey, man. You're Micah Sinclair."

I nearly barked, *"Are you kidding me?"*

But Micah'd already switched on the charm. I counted to one hundred, coincidentally about the amount of time for the whole routine: handshake, name exchange, picture, autograph, compliment, thanks, disengage.

"Stay here," I said. "I'll be right back."

I went into the flea market and walked around until I found what I was looking for.

When I came back to the bench, Micah was chatting with a girl about my age who'd taken my spot. He saw me, touched her shoulder, told her it was great to meet her, and nodded toward me. The girl took her cue and cleared out.

I shoved a paper bag at him. "Put these on."

The sunglasses weren't the most attractive, but they were cheap and dark. The baseball hat had a pickle embroidered on it. I could have bought a plain hat, honestly. But I liked to think a hat with a pickle on it might encourage Micah to keep a low profile.

"What's all this?"

"Portable privacy."

"Does it bother you?"

"Only when I'm with you." I punched him, teasing. "And no, but I wanted to talk."

"Here?"

"Okay, fine. Later then."

"No, here's good. Unless you're doing this in public so you can break it off with me where I won't cause a scene."

I crossed my arms. "Do you really think I'd break things off with you right now?"

"I thought I might have freaked you out."

"Did you mean it? Or was it just the sex?"

"It wasn't just the sex. I mean, it was, but—"

"I don't want to put you on the spot. You can take it back. You've probably said it so many times, and it slipped out."

He took my hands and his big black bug eyes peered into mine. "I've never said that, except to my family, but you know, not like that." He laughed nervously.

"But?"

"But I've said it in my head over and over again since I met you. I know. Love at first sight. It's the worst cliché. I've fought to keep myself from saying anything like that to you. And then it slipped out. I'm sorry. It's not really fair to you. I hoped you'd eventually catch up to me."

I rubbed his hand. "Look. I hope you'll take this the right way. I don't believe in love at first sight. And believe me, if there was such a thing, I felt it, too. I knew it when you first knelt down on the sidewalk that day. But that's not love. That's attraction or chemistry maybe. Or infatuation. And getting to know you is as intoxicating as a drug. But love isn't a feeling."

"You're infatuated with me?"

"Duh."

"I'll take that." He grinned.

Admittedly, it was nice to hear those three reassuring words, but I wondered if he'd feel the same way in two weeks, after our first fight or after he'd gone on tour for a month away from me. I looked through the black plastic to where I knew his eyes hid in darkness. "I want to say the same." I couldn't read his reaction through the disguise, but his mouth tightened, so I offered all I could. "I have a good feeling if I ever do, you'll be the one."

He relaxed as though that were enough of a profession for now. But in my mind, I was picturing my dad. He told my mom he loved her, but he'd never made a promise to honor her, and when a stronger external pressure exerted its force on him, fighting for his American family proved too hard, and his flimsy feelings of so-called love caved right in. How could I trust in feelings? How could anyone prove that they exist? How could anyone promise they would last?

I believed physical attraction and love were temporal. Nobody went around making professions of eternal physical attraction. That would be ludicrous. Sure, some people got lucky and the span of their feelings for each other outlasted their natural lives.

But what I longed for was more akin to a long-lived friendship, something like what I had with Zion, but more intimate. I worried Micah would prefer a lightning-flash, short-lived passionate affair. I could have given him that if I hadn't started to want more.

So much for taking things slowly. Now instead of feeling like we were tentatively working toward a steady relationship, I'd likely always brace for the inevitable end. Micah went so fast, sooner or later, he'd burn out and move on. I couldn't think of a thing in the world that would convince me otherwise. I smiled anyway and hid all signs of internal waffling.

I suddenly became aware of the time. "Micah, I'm going to have to either find a snack soon or eat an early supper."

He texted his driver while I texted Zion to let him know we were leaving. The driver dropped us at a Mexican restaurant around the corner from Micah's townhouse. After a dinner of tacos, we ditched the town car and walked back. The evening sky had just begun to grow dim, and the afternoon heat hadn't quite dissipated. We chatted as we strolled companionably though not hand in hand.

"I moved here after our first single took off." His eyes scanned the buildings along his street. "I'd been living in a one bedroom in Crown Heights for a while."

"Why'd you decide—" I stopped walking. A boy with mop hair and fish belly translucent skin leaned against Micah's stoop rail, blotting his brow with the front of his shirt. As soon as he dropped the fabric, his eyes met mine. He heaved himself onto his feet and began down the sidewalk, fumbling for a camera that obviously hadn't been prepared for this moment.

Micah never broke pace except to turn back and wait for me to catch up. By the time we reached the steps, the boy had taken control of his camera and shot several pictures. Micah reached out his hand. "Hello. What's your name?"

The kid swallowed and shoved his hand into a small backpack, producing a bent notepad. "My name is Jim." His hands shook as he poised a pen above the paper. "I contribute materials to FanBlogger.com. Have you heard of it?"

Both Micah and I shook our heads. Micah twisted his mouth. "Are you with the press?"

"We're a kind of news organization driven on one-hundred-percent reader-submitted content. I wanted to ask you some questions."

Micah relaxed and beamed the smile he gave the public. It was a beautiful smile, but I'd seen the real deal. This smile didn't come close. "Sure. What would you like to know?"

Jim dug his phone out of his bag and brought it back to life. "By any chance, have you seen this article? It was uploaded to FanBlogger earlier today."

"May I?" Micah reached out and took the phone. I leaned over to see what it said.

Micah Sinclair Blows Fans Off Outside Club.

Micah licked his lips. "Is this about Tuesday?" Jim nodded, and Micah handed the phone back. "I wasn't at my best. You can certainly print that I appreciate my fans, and I'd like to apologize to those two girls. It was just a bad night."

I stepped up. "It was my fault."

Micah threw his hand out in front of me, like we were in a car that stopped short. "Jo."

Jim tilted his head and appraised me. "You were the girl in the background, right? You're Jo Wilder, the paparazza seen with Micah last week?" I didn't have a chance to answer one way or another. Jim went on. "There were divided opinions about that. I thought it was you." His hand drifted to his camera, no longer shaking. As he gripped it and turned it around, he asked, "So are you two dating?"

Micah moved toward the steps. "No."

"Did you hire her as a personal paparazza?"

"We're done here." Micah shot me a glance, and I followed him up to the front door.

"Or Miss Wilder, are you looking for a breakout inside scoop?"

We ignored the question while Micah dug in his pocket for his house key. As he slid it into the lock, Jim threw out, "I guess I'm going to be forced to print that you *are* rude to your fans."

The door opened, and Micah stood back to let me through. As soon as we had a wall separating us from Jim, I turned on Micah. "Why'd you say we weren't dating? What happened to not keeping any secrets from the media?"

Micah pressed his lips together. "Jo, I didn't mean—"

"You talk with them about all the other girls you date. Am I somehow not good enough?" I leaned against the wall and slumped. The whole encounter with Jim had stressed me out more than I'd expected it might. And he was pitiful compared to the real paparazzi. Yet still better than me.

Micah moved into my space and pushed my hair out of my face. "Don't you know you're different than all the other girls I've ever dated? I just want to protect this. Once we open up about this, it's going to be like that all the time. For a while at least. And they'll dig, Jo." He laid his hands on either side of my face and looked into my eyes. "And I want to keep this for myself as long as I can."

I relaxed. "I'm sorry. How do you deal with that all the time? It's—"

"The price of fame." He pulled me into a hug, and I forgot about Jim. "Hey." He leaned back. "I bought season one of *Seinfeld*. You owe me a sitcom."

I laughed. "All right."

"Feel like dressing up for it?" He held up the sack from the flea market with an eyebrow waggle.

"Maybe later." The encounter outside had left me out of sorts. "I'd really love to just snuggle up. That okay?"

He lifted my hand and kissed my fingers. "Anything you want."

Chapter 21

The drive to Micah's parents' reminded me of something out of the *The Sopranos* until we got into Woodbridge where all the houses we passed had a similar weary look. His driver parked behind two other cars, and before we got out Micah stopped me for a second. He took my hand and winced. "This is going to be weird."

Instead of going up to the front door, he walked around the side through a gate and into the backyard. As soon as we closed the gate, a woman screeched, "Micah's here!" A tall blonde rushed over and grabbed Micah's face in her hands, fussing over his weight and his lack of communication for a full minute before she seemed to even notice I stood beside him.

Clearly Micah's mom. It was uncanny how much Micah took after her. After seeing him next to Eden, I didn't know what to expect. Mrs. Sinclair looked like she'd stepped out of a *Better Homes and Gardens* magazine from the fifties. Hollywood sunglasses and an oversize sun hat shrouded her face. Maybe my reputation for shooting candid photos had preceded me, but I didn't have my work camera with me. And if I had, Andy wouldn't want any photos of Micah's mom anyway.

I was glad I'd put on a sundress, ignoring Micah's pleas for me to wear the piece of cloth he'd bought me at the flea market.

I'd worn that for about five minutes the night before—five minutes before he'd peeled it right back off me.

"And who's your friend?"

"Mom, this is Josie. Josie, Mom."

I put on my sweetest meet-the-parents smile. "Nice to meet you, Mrs. Sinclair."

She waved her hand, "Oh, you can call me Peg."

Eden had already arrived and sat on the patio next to an older man I assumed must be their dad. He was reading an actual newspaper.

Peg hollered over. "Look, Howard. Micah's brought a girl with him."

Micah's dad folded back his newspaper. "I have eyes, Peg."

Peg wasn't having it. "Howard."

Howard grunted and put the paper down. Then I saw the dark hair that Eden had inherited. From what I could tell, she'd also gotten a fair portion of her dad's more withdrawn personality. Micah claimed all the bubbling vivaciousness from their mother.

When Howard came around to shake my hand, he did a solid job of pretending he wasn't put out. "It's very nice to meet you, Josie." And then he retreated to his chair and disappeared behind his paper.

Secretly, I loved this display of long-suffering matrimony. Ridiculous as it might seem, this was my dream. I had no use for empty professions of love. I wanted a committed relationship through good times and bad, in sickness and in health. Not for as long as we both had swooping feelings. Couples like Peg and Howard might seem bored with each other on the surface, but I'd observed enough older couples to recognize an invisible yoke tied them together and made them as dependent on one another as if they were a pair of conjoined twins.

Peg looked from Micah to me and back. "So where did you meet?"

Micah's eyes twinkled. "She was walking the street."

Undaunted, Peg followed up. "Which street?"

Micah led me over to the patio table and held out a chair for me. Eden greeted me with a wicked grin. "Hey. I noticed our trick didn't pan out."

Micah said, "She's got you turning tricks, too?"

"Goodness! Look how pretty Josie's hair is," Peg said. "Eden, look at how she manages to keep her curls so untangled. What do you use, Josie?"

Eden's rueful expression nearly made me do a spit take. I got the feeling this wasn't the first time she'd been on the receiving end of an inadvertent insult. Her mouth twisted into a half smile. "Come inside, Josie. There's plenty of food."

Peg's hands flew up. "Oh, yes. Come on inside."

All of us except Howard went in through the sliding doors into a family room that had time-traveled from the 1970s. I followed along to a more recently renovated kitchen. On the island sat an assortment of choices: a Crock-Pot filled with melted cheese and specks of red pepper, a casserole dish of miniature hot dogs in some kind of brownish-red molasses, fried white bread filled with either mayonnaise or cream cheese, and bags upon bags of chips.

"Help yourself," said Peg. "And we have strawberry soda, or if you'd like, I can make you a nonalcoholic margarita."

"What's in that?"

"Mostly sour mix and 7UP."

I stared at all the poison, trying to figure out the nicest way to insult this woman. But then Micah casually announced, "She can't eat any of that, Mom. She's diabetic."

Eden frowned. "Lucky."

Peg declared, "My cousin's diabetic. She has to get shots every day. Do you?"

"No, ma'am."

Micah laughed. "She's part robot." He went to the fridge and started pulling things out. "How about some milk and . . ."

It was cute watching him try to figure out what I could eat based on the limited time he'd spent with me. He pulled out celery and peanut butter and a deviled egg.

"Mom, do you have any wheat bread or crackers?"

Eden said, "Can you fix me something, too?"

Peg touched Eden's forehead. "Are you feeling okay, Eden? You look a little pale."

"I always look pale, Mom."

"You're not sick, are you?"

Eden made eye contact with me for a second. "I'm fine, Mom."

Once Micah handed us each a plate and a cup of milk, Eden said, "Come with me, Jo. I want to show you those pictures I told you about."

She walked toward the front of the house into a sitting room where a digital frame flipped through random pictures of Micah and Eden. Some were from when they were children. Micah held a guitar in most of them. But when he didn't, he made funny faces or stood in front of accidentally inappropriate road signs or intentionally inappropriate props.

"Aw. That was taken the summer before Micah left home." A younger version of Eden and Micah sat on the driveway in front of this very house. Eden's hair was shorter, curlier. Her arms and legs were sticks. The girl next to me now had filled out, or she was putting on weight.

"How are you feeling?"

Her hand passed over her belly reflexively. "Good. I mean, I'm sick half the time, but the doctor says everything's fine." She dropped her voice. "I heard the heartbeat on Friday. I wish Adam could've been there. But he'll be home this week."

"So . . . you really are pregnant?" It weirded me out that of all the people in this house—her entire family—the only person who knew her secret was me—the tabloid media, her enemy.

Her laugh came out like she'd been given the Heimlich maneuver, fast and hard. "Did you think I was lying?"

I shrugged. "When we first met, all you knew was that I worked for Andy. Knowing your history, it crossed my mind you might have set me up to hand him a story that could be easily proven false."

She touched my wrist. "I want you to know that I've grown to trust you, but you're right that at first, I worried." She sighed. "Nothing personal, but it wasn't ideal having you of all people discover us. We were idiots to talk about it while you were wandering around. I appreciate that you kept it quiet."

"Of course."

"I would've loved to tell my family about it today, but next week is soon enough. Adam will want to be here. He'll get all the credit and move one more rung up the ladder of my mom's esteem."

"It's great news."

"Speaking of my mom's esteem . . . I finally had something over Micah, and then he turns up with you."

"What do you mean?"

She rolled her eyes up to the ceiling. "You have no idea." She sat in one of the wingback chairs and tucked her bare feet under her knees. "She used to nag at me relentlessly to find a guy. Any guy. Seriously, she couldn't let it go. But Micah could do nothing wrong." She chuckled. "Thank God for Adam."

"Hasn't Micah ever brought home a girl?"

She stood and walked to the edge of the room to peer up the hall. "Listen. About that email I sent you last week . . ." She blew out her lips. "I'm glad I didn't make you go running for the hills. But I was right, wasn't I? I mean, he looks like he's on a sugar high whenever he sees you."

"He's the most transparent person I've ever met."

"Yeah, he is."

"I still don't know what he sees in me. It's hard to keep up."

She bit her lip and appraised me a moment. "I really like you, Jo. But I hope you'll be careful with him."

I still didn't know if she was worried about me or Micah. "I'm trying."

Micah hollered up the hall. "Did you guys leave?" He entered the living room. "Come outside with everyone. Mom wants to take a picture of us."

I glanced at the picture frame as we walked out, wondering if one day my face would rotate through, marking today, frozen forever this way. Or would I rotate right back out of Micah's life?

Peg stood in the yard, fussing with a string of Christmas

lights that inexplicably decorated her rose bushes. She waved us over and proceeded to pose us in various configurations: Micah with Eden, Micah with me and Eden, Micah with me.

Between shots, she stared at the camera, perplexed. "Howard, I don't think this is working. I click it, but I don't see a flash"

Howard didn't look up from his paper. "Peg, it's broad daylight. You don't need a flash."

I should have offered to take the pictures for her, but I got the feeling she enjoyed the whole ceremony of it. She pushed me next to Eden, saying, "I wish Adam could have been here. Where'd he go this time?"

Eden shrugged off Peg's attempts to lay her hand on my arm. "He's in Japan, Mom."

Peg took three steps back and peered into the viewfinder. I cringed when she put her finger over the lens. "I don't understand why he'd want to spend so much money to fly to Japan just to play music." She snapped the picture and then held the camera a foot from her face. "Howard, the pictures are all pink, now."

"Mom, they pay Adam to play music in Japan, too."

Peg handed the camera to Howard to mess with. Howard laid down his paper and weighed in on the conversation. "Micah makes a good living, and he's never gone for long. Why can't Adam play closer to home?"

Eden's lips were so firmly pinched, I thought she might pull a muscle in her face.

Micah stepped in, "Adam's band is world famous, Mom. I'd love to headline a show in Japan."

Peg poured herself a glass of some bright green concoction with floating chunks of squares I hoped were fruit—pineapples? "Micah, how could you court such a lovely young lady if you're running all over the world?" I blushed to the roots of my hair and stared at my shoes. She added, "It's a wonder Eden ever managed to set a date for her wedding."

My head jerked up, and I looked from Eden to Peg. Howard had handed the camera back to Peg, and she messed with the settings again, completely oblivious of the bomb ticking down around her. If I asked her the date, I'm sure she would have told me. What could Eden do? And why shouldn't I ask it? Eden held my gaze.

Howard broke the silence. "Peg, I don't think the kids are announcing their wedding date."

Peg pursed her lips. "Oh, well. We're with family. There's no reason to hide anything here." She raised the camera, again. "Now, everyone smile."

After a nice afternoon with the Sinclair family, the driver picked us up to take us to Park Slope. On the way, Micah's phone rang, and he winced when he glanced at the call screen. "This can't be good." He hit Answer, "Hi, Sandy. What's on fire?" The voice on the other end sounded like a mosquito, shrill and busy. "Right. I know, but—" He dropped his head in defeat. "Okay. It won't." And he hung up.

I took his hand. "Trouble?"

"My agent. She's pissed about how I handled Jim yesterday. She said she knew about the disgruntled fan blog but wasn't worried because nobody takes that site too seriously. And it would have blown over if I hadn't given him anything to go back to his blog with."

I shrugged. "FanBlogger? You probably wouldn't even be able to find that through a Google search. I wouldn't worry about it."

"Yeah. I'm not." His face said otherwise.

"You're always amazing with fans. It's not like they'll all turn on you overnight because some people are telling stories on some remote blog." When that didn't seem to reach him, I added, "I can promise you it's nothing Andy would ever want to pursue. Small potatoes." But in all honesty, if Micah's agent had found the story, Andy would have, too. And during a slow news week, he could very well milk a story that made Micah appear like an ungrateful brat. And he'd probably expect me to back it up.

Micah wrapped his arms around me. "Seriously. It's no big deal." But the air sparked with nervous energy, and we rode in silence for a while.

When his phone rang again, he sat up and spoke in monosyllabic answers.

"Yes."

"Six."

"No."

"Fine."

This time, he hung up smiling.

"What was that?"

"You have to wait and see." The mischievous tone returned to his voice. He asked the driver to turn on the radio and started singing along with a Steve Miller Band song, ignoring my interrogating eyes. I leaned my head against him and felt his shoulders relax.

When we got to his place, he practically giggled as he unlocked the front door. Heavenly smells floated from inside his apartment, and he dragged me to his kitchen.

I followed confused. "What's going on?"

A stranger stood in the kitchen wearing a white chef coat and chopping an onion. "Good evening, ma'am," he said to me. "Sir."

Micah's glee exploded all over his face. "Josie, this is Pratosh. He's going to cook for us."

"Pratosh?" I tested out the rusted hinges on a gate that had closed years before and asked, *"Niṅṅaḷ Malayāḷi ākunnu?"* Are you Malayali?

Without glancing up from the counter, he asked, *"Niṅṅaḷ Malayāḷa sansārikkumēā?"*

I tried to come up with the response, but it had been too long. "No, I can't anymore." Time had eaten away at another connection to half my identity and stolen another piece of my dad away from me.

Micah's eyebrows pressed together as he tried to make sense of the conversation, so I filled him in. "He asked if I speak Malayalam. You hired a Malayali chef?"

"I thought I'd surprise you with something completely different."

I shook off the unwanted emotional intrusion. "I haven't spoken Malayalam since—" My traitorous voice made me sound upset when I wasn't.

Micah looked horrified. "Oh. I'm sorry. I figured—"

"No, it's fine. It's a lovely reminder. I haven't had Kerala cuisine since I was a kid."

I scanned the foods lining the counter, surprised that it all looked like something I could eat. After the afternoon at Micah's mom's, I'd worried I was always going to be rummaging through cabinets for leftovers and accidentally edible extras. "Pratosh, this all looks wonderful. Thank you."

Pratosh placed a bowl in front of Micah. "I'm mixing together ginger, green chilies, turmeric, and coconut milk." He stirred the mixture and handed the bowl to Micah.

I tilted my head as Micah began to whisk the ingredients. His ebullient grin returned. "Pratosh is going to teach me to cook."

It wasn't lost on me that what Pratosh was teaching Micah to cook was healthy food. Pratosh emptied a plastic bag of shrimp into another bowl. "Ma'am, do you eat shrimp?"

"Yes, Pratosh. I love shrimp."

He rinsed the shrimp and passed them to Micah. "Drop these into the sauce to coat."

They worked together cooking the shrimp, tossing the salad, plating the meal, and serving it onto the table.

Micah set out glasses. "What do we have to drink, Pratosh?"

"Strawberry-lemon-infused water, sir."

Pratosh set a pitcher of pink water on the table, and Micah poured me a glass.

I took a sip. "Wow. This is amazing, Pratosh. Do you know how much sugar is in this?"

"Three grams per glass, ma'am."

"Unbelievable." It tasted sweet and so cold and delicious.

Micah couldn't contain his happiness. "You like it?"

I leaned over the corner of the table and met him for a kiss. "I can't believe you did this. It's incredible."

"Pratosh, what's for breakfast?"

"It's a surprise, sir."

Breakfast? "Pratosh, are you staying here?"

"No, ma'am."

Micah explained. "Pratosh specializes in tailored menus. I hired him to come cook us dinner, but also teach me to fish, so to speak. I don't want you to have to dig up peanut butter and crackers ever again."

"I don't know what to say. Thank you. I'm blown away."

"Oh, and Pratosh, did you do the other thing?"

"Yes, sir." Pratosh opened the fridge and displayed a stack of plastic restaurant-like boxes. He pulled one out. Inside, he'd packed an assortment of small foods. It looked like an elaborate snack box. The one he showed me had a small sandwich of some variety made with wheat bread, a couple of carrot sticks, a small box of milk, and almonds.

Micah said, "So you don't go hypo."

"Go hypo?" I cracked up. "Have you been researching?"

"I wanted to understand what you're dealing with. I don't know how you do it, Josie. I'd lose my mind. But you just deal with it. You're incredible."

"You are. I am overwhelmed."

"Well, let's eat. The shrimp is getting cold." He looked over at our chef. "Pratosh, how do you say *shrimp* in Mala—" He made a face at me.

I helped him out. "Malayalam."

Pratosh said, "*Cem'mīn.*"

Pratosh and I exchanged an amused glance when Micah tried to repeat it. Undaunted, he asked, "How do you say, 'You have beautiful eyes.'"

"*Niṅṅaḷ manēāharamāya kaṅṅukaḷuṇṭ.*"

Micah's face dropped. "What about just 'beautiful.'"

"*Manēāharamāya.*"

Micah repeated it, kind of. Close enough anyway.

I said, "*Nandi.* It means 'thank you.'"

"Why do you get the easy one?"

I ran my finger across his cheek. "Micah, you are *manēāharamāya.* And not bad looking either."

As we ate, I told him more about my trip to Kerala as a child.

"I was only there for a week, but those memories are more vivid to me than most of my memories of high school."

"We should go there."

"I'd love to go there with you." I pictured myself introducing Micah to my dad and wondered if we'd end up in the same shouting match Dad had had with his father. It's funny who we let influence our lives.

I thanked Pratosh for the wonderful meal and said to Micah, "It was sweet of you to do all this. Thank you for going to all the trouble."

"You asked." He poured himself another glass of the strawberry-lemon drink.

"What?"

"The first night you stayed here. Or that morning. You asked me to have more food."

"I did?"

"You scared the hell out of me that morning. This is something I can do, Josie. This doesn't have to be so hard. Okay?"

"Okay."

"I want to make you happy. And healthy. And just . . . here."

After we burned off the calories from supper and spent ourselves so thoroughly Micah fell asleep even before me, I snuggled against him and processed everything I'd experienced during the day. Micah's family proved that he'd been raised with an example of a long-term stable relationship, and yet so far in his life, he'd chosen to pursue short-lived shallow affairs that meant nothing. Why had he singled me out for his first attempt at something real?

Meanwhile, I was the offspring of a broken home, always on high alert to stay away from anyone who might turn out to be like my dad. So why had I gone straight for the one guy who'd burned through probably dozens of women, proving time and time again that he couldn't be counted on to make a failing romance work?

More importantly, why was I letting him lure me in?

It troubled me that I wasn't troubled. Despite all the historical evidence against him, I wanted to trust Micah. But I couldn't figure out for sure whether my desire to trust him was blinding me to any warning signs. Was it all wishful thinking?

If I told him I'd had fun, but now I wanted to move on, would he let me go like he had with so many others? Or would he fight for me?

He made a snuffling sound and threw his arm up over his head—something I'd noticed he only did when he was here in his own bed, safe and content.

Tomorrow after work, I'd talk to him about how I was feeling. I closed my eyes and lay awake for another hour, already rehearsing every word.

Chapter 22

In the morning, I nearly cried when Micah set a plate of pancakes on the table before me. Pratosh had shown him how to make them with whole wheat flour, pears, and ginger. He'd jumped out of bed before I woke up and brought me my glucose meter. By the time I'd showered and dressed, he had half the batter sizzling on some kind of state-of-the-art griddle.

He kissed me on the forehead before he joined me with his own plate. "You once told me you hadn't had pancakes in fifteen years."

As we ate the decadent and only slightly burned food he'd created (mostly) with his own hands, we had the most wonderfully banal conversation.

I took a bite and moaned with pleasure, and then asked, "What are you going to do today?"

"I plan to burn off this breakfast in my gym, then work on a song I'm writing. Aaaaaaand then I'm going to take a long afternoon nap." He stretched as if he was going to go to bed the second I left.

I got the impression he threw in the mention of a nap to keep me from interrogating him about the song, so I asked, "What about this song?" His cheeks rose in the first signs of an underground smile, and I knew he was up to something.

Once we were done eating, he sent me off to work—with my snack box and a kiss.

As the driver whisked me away from Micah's form, receding on the sidewalk, I took stock of my incredible luck—like I'd won the lottery without ever buying a ticket. Could there be a better person in the entire world than Micah? I didn't think so.

I entered the office for the first time in nearly a week, feeling like I'd been on vacation. I hadn't seen Zion since Saturday. He gave me a funny look when I passed him, so I grabbed him by the elbow. "I need coffee. Come with me."

We walked together up to Washington Square Park. He peppered me with questions about Micah all the way, and I told him about driving out to New Jersey and about Pratosh. By the time we got into the park, Zion had all but named our children.

We settled on a park bench to watch people walk their dogs. Zion bumped my shoulder. "Sounds like you're really happy. Micah's quite the catch, huh?"

"Yeah, he is. But what's going on with you and Adrianna?"

He stretched his arms across the back of the bench, one foot crossed over his knee, pleased, downright cocky. "All right. So you know how she followed me on Twitter?"

"Yeah."

"We started flirting. A lot. It veered off into a very *not* gray, very *not* euphemistic, very, very hot conversation. She said she wanted to meet up with me."

"When was this?"

"Last Friday. I got nervous though and told her the truth. I explained that I'd never been with a woman before, but that I was willing to give it a try. I wanted her to be prepared in case there was an epic failure to connect."

"So what happened?"

"Friday night, I agreed to meet her at a bar. When she showed, I didn't even recognize her at first. You've seen her now. She changes like a chameleon. We found one of those round booths where we could talk. I scooted beside her, and next thing I knew, she kissed me."

I elbowed him. "How was it?"

His eyelashes fluttered. "If she'd been dressed in her pop diva magnificence, it would have made me question my identity. But as it was, it felt right. It felt natural. And I knew then."

"That she's . . . ?"

"One hundred percent boy."

"I knew it!" I'd seen her perform her reverse Madame Butterfly in our apartment, so I wasn't surprised, but still. I felt a stab of remorse for my curiosity. "Oh, my Lord, Zion. I'm sorry for being so nosy. It's none of my business."

"Have you ever noticed you only ask the invasive questions when you have no intention of publicizing them? You're the worst reporter."

I knocked him with my shoulder. "Takes one to know one." Zion was sitting on top of a powder keg.

"Ha, yeah. I reckon I'm a spectacular failure in this regard."

The fact that two tabloid reporters knew her secret raised an important question. "How does that work, exactly? She's a very public figure."

He shrugged. "I mean, there have always been rumors, but I figured if they were at all true, she would have gotten caught a long time ago. Can you imagine how many people have to work with her on wardrobe for a single concert?"

"And you have no desire to make a fortune off this information?"

"No way. She's savvy. She's prepared for the story to come out eventually. And she'll share it herself when the time is right. But it would disrupt her career and totally kill her ability to drop into public incognito. And that would kill my chances of having a semi-normal relationship with her. So no. I won't print this story. And I'm trusting you won't either."

"Nope. But why is she trusting us with such a huge secret?"

He leaned his elbows on his knees, hands clasped around his coffee cup, and turned his head up toward me, squinting against the bright sunlight. "Adrianna trusts you because Micah trusts you. Simple as that."

"And why does she trust you?"

"She doesn't have much choice, does she? Unless she wants to spend her life locked away, sending text messages. From what she told me, she's tried it that way, and she's willing to take calculated risks. I've given her my word. I told her I didn't care one way or the other what was going on with her, but she could tell me. Either way, I want to be with her. And she's told me everything."

I arched an eyebrow. "Everything?"

"Yeah. Her whole story."

We sat in silence while a million questions processed through my brain. None of them seemed appropriate. But this was Zion. "Can I ask you something?"

"Ask me whatever."

"Is she interested in changing?"

"Doesn't seem to be. She joked that she's a heterosexual girl trapped in a gay man's body."

I snorted.

"She's really funny." He didn't laugh. Instead, he stared at his fingernails. "Turns out I must be part heterosexual guy because I like her exactly the way she is." He must have felt as conflicted in the past week as I ever did, but he'd kept it hidden.

"And so she's, uh—" I blew through my lips, trying to find the right way to ask it.

But Zion read my mind. "Does she identify as female?"

"Is that a terrible question?"

"She'd tell you herself if she were here. Sometimes she identifies as female. Not always."

"Am I going to have to figure it out? Like should I refer to her with different pronouns?"

Zion laid a hand on mine and rubbed my thumb. "You don't need to worry about anything. She'll appreciate that you care enough to want to respect her, but she's easygoing. People make worse mistakes than grammar." He shook his head. "And I always thought I had things hard. I can't even imagine dealing with that. But she just does."

His comment reminded me of Micah's reaction to my own burdens. And that brought home just how important this was to Zion. I could get the nuances of Adrianna straight in time. Only one thing mattered right now. "You really like her?"

"Yeah. I don't know how strongly she feels about me, but I figure she's taking a pretty big risk if she's not interested in giving things a chance."

I processed all that, shaking my head at how complicated and simple everything could be at once. "You make it look so easy, Z." My current drama paled in comparison to what he'd been dealing with.

"Why borrow heartache?" Zion shrugged and tossed his coffee cup into the trash.

His honesty encouraged me, so I dug the snack box out of my backpack and showed it to Zion. "Would you look at this?" It was such a tiny thing. Micah hadn't even packed it himself. Pratosh had done all the work. But it filled me with happiness.

Zion popped the lid and smiled at the finger sandwiches and cut vegetables. "He really seems to care about you."

I debated whether or not to confess, but this was Zion, so I blurted it out. "He told me he loves me."

Zion handed back the snack box with an inscrutable expression. "And?"

"I've been thinking about it a lot." I swallowed down a lump. I'd been resisting the idea that anyone could fall in love so quickly. And Micah had been careful not to say it again, except when it slipped out in those moments of transcendence. "I mean, what does love even mean if you can feel that way in a matter of days?"

I poked around at the contents of the snack box and nibbled on a square cheese sandwich, something my mom would have made me when I was in school. I realized I was crying. And not just a wistful moistening of my eyes. Tears rolled in heavy drops down my cheeks.

Zion reached over and wiped away a tear. "Honey, do the words really matter? You're holding evidence that you're important to him, that he's conscious of what you need. Isn't that something worth considering?"

A laugh burst out because this one ridiculous thought passed through my mind. "Are you saying, the snack box is love?"

He took my hand. "Jo, I'm like you. I don't put much faith

in professions, but I put a lot of faith into actions—and so do you. I think Micah's trying to show you what the words mean to him. He's trying to show you he can be there for you. Do you trust that?"

I wanted to think I could trust him, but that would have to come in time. "I think he's sincere." I took a shaky breath. "And I think I feel the same way, too. Is that crazy?"

He gently knocked my forehead. "Don't ruin a good thing, Jo. If you know, you know. You should tell the boy the words he wants to hear."

I did know. I was in love with Micah. I'd never known anyone like him. "I want to. And I will. Today."

And just like that, the fear I'd harbored lifted from my shoulders. My mom's life wasn't mine. And besides, when things were good with my dad, she'd been truly happy. For over ten years, she'd been in love with him. She'd never told me she wished she hadn't ever met him. I wouldn't project potential future heartache onto today. I had a choice in the matter. I could choose to be happy for now.

As soon as Zion and I arrived in the office, Andy stuck his head out. "Jo, is that you? Come in here."

Since he'd sent me such a complimentary text about my work on Friday, I didn't think he'd yell at me or fire me. I hoped he'd tell me I could go out on the usual rounds.

"Jo, what do you know about Eden's pregnancy?"

I stopped dead in his doorway. "What?"

"Eden Sinclair? She's pregnant."

"I'm sorry? Why do you think that?"

"Derek. He followed her to her gynecologist and saw her buying prenatal vitamins. It's not rocket science."

I slowly walked into his office. "What do you intend to do with that information?"

He sneered at me and transformed into the ugliest human being I'd ever seen. "Print it, obviously."

My mind reeled. If he printed that now, Eden would be taken completely by surprise. And she'd certainly think I had something to do with it. "But you have no hard evidence. She could have bought those vitamins for someone else. Or to fool you. It would be libel. You could get sued." I was throwing everything I could out there.

"Sued? She'd have to prove that it wasn't true. And if it's not true, she'd have to prove that I didn't believe it was true. And I believe it. I think it's very, very true."

"Andy, you can't print that. I'll get you a better story."

He glanced down at his tablet, and I knew he was about to shut me out. "Keep talking."

I licked my lips, weighing all the options. In my head, I screamed *Shit shit shit!* I did have a better story, and it briefly crossed my mind to throw Adrianna under the bus. The buzz from that story would steamroll over anything about Eden and would occupy the paper for months. Andy would commemorate me with medals of honor. But I couldn't do that to her or to Zion. Not because it was his story to break, but because he never would. And it turned out Andy was right. I didn't have whatever it took to ruin someone's life for sport. It would be unfair to Adrianna, and I'd never forgive myself for turning her over to the firing squad. When and if she wanted to share her story, that should be her prerogative.

There were two other far less explosive stories in my possession. Praying one or the other might throw him off the scent, I lobbed the weaker of the two. "I found out yesterday that Eden's set her wedding date."

Andy didn't stop scrolling through photos. "When is it?"

My eyes closed in resignation. "I don't know. Soon."

"Then that's not really news, Scout." He yawned. "Everyone knows they're getting married. Nobody knows she's having a baby."

In desperation, I threw him my last bone. "I know who Micah's dating."

His eyes shot up. "Yeah?"

"Would you postpone the story on Eden for another week if I share that information?"

He snorted. "Are you trying to bargain? This is why I pulled you off covering these people. We should be printing both stories."

"You can print both stories, just not at the same time. One week, Andy. That's all."

He tapped his pen, weighing the options. Honestly, I couldn't believe my ploy was working. Eden's pregnancy would be a bigger story than Micah's next girlfriend, especially since it was me. But he finally said, "Fine. If you tell me right now who Micah's dating, for the record, and if you'll confirm Eden's pregnancy, for the record, I'll push Eden's story."

I exhaled, hoping he could be trusted. "Can I get that in writing?"

"Are you shitting me? Jo, you work for me. Remember?"

I wanted to punch him in the face, but I needed the paycheck. And the health insurance.

"Do I have your word at least?" Desperation colored my voice. If I lost Eden's trust, I'd never get it back.

I prayed Micah would forgive me for what I was fixing to do. He'd always been so open to the media. Of the two of them, Micah would be less bent out of shape from overexposure.

"Sure." He crossed his arms. "So Eden's pregnant?"

I nodded. The blood drained from my face. I couldn't believe I was betraying Eden to keep her story from coming out sooner.

"How long have you known?"

I looked at my feet. "A week."

"Jesus, Jo. I should fire you."

My chin jutted out, and I stood a little straighter, daring him to try that. I'd love to write that report up for HR. *Fired for failing to expose secrets shared in confidence.*

Andy ran his tongue across his teeth. "Is she married?"

"That's not part of the bargain."

His lips puckered. "Fine. Who's Micah dating?"

I'd promised him, but that didn't make it easier to take the plunge—I was wagering a relationship that hadn't quite gotten airborne, and on top of that, I was about to become the story. But what could I do? Andy left me no choice, so I gritted my teeth and said, "Me."

His mouth slowly twisted into an approximation of happy. "Wow. I thought it would take more than that to get an admission from you."

"What do you mean?"

"You two have been seen all over Brooklyn. But I couldn't confirm anything. Not until you just did."

My mind raced through every gesture, every kiss. "You've been following me?"

"I'd hardly need to. From the online traffic alone, we could have run a speculative piece. But this is better."

I didn't know how. But whatever worked. In fact, if he was going to run it anyway, I felt like I'd at least used the little influence I had for good. Micah and I hadn't done anything in public that I wouldn't want my mom to see in the papers. "Great. So you'll run that and hold off on Eden, right?"

"Yeah."

Crisis averted as much as possible, I relaxed. "Thanks, Andy."

He grinned, and I swore his teeth looked razor sharp. "No problem."

Chapter 23

The entire staff watched me as I exited Andy's office. I wanted to call Micah to give him a heads-up, but more urgently, I needed to contact Eden immediately to warn her that Andy knew, but I certainly didn't want the hungry wolves to overhear my conversation with her, so I jumped in the elevator down to the lobby, searching for her contact info in our email chain.

When I got out to the street, I dialed the number, but as I was about to hit Send, a man approached me. "Jo Wilder?"

I looked up from my phone and squinted at him, trying to place where I knew him from. All at once I recognized him as one of the paparazzi from a competing newspaper, but I couldn't remember his name. We'd met at some event or another, jockeying for the same photos. "Yes?"

He snapped my picture. "When did you first sleep with Micah Sinclair?"

"What?"

"Are you still sleeping with him? How would you characterize your relationship?"

What had Andy published? I turned away from the reporter and walked down the sidewalk back toward the building. "No comment."

"What do you know about the other women?"

"Leave me alone." I tripped over my own shoes, but caught myself. My hands started to shake.

He kept pace with me. "Where is Micah now?" He turned and started walking backward as his camera clicked in bursts. "Were you working undercover? Did Andy Dickson send you in on assignment? Pretty choice assignment."

I put my hand up to block the shot, and nearly walked into a woman holding a small boy by the hand. When I stopped to let her by, he asked. "What's it like working for Andy?"

I turned to face him. "Off the record?"

He dropped his camera to his shoulder. "Yeah. The guy's a genius."

"It sucks. It really sucks."

"Are you thinking of leaving? Could I give you my card in case they need to replace you? I'd be willing to sleep with celebrities to get the story."

I finally made it to the lobby doors and ditched the pest. I hid in the stairwell and pulled up our website on my phone. Right on the front page, the headline read: "I Slept with Micah Sinclair."

I'd never said that. I'd never given Andy any details about my relationship with Micah, and my name accompanied a single statement, which I'd also never exactly said: *"I'm dating Micah," says* Daily Feed's *own Jo Wilder.* At the top of the page an image was slowly loading, knocking that one sentence farther down. The reception was terrible in the stairwell, so I stepped into the lobby.

Midmorning and midafternoon were the best times to publish a click-bait story. The traffic on the site would hammer our servers. Andy had posted this the minute I'd left his office. He'd only been waiting for me to take the bait.

The image finally finished loading, and I stared at a picture of Micah, asleep, half-naked on his own sofa, draped in a crimson throw. My blood ran cold.

As I waited for the elevator, my phone rang, incoming number unknown. I answered it anyway. "Is this Jo Wilder? Hi, I'm a reporter from the—" I hung up, cursing the vultures. How'd he get my cell phone number?

The minute the elevator doors opened on our floor, I rushed into the newsroom and burst into Andy's office. "Andy, how did you get that picture? I took that on my personal camera. You have to take it down!"

He smirked. "Oh, did you? Then why'd you upload it to the server here?"

I combed through my memory. Had I used my personal camera? It had been early. I'd been so hungry. I'd reached into my bag and . . . I couldn't remember. Maybe I'd taken out the wrong camera. And then Zion had uploaded everything. Everything.

I had to sit down. Dizzy. "You can't publish that, Andy."

"It was that or we run the story on Eden. You chose that story."

I balled my hands into trembling fists. "You have to pull it"

He sat down. "No. I don't."

He didn't understand. How could he? I hadn't explained it right. "Andy, I'm not just sleeping with Micah. I'm not one of those girls. We have something really special, and this is going to ruin everything. He's going to think—" My hand flew to my mouth as I realized how this story would distort my intentions with Micah all along

Andy closed his eyes and shook his head. When he looked at me again, I thought I saw pity. "Go read the article, Jo. Tell me if you really believe all that when you're done."

Zion waited for me outside Andy's office. "Josie? Are you okay?"

"Zion, what did Andy write?"

He laid a hand on my arm and looked into my eyes. "Remember what Andy does, okay? It might not be so bad."

I pushed past him to my workstation and powered up my laptop. The story loaded, and I started reading. Under the giant picture I'd taken, the statement I'd allegedly made was followed by: *Has Ms. Wilder gone "undercover"? The photo she submitted (above) gives us a fly-on-the-wall view of a morning-after with Micah Sinclair—although as documented below, this is hardly a unique perspective.*

Several smaller images scattered down the page. It was a collection of tales. A collection of cautionary tales. Each had a small paragraph to the left or right.

Micah used me for sex when he toured in France. Yeah, the sex was amazing. But he left me behind when the tour ended.

I spent three months with Micah. I thought we were having fun, but one day, he told me to stop calling. He never gave me an explanation.

All of the women were attractive. In a couple, Andy had found pictures of them with Micah. He stood smiling next to every quote. Every damning quote.

At the very bottom, I was horrified to find the picture of Victoria Sedgwick I'd taken a little over a week ago. My name ran sideways along the edge, adding a cruel irony to the entire situation. Victoria's statement knocked the wind out of me. *I thought we had something special. I really thought I loved him. I thought maybe he loved me, too.*

I remembered shooting that picture of her. I thought she'd glared at me with envy when she saw Micah with me. What had her expression really meant? Was she nursing a broken heart?

Andy was right to pity me. I was just another one of Micah's girls. My statement at the top of the article made me seem like a naïve fool—or a calculating snake. And that picture of Micah, draped in his crimson blanket. He looked like a king on his divan, waiting for his harem to come feed him his grapes.

I turned and threw up all over the floor.

Zion closed my laptop and took it out of the dock. He slid it into the computer bag and started gathering my other things.

"What are you doing?"

"Taking you home."

I looked at the mess on the floor. "Oh, God. I have to clean this up."

"No, you don't. The custodial staff has been called. Come with me."

We walked out front, and he hailed a cab. As soon as we got in, he started talking.

"What are you thinking, Jo?" His voice sounded like cotton. Cotton from miles away—from the land of cotton. I started to giggle hysterically.

"Josie." Zion turned my face toward his. He seemed so far away. In slow motion. Blurry. Dim. I stared out the window and watched the buildings pass. In the distance, my phone rang. And rang.

When we got home, he led me to the sofa and plumped a pillow behind me. He grabbed my glucose meter and pricked my finger. I watched him, but it was like it was happening to someone else.

"Did you eat any lunch, Jo?"

He found my bag and pulled out a glucose tab. "Take this. Now, Josie."

I put it in my mouth and swallowed it. He brought me a juice box, and I drank that, too. He could have handed me a plate of chocolate cake and a pint of beer. I would have eaten it all. I didn't care.

After about fifteen minutes, the world rushed back at me. "Zion?"

He came out of his room. "Oh, thank God. How are you feeling?"

"What am I going to do?"

"Right now, you're going to rest. And I'm going to make you some lunch. Then we're going to talk about it."

I closed my eyes and focused on breathing, in and out. The pain I felt after less than two weeks only proved that there was no amount of happiness that could lessen the blow of losing it all. Was it as recently as that morning I thought I'd be content with being happy for now? How could I be happy for now if it meant one day I'd be living unhappily-ever-after?

Earlier that morning, I was ready to fall into a feeling. Worse, I'd nearly excused my mom's heartbreak due to her decade of romantic fulfillment. I was furious with myself for betraying her for a fleeting emotion. I strengthened my resolve to fight that feeling. Snack boxes. How'd I allow myself to confuse food with love?

As I calmed enough to drift off for a bit, Zion handed me a plate and sat next to me. "You ready to talk?"

He'd made some kind of burrito. It wasn't as fancy as pear-ginger buckwheat pancakes, but he hadn't paid anyone to make it for me. And he didn't make a big deal out of it. He just did it because he truly loved me.

"Zion. Have I ever told you I love you?"

"Aw. I love you, too. I hate to break it to you, though. You're not my type."

I guffawed. "That's a pity. Life would have been so much easier if I were."

"Yeah? You want to get with all this?" He struck a ridiculous pose, shoulder dropped, cheeks sucked in, eyes batting in exaggeration.

"Who wouldn't?"

"True. But I think there's someone else you like more than me. Or at least you did."

"Yeah. I did."

"And now? You're not going to let that article change your feelings, are you?"

"My feelings?" It came out a sob. "Zion, he was just using me. Didn't you read the paper? He strings girls along, letting them think he loves them. And then he dumps them. And I'm one of those girls. Lord. I'm so stupid." Tears welled up in my eyes for the second time that day.

Zion went into the bathroom and brought me a wad of tissue paper. "Did we read the same article?"

I wiped my eyes and sniffed. "Why?"

He resettled himself beside me and squeezed my knee. "Yeah, he's been with a string of women. You already knew that. And those relationships all ended. You already knew that, too. And those women are now talking about it to the media. All factual."

Every word he said hurt, but I took a deep breath, interested to hear how he'd spin this nightmare. "Go on."

"At least two of those girls were groupies. They sort of advertise a no-strings-attached arrangement, you know? You don't know what Micah may have promised them. Probably nothing. They got exactly what they wanted from him. You notice none of the girls who moved on to a bigger rock star were interviewed? Why not? Why only the couple who are no longer featured in any gossip stories?"

He made a little sense, but I wasn't convinced. "So what? So they're bitter. That doesn't exonerate him at all. How can I know he isn't going to have his fun with me and then drop me, too? Look at Victoria Sedgwick. She was with one of Adam's band members last time I checked. And she claims Micah was in love with her. How am I any different?"

"She said she was in love with Micah and that she *thought* he loved her. Doesn't mean he did. And come on. Victoria Sedgwick is the biggest hanger-on. You don't know if she's even still with that band member. If she is, I wouldn't doubt she's trying to work her way up to Adam himself."

I snorted. As if anyone would get Adam to look away from Eden.

And then I remembered what Eden had said about the way Micah looked at me. And how he'd never brought a girl home. And how he'd never said he loved any of those girls.

My phone rang again. I reached into my pocketbook, hoping despite my misgivings that it would be Micah. But when I saw the incoming call was from my dad, I hit Ignore and threw the phone onto the coffee table. I couldn't deal with a lecture from him on top of everything else. I couldn't think of anything he could do but make me feel worse.

It pissed me off that just by calling, he'd already said everything to me. I knew he'd tell me to think of the shame I was bringing to him and to my family. He'd tell me to change my behavior and stop being seen with someone who disgraced me. And a small part of me wanted to pick up the phone and call him to tell him it was over with Micah so I could hear him say, "*Nalla*. Good," as if I'd done something right for a change. And then maybe he'd be proud and accept me again.

But I was thirty-three, and he'd stopped pretending to be my dad half my life ago. He couldn't tell me how to live my life or who I could love. I wasn't about to make the same mistake as him.

Then I thought, maybe I knew what he'd say to me, but he needed to hear what I had to say to him. I grabbed my phone and hit the call button. As I listened to the weird ringing, I realized it must have been past ten p.m. his time. How was he even hearing this story already?

The phone clicked through. "Anushka, baby doll." I hadn't heard his voice in a couple of months, and it always took me by surprise. Even when he was angry with me, he always moderated his tone, sounding warm and comforting. The main problem with my dad wasn't how he treated me. But it was easier to pretend he was a horrible person than to admit that I still hadn't forgiven him for never being there.

"You called?"

"Yes. I am calling you to talk about what is happening with this boy." His English had been nearly flawless, though accented, after his years living with my mom. He'd reverted to the heavier Indian accent, but it was evident he hadn't spent much time thinking in English lately. His singsong intonation sounded more like his family than him. He'd fully assimilated into his home culture. What would he do with a daughter like me?

"There's nothing to discuss. It's a tabloid article. I've done nothing wrong."

He said something in rapid Malayalam, and a woman's voice nattered in the background. "Anika, people, they know you are a Namputiri. They read this article, and they will see it as a reflection on my family. I will hear about this tomorrow."

I regretted calling. "Dad, you don't get to have this both ways. You don't get to make me a part of your family only when I'm bringing shame down on you. If you wanted me in your family, you had that choice years ago. And you left."

Zion walked behind me and rubbed my shoulders. I was grateful for his presence in my life. Even though he was my age, he'd been more of a father to me than this man on the other end of the phone. He'd looked out for me, celebrating my victories and commiserating during my failures. He'd advised me and fed me and housed me and literally saved my life.

My dad started to speak again, but I didn't need to hear anything he said. Even if he said he was wrong, that he'd made a mistake years ago or only today, I didn't care. I didn't need his recognition anymore. In a weird way, more than anything Zion had said, it was my dad's disapproval that led me to conclude that I needed to give Micah a chance to fight his corner. I always did like to play devil's advocate.

"Dad, I have to go. There's someone I need to talk to." I hung up and stood. "Zion, I'm going for a walk."

I walked to the subway and took the G train south to Park Slope. I didn't know if Micah would still be home, but I wanted to talk to him face-to-face. There was too much potential for misunderstanding.

When I turned up his street, I immediately spied a cameraman sitting on the lowest step in front of his door. Another reporter leaned against a tree across the street. I wheeled around before they saw me.

I doubled back to the coffee shop on the corner and ordered hot tea. At a table near the far wall, I stared at my phone, trying to decide who to contact first. Micah or Eden. Neither one had tried to reach me. The article had only been out a few hours. Maybe they hadn't seen it. Or maybe they were trying to figure out what they were going to do about it.

The only thing in my notifications, besides a dozen calls from unknown numbers, had been a mention on Facebook. I opened that up to find that Marisa Bennet, Mom's bitch of a neighbor, had dropped the article about Micah on my mom's wall. *Nice to see Josie Wilder is making the most of her time in NY.*

I grimaced at her tackiness. Yeah, so my mom had proudly posted every single thing that my name ever appeared on for all the world to see, with the very blatant exception of this latest article. Marisa wasted no time attempting to slut shame my mom through me. But my mom had spent the better part of her life dealing with bitches like Marisa, and her response was possibly the greatest thing to happen since the whole debacle began.

Come on, Marisa. You know you'd hit that if the opportunity presented itself.

If I'd had any temptation to defend myself, that mic drop allowed me my first solid laugh of the day. I was still chortling when the phone rang again. I didn't recognize the number, but had a crazy, fleeting worry that Micah might be trying to reach me. I hit Answer, and the man's mosquito voice droned on immediately about the money they'd pay me for an in-depth interview. All I had to do was sell them a slice of my life.

I hung up, and blew on my tea, wondering if I should wait out the reporters on Micah's stoop or push through and knock on his door. Before I could make up my mind, Zion texted me a link to a competitor's site with a video of Micah posted in a sea of targeted ads. *This Williamsburg woman controlled her glucose with one weird trick.*

The headline read "Fame-Whore Micah Sinclair Confirms He's Dating Tabloid Photographer Jo Wilder." My fingers shook as I fished my earbuds out of the side of my pocketbook and hit Play on the video.

Micah opened his front door, dressed in a pair of faded skinny jeans and a white T-shirt with a red Japanese sun on the front.

At least he hadn't stepped out in his pajamas.

He approached the cameraman closest to him, offering his hand. My mouth dropped open at the unfolding shark attack, and I thought, *Run, Micah, run!* but he couldn't hear me.

He tapped the cameraman on the shoulder when his handshake went ignored. "Hey. Sam, right? What's going on?"

The cameraman shooting the video moved in closer and called out the question they'd been sent to ask. "Do you have any comments on the article posted in the *Daily Feed* today?"

A shadow of confusion passed across Micah's face, but he controlled his features quickly. "I'm sorry. I'm not aware of any article. What do you wanna know?"

"Is it true you're currently dating Jo Wilder?"

Micah's smile broadened. "Is that what brings you here? Is that the news of the day?"

"She's quoted saying you two are dating."

Micah turned up the sidewalk and started walking. "If she's saying that, it must be true, right?"

The first cameraman started walking backward shooting pictures or video. He asked, "Do you want to comment on it?"

If they'd rattled Micah, he didn't show it. With his usual charm, he calmly told them, "If you don't mind, I'd like to talk to her about all this before I comment."

They tag-teamed the questions as they pursued him, pressing for the real scandal and hoping to get a reaction. "What about the other women in the article?"

He didn't stop walking. If it had been me, I would have stopped. He just said, "As I said, I haven't read the article you're referring to."

But then the reporter recording the video asked, "Are you sleeping with a tabloid journalist to get more media coverage?" and Micah shot him a dirty look.

The other reporter alley-ooped with "Are you sure she didn't sleep with you to get that insider photo?"

Micah picked up his pace and turned his back on them both, but the camera followed him to the end of the street until he opened a door and went into a coffee shop.

This coffee shop.

Chapter 24

Two cameramen hung around on the sidewalk outside the huge front window, pacing back and forth like prowling wolves. From where I sat, the entire barista island obscured my view of the door, so Micah could have come in while I was messing with my phone. A terrifying, wonderful thought crossed my mind: *He could be sitting at a table on the other side of this very room.*

And if he was, he'd probably be pulling up the article and learning how badly he'd been portrayed. As hurt as I was by that story, I could imagine he'd feel even worse—taken completely off guard and betrayed.

I stood and walked along the counter toward the front. I peered around the corner. Sure enough, he'd taken a seat in full view of the two cameramen and held his phone in front of him as he read. I glanced outside surprised those two hadn't breached the entrance at my appearance. Andy would have expected any of his staff to take a seat at the next table with the video rolling—until the staff kicked us out or called the cops.

Micah lifted his eyes from his phone and saw me. "Josie." The careful composure he'd held in front of the two inquisitors broke—his tight mouth melted into a frown, and his nostrils flared as he sucked in air. I couldn't tell if he was relieved or pissed.

He stood and indicated the chair across from him.

"Hello, Micah." I set my tea on the table and scooted in. The speech I'd memorized on the way over threatened to evaporate the longer I looked at him. And dear Lord, I could smell him. I swallowed hard. "Can I go first?"

He shifted in his seat slightly but didn't hesitate. "Yes."

I'd intended to question him about all the girls straightaway, but after seeing what that article was doing to him—and all because of me—I knew I couldn't grill him until I'd set the record straight about why that article had even published. I needed his absolution before I could even consider giving him mine.

"First, that picture of you on your sofa. I swear I didn't know I'd taken that on my work camera. Zion accidentally sent it in with all my other pictures on Friday."

His expression remained inscrutable. Did he hate me? I pressed on.

"And I had no idea Andy was writing *this* article. I did tell him we were dating—he already knew it anyway—and I knew he'd write something about it, but I didn't know it would be so bad. I promise you, no matter what it looks like, I did *not* start seeing you with the intention to get some kind of inside story."

He blinked twice. "Really? This article comes out, and you're worried that I'm going to be mad at you?"

A weight lifted from my shoulders. "You're not mad?"

He put his hand out, and I took it. "Josie, it was only a matter of time before the media figured this out. And you had to know when the story broke, it wasn't going to flatter either of us."

"Micah, even the reporters from other newspapers assume I infiltrated your family to exploit you from the inside."

"Eden thought the same thing at first. You might hit a rough patch with her after all this, to be honest. But if you were going to exploit me or my friends, you'd think you'd go for juicy secrets. Why would you start a relationship and then report on that relationship? When you start printing things about my secret basement gym, we'll have words." He winked.

"Eden thought I was a spy?" I felt sick. The impending article about her pregnancy would only confirm her suspicions and fuel her hatred of me. For a heartbeat, I considered telling Micah everything, but then I remembered the whole reason Eden wanted to keep the secret was so she could be the first to tell her family. I'd only be making things worse if I blew her moment with her big brother. Plus, I had time to warn her still. Adam would be home soon, and Andy promised me a week.

Micah shrugged, completely oblivious to the land mines I was navigating. "You have to know how much she hates your boss and by extension everyone in your profession. But you must have done something to win her over. She thinks you're great."

"Not after this, I'm sure."

"Josie, you didn't share anything I wouldn't have told them myself if they'd only asked me. But obviously, it wasn't even interesting enough to them as a story on its own. Though I wish it had been."

"Yeah."

He retracted his hand and sat up like a schoolboy. "I suppose you have some questions for me."

I sipped my tea, parsing through the long litany of questions I'd intended to press him with, but sitting here face-to-face with him, everything Zion had said echoed in my mind. I settled on something simple but important. "Did you ever tell any of those girls you were in love with them?"

He leaned toward me, elbows on the table. "No. And I wasn't."

"They all sounded like they believed you were. Or at least as though they thought you cared more than you did."

"They're romanticizing the past, Jo. They may believe what they're saying, but none of it is exactly true."

I pulled the article up on my phone and asked, "Did you abandon Annie in France?"

"No. I abandoned her in Spain."

I flinched.

He frowned. "Sorry. Bad time to joke." He shifted and threw a glance at the cameramen outside, but he didn't seem to register they were there. He could have been watching the waitress pouring coffee a table over.

His eyes never lost that intense faraway look as he thought

back. "I met Annie when I toured with Adam's band. She wanted to ride with us for a few days. I wasn't seeing anyone else at the time, and I'd grown bored of traveling with those guys, stir-crazy." He scratched the scruff on his chin. "She was really nice—and there. And I really like sex. Okay?"

I winced even though none of this was new information. I'd always known his reputation, but there'd never been so many faces bringing his cartoon-like promiscuity to life. And Micah didn't cast his eyes down or blush or show any signs of shame. His eyes locked on mine. "Look, I was twenty-nine, playing huge stadiums for the first time in my life, and I didn't tell her not to follow us across the South of France to Barcelona. I wasn't in love with her, and I never promised her anything."

"So you left her there?"

He sipped his coffee as a couple passed by our table on their way to the door. Then he resumed. "Actually, I asked her to come with us to New York, but she had family in France. She chose to stay behind. We emailed for a little while, but we had nothing at all to talk about. We were never really together. If she says I was using her, I could say the same about her. It might not be a storybook romance to write home about, but she wasn't upset when it ended."

I processed that and accepted it. If I was going to judge any-one for a series of meaningless physical relationships, I'd need to sit Zion down and have a talk. I'd never judged anyone else for separating sex from romance, so I needed to grant the same forgiveness to Micah, no matter how it felt. "So what happened with . . . Martina? She said you were together for three months before you told her to stop calling."

He pressed his lips together. "Yeah. So, not so much."

"She's lying?"

He exhaled through his nose, half laugh, half snort. "Martina showed up at some point at a show. She made it clear she was interested in coming to my room. I wasn't seeing anyone else at that time. And did I mention I really like sex? I'm pretty sure I did."

I clenched my fists together and relaxed them. "So you started to see her?"

He pinched the bridge of his nose. "No. She started to see me."

"What?"

"She was always there at all the shows we played. I don't know how long that went on. She says three months. It could have been. It wasn't a consecutive three months. It was a night here and there. And after a while, we'd hang out some. We went out to eat or did something in town to blow off steam. But I never saw her between towns.

"And then during a hiatus, I started seeing Lauren—who isn't interviewed in this article, you'll notice. Things didn't work out with Lauren either, but that's another story. The next time Martina came to a show, I told her I was in a relationship and couldn't hang out with her."

"Did she keep trying?"

"I guess. I never thought she was looking for anything more than a hookup. She didn't even have my phone number or email, so I wouldn't have told her to stop calling. I might have told her she shouldn't keep trying to hang out. I don't mean to freak you out, but there are a lot of women like Martina at shows. They aren't usually looking for a long-term relationship."

"And you like sex." I raised an eyebrow at him. "What about Victoria? She didn't seem to be in it for the sex."

He fell back in his chair. "You may not believe me, but I have no idea what Victoria is talking about. Maybe she thought they asked her about someone else. I've never had anything with her. Ever. Maybe she wanted to be featured in a story. I swear." He held my gaze for a beat and said, "You're going to have to decide if you trust me more than a quote in a tabloid article, Jo."

A knock on the window caught my attention. A cameraman had pressed his lens up to the glass, pointed right at us. I sorely wanted to give the guy the finger, but all that would accomplish would be getting my picture in the paper looking like a jerk. Nobody would see it from my point of view. They'd never see that guy spying on us. On a sudden impulse, I lifted the strap off the back of my chair and grabbed my camera out. I pointed it right back at the paparazzo in the window and clicked a photo.

Micah laid his hands on the table and stared at his thumbnail as if it held magical properties. "Jo, are you going to want an explanation for all of these? I know it sounds terrible, but for the past couple of years, women have literally thrown themselves at me. I can't change all of that. But it's not like we spent a lot of time talking about our futures."

"So you're just a man-whore."

"I'm a man-whore?"

"Yes. You are a man-whore who really likes sex. Did I mishear you?"

He coughed. "With you, I love sex." He touched my arm, and a chill traveled up my spine. "But Josie, I'm not some kind of sex addict. You don't have to worry about me here or out on the road. I've got some self-control."

I thought of the first night we spent together, sleeping in my room. "Yeah. I believe that."

"I want to be with you, only you. You're special to me." He reached across the table for my hand. "Josie, I love you."

The sincerity in his eyes gave me pause. For that moment, I trusted him completely. I opened my mouth to tell him I loved him, too, but then the door swung open, and a man took a seat at a table across from us. He laid his phone in front of him and began flipping through the sugar packets with interest—which was odd because he hadn't ordered anything to drink.

"I've got to get out of this fishbowl, Micah." I stood to gather my things.

Micah jumped up. "Will you walk with me to my place at least? Can we finish this conversation?"

As we left the coffee shop together, the cameramen divided and conquered. One approached Micah. The other walked beside me. I ignored the guy peppering me with questions and lifted my camera to shoot video of the other guy, clearly harassing Micah all the way up the street.

"How long have you been seeing each other? Did you start dating Jo before you broke up with Isabelle?"

Micah got the easy questions. My inquisitor wanted to know if I was using Micah for sex or if I was using sex to further my career. Watching all this unfold through my lens placed it at a distance, like watching someone else's life being torn to shreds. I lowered the camera out of curiosity to see this person's eyes. I wanted to know what it would look like to no longer have a soul.

It was a miscalculation. As soon as he saw my face, his strategy deviated, and he asked, "You're not stupid enough to have fallen in love with him, are you?"

I'd almost made it to Micah's townhouse without giving them anything, but the new line of questioning took me by surprise, and the tears burst forth as we neared the steps. Micah led me inside and slammed the door behind us. We hadn't exchanged a single word in those harrowing five minutes.

He wrapped his arms around me, whispering, "It's okay. It's okay."

But it wasn't okay. I broke free and sat on his sofa. Micah ran into the kitchen, and I waited, running my fingers through the soft underside of that damn crimson throw. I pulled it to my face to wipe away tears, but the smell of Micah overpowered me.

He sat beside me with one of those snack boxes, and I stared at it. Without looking up, I said, "Micah, I know you love me." I lifted my eyes. His blue eyes were so pretty. And his lips—God, his lips. "At least for now."

His face fell. "You don't think my feelings for you will last?"

"I know you think they will. And you might be right. If this were any ordinary relationship, we might have a chance to figure that out."

"What are you saying?"

"I love you, Micah." My voice had given up trying to sound emotionless. I wiped a tear off my face with the back of my arm. "Believe me when I tell you I want to make this work."

He smirked in his adorably bratty way. "I knew it." When I didn't smile back, he shifted. "But?"

"Micah, for the short time I've known you, you've done everything right, and if I thought this could last, I'd stay." I straightened my spine and steeled myself like I used to whenever I had to chase people down with my camera. Steeling myself for the kill. "But I don't know how to deal with any of this. I can't tell up from down. I can't keep going forward like this. I need some time to get my head together. Can you give me some time? Away from all that?" I pointed toward the front where right now, those two men who were just doing their job (God, how many times had I said that?) were waiting to pounce.

He stared at his feet and didn't speak right away. Finally, he said, "I'll give you all the time you need, Josie. Whatever you need. I know you'll eventually come around. When you do, I'll be waiting." He wrapped his arms around me and hugged me for a solid minute.

It would have been so easy to fall into him. Pratosh could cook for us, and we'd kiss and kiss and kiss. I wanted it so bad it hurt.

But I needed to take care of myself first. And I was damn good at forgoing temptation.

I grabbed my gear and stood. "I need to go."

Micah called his service, gave me one last big hug inside, told me again how much he loved me, and then walked me out through the onslaught.

Those two guys were still rolling tape as we death-marched to the waiting car. They started in on Micah first. "What's going on, Micah? Are you guys still together?"

Despite my best efforts, my lips trembled. I gritted my teeth, but before we'd made it to the car, I lifted my hand involuntarily to wipe a tear off my face. Then the camera was in my face. "Josie, did Micah dump you?"

Micah pressed between me and the camera. "Give her some space, guys. Come on." He shielded me until he had to open the door. As soon as he moved out of the way for a heartbeat, the camera filled in the empty space.

When the door closed, I heave-sobbed, submitting to the emotions I'd bottled up for the past hour—and the past fifteen years. The driver asked me for the address, and I lifted my head to give it to him. A reporter loomed in the right side of the windshield, camera pressed to the glass, recording my complete breakdown. Micah passed in front of the car and grabbed the guy by the elbow, jerking him away.

As the car drove off, I turned and watched as Micah, red-faced and angry, yelled at the reporters while they stood by recording it all.

Chapter 25

Naïvely, I thought I could go home and decompress. Alone at my apartment, I could brew some tea, take a hot bath, shut out the world. And wait for the world to forget about me.

But when the car pulled up at my apartment, photographers I'd worked with at other events were hunkered down outside my apartment. One of them had a big fancy camera—the kind with an external microphone. I lowered my eyes and put my hand up to block my face. While I punched in my key code, they pestered me with their fascination. They wanted to know if I'd intentionally dated Micah to get a story. They wanted to know if I'd fallen in love while in the trenches. They wanted to know if we'd split up because I didn't need him for anything anymore. Or had we split up because he no longer needed me?

Apparently, they were building the story of beauty and the beast, and they hadn't yet decided which part I'd played.

A woman who'd bothered to wear a nice two-piece suit pushed through to ask me, "Jo, what on earth were you thinking?"

The oppressive shit storm might have relented if those rubberneckers outside Micah's hadn't captured video of his alleged ex-girlfriend blubbering in the back of the car he'd deposited me into. Throw in video of an angry Micah yelling, "*Just leave her alone now,*" and you've got a recipe for the kind of chum that draws more sharks.

The reporters supplied their own narrative, painting Micah as a shallow playboy who'd dumped me in the same way as he'd dropped every other girl.

Exhibit #1: *Inside Scoop* posted the headline "Micah Sinclair Adds Another Notch to the Bedpost. Who Wants to Be Next?"

Exhibit #2: *The Dish* said "Coyote Micah Sinclair Gnaws His Own Arm Off in Record Time."

Micah made no comment to dispel that interpretation, taking the brunt of the gossip. And nobody wanted the nuanced truth over a sensational lie anyway.

My phone turned into something that reminded me more of a sex toy than a communication device. I could ignore the chatter about me online, but the reporters kept intruding into my real life with their incessant attempts to milk an easy story, even though it wasn't even big news. And I had one bitter thought— seeing cutthroat reporters in action brought home how badly I'd always sucked at this job. And I knew I couldn't keep doing it.

But the road to freedom was paved in quicksand. I emailed Sang Moon-Soo to ask him again if he had space for me in his department. He'd published both articles I'd sent him, so I knew he was happy with my work. He wrote back, "Not yet. Unless you want to work freelance."

I didn't. I needed the health insurance of a salaried job, and with nothing else to fall back on, I had to suck it up and go in to the office.

As soon as I got to my workstation, Kristin and Jennifer were kind enough to come over and give me a hug, telling me not to worry, everything would blow over. Kristin whispered, "And we're both dying of jealousy that you got to shag that beautiful man."

Leonard kept me amused with his nonstop tales about all the times he'd almost been a part of the story.

Not surprisingly, Derek sided with the scumbag reporters, insisting I'd brought it all on myself. "You forgot your place, Jo. You're the scenery, not the main attraction."

Sitting at my desk, sharing the same hemisphere as Andy made me feel nauseated. But until the vultures lost interest, the attention made it impossible for me to work outside. When Andy eventually asked me to come into his office, he seemed neither contrite nor malevolent. For him, it was just another day.

He shuffled some papers on his desk, not even bothering to look me in the eye. "I know I've been a little hard on you lately, Scout."

He had a nerve to act like he'd only slighted me. "Is that what you call throwing me under the bus with that article?"

Now he looked up. "I've been worried that you lack the guts to do this job. The fact that you were so willing to put yourself directly in front of that bus to derail a better story concerns me."

"I thought you said the Micah story was better."

His lip curled in amusement. "Hardly. The story wasn't better. Having it come out yesterday, though . . . especially with that whole circus last night. Well, it all makes today's story that much more potent." He barked a harsh laugh. "Congratulations, you finally brought me something useful, Scout."

My mouth felt dry. "You wouldn't go back on your word. You promised."

"I promised I'd push Eden's story. And I did."

"You promised you'd push it till next week!"

"Your words, not mine."

"You bastard. If you run that story . . ." I searched for a suitable threat. "I'll write a scathing report on you and send it to HR."

He chuckled. "Oh, you'll tell them I did my job? Who do you think brings in the money to pay their salaries?"

"You are a pathetic little man." I gritted my teeth and choked back threats to shove a pen up his ass. "You have no ethics, no integrity." I realized I sounded like L.L. Stylez, and a light went off in my head. I needed to leave with or without a fallback. I could go home to Atlanta if it came to that. I put my hands up. "I can't do this anymore. You're a poison, Andy." And now I channeled Eden.

He yawned. "Anything else, Josephine?"

I wondered if I could get off on a plea of temporary insanity, but I counted to three and resisted the strong desire to strangle him. "I hope one day you'll get what's coming to you, Andy."

As I turned to go, Andy said, "Wait a minute."

I stopped in the doorway, praying he'd reconsider running the story about Eden to keep me there.

But all he said was "Leave your camera here. It's not your property."

I dropped the camera on his desk and walked out the door. When I got halfway across the room, my knees wobbled. I put my hand on a desk and caught myself.

Zion jumped up and put his arm around my back, taking my weight and helping me to a stool. "Are you all right?"

I laughed, but only to keep from crying. "I think I just quit."

"What?"

"I kind of told him I hope he dies." I stewed in my indignation. "That dirty little man is planning to run a story he promised me he wouldn't run until next week."

"The story about Eden?"

"Yeah. How'd you know?"

"Because it's already live." He went to his desk and fetched his tablet.

I read the first lines, heart sinking. *Eden Sinclair pregnant? Josephine Wilder, a day after her breakup with Micah Sinclair, has confirmed the news. There is still some speculation . . .*

"Oh, holy shit. He totally used me! This is completely misconstrued."

A photo loaded with my name sideways along the edge. That picture of Adam with his arms around Eden, hands flat on her midsection. The quality was subpar because Andy had to zoom in so far on that photo. I should have known he'd figure it out. I should have deleted it when I had the chance.

I read the text again. "Now I get it. He totally planned this."

Zion rubbed my shoulders. "Josie, you need to calm down."

I was shaking from anger. "That fucker. I'm going to bring him down."

"Go home. Get some lunch. Take a nap. Those are my orders. Okay? Do you hear me?"

I nodded, but I had no intention of going home. I dropped from the stool, trying to figure out how I'd ever fix this. "I'll see you later, Zion."

Zion called after me. "Go home, Josie. Don't try to do anything right now. Wait until it blows over."

But I was already emailing Eden before I'd left the building.

> Eden,
> I swear I had nothing to do with the article
> that posted today. I didn't break the news to
> Andy. He had someone following you and figured
> it out.
> Please call me.
> Jo

She didn't respond. I wasn't surprised. I hadn't talked to her since Micah's story ran, assuming I'd have time over the next week to figure out how to explain it and warn her to go ahead and share the news with her family when Adam came home. For all I knew, she'd already written me off the day before when the story on Micah ran, and this article was the final nail in my coffin. It looked so bad, even Micah might conclude Eden's suspicions had been justified all along.

I dodged a lone reporter, jumped on the subway to Park Slope, and walked to Micah's. There were no cameramen out today. I figured they'd all be swarming outside Eden's door. If I brought the paparazzi nightmare to her stoop, she really would never talk to me again. I knocked on Micah's door, but there was no answer, so I sat and waited. He'd have to come out or come home eventually.

After an hour, a woman approached and started up the steps. She wore a housekeeping outfit and carried cleaning supplies.

I stood. "Are you Anna?"

She nodded.

"Can you let Micah know I'm out here?"

She let herself in and then peeked out. "Mr. Sinclair is not home."

The temperature had dropped as a dark cloud obliterated the sun. I walked down to the corner coffee shop, ordered a hot tea, and sat at a corner table near the front, hoping lightning might strike twice and Micah would stroll in again. I took out my phone and started an email to Kate in human resources.

Kate,

I'd like to file a formal complaint against Andy Dickson. In the past week, he has asked me to skirt journalistic ethics on a number of occasions. I realize the company turns a blind eye to his activities since these actions increase the revenue for the company, but nonetheless, I feel it's important to document his bad behavior.

1. Last week, he asked me to give him information that was off the record after I had lunch with a musician he obsessively (and psychotically) hounds.

2. He also rewrote a story I'd submitted, changing the tone of it from neutral and newsworthy to vicious and derogatory. And he disregarded the photo I'd submitted. Instead, he combed through my files and found the most unflattering one. He then posted the story with my name on the byline, misrepresenting my work.

3. Finally, he made a verbal promise to me on Monday that he would not run a story (about that musician he stalks) until next week provided I give him some information for another story. And even though I upheld my end of the bargain, he went against his word and posted both stories anyway. This has had serious ramifications on my personal life.

Please consider taking action against him.

Jo Wilder

Reading it back, I realized how insane it all sounded. Most people would rightfully say I was only bitching about how the sausage was made. Complaining about a lack of ethics in tabloid journalism was akin to complaining about a lack of dryness in water.

I sent it anyway. More than likely, I was already out of a job. If Andy hadn't taken my statements as a resignation, surely, he'd started the paperwork to have me terminated.

As I swirled my tea, I began to relax. For the first time in a day, nobody pursued me. Nobody expected me to be anywhere. Nobody expected me to hunt humans for sport. I was nobody. I had no agenda. It felt liberating. And it gave me time to think.

I stared at the picture of Micah in concert I'd used for my screen saver. It took me right back to that moment before we'd been together, back to when I thought I'd have been happy to spend one blissful night with him. Why did everything have to get so complicated?

My heart wanted Micah. I was miserable without him. It didn't take a genius to realize that he'd likely be the great love of my life. If I let him go, I'd probably regret it forever. On the other hand, forever with Micah might turn out to be a month. He'd burned through so many women so fast. What if he tired of me and my pain-in-the-ass never-ending disease? Was it worth the risk? Was "happy for now" enough?

I could honestly say it beat the shit out of "unhappy for now."

Still, he came with so much baggage. I wasn't just dating him. I was dating the media, and through them, the entire world. And I was dating his sister, to be honest. But Micah knew how to handle the media. They'd grow bored with us in time. And if I could get Eden to stop hating me, I'd be friends with my boyfriend's sister. So there was that.

I closed my eyes and resolved to filter out the less valid objections, throwing out fears of the unknown and external pressures I had no control over. And that's when it hit me: I'd done everything to Micah I'd worried he'd do to me. And in the process, I'd behaved exactly like my dad—for different reasons, to be sure. I'd let everything outside our relationship drive me away from Micah.

And he'd done nothing but show me devotion.

But it was very possible that the double-barrel shotgun stories in the paper two days in a row had opened a fatal wound in my relationship with him. And I couldn't find him to assess the damage or repair it. I needed to find him and explain everything.

It suddenly occurred to me that I had access to world-class celebrity stalkers. I texted Zion, *I can't find Micah. Call or text me.*

Within minutes, he wrote, *Josie where are you?*

I went to talk to Micah but he's not home. Do you have any idea where he might be?

Go home, Jo. You can deal with it later.

Can you contact Adrianna and ask if she's seen him?

My phone rang a minute later. Zion.

"Josie, Adrianna's not answering my calls. I'm sure she thinks the bus is coming for her tomorrow."

"Why would she think that?"

"Think about it, Jo. First Micah. Then Eden. She doesn't know you're not giving up the information. I think Adrianna's going into a media blackout just in case."

"Oh, God."

"Don't worry, Jo. Tomorrow there won't be a story about her, right? Because neither of us have given it to him. And these stories will blow over, too. Go home and wait it out."

"Zion, the stories will blow over for the rest of the world, but Eden will never forgive me. And I can't blame her. She can never get back the moment when she and Adam would tell their parents first. And how can I prove to her I wasn't the one who leaked?" I choked back a sob. "I need to go see her. What if Micah's with her? What if she convinces him I'm everything she feared?"

"Stay where you are. I can come get you."

I knew if I told him where to find me, he'd take me home, so I lied. "You're right. I'll go home and wait for you."

There was only one place I could go if I wanted to deal with the fallout. It took me about an hour to take two subways to Brooklyn Heights and walk six blocks to Eden's apartment. As expected, a cameraman perched outside, biding his time. And it was Derek.

He wouldn't let me go by without a challenge. "Hey, Jo. What are you doing here?"

I shot him a dirty look as I passed and climbed the steps. The air outside smelled of cigarettes. Inside, voices rose in argument, and I feared I might be too late. My hand trembled as I knocked.

Eden opened the door slightly. "No fucking way."

"Eden, can I talk to Micah?"

"He doesn't want to talk to you. Go back to the sewer with the other rats." She closed the door, and the arguing started again inside, louder, but still muffled. I glanced at Derek, then put my ear to the door. A low male voice rumbled, but I couldn't make out the words. I stood outside and waited, hoping. I thought about knocking again, but Eden would just answer and send me away.

Defeated, I turned to leave. My legs felt like Jell-O as I descended the steps and walked up the sidewalk.

Derek followed behind, asking me, "Jo, are you trying to get Micah back?"

My stomach rumbled, and I realized how hungry I was, absolutely ravenous. I didn't have anything in my bag with me. Not a snack box. Not a single bag of gummy bears.

The camera floated in my peripheral vision as Derek kept pace alongside me. "I guess Micah's not a big fan of the media now either, huh? Good job finally breaking him of his famewhore ways."

My legs started to shake again, and I stumbled. Each step I took felt heavy. I had the ludicrous thought that the gravity of the earth had increased. I put a hand on a tree for balance and pulled out my phone to call Zion, but my hands shook too hard. And I couldn't remember how or what I was doing. I leaned against the tree and slumped to the ground. I just needed a few minutes so I'd stop feeling so dizzy.

The townhouse door opened, and Micah emerged with

Eden's hand wrapped around his bicep. He stopped and peeled her fingers off, yelling, "It's my decision, Eden."

She let go of him and shouted, "You never think, Micah. I'm just asking you to take some time and think."

But he was already halfway down the steps, casting his eyes frantically up and down the street. He shot a shitty look at Derek and then looked down at me. "Oh, my God. Josie!"

He ran down the sidewalk and fell on his knees, screaming at Derek, "You just stood there and rolled tape? Did you call an ambulance?"

Derek laughed. "Hey, man, she's drunk."

"She's not drunk, you asshole."

Micah bent down and grabbed my phone off the sidewalk. He punched in the numbers and then paced around with one hand tearing out his hair. "Zion, it's Micah." Pause. "Yes, she's here with me. What should I do? Should I call an ambulance?" His panicked sobs slowed as he listened. Finally, he nodded, and said, "Okay. Thanks." He dialed again, "Eden, I need you to do me a favor."

He spoke to her for a couple of seconds. Then he sat flat on the ground and lifted me in his arms, across his lap, caressing my hair and talking. "Josie. Oh, God, are you okay? Can you sit up?"

He leaned forward and laid a kiss on my forehead, then rocked me until Eden came outside and gave him a glass of orange juice. He stroked my hair while I sipped on it. After a few minutes, I sat up on my own. Together, Eden and Micah looped their arms around me and helped me stand up and walk back up the steps into the townhouse.

Once inside, Micah sat me on a sofa and dropped beside me, elbows on knees, looking like he'd been through hell. He wiped his face with the back of his hand. "Josie, I'm so, so sorry."

He threw a glance at Eden. Eden backed out of the room and left us alone.

Micah's voice broke when he started to talk. "Josie, you scared the hell out of me. When I saw you lying on the ground, I thought the worst." He grabbed my hands like he wanted to make sure I wouldn't leave. He pulled me toward him, and his arms around me made me feel safe and protected. I wrapped my arms around him, too. He hugged me tight, and his heart beat fast in his chest.

"Micah." I leaned back to look into his eyes.

A tear rolled down his cheek. He scrubbed it off and swallowed. "Yesterday, when you asked for time, I let you go because I believed you'd come back in time. And I know I said I'd wait for you. I meant that. I would wait for you for the rest of my life. But today I realized I could lose you, for real, forever. And what if you never came back? You're everything to me. I love you, and I need you." He held my face in his and said, "Anika Jo Wilder, I don't want to wait for you."

He was right—today might be the only day we ever had. I tasted the tears running over my lips. "Micah, are you going to still want this tomorrow?"

"Tomorrow." He laid a kiss on my forehead. "And the day after that. As long as you'll have me. No, longer than that because I won't let you go again without a fight."

He'd just said the magic words. "You won't have to. I love you, and I trust you. And I need you, Micah. I can't possibly live without you."

He smiled that big smile, the one that made his dimple appear.

Then he kissed me proper. And, oh, how I'd missed that. But we had a mess to clean up. "Micah, can we talk about the news story? I want to explain everything to you. And to Eden."

Before we'd made a move, a knock on the door brought Eden back through the living room, and I worried for a moment it might be Derek, invading her personal space further. I followed Eden to the foyer, relieved to discover Zion standing in the open doorway. There was no sign of Derek or any other paparazzi out front.

Eden led us all into the kitchen. Despite everything, it took me a moment to recover from the shock of seeing Adam at the table, nursing a beer in his own home. I hadn't realized he'd come back from Japan already.

Micah said, "You remember Josie, right? You guys met two weeks ago."

He nodded, and then his eyes tracked Eden. I guessed he planned to follow her lead where I was concerned. Was I still the enemy? Had she forgiven me? Or did she just feel bad for my collapse?

Micah held a chair out for me, and I sat. Zion had brought my glucose meter. While I messed with that, Micah went to the fridge and rummaged around. He came back with everything he could find and laid it before me. A cornucopia of options. My numbers were still low, so I grabbed the lone piece of fruit but snagged a couple of pieces of cheese as a chaser.

Once he had me all settled, he came back, and the four of us sat around the table, occupying our hands with our food and drinks, waiting for someone to break the ice.

Finally, I said, "Eden, I want you to know that I didn't tell Andy about you. He had Derek following you, and they saw you coming from the OB/GYN and then watched you buy prenatal pills. He wanted to run the story on Monday, but I worked out a deal. He promised he wouldn't run the story about you for another week. But he broke the promise."

"What was the deal?" She gripped her beer bottle and took a swig.

As hard as it was, I maintained eye contact with her. I needed her trust. "First, I had to tell him who Micah was seeing." I licked my lips. It sounded every bit as bad. "Knowing that it was me, I figured that was my information to give. Little did I know, he had already figured that out and only needed me to confirm it."

"That makes sense."

"But there was one more thing." I took a sip of juice, postponing the inevitable. "He asked me to confirm that I knew you were pregnant."

She sucked on her teeth, glaring.

"I figured it was better to buy you the week. You were planning to tell your mom and Micah soon. And he wouldn't postpone the story forever. But he obviously had nothing but circumstantial evidence, and he tricked me into giving him the proof. And I'm very sorry."

Her expression darkened. I wished I could go back in time and do everything differently. How could I go on with her hating me? I was prepared for her to shut me out, but instead she relaxed and took my hand. "And I'm so sorry about what happened before. I had no idea you were so sick."

"I know. And I understand why you were angry. Under the circumstances, you had every right to be."

Zion interrupted, phone in hand. "Hey, guys. I got a text from one of our coworkers. Derek just posted video on the site."

Eden threw a sideways glance at Adam. "Can you grab my tablet?"

Adam hopped up and came back a moment later. It amused me that one of the biggest rock stars in the world turned into a puppy around Eden. I looked over at Micah and recognized that same expression on his face. I thought he'd do anything I asked of him.

Eden's fingers flew across the device until she had the video up from earlier. She motioned for me to come around the other side of the table, and I watched over her shoulder as she hit Play.

Typically, Andy had gone for the most vicious headline:

"Micah Sinclair's Ex-girlfriend Stalks Him, Passes Out Drunk on the Street."

I cringed seeing myself stagger down the steps. She upped the volume when Micah came out. Then Derek said, "Hey, man. She's drunk."

The video ended, and Eden narrowed her eyes. "Does Andy know you're diabetic?"

"Yeah. Why?"

She smiled for the first time since I'd gotten there. "Would he really think you were drunk?"

"Yeah, he's an idiot."

She locked eyes with me, and I could see the wheels spinning. "How badly do you want to keep your job?"

"Actually, I think I might have already quit."

"You think? What did you say?"

"I basically told him, 'I hope you die,' and walked out of the office."

Her lips twisted as she worked that out. Then her expression softened, and she nodded. "Jo, would you like to get even with Andy?"

I locked eyes with her. "Absolutely."

Chapter 26

Mr. And Mrs. Howard Sinclair
Request the honor of your presence
At the marriage of their daughter
Eden
To
Adam Copeland
Saturday the nineteenth of September
Private location—contact Adam or Eden for details

Adrianna handed me the wedding invitation when she buzzed up the next morning, wearing a brown uniform and holding a clipboard under one arm.

I stood back to let her in. "You didn't have any trouble with the paps downstairs?"

"Oh, no. I go all over the place like this. You wouldn't believe how few people take note of the UPS guy. I throw this on, and I could walk right up to a counter and order lunch."

"Do you think that would work for me?" We'd all agreed I couldn't be seen with Micah until this farce played out since Andy thought we'd broken up. A nice disguise might let us cheat.

She giggled. "I don't think so. You'd look like you were wearing a costume. The beauty of my disguise is that it's so different from what people expect to see. When I'm Adrianna, I'm so ridiculous that nobody notices me hiding in plain sight."

I scratched my head. "When you're Adrianna? Who are you now?"

She tapped the name tag on her chest. "I'm Andrew."

"How do you manage to keep it all straight?"

She cocked her head. "Oh, honey. This is how I've lived for years."

"Lord. It must be so hard."

"Yeah. But sometimes I meet someone magical, like Zion, who sees through all this. And that makes it all a little easier."

One day I'd get her to tell me her whole story. But it wouldn't be today. I needed to get into the office.

Adrianna picked up the invitation. "There are more of these. If things don't work out today, we'll have to find another way."

I took it from her and slid it into my pocketbook. "Thanks for your help on this."

"My pleasure. I'd do anything for Adam, and I miss the fun we used to have messing with the tabloids."

She gathered her things and put her cap on. I had no doubt she'd dissolve right back into the crowd. I didn't envy her complicated existence, but I envied her ability to disappear at will.

But today, I needed to be conspicuous. I wanted to wear makeup to effect a hangover, but both Eden and Micah regretfully informed me that my complexion was sallow enough already. An evening in a near coma had taken care of my healthy glow.

Micah had asked me if I was even up for shenanigans, offering me an out. "You could just come home and hang out with Oscar and Felix and me."

But I was up for it. I had my own reasons to exact revenge on Andy fucking Dickson. And it didn't hurt to know that Eden would forever love me for going through with it. She deserved her own revenge.

I returned to the office before noon. Zion sat at his desk already and gave me the slightest chin raise in greeting. I slipped the invitation out of my pocketbook to lay it on his desk, but he shook his head. I ran my eyes over to Derek's desk. He wasn't there. Crap.

Zion said a little too loud, "Josie, why aren't you at home? You look terrible."

Andy flung open his door and stared at me. "You? Get in here, now."

I dropped my head down, feigning shame and fear. "Yes, sir."

He waited until I'd entered the office and then slammed the door. He rounded his desk and faced me. "First, you send a complaint about me to HR. And now, you're back? Are you hoping to pick up your last paycheck? Or turn in your credentials? One of those might be an option."

His face had turned the color of eggplant. All the times I'd fought back tears in this office, and I couldn't cry at will. Instead, I scrunched my face up and sniffled. "You were right about everything."

"What?" A piece of spittle stuck to his lower lip, but he wasn't the least bit self-aware. "You finally figured out they don't give a shit about you, right? That act Micah put on for the cameras was just for show, wasn't it? What happened? Did he stop answering your calls? Or did he actually tell you he didn't want to date some psycho stalker who showed up drunk at his sister's house banging on the door after she gave up all his family's secrets?"

I bit my tongue so I wouldn't say, "You gave up all his family's secrets." I had a response better than words. "I understand you might want to fire me and—"

"Damn straight. Your behavior has been completely unacceptable, Jo."

I added an extra waver to my voice. "About yesterday . . ."

His nostrils flared, and I watched the light go off in his head. "That video is undeniable proof that you're completely unsuitable for this line of work. I'll be adding it to my counter complaints to send to HR."

I reached toward him. "Oh, please. Don't." I worried I might have veered into melodrama. "I swear I wasn't drunk. I hadn't eaten in hours, and I went into hypoglycemic shock."

He hesitated. He'd already gone on public record accusing me of intoxication. He'd have to retract the story if he chose to believe me. His tongue ran across the front of his teeth. He stepped to the door. "Derek, get your ass in here."

I craned my neck and saw Derek shoving back a Styrofoam box of street meat. He hopped up, wiping his lips with a napkin, and entered Andy's office. "What's up? Oh, hi, Josie." Just like that, as if he hadn't stood by and filmed me slipping into a coma.

Andy didn't mince words. "Derek, you said Jo was drunk last night when you saw her. She claims she was in some kind of shock."

"Hypoglycemic shock," I offered helpfully.

Derek scoffed. "You saw the video. She was tanked, staggering all over the sidewalk. Classic drunk."

"Thanks, Derek. You can go."

Andy wiped the spittle off his lips with the back of his hand. "Look. You were upset. You mistook a media slut's interest in you as something real. It could happen to anyone." He chuckled. "Well, not really, but you're about the most naïve journalist I've had the misfortune to hire."

"You're right. I—" I couldn't deny that, not out loud anyway. Not if I wanted him to believe Micah had dumped me.

"So you got a little drunk and threw yourself at him. It's embarrassing. I can understand why you'd want to play it off as some kind of illness."

"Andy, I wasn't drunk."

His eyes lit up with glee. "I hope you felt humiliated seeing it all over the Internet. I sure did enjoy it." His lips curled into a nasty sneer. "You never should have crossed me, Jo."

I couldn't stand to look at his face another second, so I pushed him to act. "What are you going to do, Andy?"

"I'm going to fire your ass." He smiled, though on anyone else, one might call that expression a frown. "Now, get out of my office."

I fought my own expression of joy as I walked out of that snake pit for good. I covered my mouth as though hiding my tears. It was the only way I could keep from laughing.

Zion asked, "Is everything okay, Jo?"

Derek looked up from his pile of lamb strips with pieces of rice adhering to his chin.

I sniffed. "Andy just fired me. This has been the worst goddamn twenty-four hours of my life."

"Oh, man. Do you need me to do anything to help you?"

"No. I suppose I'll be all right." I started toward the door, but stopped. As if I had an afterthought, I produced the wedding invitation from my pocketbook and dropped it on Zion's desk. "This came in the mail yesterday. I've been carrying it around, wishing Micah might take me back." I wiped imaginary tears from my dry eyes. "But there's no way I'm going to go—not after everything. Maybe you could take my place. If you can figure out where it is, take lots of pictures and publish them everywhere."

"Is that what I think it is?" He hadn't made use of his acting skills since we'd performed in an off-campus production of *Jesus Christ Superstar,* but this job didn't require thespian chops. And he was killing it.

I dropped my face into my hands. "I can't fucking believe this is happening." I'd like to thank the Academy . . .

Zion jumped off his stool and wrapped an arm around my shoulder. "Let me at least walk you down and help you get a cab."

We walked down to the elevator together and both climbed in. When the doors closed, I asked, "Do you think he'll take the bait?"

Zion snickered. "We'll know soon enough. I left my web cam running."

I got out of the elevator on the second floor and hugged Zion. "Sorry to leave you here to deal with this shit. I'll see you at home later."

And then I walked away from that festering soul suck. I stretched my legs and stood a little taller. I'd done my part. Now I could only wait and see. And hope everyone else lived up to their end of the plan.

We couldn't meet at Micah's or Eden's because they were so often under surveillance, and I still had a few reporters following me home. So we texted or talked on the phone. But we only did the latter when we were sure nobody could overhear us.

Zion sent us all a video showing Derek picking up the wedding invitation and reading it. Derek's eyes bugged out of his head, and he looked over his shoulder at the entrance to the office. Then he disappeared. I wondered if he photocopied it or took it straight to Andy. Zion said that the invitation sat on his desk when he returned.

Would Andy print the wedding invitation and run a story leaking the date, or would he go for the bigger story? Would he try to get exclusive photographs of a private wedding?

We got our first hint later that night when Eden's parents called to find out why a reporter was asking about a secret wedding. Confused by the question, they'd told the reporter they had no idea what he was talking about. Eden would have told them to say exactly that if she'd wanted to loop them in any sooner. She said they'd more likely screw it up if they had a script to follow.

For the next two weeks Eden worked behind the scenes to organize everything else while I waited for time to pass. She called to let me know she'd taken a walk to the Brooklyn Botanical Gardens where she conspicuously spoke to directors at the all-glass Palm House. She'd already booked the hall after calling around and finding a venue that could accommodate her needs at short notice, but she wanted to make sure Andy's sleuths would have something to work with.

Adam and Adrianna were busy writing music and filming on location. Micah had performances, and reporters hounded him for a comment about the breakup with the girl he'd recently been linked to—me—but he charmed his way around them. His picture still showed up in the gossip pages, but mostly "seen out and about."

It killed me that I had to stay away from him all this time. He called every day and occasionally sent me text messages, like *Would you rather go to Bali or Scotland? This is not a hypothetical question.* But I missed seeing him. I second-guessed my involvement in this prank every time I had to resist an urge to show up on his doorstep.

Meanwhile, I saw Zion off to work in the morning, shuffled around the apartment, and went running. In the afternoon, I wandered the streets observing people. At night, I shot pictures of the Brooklyn Bridge. And every day, I watched my bank account dwindle.

Once my connection to Micah appeared to be severed, my phone quickly stopped ringing, and the reporters cleared off the sidewalk outside my apartment. Even when I saw paps I knew out on the street, they looked right past me. Without Micah beside me, my value to them dried up. Once again, I became a footnote to someone else's celebrity. A historical anecdote. As it turned out, that didn't bother me one bit.

After a week of near solitude and anonymity, my phone rang with an unknown incoming number. I almost ignored it, but curiosity got the best of me.

I hit Answer and hesitantly said, "Hello?"

"Josephine? Hi. This is Lars Cambridge of the *Rock Paper*."

I sat up. "Lars?"

"Yeah, hey. I'm glad I caught you. Listen, Micah sent me a link to the article your paper posted about you."

A top editor at a huge magazine was calling to talk to me, but he only wanted to talk about a tired personal scandal. I sighed. "I'm not commenting on that story, Lars."

"No, of course not. I'm not interested in the story. But I really liked the photographs credited to you. The one of Micah is stunning. Like something that should hang in the Louvre, not on the gossip pages."

"*Thank* you." I said it as a vindication for what I'd thought and quickly added, "That was exactly what I was thinking when I shot it. It's impossible to take a bad picture with a subject who already looks like a work of art."

He laughed. "Yes. But I also saw your breathtaking photo of Victoria Sedgwick. I've seen her many times before, but I'd never noticed how poignant a figure she cuts. You are way too talented for a second-rate newspaper."

"That means a lot, Lars. I didn't mean for either of those pictures to post in the paper. It was—an unfortunate confluence of events."

"I'm glad they did, or I might have missed seeing them. Look, I can't promise you anything, but I'd like to take a look at your other work. I have an idea for you, but I need you to send me whatever you can."

I slumped. "Most of my work is owned by the *Daily Feed*." I combed through my mind and tried to think what I had on hand. "But I have been building a portfolio. I can send you all of that. It might not be much."

"Great. I look forward to it." He gave me his email address, and I promised to get it to him right away.

Before he hung up, he said, "I hope things are good with Micah."

"You know the papers distorted what happened." Even as I said it, I caught the poetic justice of the situation.

Lars kindly left the obvious lesson aside. "Micah told me."

"What did he say about me?" I could hear Micah saying, *"Positively shameless fishing, Wilder."* But I was desperate for any glimmer of Micah. I missed him so much.

"He said you were a talented photographer and far too ethical to be working for Andy Dickson. And he said you were too good for him."

"I think we both know that's not true. Micah's a gem."

"Like I said, I hope things work out for you both."

I buried myself in the task of putting together a collection of photos that would show Lars my best work: the little girl with her face painted, the monks at Times Square, the chess players, the girl chasing her dog, paparazzi harassing Micah, Eden and Micah performing together, Micah floating like a god across the top of the crowd. Micah's beautiful, beautiful face as the spotlight lit him from above and hands reached for him from below.

I couldn't take it anymore and grabbed my phone. I texted, *Where are you? I'm coming to find you.*

He wrote back, *One day at a time there, Micaholic. I'm sending you something to keep you occupied.*

The next day, a nonpostmarked letter arrived containing a single ticket to a matinee showing of one of the worst plays Off Broadway. Box office sales had been so poor that the show would be pulled by the end of the week, but it would kill time. So I took a series of subways to Times Square and disappeared

into the dark and empty theater. Despite the dearth of spectators, the usher directed me to my seat at the very back of the
balcony, all the way at the end. Crappy seats at a crappy play
all alone.

But as the show started, someone sat next to me and put his
arm around me. I spun toward him so fast, I nearly fell out of
my chair. Micah sat there looking extremely pleased with himself. I wiped the cocky smirk off his face with a kiss. We didn't
see any of the play, and yet I'll never forget it.

After that, whenever Micah had a free day, I'd wake to find
either an envelope or a text message with mysterious instruc-
tions that would inevitably lead me to him. And he took me
on a personal tour of the city—Brooklyn anyway. We swapped
stories about our pasts for hours in a private meeting room at
the Brooklyn Public Library. We made plans for our future in
a balcony pew at Plymouth Church. And, more than once, we
toured the facilities of the local hotels—where we barely spoke
at all. Sneaking about added a level of excitement and daring to
an already thrilling romance. Every day I fell more in love with
Micah. And the next two weeks flew by.

On the Friday before the big event, Adam and Eden quietly
stole to the clerk's office and registered for a marriage license.

On Saturday morning, I sat in my pajamas and watched Zion
get dressed to head out. In Andy's world, I no longer had any
reason to be attending Adam and Eden's wedding, so I'd be sitting this one out. Zion promised there would be video.

And if all went according to plan, there'd be plenty of it.

I tried to distract myself with Internet games. Then I went
for a jog, fighting the temptation to head down toward Prospect
Park. Zion texted me periodically.

The eagle has landed.

I wrote him back, *Don't you dare talk in code. What's happening?*

*Andy's lurking outside the building taking pictures of the
guests.*

Is he buying it? I chewed on my thumbnail, waiting to hear
the answer. Everything hinged on Andy's complete belief.

Adrianna just showed up in a ridiculous pink taffeta brides-maid dress. That seems to have sealed the deal.

He sent me a snippet of video from his phone. Andy had found a place to perch right outside the building. It would have been a great place to get exclusive photos or video of a private wedding. Zion scanned the entire venue with his camera. The seats filled as classical music played. A "wedding photographer" moved around the room with his professional equipment. Adam stood at the front, waiting. Micah flanked him on one side, Adrianna on the other.

The wedding music began to play. Zion's video cut off, and I imagined Andy snapping photos of Eden in her last-minute gown. And then I watched the clock for several hours.

Finally, Zion opened our apartment door and dropped onto the sofa. "That was incredible."

"Everything went well?"

"Incredible. Adrianna said she'll have everything ready by tomorrow. I'm just hoping Andy doesn't post anything tonight. I don't suppose we'd be so lucky that he'd wait until Monday."

We weren't. Sunday afternoon, it came out. He'd gone all out. The website had the photocopied image of the wedding invitation and an article about how clever Andy had found the venue and gotten the exclusive photographs of Adam Copeland and Eden Sinclair's wedding. He posted video of Eden walking down the aisle and apparently exchanging vows with Adam. The only sound accompanying the video came from outside the venue—the wind rustling through the trees, people talking in the distance, Andy grunting with exertion.

Adrianna sent frantic texts, saying it would be another hour. Then another. Zion paced the floor. Finally, I got the text and saw Adrianna's tweet.

Check out my new music video.

And there it was—the music video she and Adam had shot over the past three weeks. The final scenes had been taken from the staged wedding the previous morning.

The video told a story. At the beginning, Adrianna and Adam appeared together like a happy couple. They even kissed, chaste.

Then Eden entered the scene, and Adam's interest in Adrianna clearly waned as he spent time with Eden. Adrianna stood by helpless as she watched this developing. I recognized this as the narrative that Andy had tried to manufacture three years before when he'd revealed Eden's relationship with Adam.

When the chorus came around, Adrianna held a wedding invitation. She dropped it, and the camera zoomed in on the prop to show the words. And as she sang the lyric *"always a bridesmaid, never a bride,"* the video switched to Adrianna standing beside Adam, as Eden walked down the aisle in a costume wedding dress.

It was a thing of beauty.

Within an hour, the video, along with Andy's story, had gone viral. He'd get a ton of traffic from this embarrassment, but it would be a Pyrrhic victory for him. Adrianna would get even more publicity from it, and Andy would look like a total jackass.

If he got fired after that, it would just be icing. He'd never live this down.

Zion made me some popcorn, and as I settled in to read the competitors' sites gluttonously, the intercom buzzer sounded. Zion got up and pressed the button. "Yo."

Micah answered, "Yo," and Zion let him in.

He scooted in next to me, and I slouched against him. "How's Eden doing?"

"Never better. Thanks for all your help."

I laughed. "All I did was get fired. Y'all were amazing."

"Yeah, we were."

Zion said, "Guys, you've got to look at *The Watch Dog*."

The headline read "How Far Is Too Far?"

The now viral story of an established tabloid journalist mistaking the making of a music video for an actual wedding raises important questions about the entertainment news industry. The incestuous nature of celebrities with the paparazzi often clouds . . .

My eyes glazed over. "Too wonky."

Zion tapped my foot with his. "Oh! Read this one!"

My Facebook dinged, and a message popped up from Zion with a link to an article at *Inside Scoop.*

Inside Scoop *has followed up on earlier stories posted in the* Daily Feed *and has made a shocking discovery.*

Weeks ago, Derek Peterman of the Daily Feed *shot* <u>this video</u> *of tabloid journalist Josephine Wilder passed out in front of Micah Sinclair's apartment. In the video, Mr. Peterman mocks Ms. Wilder for being drunk. Since this incident, Ms. Wilder, who was also a reporter for the Daily Feed, has been terminated for this unseemly behavior.*

However, Ms. Wilder's medical records were released to us earlier this afternoon. Ms. Wilder is a diabetic. Sources say she was not intoxicated, but suffered from hypoglycemia, brought on by extremely low blood sugar.

Asked for a comment, Mr. Peterman said, 'But she didn't look like she was sick. How could I have known?'

Coworker Zion Knight told Inside Scoop *that Ms. Wilder had been under stress after her boss Andy Dickson released a story she'd negotiated to run at a later date. Mr. Knight gave no further details about this story.*

We were unable to reach Mr. Dickson for further comment.

I held my hand up for the high five. "Zion, way to turn the story in on itself."

Zion beamed. "Hey, you use the weapons at your disposal."

On Monday morning, reporters dug up Adam and Eden's marriage license and began to raise questions about intent. Before a counter story could emerge to vindicate Andy's misinterpretation of events, Eden stopped on the street to answer the questions lobbed at her. Nobody bothered to ask her why she'd started talking to the reporters—although Andy would have surely noticed this deviation in character. The hardworking reporters were just happy to have a quote to turn in to their editors—especially the long-sought-after announcement of Adam and Eden's wedding date, set to coincide with the two-year anniversary of their engagement in October. "*We've al-*

ready booked the hall, and invitations were sent out ages ago."
This was true. But she'd also only invited trusted family and
friends.

Other articles about Andy would follow. And they'd fade into
the background. I didn't think anything would change, except
that Andy Dickson would know what it felt like to be on that
side of the story.

But with his name now a part of the cultural debate, his life
became fair game to the kind of reporting he'd perfected. Over
the next several days, reporters followed him around with cameras, peppering him with questions and egging him on for a
reaction. If Andy had learned anything over the years, he should
have known not to engage. But whether due to his own van-
ity or blind ignorance of his situation, his responses were often
ugly, and the public wasn't on his side.

Celebrities he'd burned in the past joined in, and soon stories
about his behavior came out. Accusations of blatant harassment
or misleading claims piled up, and when the investigative reporters began to dig into Andy's personal life, more than one
embarrassing skeleton fell out of his closet. I guess he figured
nobody would ever have any reason to wonder what he charged
on his credit cards, but apparently America loves to point and
mock a certifiable villain with an eHarmony subscription.

Honestly, I almost felt bad for the guy. Almost.

Epilogue

Concert photographer. It sounds pretty cool, doesn't it? Too cool to be an actual job, right? Think again.

A month after I lost my job, Lars Cambridge followed up with me about doing some work for his magazine. He'd also forwarded my photos to Stuart Michaels with my permission. I'd worked it out with Stuart to display the photo of Micah in one of his upcoming shows. As a settlement in the wrongful termination suit against the *Daily Feed*, I'd gotten all my pictures back. It thrilled Micah to become an actual work of art. Stuart said he'd be happy to consider future work. Maybe one day, I'd be able to put together a show of my own.

I'd been a professional photographer for years, but for the first time I felt legitimized—like I might finally get the blessing of my dad. But of course, I no longer needed it. I had all the approval I needed from industry professionals, my boyfriend, my best friend, and of course my oversharing mom.

Still, I sent photos and articles to Dad. I liked to think he was secretly proud of his legacy.

Lars had offered me an open-ended freelance gig. I'd have to get my own medical insurance through the state's marketplace exchange, but it beat being unemployed. I'd already covered a couple of huge acts, wearing my credentials into the press pit and working with incredible equipment. My art degree hadn't

been a complete waste of time and money after all. Of course
the pay was uneven, but good when I got the right jobs.

Tonight I had the best job.

Positioned where I stood, I could get great shots of the entire
band plus the faces of the people floating on their backs, carried
across the top of the crowd. They laughed as hands pushed them
like a living conveyor belt to the back of the theater. Where the
human surfboards went from there remained a mystery.

Micah hauled another volunteer onto the stage, and the process started over again. Photographing his shows always gave
me ample material. The fans were as interesting as the band.
And I'd grown to like the music.

Tonight, like every night, Micah fed the crowd energy. He
looked my way and winked. I shot the picture.

He hit the last note and turned around to the band with a
nod. They started playing something new to me. His reper-
toire was bottomless. Every night, they played fan favorites and
sprinkled in some of their older songs or some new song they
were trying out.

Micah said, "I'm a little nervous about this new song. Normally, I don't have to sing to my muse."

It took me a second to parse his meaning, and by then, he'd
pulled the microphone from the stand and walked to the corner
where I perched with my camera. I let it drop, and it smacked
me in the gut. Everyone in the audience looked at me.

Micah threw his guitar around his back and sat down in
front of me. "This song is called 'Josie.'"

I flipped on the video on my camera to capture the audio.
And he started to sing.

> *"I've got a crush*
> *on her cinnamon curls*
> *It's a sugar rush*
> *And I'm high on a girl"*

The band echoed his last words. He took my hand and broke
into the chorus.

*"Jo-Jo-Josie
Devil from Georgi-a
Can't live without you
ñān ninne snēhikkunnu"*

As he sang, I twined my fingers with his. But my hands flew to my face at the Malayalam for "I love you." I hadn't heard those words in years, and he gave them back to me in the sweetest way possible. But he didn't need to write me a song to tell me how he felt.

He'd been a rock for me, through crazy times that might have shaken any other guy. He'd literally carried me when I was at my lowest. And right here, at his highest, he wanted me. He needed me.

He'd proved himself to me every day over the past six months. When the tabloids tried to paint me as his next groupie, he went and outfitted his tour bus to accommodate his "road wife" with a veritable pharmacy of insulin and healthy snacks. When the tabloids lost interest in me and tried to catch him with other women, he invited me to come live with him. When they ran stories about his gold-digger-hanger-on girlfriend, he brought me breakfast in bed. And when the girls flirted with him at the meet and greets, he flirted back, but he left with me.

And every day, he religiously updated his daily log with my glucose readings. And sat beside me, rubbing my back while I recovered from light-headedness. And drove me to the edge of insanity with just a touch.

And every night before I fell asleep, he whispered the same words in my ear:

"I will love you tomorrow—and every tomorrow after that."

Acknowledgments

If a picture is worth a thousand words, I'd need a thousand pictures to express my gratitude to my editor, Wendy McCurdy, for her continual faith and expert guidance. Kensington is a landscape of infinite support. Thanks especially to marketing geniuses Jane Nutter and Lauren Jernigan for spotlighting my work, to Paula Reedy, a portrait of production prowess, and to Steven Zacharius, a perfect model of encouragement. Out on location, I was lucky enough to click with Jen Halligan, publicist extraordinaire.

I owe an enormous debt to Kristin Wright, Kelli Newby, Laura Heffernan, Susan Bickford, and Rachel Reiss. I'm forever aware of the watermark you each left on my words. You all were instrumental in developing this book from a negative into a positive. You give me flashes of inspiration and never tell me to shutter up. (Sorry, you know I can't f-stop with bad puns once they start shooting.)

Special thanks to Tara Sim for consulting on Indian-American culture and Sarah Marsh for her input on living with diabetes. Any errors in representation are entirely on me.

To my family, I appreciate that you never complain when I disappear into my metaphorical darkroom to expose the world of my imagination.

And to my extended writing family, the CD and the Pitch Wars community, you all keep me focused and balanced. Thanks so much for your constant generosity and bursts of sanity.

I'm deeply thankful to everyone at Dystel, Goderich & Bourret, specifically Rachel Stout, Jane Dystel, and Mike Hoogland, for zooming in on my work and shepherding me through this process.

Most important, thank you, reader, for allowing this author to capture you for a moment in time. Without you, our stories would be like a roll of film in a forgotten canister.

Any book's acknowledgments are limited to a snapshot. Many more people, from copy editors to designers, will be involved with the production of this book before it's finally released. To anyone who's out of frame, please know that I'm eternally grateful. I did not do this alone.

A CRAZY KIND OF LOVE

Mary Ann Marlowe

About This Guide

The suggested questions are included
to enhance your group's reading of
Mary Ann Marlowe's *A Crazy Kind of Love*.

DISCUSSION QUESTIONS

1. What do you think of Jo's job as a tabloid photographer? Do you understand why she took this job, even though she is such a talented artist?

2. Why does Micah help Jo get a picture of Maggie Gyllenhaal in the first chapter of the book?

3. Are Micah and Jo using each other—Jo for her job, and Micah to get publicity for himself?

4. Why does Jo try to keep her father a secret? Do you understand why he behaves the way that he does? How has this affected Jo?

5. Can you imagine photographing celebrities for a living? Would you be any good at it? What would be fun about it and what would be the drawbacks?

6. What do you think of Andy as a boss? Who was the worst boss you've ever had, and what made him or her so bad?

7. What do you think of Zion as Jo's roommate? Is there anyone in your life who plays a similar role?

8. If you were a member of the paparazzi, which celebrity would you most like to snap a picture of? How far would you go to get this pic? Where would you draw the line?

9. Do you sometimes read the tabloid papers and celebrity magazines, or at least sneak a peek while standing in the grocery store line? Which one is your favorite? What makes this kind of media so irresistible to so

many people? Do you have a favorite place to indulge—
i.e., mani-pedi, hair salon, bathtub, waiting room for a
doctor's appointment, etc.?

10. Can you imagine dating someone really famous? How
    would this change your life—or would it?

11. If you have read both *A Crazy Kind of Love* and *Some
    Kind of Magic,* whose story do you find more romantic,
    and why—Micah and Jo's or Eden and Adam's?

Do not miss Eden and Adam's story in

SOME KIND OF MAGIC

By
Mary Ann Marlowe
Now available in bookstores and online!

What if you could seduce anyone in the world. . . .

**In this sparkling novel, Mary Ann Marlowe introduces a
hapless scientist who's swept off her feet by a rock star—but
is it love or just a chemical reaction . . . ?**

Biochemist Eden Sinclair has no idea that the scent she
spritzed on herself before leaving the lab is designed to enhance pheromones. Or that the cute, grungy-looking guy she
meets at a gig that evening is Adam Copeland. As in *the* Adam
Copeland—international rock god and object of lust for a million women. Make that a million and one. By the time she learns
the truth, she's already spent the (amazing, incredible) night in
his bed. . . .

Suddenly Eden, who's more accustomed to being set up on
disastrous dates by her mom, is going out with a gorgeous celebrity who loves how down-to-earth and honest she is. But for
once, Eden isn't being honest. She can't bear to reveal that this
overpowering attraction could be nothing more than seduction
by science. And the only way to know how Adam truly feels is
to ditch the perfume—and risk being ditched in turn. . . .

Smart, witty, and sexy, *Some Kind of Magic* is an irresistibly
engaging look at modern relationships—why we fall, how we
connect, and the courage it takes to trust in something as mysterious and unpredictable as love.

Read on for a preview. . . .

Chapter 1

My pen tapped out the drumbeat to the earworm on the radio. I glanced around to make sure I was alone, then grabbed an Erlenmeyer flask and belted out the chorus into my makeshift microphone.

"*I'm beeeegging you . . .*"

With the countertop centrifuge spinning out a white noise, I could imagine a stadium crowd cheering. My eyes closed, and the blinding lab fell away. I stood onstage in the spotlight.

"Eden?" came a voice from the outer hall.

I swiveled my stool toward the door, anticipating the arrival of my first fan. When Stacy came in, I bowed my head. "Thank you. Thank you very much."

She shrugged out of her jacket and hung it on a wooden peg. Unimpressed by my performance, she turned down the radio. "You're early. How long have you been here?"

"Since seven." The centrifuge slowed, and I pulled out tubes filled with rodent sperm. "I want to leave a bit early to head into the city and catch Micah's show."

She dragged a stool over. "Kelly and I are hitting the clubs tonight. You should come with."

"Yeah, right. Why don't you come with me? Kelly's such a—"

"Such a what?" The devil herself stood in the doorway, phone in hand.

Succubus from hell played on my lips. But it was too early to start a fight. "Such a guy magnet. Nobody can compete with you."

Kelly didn't argue and turned her attention back to the phone.

Stacy leaned her elbow on the counter, conspiratorially talking over my head. "Eden's going to abandon us again to go hang out with Micah."

"At that filthy club?" Kelly's lip curled, as if Stacy had just offered her a *non*-soy latte. "But there are never even any guys there. It's always just a bunch of moms."

I gritted my teeth. "Micah's fans are not all moms." When Micah made it big, I was going to enjoy refusing her backstage passes to his eventual sold-out shows.

Kelly snorted. "Oh, right. I suppose their husbands might be there, too."

"That's not fair," Stacy said. "I've seen young guys at his shows."

"Teenage boys don't count." Kelly dropped an invisible microphone and turned toward her desk.

I'd never admit that she was right about the crowd that came out to hear Micah's solo shows. But unlike Kelly, I wasn't interested in picking up random guys at bars. I spun a test tube like a top, then clamped my hand down on it before it could careen off the counter. "Whatever. Sometimes Micah lets me sing."

Apparently Kelly smelled blood; her tone turned snide. "Ooh, maybe Eden's dating her brother."

"Don't be ridiculous, Kelly." Stacy rolled her eyes and gave me her best *don't listen to her* look.

"Oh, right." Kelly threw her head back for one last barb. "Eden would never consider dating a struggling musician."

The clock on the wall reminded me I had seven hours of prison left. I hated the feeling that I was wishing my life away one workday at a time.

Thanh peeked his head around the door and saved me. "Eden, I need you to come monitor one of the test subjects."

Inhaling deep to get my residual irritation under control, I followed Thanh down the hall to the holding cells. Behind the window, a cute blond sat with a wire snaking out of his charcoal-gray Dockers. Thanh instructed him to watch a screen flashing more or less pornographic images while I kept one eye on his vital signs.

I bit my pen and put the test subject through my usual erminator-robot full-body analysis to gauge his romantic eligibility. He wore a crisp dress shirt with a white cotton undershirt peeking out below the unbuttoned collar. I wagered he held a job I'd find acceptable, possibly in programming, accounting, or maybe even architecture. His fading tan, manicured nails, and fit build lent the impression that he had enough money and time to vacation, pamper himself, and work out. No ring on his finger. And blue eyes at that. On paper, he fit my mental checklist to a *T*.

Even if he was strapped up to his balls in wires.

Hmm. Scratch that. If he were financially secure, he wouldn't need the compensation provided to participants in clinical trials for boner research. *Never mind.*

Thanh came back in and sat next to me.

I stifled a yawn and stretched my arms. "Don't get me wrong. This is all very exciting, but could you please slip some arsenic in my coffee?"

He punched buttons on the complex machine monitoring the erectile event in the other room. "Why are you still working here, Eden? Weren't you supposed to start grad school this year?"

"I was." I sketched a small circle in the margin of the paper on the table.

"You need to start applying soon for next year. Are you waiting till you've saved enough money?"

"No, I've saved enough." I drew a flower around the circle and shaded it in. I'd already had this conversation with my parents.

"If you want to do much more than what you're doing now, you need to get your PhD."

I sighed and turned in my chair to face him. "Thanh, you've got your PhD, and you're doing the same thing as me."

When he smiled, the corners of his eyes crinkled. "Yes, but it has always been my lifelong dream to help men maintain a medically induced long-lasting erection."

I looked at my hands, thinking. "Thanh, I'm not sure this is what I want to do with my life. I've lost that loving feeling."

"Well, then, you're in the right place."

I snickered at the erectile dysfunction humor. The guy in the testing room shifted, and I thought for the first time to ask. "What are you even testing today?"

"Top secret."

"You can't tell me?"

"No, I mean you'd already know if you read your e-mails."

"I do read the e-mails." That was partly true. I skimmed and deleted them unless they pertained to my own work. I didn't care about corporate policy changes, congratulations to the sales division, farewells to employees leaving after six wonderful years, tickets to be pawned, baby pictures, or the company chili cook-off.

He reached into a drawer and brought out a small vial containing a clear yellow liquid. When he removed the stopper, a sweet aroma filled the room, like jasmine.

"What's that?"

He handed it to me. "Put some on, right here." He touched my wrist.

I tipped it onto my finger and dabbed both my wrists. Then I waited. "What's it supposed to do?"

He raised an eyebrow. "Do you feel any different?"

I ran an internal assessment. "Uh, nope. Should I?"

"Do me a favor. Walk into that room."

"With the test subject?" It was bad enough that poor guy's schwanz was hooked up to monitors, but he didn't need to know exactly who was observing changes in his penile turgidity. Thanh shooed me on through the door, so I went in.

The erotica continued to run, but the guy's eyes were now on me. I thought, *Is that a sensor monitoring you, or are you just happy to see me?*

"Uh, hi." I glanced back at the one-way mirror, as if I could telepathically understand when Thanh released me from this embarrassing ordeal.

The guy sat patiently, expecting me to do something. So I reached over and adjusted one of the wires, up by the machines. He went back to watching the screen, as if I were just another technician. Nobody interesting.

I backed out of the room. As soon as the door clicked shut, I asked Thanh, "What the hell was that?"

He frowned. "I don't know. I expected something more. Some kind of reaction." He started to place the vial back in the drawer. Then he had a second thought. "Do you like how this smells?"

I nodded. "Yeah, it's good."

"Take it." He tossed it over, and I threw it into my purse.

The rest of the day passed slowly as I listened to Kelly and Stacy argue over the radio station or fight over some impossibly gorgeous actor or front man they'd never meet. Finally at four, I swung into the ladies' room and changed out of my work clothes, which consisted of a rayon suit skirt and a button-up pin-striped shirt. Knowing I'd be hanging with Micah in the club later, I'd brought a pair of comfortable jeans and one of his band's T-shirts. I shook my ponytail out and let my hair fall to my shoulders.

When I went back to the lab to grab my purse and laptop, I wasn't a bit surprised that Kelly disapproved of my entire look.

"I have a low-cut shirt in my car if you want something more attractive." She offered it as though she actually would've lent it to me. Knowing I'd decline, she got in a free dig at my wardrobe choices. We were a study in opposites—she with her overpermed blond hair and salon tan, me with my short-clipped fingernails and functioning brain cells.

"No, thanks. Maybe next time."

"At least let me fix your makeup. Are you even wearing any?"

I pretended she wasn't bothering me. "No time. I have a train to catch."

She sniffed. "Well, you smell nice anyway. New perfume?"

"Uh, yeah. It was a gift." Her normally pouting lips rounded in anticipation of her next question. I zipped my computer bag and said, "Gotta go. See ya tomorrow, Stacy?"

Stacy waved without turning her head away from whatever gossip site she'd logged on to, and I slipped out the door.

As I stood on the train platform waiting for the 5:35 Northeast Corridor train to Penn Station, I heard someone calling "Hello?" from inside my purse. I fetched my phone and found it connected somehow to my mom, whose voice messages I'd been ignoring.

Foiled by technology and the gremlins living in my bag, I placed the phone to my ear. "Mom?"

"Oh, there you are, Eden. I'm making corned beef and gravy tonight. Why don't you come by before you go out?"

I didn't know how to cook, so my mom's invitation was meant as charity. But since she was the reason I couldn't cook, her promise of shit on a shingle wasn't enough to lure me from my original plans.

"No, thanks, Mom. I'm on my way into the city to hear Micah play tonight."

"Oh. Well, we'll see you Sunday I hope. Would you come to church with us? We have a wonderful new minister and—"

"No, Mom. But I'll come by the house later."

"All right. Oh, don't forget you've got a date with Dr. Whedon tomorrow night."

I groaned. She was relentless. "Is it too late to cancel?"

"What's the problem now, Eden?"

I pictured Dr. Rick Whedon, DDS, tonguing my bicuspid as we French kissed. But she wouldn't understand why I'd refuse to date a dentist, so instead, I presented an iron-clad excuse. "Mom, if we got married, I'd be Eden Whedon."

Her sigh came across loud and clear. "Eden, don't be so unreasonable."

"I keep telling you you're wasting your time, Mom."

"And you're letting it slip by, waiting on a nonexistent man. You're going to be twenty-nine soon."

The train approached the station, so I put my finger in my ear and yelled into the phone. "In six months, Mom."

"What was wrong with Jack Talbot?"

I thought for a second and then placed the last guy she'd tried to set me up with. "He had a mustache, Mom. And a tattoo. Also, he lives with his parents."

"That's only temporary," she snapped.

"The mustache or the tattoo?" I thought back to the guy from the lab. "And you never know. Maybe I'll meet Mr. Perfect soon."

"Well, if you do, bring him over on Sunday."

I chortled. The idea of bringing a guy over to my crazy house before I had a ring on my finger was ludicrous. "Sure, Mom. I'll see you Sunday."

"Tell Micah to come, too?"

My turn to sigh. Their pride in him was unflappable, and yet, I'd been the one to do everything they'd ever encouraged me to do, while he'd run off to pursue a pipe dream in music. So maybe they hadn't encouraged me to work in the sex-drug industry, but at least I had a college degree and a stable income.

"Okay, Mom. I'll mention it. The train's here. I have to go."

I climbed on the train and relaxed, so tired of everyone harassing me. At least I could count on Micah not to meddle in my love life.

Chapter 2

At seven thirty, I arrived at the back door of the club, trailing a cloud of profanity. "Fuck. My fucking phone died."

Micah exchanged a glance with the club owner, Tobin. "See? Eden doesn't count."

"What the fuck are you talking about?" After two hours fighting mass transit, I'd lost my patience. My attitude would need to be recalibrated to match Micah's easygoing demeanor.

Micah ground out his cigarette with a twist of his shoe. "Tobin was laying a wager that only women would show up tonight, but I said you'd be here."

I narrowed my eyes.

Micah's small but avid female fan base faithfully came out whenever he put on an acoustic show. His hard-rock band, Theater of the Absurd, catered to a larger male following and performed to ever-increasing audiences. But he loved playing these smaller rooms, bantering with the crowd, hearing people sing along with familiar choruses.

Before Tobin could get in on the act, I blurted, "Can I charge my phone in the green room?"

I made a wide berth around Tobin's plumage of cigarette smoke and followed Micah down the shabby narrow back hall. Dimly lit eight-by-eleven glossy posters plastered the walls, advertising upcoming bands and many other acts that had already passed through. Nobody curated the leftover fliers although hundreds of staples held torn triangles of paper from some distant past. A brand-new poster showing Micah's anticipated club dates hung near the door to the ladies' room. That would disappear during the night as some fan co-opted it for him to autograph, and Tobin would have to replace it. Again.

The green room was actually dark red and held furniture that looked like someone had found it on the curb near the trash. And it smelled like they'd brought the trash, too. God knew what had transpired in here over the years. I tried to touch nothing. Micah flopped down on the sofa and picked up a box of half-eaten Chinese food. His red Converse tennis shoes and dark green pants clashed with the brown-gold hues that stained the formerly whitish sofa.

I plugged in my phone, praying I'd remember to fetch it before I left. I fished out some ibuprofen and grabbed Micah's beer to wash it down. I waved off his interest in the drugs I was popping. "Birth control," I lied.

Without looking up from his noodles, he said, "Oh, good. I was starting to worry you'd joined a convent."

When Micah finished eating, he led me to the front of the club and put me to work setting up his merch table. His band's CDs wouldn't sell, but his self-produced EP of solo work would disappear. Mostly for girls to have something for him to autograph. They'd already own his music digitally. A suitcase filled with rolled-up T-shirts lay under the table. I bent down and selected one of each design to display as samples.

Micah moved around onstage, helping the club employees drag cables and whatnot. Not for the first time, I envied him for inheriting some of Mom's Scandinavian coloring and height, while I got Dad's pale Irish skin and raven hair. Micah repeated "one-two-three check" into the mic a few times and then disappeared around back to grab one last smoke before he had to transform from my sweet older brother into that charismatic guy who held a crowd in the palm of his hand.

Right before the doors opened to the public, one of the guys I'd seen setting up the stage stopped by the table and flipped through the T-shirts and CDs. He picked up Micah's EP and then raised dark brown eyes. "Micah Sinclair. You like his music?"

He wore faded jeans and a threadbare T-shirt from a long-forgotten AC/DC concert under a maroon hoodie. His black hair fell somewhere between tousled and bed head. I saw no traces of product, so I assumed he came by that look through honest negligence rather than studied indifference.

My quick scan revealed: too grungy, probably unwashed, poor. I resisted the urge to pull the merch away from his wandering fingers. But I wouldn't risk the sale, so I leaned in on my elbows, all smiles.

"He's amazing. Will you get a chance to hear him perform?"

"Oh, yeah. Definitely." He set the EP down and held out his hand. "I'm Adam, by the way."

I wrapped my hand around his out of sheer politeness and proper upbringing, but I couldn't help laughing and saying, "Just so you know, my worst nightmare would be dating a guy named Adam."

He quirked his eyebrow. "That's kind of discriminatory."

"My name's Eden." I waited a beat for the significance to register, but I guess any guy named Adam would've already dealt with such issues of nomenclature. His eyes lit up immediately.

"Oh. Seriously?" He chuckled, and his smile transformed his features. I sucked in my breath. Underneath the dark hair, dark eyes, and hobo wardrobe, he was awfully cute. "I'll rethink that marriage proposal. But could I get you anything? You want a beer?"

This was a new twist. Usually, the ladies were offering drinks to my brother. I loved getting the attention for a change. "Sure. Whatever lager or pilsner they have on tap."

He walked off, and I snickered. *Maybe some guys like pale brunettes, Kelly.* As he leaned against the bar, I assessed him from the rear. Tall enough, but too skinny. Questionable employment. Either an employee of the club, a musician, a wannabe musician, or a fan. Shame.

Micah strolled up. "Is everything ready?"

I forced my gaze away from Adam's backside. "Are you?"

He scratched his five-o'clock chin scruff. "That's the thing. I may need some help tonight. Do you think you could maybe sing backup on one song? I was hoping to harmonize on 'Gravity.' "

"Sure." What were sisters for? I had his whole catalog memorized, even the music from his band, although that music ran a little too hard rock for my tastes.

Micah left me alone at the merch table, and Adam returned with a glass. "Did I just miss Micah?"

He'd pulled his hoodie up so his face fell into shadow, giving him a sinister appearance. With the nonexistent lighting in the club, I could barely make out his features. This odd behavior, coupled with his interest in my brother, made me worry maybe he was in fact one of the crazy fans who found ways to get closer than normal, and not, as I'd first thought, an employee of the club. How had he gotten inside before the doors opened?

Before I could ask him, a woman's sharp voice interrupted. "Will Micah be coming out after the show?"

I looked toward the club's entrance, where people had begun to stream in. I took a deep breath and prepared to deal with the intensity of music fandom.

"I assume so. He usually does."

She didn't move. "It's just that I brought something for him." She held up a canister of something I guessed was homemade. I'd advised Micah not to eat whatever they gave him, but he never listened. And so far he'd never landed in the hospital. I knew his fans meant well, but who knew if those cookies had been baked alongside seven long-haired cats?

"I could take it back to him if you like." I made the offer, knowing full well it wouldn't do at all.

"No. Thank you. I'll just wait and give them to him later. If he comes out." She wandered off toward the stage.

I spotted one of Micah's regular fans, Susan something-or-other, making a beeline for the merch table. She looked put out that I was there before her. "Eden, if you like, I'm more than happy to man the merch."

I never understood what she got out of working merch for Micah. He didn't pay except possibly in a waived cover charge.

And she was farther from the stage and possibly distracted from the performances. Perhaps it gave her status. Whatever it was, it made her happy, and I was glad to relinquish the duty to her.

"Thank you, Susan."

She beamed. "Oh, it's no problem." She began to chatter with the other women crowding up to the merch table. I overheard her saying, "Micah told me he'll be performing a new song tonight."

Adam caught my eye, and we exchanged a knowing smile. So okay, he wasn't a fan. He stepped beside me as I walked to the bar to get a seat on a stool. "So you're not the number one fan, then?" he asked.

I smiled. "Of course I am."

Before we could discuss our reasons for being there, the room plunged into near-total darkness, and Tobin stepped onto the stage to introduce the opening act, a tall blonde whose explosion of wild hair had to weigh more than the rest of her.

She pulled up a stool and started into her first song without further ado. Out of respect, I kept quiet and listened, although her performance was a bit shaky, and the between-song banter didn't help. It pleased me that Adam didn't turn to me to say anything snarky about the poor girl or talk at all. I had to glare over at the women hanging around the merch table a few times, though. They'd shut up when Micah came on, but they didn't seem to care that other musicians preferred to play to a rapt audience, too.

In the time between acts, Adam ordered me another beer. At some point he'd dropped his hood back, but with the terrible lighting in the club, I had to squint to see his face. Normally, I wasn't a big fan of facial hair of any kind, but Adam's slight scruff caused my wires to cross. On the one hand, I worried he couldn't afford a razor out there in the cardboard box he lived in. On the other hand, I had a visceral urge to reach up and touch his cheek. And run my finger down the side of his neck.

He caught me staring when he leaned closer to ask me how long Micah had been performing.

I wasn't sure what he was asking, so I gave him the full answer. "He's been singing since he was old enough to talk. He started playing acoustic when he was eleven, but picked up electric when he was fifteen. He formed a metal band in high school, and the first time they performed live anywhere beyond the garage was a battle of the bands."

Adam's expression changed subtly as I recounted Micah's life history, and I could tell he was reassessing my level of crazy fantardness. I laughed and said, "I told you I was his number one fan."

His smile slipped, but he managed to reply politely. "He must be very talented."

Something about the timbre in his voice resonated with me, almost familiar, and I regretted my flippant sarcasm.

Before I could repair my social missteps, the lights faded again, and the girls near the stage screamed in anticipation. A spotlight hit the mic, and Micah unceremoniously took the stage. He strummed a few notes and broke directly into a song everyone knew. The girls up front sang along, swaying and trying to out-do each other in their excitement.

Adam twisted around and watched me, eyebrow raised. Maybe he expected me to sing along, too. I raised an eyebrow back and mouthed the words along with Micah. Wouldn't want to disappoint him. Finally, Adam straightened up to watch the performance, ignoring me for several songs.

Micah performed another well-known song, then a new one, introducing each with some casual-seeming banter. I knew he planned every word he said onstage, but the stories he told were no less sincere for that. He controlled his stage presence like a pro.

Before the fourth song, he announced, "This next song requires some assistance. If you would all encourage my sister, Eden, to come join me, I'm sure she'd hop up here and lend me a hand."

The audience applauded on cue. As my feet hit the floor, Adam's eyes narrowed and then opened wide as he did the math. I curtsied and left him behind to climb up onstage to perform— Micah's support vocals once again. Micah strummed a chord, and I hummed the pitch. Then he began to play the song, a beautiful ballad about a man with an unflagging devotion to a woman. The ladies in the front row ate it up. Micah knew I got a kick out of performing, and I suspected he asked me up so I could live his musician life vicariously.

When the song ended, I headed back to the anonymity of my stool. The hard-core fans all knew who I was, but if they weren't pumping me for information about Micah, they didn't pay much attention to me. There was a fresh beer waiting, and I nodded to Adam, appreciative. He winked and faced forward to listen to Micah. That was the extent of our conversation until Micah performed his last encore and the lights came back up.

Then he turned back. "You were right. He's very talented." He tilted his head. "But you held out on me. Your opinion was a little bit biased."

"I was telling you the truth," I deadpanned. "I am his number one fan."

"You two look nothing alike. I'd never have guessed."

"We have a crazy mix of genetics."

As we chatted, the area behind us, near the merch table, filled up with people waiting for a chance to talk to Micah, get an autograph, or take a picture with him. The lady with the cat-hair cookies had nabbed the first place in the amorphous line. I scanned the rest of the crowd and discovered that Tobin had lost his bet. A pair of teenage boys holding guitars stood on their toes, trying to get a glimpse of Micah over the heads of the other fans, but he hadn't come out yet. They were most likely fans of his edgier rock band, taking advantage of the smaller venue to meet him, pick his brain about music, and have him sign their guitars. They'd still be competing with at least thirty people for Micah's time.

If I wanted to go home with my brother, I'd be hanging out a while. I could still catch a train back to New Jersey, but Micah's place in Brooklyn was closer. I decided to stay. It had nothing to do with the cute guy paying attention to me. I just didn't want to navigate Manhattan alone and drunk.

Adam leaned in and asked, "So what do you do? Are you a musician, too?"

"Actually, no. I'm a biochemist."

"Finding cures for Ebola?"

That caught me off guard, and I snorted. "No, nothing like that." I didn't know what to tell him about what I actually researched, so I half lied. "My company's developing a perfume."

"What's it like?"

I scooted over. "I'm wearing it. Can you smell it?"

He met me halfway, eyes dilating black. I knew I shouldn't be flirting. He didn't appear to meet a single one of my criteria and, in fact, actively ticked boxes from the "deal-breaker" list. I didn't want to lead him on only to have to give him the heave-ho in the next thirty minutes.

He took my hand and kept his dark eyes on mine as he lifted my wrist up to smell the fragrance Thanh had given me. "Mmm. That's nice."

Without dropping his gaze, he brushed his lips across my skin, and an electric current shot up every nerve in my arm. I drew my hand back, shrugging off the shiver that hit me like an aftershock. "And you? What do you do?"

He laughed and scratched the back of his neck. "Well, I'm a musician."

I blinked back my disappointment. From Adam's appearance, I hadn't had high hopes, but he might've been dressed down for a night out. Way down.

On my list of suitable professions for my prospective mate, *musician* wasn't at the absolute bottom. There were plenty more embarrassing or unstable career choices. I wouldn't date plumbers or proctologists for obvious reasons. Salesmen either because, well, I didn't like salesmen, but also because their financial situation might be uncertain. Plus they tended to travel. My ideal guy, I'd decided, would be an architect. But there weren't many of those swimming around my apartment complex in Edison, New Jersey.

I had nothing against musicians. On the contrary, I loved

them. I'd supported my brother in his career, but the lifestyle was too precarious for my peace of mind. Even the most talented had a hard time making ends meet. Traveling and selling merchandise became a necessity.

Which is why I never dated musicians.

Unfortunately, all the doctors, lawyers, and architects I encountered were usually not interested in jean-clad, concert T-shirt wearing me. This train of thought brought me around to the realization that I'd judged Adam for dressing exactly the same way.

Micah saved me from sticking my foot in my mouth when he appeared at our side. "Adam! I'm glad to see you here. I see you've met my sister." He turned to me. "Eden, do you mind if I steal him for a few?"

Adam threw me a glance. "Will you be here when I get back?"

The jolt of butterflies this simple question gave me came wholly unexpectedly. "I'll be here. I'm leaving when Micah does."

He flashed a crooked smile at me, and I traced his lips with my eyes. He was going to be trouble.

They headed toward the green room, leaving me as confused as Adam must've been when I went onstage. I didn't know who he was, or why my brother wanted to see him.

I weighed the possible options.

Option one: The most logical explanation was that Micah was hiring Adam to temporarily replace his bassist, Rick, who was taking time off to be with his wife after the birth of their first child. I congratulated myself for solving the mystery on my first try.

Option two: Maybe Adam was a drug dealer. No, other than smoking and drinking, I'd never known Micah to try a recreational drug. And surely, this wouldn't be an ideal location for such a transaction. Besides, Adam already said he was a musician. Option one was looking better and better.

Option three: Or maybe Adam was a homeless man Micah was going to take in out of charity. A homeless man who'd just bought me three beers. I rolled my eyes at myself, but then felt awash with guilt. He probably wasn't homeless, but it did seem like he might be struggling to get by, and I'd accepted three drinks I could've easily afforded. *Good job, Eden. Way to drive a man to starvation.*

Every new option I came up with to explain Adam's presence here defied logic and stretched the imagination. I gave up and watched the crowd thin. When Micah and Adam came back out, the bar was empty, save me and the staff.

Micah poked me. "We're going over to Adam's. You can come or just go straight back to my place." He bounced on his feet. I looked from him to Adam, standing relaxed up against the bar. From the looks of things, Micah had a boy crush. I might be interrupting a bromance if I tagged along.

Adam stepped toward me. "I have a fully stocked bar, and I don't like to drink alone." His smile was disarming. The whole situation seemed so contrived, and I had to wonder whose idea it was.

Micah stifled a yawn. "Come on, Eden. Just for a drink. Let's go see how the other half lives."

Did he know what that expression meant? "Okay, but let's get going. Some of us have been awake since this morning."

Connect with U(s)

Visit us online at
KensingtonBooks.com
to read more from your favorite authors, see books
by series, view reading group guides, and more.

Join us on social media
for sneak peeks, chances to win books and prize packs,
and to share your thoughts with other readers.

facebook.com/kensingtonpublishing
twitter.com/kensingtonbooks

Tell us what you think!
To share your thoughts, submit a review,
or sign up for our eNewsletters, please visit:
KensingtonBooks.com/TellUs.

NOV - - 2017